The Dead Man's Deal

A Witherspoon Mansion Mystery

Book 1

Jax Daniels

Cover art by Tim Neil

To Russ

ACKNOWLEDGEMENTS

I would like to thank Jennifer, Denise, Jason, Laura, and Carolyn for their insights, suggestions, and patience, Jeanette and Glenn for being awesome parents, Russ for his love and guidance, Bert and Savannah for their adherence to strict schedules, and the folks of Assent who showed me the path I want to walk. This book wouldn't exist without you.

Chapter One

IT HAPPENED AGAIN last night.

I sprawled lifelessly on my sofa, without the nerve to sleep alone in our ... *my* king sized bed the last few months. Will passed away unexpectedly last November. Since then I had spent miserable and depressed days flipping emotionlessly through TV channels, napping on and off as the rest of the world hummed and buzzed about its business with a vitality, or even vague interest, I no longer possessed. Driven from the world by my anguish, driven from the bed by my loneliness. As a result, I made my camp on the davenport.

But lately, in maybe the past week or so, this weird experience, or dream, or *something* kept happening. Just as I dozed off, just after the late-night host said his goodbyes, just as my attention lost its already tenuous mooring, it happened again. The TV and all the lights in the room popped and dimmed, as if a sudden brownout had hit the city. Then the clasp. Cold, very cold fingers clutched my forearm, just above my wrist. Just as it had the nights before.

I jerked upright. My heart raced as panic filled me. *Let go of me!* I looked down but saw nothing. Though I could see no indentations on my skin the grip remained tight and unyielding. I lurched off the sofa but the clutch never wavered. I felt trapped. I felt helpless. I felt like I was losing my mind. As I gasped to scream—another pop. The lights and TV brightened and the grip vanished.

Just as they had the other nights.

What the hell was happening to me?

~ ~ * ~ ~

A persistent knock on the front door roused me. Despite my wide-eyed fear of things that go bump in the night—now all so very real to me—I had managed to fall asleep—well, not so much fall as pass out from exhaustion. Until he returned.

"Mrs. Witherspoon?" he called from the outside. "Mrs. Witherspoon? It's me. Nathan. Nathan Marble. Remember me, Mrs. Witherspoon? Today's the big day."

Nathan Marble had introduced himself to me just last week. He spoke with this squawky, annoying, Boston accent that seemed to vibrate my spine. I strive to be tolerant, but his voice would have annoyed Gandhi. Despite my lack of desire to move from my sofa, his voice pulled at me like a puppet's strings. Anything to stop that sound.

"Ah," he said as I opened the door. "Mrs. Witherspoon. How are you today?" Actually, he said, "Mrs. Withahspoon. How ah ya tahday?" But I'll translate, since Bostonians seem to have some aversion to the letter "r".

"Mr. Marble. This really isn't a good time—"

He wagged his finger. "Now, now, Mrs. Witherspoon, we discussed this, yes we did." Without invitation he pushed through the unlocked door into the small foyer. "It's the big day. And you won't regret it, I promise you. You surely won't."

If Mr. Marble brings a door-to-door salesman to mind, my job is done. He's not, as it turns out. He's the executor of my husband's estate. Not a salesman, but always in sales mode. He kept selling me to see, well, something. Something my husband owned, something I hadn't known about. Something, I took it, big.

"Let's take a drive," he said. "It will make you feel better, I promise. Get out of the house, get some fresh air. When's the last time you've been out of the house?"

Pushy man, don't you think? But to be honest, it had been months. I'd had groceries delivered, not that I'd been all that hungry. I hadn't wanted to do anything. I hadn't wanted to eat anything. I hadn't wanted to drive anywhere. I just wanted Will back ... *God, I miss him.*

Seeing my reluctance he pressed. "Please, Mrs. Witherspoon, this is what Will wanted. He left this for you."

I rubbed my face with my hands to hide the giant yawn behind them. "May I take a shower first?"

"Yeah. Sure. I'll, uh ... I'll just sit here and wait."

I rolled my eyes but slowly shuffled to the bathroom. As I ran the water I could hear him going on and on, about what a great day I would have and how surprised I would be. Lost in thoughts and memories, I didn't bother to answer. Not once had my husband ever mentioned Mr. Marble. Not once had he mentioned keeping something separate from our life together, something I would learn about only with his passing. I mean, I had always known we had money. Not millions, mind you. But enough. I assumed it was tied up in an apartment building or some commercial property, something bringing in a small, steady stream of income. Mr Marble's insistence seemed far too intense for a simple real estate investment. And why would Will have hidden something more important from me?

I stepped into the warm shower, wishing the water would wash away the loneliness I felt. Hell, just breathing was hard. I was done with the tears. What remained was just the shell of the woman I used to be. Hollow. Lifeless. Distant.

Still that irritating man talked in the background. Even though I couldn't make out anything he said, his brittle voice pushed me to get the shower over quickly and get him out of my house. I showered, toweled off, ran a comb through my wet brown hair and let it be. I hurriedly donned jeans, a t-shirt (both of which draped off my new, thin frame), and tenny runners. Anything to get this over with so I could slump back into my sofa and mindless meat-head TV shows.

"There you are!" he said as I made my appearance. "And don't you look lovely this morning? Shall we get something to eat? Breakfast perhaps?"

"Please," I held up a hand. "Let's just go."

"You're the boss, you are, you are." He bounded for the front door and held it open for me. With a sweeping gesture he said, "Ladies first."

The drive to Uptown wasn't long—thank God!—but that man chattered the entire ride as we wandered about the Garden District of New Orleans, away from my protective shotgun home in the Irish Channel. Usually the auspicious homes, lush gardens, and grand oak trees would distract me. But that *voice* ... I was tempted to bludgeon him with my wallet. Good thing I wasn't armed.

He finally slowed the car and made a left down a very narrow lane or service road between two large and stately looking manors. He slowly steered the white gravel path between very tall hedges of cypress. Once clear I could see it. A mansion. You would never see it from the street, tucked away in the middle of the block.

As the wheels crunched over the horseshoe driveway I could see details more clearly. Huge porches wrapped around the lower and second floors, with matching wrought iron scrollwork as railings. French doors dotted both levels. But it was run down. Decrepit, actually. The dreary paint was chipping and mold darkened most of the north side. The ironwork was rusted completely through in sections, with panels dangling or missing completely. A few gaslight sconces still worked, but most clung limply to the siding. The thick, dead bougainvillea swallowed a good portion of the upper floor. The building looked crooked, listing slightly to one side. Not uncommon here in New Orleans; if you aren't actively remodeling your home, it's actively decaying. That's just the way it is, here.

Mr. Marble eased to a stop in front of a once grand wooden staircase leading to an expanse of porch and a dramatic double door entry. I couldn't help but notice the spider web transom arching above it. Standing beneath was an elderly man dressed in, I kid you not, a tuxedo. Black tails, black bow tie, and white gloves. The only thing missing was a top hat.

"Ah, good morning, Mr. Wilson," Mr. Marble called as he exited the car.

Mr. Wilson gave a bow. "Greetings, sir." The posh English accent complemented the formal attire perfectly. He continued around the vehicle and finished opening the car door I'd opened myself before realizing his intent.

"Oh, sorry," I said grinning awkwardly, uncertain as always on etiquette, including if an apology was in order.

"Madam," he gave a bow as I stepped out of the car.

"Mrs. Witherspoon," Mr. Marble announced, "please meet Mr. Wilson."

Watching Mr. Wilson's face made it clear I wasn't the only one bothered by the annoying quality of his voice. The old man winced. "Must you do that, sir?" He turned his attention to me. "Please to make your acquaintance, madam."

"Same, here," I said as I held out my hand. He just looked at it, nervously, then at me, then at Mr. Marble.

"Uh," Mr. Marble cleared his throat, "you don't shake hands with the butler."

"Butler?"

Mr. Wilson bowed again. "At your service, Madam."

"Let's take a look inside, shall we?" Mr. Marble waved an open hand to the front door. "Please, after you."

The stairs creaked in miserable protest under our combined

weight. Mr. Wilson stood aside as he opened the door. I thanked him as I stepped into a grand entryway. Well, once grand, maybe one hundred years ago. Now it appeared faded and worn. The thick staircase curving gracefully into the hall, its finish discolored in hues of grey with no polish or shine. Cobwebs delicately dangled from the doorways leading to other rooms. Flowery wallpaper peeled away from the wall in spots and missing altogether in others, exposing the lathe and plaster walls beneath. I would have been appalled if the very look of the place didn't match the very feel of my soul.

Just as I turned to Mr. Marble to tell him I'd seen enough and wanted to go home, two women entered the room, one right behind the other.

"Yes, yes," Mr. Marble said to them. "Please come in and meet the new master of the house." He turned to face me. "Unless you prefer mistress of the house?"

"I, uh," I didn't get to answer, really.

"Mrs. Witherspoon, meet Mrs. White. She's the cook."

Mrs. White was a short, stocky, black woman with her salted hair pulled tightly away from her face in a perfect bun. What struck me were her eyes, which almost popped out of her head; she looked like she was in a constant state of surprise. She wore a faded frock under a full bib apron. She gave me an awkward curtsy. "Ma'am," she said.

Mr. Marble scooted us down a person. "And this is Mrs. Black, the maid."

"Mrs. Black?" I began to suspect these were not their real names.

Mrs. Black had the classic witch appearance. Long grey hair, set in a braid that draped over her right shoulder. Tall, thin, frail looking, with a beaked nose sporting a pair of pince-nez glasses with coke-bottle lens. Her owl-like grey eyes perfectly matched her hair. She, too, curtsied, spreading her black skirt (which swept to the floor) with bony fingers. "I'm quite pleased, madam," she nearly cackled.

Mr. Marble turned to Mr. Wilson. "And where are Smith and

Wesson?"

I raised my eyebrows at the names.

"Where you'd expect them, sir," he sighed disapprovingly.

Mr. Marble seemed miffed. "It was just the one day!"

"I understand, sir. But with the upcoming tournament they are quite distracted."

Those words had barely left the butler's lips when a thunderous boom rocked the building.

Mrs. White exhaled an hiss. "Them boys are at it again." Her sultry voice contained a distinct island accent, which turned her *th*s to *d*s. She turned to Mr. Wilson, put her hands on her hips and nearly yelled, "I don't mind meetin' the maker, but I'll be damned if I do it in a hundred pieces!"

"Now, now," Mr. Marble said, back into his full, grating tone. "Let's not lose our tempers in front of Mrs. Witherspoon."

"Hm!" she huffed, then turned to me. "If you'll excuse me I need to get lunch on. Ma'am," she gave a curt nod and stormed off. As she left her voice trailed off, "Indeed, better get lunch on the table before Mrs. Witherspoon hightails it outta here. If that is her real name!"

I stood, mouth open, at the comment. "Said *Mrs. White*," I thought aloud. I almost laughed.

"Now, now, dear," Mrs. Black called to her, then put a hand on Mr. Marble's shoulder. "Things are a bit tense around here these days. They'll settle back down. You'll see."

Another boom, bigger this time, shook the enormous crystal chandelier above us. It swayed precariously back and forth, reminding me of Poe's pendulum. Instinctively, I moved out from under it. I noticed everyone did.

"Okay, well," Mr. Marble said and he rubbed his hands together, "let's go meet Mr. Smith and Mr. Wesson, shall we?"

Mrs. Black bowed. "I'll prepare your room. Welcome home,

madam." And she walked away.

"What did she mean by that? Welcome home?" I asked, following Mr. Marble through a maze of rooms and doorways until we reached what appeared to be a closet. Mr. Wilson followed quietly. "Oh, that?" He waved the air. "Never mind that." He opened the door revealing not a closet but rather a staircase, narrow and damp, leading down. *Geez Louise, there's a basement?* "Please. Follow me."

Mr. Marble trotted down the staircase into an expanse of a room filled with what looked to me like magician props. Tall boxes painted in gaudy colors and designs, labeled "The Amazing Zingo" or "The Mysterious Mr. Moustafa," hoops, unicycles, platforms, and balls formed a maze.

The twisted path led to another door. Mr. Marble knocked, interrupting muffled words leaking through. After a beat someone called, "Come in!"

The three of us entered a laboratory. You've seen it in the movies. White walls, stainless steel cabinets and drawers, microscopes, test tubes, petri dishes, laptops and monitors, machines that go "ping", and one of those rabbit ear antennae thingies with electric arcs traveling up then vanishing, one after the other.

"What the—", I said. I couldn't help myself.

I almost missed the two men in lab coats standing side by side.

"Mrs. Witherspoon, please meet Mr. Smith," Mr. Marble gestured to one, "and Mr. Wesson."

What a mismatched pair. Mr. Smith was a very tall man, around six foot six, I'd bet. And large. Not fat, mind you, but thick and barrel shaped. The way he carried himself made me guess ex-military, even with the black hair that dangled behind him in a loose ponytail. In contrast to his white lab coat he sported black fingernails.

Mr. Wesson stood over a foot shorter. He looked trim and thin beneath his lab coat, his tousled wavy blonde hair pointed in multiple directions. He carried an iPad-y-like tablet.

The only things they had in common were the goggles pushed up on their heads and the silly grins on their faces, like children hiding something from a suspicious parent.

"And what manner of staff are they?" I asked. I mean, I don't know what the typical mansion staff includes, but I was fairly confident "mad scientists" weren't on the list.

"They, uh, well ...?" Mr. Marble stammered. "They do a number of jobs around here. Not the least of which is make *you* money." He pointed at me quickly.

"How so?"

Mr. Marble nodded to Mr. Smith. "Well, we generate revenue from our inventions," his voice pitched higher than I'd have guessed from his size. Mr. Wesson nodded excitedly in agreement.

"If I may, sir," the butler said to Mr. Marble from behind me, "officially, they create magic tricks—"

Mr. Smith cleared his throat.

"My apologies. They create *illusions* for magicians all over the world. They are quite famous in those circles."

"Right," Mr. Smith pointed to the butler, "There's that!" Again, the small one nodded rapidly.

"And *unofficially?*"

Apparently they had hoped that word made it past me without being noticed. The four men looked at each other, mumbling and grunting. Except for Mr. Wesson, who still said nothing at all. His eyes just darted about the others.

Their hesitation made me wary. It must have shown. "Oh!" Mr. Marble burst. "No, no. Nothing illegal, I assure you."

"Yeah," Mr. Smith said with a giggle. "It's not like we're down here making crystal meth or anything." The room went quiet. Mr. Wesson whacked him hard with his pad. "Ow! What? I'm just saying."

Mr. Wesson rolled his eyes.

I'd heard and had enough. "You two," I addressed the lab coats, "are responsible for the explosions, yes?"

"We're testing a new formula for hyper—"

I held up my hand, uninterested in his explanation. "And I'm to understand that, for the moment, you work for me, yes?"

"Yes, ma'am," Mr. Smith said quickly. Mr. Wesson nodded vigorously.

"Then let's keep it down until I've left. Understood?"

"Yes, ma'am—uh, wait. You're leaving?" Mr. Smith looked at Mr. Marble. "She's leaving?"

"I, er," he stammered, "haven't had a chance to talk to her yet. Please, Mrs. Witherspoon, follow me." He waved as he walked, hand high in the air. "Thank you, gentlemen!"

"Bye, bye!" Mr. Smith called after us.

Crazy bunch of people if you ask me.

Mr. Marble led Jeeves (that's what I'm calling the butler from now on, I mean, it's not like anyone is using their real names around here) and me back upstairs to the dining room, which the cook (Mrs. White, the black lady) had set up for lunch.

I wasn't hungry. At least I thought I wasn't. But when the wafts of gumbo hit my nose my stomach howled in hunger, unlike anything I'd experienced since, well, since before Will died. I had lost my appetite for so many things, eating included—I had lost over forty pounds. I even stopped enjoying my beloved beignets from the Cafe Du Monde, where we'd go every Monday morning when Will was in town. Nothing smelled good anymore. Nothing looked good anymore. And on those rare occasions when I forced myself to eat, nothing taste good anymore. Until now.

As Mrs. White heaped a ladle full of gumbo into a delicate china bowl my mouth watered. Jeeves pulled out a chair at the head of the long table and I sat. So did Mr. Marble, bowl in hand, taking the chair on my right. Jeeves and Mrs. White gave bows and left, leaving the gumbo and some steaming white rice.

Gumbo is a staple here in New Orleans. You can get it almost everywhere, in a variety of flavors, meats, and textures. Nearly all of it is okay, and most of it is very good. This, however, blew them all away. I'd never tasted gumbo like this; perfectly seasoned, perfectly spicy, perfectly thick, perfectly balanced with andouille sausage, shrimp, and okra. It coated my throat, it warmed my belly, and it healed my soul just a little.

We ate in silence. For the first time that prattling man shut up and kept quiet. Thank God. Only the settling sounds of the grandfather clock in the corner ticking away the seconds reached my ears.

I helped myself to seconds, pouring another ladle of gumbo into my bowl, then a float of rice on top. Mr. Marble smiled. "Glad to see you eating, Mrs. Witherspoon," he whispered.

At a whisper his voice soothed rather than grated. "First time I've felt like eating in a while. Mrs. White is a good cook."

"No," he said, taking another mouthful. "You'll come to find she's a *fantastic* cook. She knows exactly what to feed you and when." After another bite or two he continued. "She's also an herbalist. An herbal healer, for lack of a better term. You tell her what's ailing you, and she'll make you a tea guaranteed to cure it. Headaches, allergies, stomach ailments, cuts and scrapes. Hell, she took a wart off me once with a leaf and some ointment." He looked at his thumb. "Completely painless. Never came back."

I finished and sat back, my lips tingling, numb from the gumbo's heat. I considered having thirds. Reluctantly I decided against it.

To my right, stretching along the length of the room, towered windowed doors opening onto the patio in back. Through their laced curtains I could see the backyard, and just beyond it a small glass house. I assumed the herbs came from there. Despite the worn interior of the room, the yard looked immaculate. I envisioned this grand old home in its heyday, hosting spectacular parties with wealthy people dressed in costumes, ambling from the dining area out to the lamp-lit yard to dance, the happy music darkened by my despair.

"Quite a place, don't you think?" Mr. Marble broke my concentration.

I wiped my mouth with my napkin and scooted my chair back to face him better. "Yes. And thank you for showing it to me, Mr. Marble. But I'd like to go home now."

"But we haven't covered the trust arrangement yet."

I looked out the window, flooded with both questions and anger. This house? This was the big secret? This run down, dilapidated building and its quacky occupants? Why didn't Will mention this to me? Why wouldn't he have? I felt betrayed he'd been keeping this a secret. "Mr. Marble—," I started.

"Nathan, please. Call me Nathan—."

"—I don't care about the trust. I don't care about this house. I don't care what my husband wanted." He twisted his head, perplexed. "I was married to him for seventeen years. I thought I knew everything about him. I thought we shared everything. Now I find out that he had a separate trust, with separate money, and a possible separate life? I don't get it. I don't see why this had to be kept from me and now, frankly, I don't care."

"Please, let me—"

"You've had your shot. You sold it well. I did everything you asked. But now I want to go home."

"You stand to inherit—"

"I. Don't. Care."

He hung his head for a moment and we sat there in silence. Then Mr. Marble cleared his throat.

Jeeves entered the room. "Yes, sir?"

"Jeeves," Mr. Marble said, "can you please bring me my briefcase. I left it in the foyer."

"Indeed, sir," Jeeves bowed and left. Left me, there, with my mouth open. *Jeeves? He called him Jeeves?*

My utter shock read loudly. "Well, that's what you were gonna call him, isn't it? He'd best get used to it."

"But I never told you that."

"Nope. Didn't have to." He smiled. Not the salesman smile I'd had more than my fill of already. Rather a kind and gentle smile, the smile of a man who actually cared. "It's what Will used to call him."

I slumped in my seat and folded my arms. Another wave of anger washed over me. *Dammit.* Why couldn't I be a part of this, whatever this was? It's just a house, for Minerva's sake.

"I know," he started slowly and softly, "that you're angry. I know that you're hurt and overwhelmed. I get it. But Will is dead, Mrs. Witherspoon. It's time for you to live." I sniffed back the tears and rubbed my watery eyes. "He didn't share this with you in life, but it was his dying wish to share it with you in death." Jeeves quietly placed the briefcase on the table. "Thank you." He returned his gaze to me. "Please, just hear me out for a few more minutes. Then, if you want me to, I'll take you back. I promise."

I didn't argue, which he took as a sign of agreement. He opened his briefcase, pulled out a thick three-ringed binder, and continued. "Will and I set up this trust when the two of you married and kept it current. It was last updated—"

"How long?" I interrupted.

"Excuse me?"

"How long did you know him? Will. How long did you know my husband?"

He sighed. "Just a couple of years before he met you."

"Why did he never mention you?"

"Never mentioned me? I, well ..." It was back. That annoying, grating texture of his voice. I hadn't realized it had fully disappeared until now.

"Don't use that tone of voice with me!"

He sat back, stunned. He slowly closed his mouth and nodded. "All right." He flipped through a page or two. "How we knew each other and why isn't important right now, Mrs. Witherspoon. Please, let me get through this. Just hear me out. Hear *Will* out."

"Fine," I said curtly. My nervous thumb played with the table's fluted edge.

He paraphrased as he read. "The terms of the trust are simple. I, as your executor and accountant, am to provide you a monthly stipend of two thousand dollars. I'm also to maintain and pay your staff here at Gateway Manor," he waved his hand about to indicate the mansion, "as well as any supplies needed or used by the staff, including but not limited to food, tools, medicines, appliances—"

"Yeah, yeah. I get it. Move along."

"You, as the sole benefactor of the trust, must live here in Gateway Manor for a period no less than two years."

"What?" I cried out.

"After that you are free to live anywhere you like and you inherit completely and without restriction the rest of the trust reserves, which is a—"

"Not interested."

"But I haven't told you what you'll inherit."

"Not interested!"

"Seventy-four million dollars."

"Not inter ... *Great Gatsby*, how much?" It wasn't the money. Really. Never has been. In fact, one of the things that attracted me to Will right from the beginning was his total lack of enthusiasm to chase the almighty dollar. What shocked me was the sheer enormity of his deceit. "Where did Will get seventy-four million dollars? He was a CPA! He was good but ... *holy crap!*"

"Family money. Passed down through generations. Like this house." I must have looked like the words made no sense to me. Probably because they didn't. "Mostly the money stays in bank accounts and conservative investments. Because, like you, Will, nor his ancestors for that matter, cared about the money. So they tucked it away. Just in case."

"Just in case?"

"Yeah. Just in case. They lived mostly off interest and accumulated a little here and there. Over the years, *violà*." He handed me a pile of papers. Savings accounts statements and government bond receipts mostly. A cover letter outlined the grand total. Seventy-four million. Give or take a few hundred thousand.

As I studied it Mr. Marble continued.

"Will never cared about money. And I know he'd never marry a woman who felt differently. But I'd like to tell you what will happen, what Will had outlined in his trust to happen, if you walk away right now."

I looked up at him, and set the paper aside.

"If you leave the manor before the two year mark then the mansion is sold. The proceeds go to you. And only that. The remaining investments are to be shared amongst these charities," he said, rustling out another piece of paper, "in the distribution outlined."

I looked over the paper. I recognized most of the names. Habitat for Humanity, Red Cross, Doctors Without Borders, all charities Will and I supported in the past. The list also included an art school, a halfway house, and an orphanage in the city.

"You'd probably net ten or fifteen million from the mansion, so you'd still be set for life. That's what Will wanted." Then he mumbled, "We argued over that point a great deal, I assure you."

"So why don't I do that?" It seemed I was missing a part of the picture here. "What's the downside of selling this *dump* and giving the rest to charity?"

His eyebrows shot upwards at the word "dump" and, simultaneously, the house issued a loud settling creak. The timing unnerved me a bit. He looked skyward, eyes darting about the ceiling, and yelled, "She didn't mean it!" Then he looked at me, and cleared his throat. "Because if you sell this," then whispered very quietly, "dump", then continued, "everyone here not only loses a job, but they lose their home. They don't just work here, madam. They *live* here. Some for all of their lives."

I chewed on my bottom lip. I didn't want to kick anyone out of their home. But I didn't want to live in it, either.

Mr. Marble saw the spinning wheels in my head and rifled through the notebook again, retrieving several old documents. As I looked through them he spoke.

"The manor was built in 1823 by Thomas Tyler Witherspoon, who settled here after fighting in the Battle of New Orleans in 1814. Served with Andrew Jackson. Here," he pointed to one document. "He started with these three parcels, then purchased the next fourteen over five years. Initially it was—"

"Witherspoon Plantation," I finished, reading the description.

"Slaves, cotton, the whole works." He sat back. "Then the Civil War came."

"I take it the Witherspoons' backed the Confederates."

He tilted his head. "Um, yes and no. The sons went to war to defend their rights to the land. But the daughters and the servants, well ... There were several safe houses that started and organized passage through the Underground Railroad. This was one of them."

"Really?"

He nodded. "That's originally where the name came from. Gateway Manor." He shrugged. "It swings both ways."

I have to admit he had piqued my interest. "If I stay here, what happens to our place in Irish Channel?"

He whipped out another document. "This gives me power of attorney to manage the sale of your current house. The proceeds will add to the reserves you'll inherit in two years."

I scowled. "Will and I bought that place together."

"And all the memories of your marriage and your life together are there. But, Mrs. Witherspoon," he leaned close to me and tapped the table with his index finger. "Will *is here*."

I stared at the scattered documents again, the small flat representations of decades of lives and stories. Who was I to end all of that?

Mr. Marble handed me a pen. I straightened the power of attorney document. And I signed it. *Winki Witherspoon.*

Chapter Two

I WASN'T SURE how many hours had passed since Mr. Marble drove away leaving me in my new home. I lay on my new, puffy, and outrageously comfortable feather bed in my new, lace draped bedroom painted minty green, outlined by twelve inch ornate baseboards and thick crown molding. A gentle breeze entered through the french double doors swung open to the second floor veranda, exiting through the adjacent window. As bedrooms go, it was beautiful. It had held up better than the rest of the manor.

As time ticked by, however, I wondered how Mr. Marble had snookered me into staying. I started regretting the decision to sell the other house—*my* house—and move here. Why had Will kept this from me when he was alive while going to such great lengths to force it on me when he was gone?

Bored and utterly regretting my decision to stay I did what I'd been doing the last six months: I lost myself in his memory. Looking back on our seventeen years of marriage I tried to find a hint of this house, or a second life. I wanted to be angry. But every time I thought of those twinkling blue eyes, those perfect lips, that crooked smile, those tender kisses ... It was, *well*, magic.

I opened my eyes.

And screamed.

On the ceiling directly above me danced a cockroach.

As I scrambled in a panic out of the bed it scurried away. In the time it took me to take off a shoe it dashed across the ceiling and down the wall. When it reached the door that led into the hallway I threw. The roach acted like it saw the incoming projectile and serpentined upward, escaping the shoe's impact, arced around then straight down, and disappeared beneath the door.

I bawled. I yearned to sink back into the blissful memories of Will, but I couldn't escape this miserable hole of a house pressing in on me. Why keep something so banal, so ordinary, a *secret? I sold our home. My home. For this?* I mean, seventy-four million dollars and no one thought to have this place fumigated?

Someone knocked on my door. "Madam?" Jeeves called from the other side. "Are you in need of assistance?"

I wiped my face with my hands. "I'm fine." I'm sure my voice quaked.

"Since you missed dinner this evening I took the liberty of bringing it to you."

"I'm not hungry," I said to the door.

A moment passed. "Actually, madam, if I may be frank? I'm under strict instructions from Mrs. White to bring you something to eat. I fear that if I return with this tray of food untouched there will be great consequences on my person." I rolled my eyes. "What is the expression these days? You would be doing me a solid."

Despite my miserable state nothing is quite as humorous as hearing a painfully posh Englishman talk street. I kicked my shoe aside and opened the door. "Come on in."

Jeeves bowed before entering the door, in thanks I presumed. He smoothly glided into the room, placing a silver tray loaded with various covered dishes, utensils, and a teapot onto a small table under one of the windows. As he did so, he noticed my feet. Only one of which bore a shoe. But he didn't remark.

"I threw it over there," I pointed, feeling the need to explain. "At a cockroach."

His back quickly straightened. "Indeed!" he huffed. I felt like he thought I was making it up, but he continued. "I apologize, madam. I will have a scolding conversation with him, I assure you."

Oh. Kay? Maybe some weird, obscure British sense of humor? Before I could comment on his odd remark the scent of the food hit me like an aromatic brick. I inhaled deeply. "Wow! What did she make for dinner?"

"Mrs. White made Eggplant Parmesan, madam. A house favorite, I must say. She included a Caesar salad with homemade croutons, some chicory coffee, and a small slice of tiramisu for dessert. That, perhaps, is my favorite."

I lifted the cover on the large plate. It looked as fabulous as it smelled. "A sweets guy?" I asked him.

"Not usually, madam. No." He folded his hands comfortably behind him. "May I bring you anything else, madam?"

"No. Thank you."

"When you wish me to remove the tray simply pull the bell-cord." He gave a small nod with his head and I followed it to the headboard of the bed. A velvet piece of cloth about four inches thick with a garish gold tassel hung from the wall. I'd only see these in old movies before.

I nodded. "Thank you, Jeeves."

His eyebrows gave a quick shot up at the name. Then he nodded and left.

To say "I had dinner" doesn't begin to convey the ravenous devouring that followed, perhaps only rivaled by Cookie Monster and his treasured treat. As impressed as I was by Mrs. White's take on creole cuisine this afternoon, she awed me with her absolute spot-on version of this dish. Thick, zesty, red sauce that smothered perfectly roasted (not breaded and pan-fried, mind you) eggplant slices, topped with a blistered crown of cheese. My fears, frustrations, and roach-induced paranoia receded with each bite. Even the spider hiding behind the lacy curtains didn't upset me.

After the crisp salad and the espresso drenched tiramisu I went back to the fluffy bed and nestled myself into one of the best sleeps I'd had in months.

~ ~ * ~ ~

"*Shhhh!*"

Funny how the sound of ordering someone to be quiet is the very thing that breaks the silence. My eyes opened. The dark of my room emphasized the shadows disturbing the sliver of light beneath the door; shuffling feet made their way down the hall. Multiple pairs, it seemed. I heard voices but not couldn't make out any words. The creaking floors gave away their direction. Everyone tiptoed downstairs.

I checked my watch but couldn't make out the time. I quietly rose from my bed and went to the window where moonlight streamed in. Just after midnight.

I hadn't undressed when I collapsed after dinner, save for removing the remaining shoe. Leaning my head against the door I listened until all the movement had ended. After hiking up my way-too-big jeans I slowly cracked the door open and peered down the hall. I saw Mr. Smith and Mr. Wesson, dressed in lab coats, disappear down the staircase.

I'm not sure why I felt a compulsion to follow them, since, if I'd thought about it, I would have assumed they were just heading back to their crazy lab. But compelled I was. On my tippy-toes I made my way to the stairs.

"Gentlemen," I heard Mr. Marble's voice call to them, "glad you decided to join us." He sounded sarcastic.

"Sorry we're late," Mr. Smith said. "Wesson couldn't find his shoes."

"So why are *you* late?" The voice was Mrs. Black. The housekeeper.

"I had to help!"

"Come on," Mr. Marble said. "Let's get this house meeting started." He paused a moment. "Now, I know all of you are a little worried about Mrs. Witherspoon. I admit this isn't an ideal situation for any of us. But I implore you to give her some time."

I squatted at the top of the spiral staircase, from which vantage I could see most of the "house meeting" attendees, or at least their backs. I couldn't see Mr. Marble unless I bent farther forward, but then they might see me. I decided to wait and eavesdrop a bit longer.

"Time?" Mrs. White growled. "We don't have time." A number of members nodded and others mumbled sounds of agreement.

"Now, now, listen to me," Mr. Marble said. "We do so have time. We'll just have to adjust the schedule a little." He didn't have that grating quality to his voice but definitely was trying to sell them something.

"The tournament is next month," Mr. Smith said, "We really need a time machine."

More mutters of agreement.

"We don't even know if she's the right one!" Mrs. Black.

"We don't like her!" That came from a voice I didn't recognize. It was small and tinny, and comically French. From a child, a little boy, perhaps?

"That is your own fault," Jeeves said. "I explicitly told you not to try to introduce yourself until she was prepared to meet you."

"*Will* loved us," retorted the small voice.

"Will was raised with you," Jeeves said. I leaned down a bit farther, crunching my neck, hoping to see the voice's owner. Who on earth was Jeeves talking to?

"I'm not convinced," Mrs. Black said, "that she's the right one. I think you're backing the wrong horse. *I* hold the most experience now. I should be selected."

"That's not a bad idea," Mr. Smith said. "Black could represent the house this year, then maybe we can get Witherspoon ready for next year."

"This isn't a popularity contest," Mr. Marble said. "Only the champion of the house may represent it." No one said anything, to my dismay, because a little more explanation would have gone a long way.

"You're certain she's the one?" Mrs. White asked. "How do you know? You weren't there when Will died. You don't know that he passed on his talents to her."

"Are you kidding me?" Mr. Marble said. "Look around! This place is falling apart."

"It's mourning losing Will."

"It's mourning because *she's* mourning." He paused. "Guys, back me up." I guess he was speaking to Smith and Wesson. "Tell them what you told me. About the energy signatures."

Mr. Smith coughed. "Ah, well, every year Wesson and I assess the condition and strength of the house by using the spectrograph to go over the energy signatures—"

"Please," Mr. Marble interjected. "The results."

"It's different."

"What's different?" Jeeves asked.

"The wavelength, the amplitude, the frequency—" I spied Wesson tapping on his pad. "Oh, and its color. Now it's bluish," Mr. Smith added.

"That could mean it's tied to any one of us!" Mrs. Black said, angrily.

"In case you've forgotten let me be clear," Mr. Marble said. "The energy of the house is tied to the champion of the house. That is always, *always*, someone of the Witherspoon family. And since the color of the signature has changed, that implies that it's been passed to a Witherspoon not in the blood line. A wife, in this case. *That* would be Winki."

Mr. Smith chortled. "What kind of name is *that, anyway?*" I rolled my eyes. I get that a lot.

"That," Mr. Marble emphasized, "is an excellent question and one that you might ask her to start *getting to know her.*" Mr. Smith snorted and sat back, folding his arms. Mr. Marble continued. "We had great aspirations for the tournament this year, I know. But we'll just have to start over." The room roared in disagreement. My brain roared as well. What the hell was this tournament? All I could envision was men clad in metal and jousting on horseback.

"Will was a level forty-two!" Mr. Smith shouted. "You want us to enter back as a level *one?*"

"If we show up with a level one champion," Mrs. White said, in a worried, shaky voice, "they'll know our house is weak. Everyone! And that damned Malador will pick us off, one by one!"

That riled up the whole group. More yelling, more finger pointing, more feverish pacing.

Mr. Marble gave a shrieking whistle to get their attention. "That's enough!" he bellowed.

The room went deathly quiet.

"First," he said calmly, "since we've done no training, no prepping, and no practicing, we have no idea what level she really is." No one seemed very persuaded by that. "Second, it isn't about what level you *enter* the tournament. The show of power is all in what level you *leave* it." That did seem to mollify them a bit. He let it hang in the air a moment, then continued. "Now. I propose that we organize and itemize what needs to happen when."

Enough. "Don't I get a say?" I calmly descended the stairs, no longer able to just sit and listen.

All eyes turned to me. Those who were seated stood. I heard

Mrs. White moan, "By the devil! She was there all the time!"

"Well?" I asked. "Why aren't I being included in the 'we' who decide what happens next?"

Mr. Smith looked upward at the ceiling. "Fine bunch of lookouts you are." I had no idea what or who he was talking too—maybe he had very tall invisible friends? I was more focused on the annoying man who had disrupted my entire life and apparently intended on running it for me from now on.

He opened his mouth, then closed it, as if the words wouldn't come out. He haltingly held up his hands. "Please. Winki, we need to talk about—"

Then it happened. *Again!*

An audible pop filled the room and all the lights dimmed dramatically. I gasped as the cold and icy grip crushed my arm with *tremendous* force. I screamed and screamed, filled my lungs with air, and screamed again. I could feel the clasp breaking my arm. Through my agony I realized the others hadn't seen the lights dim. They hadn't noticed anything change. Other than me. Hysterical me.

"Winki!" Mr. Marble ran to me where I writhed on the floor. "What is it? What are you feeling?"

"It won't let go!" I yelled. I stared at my arm, hoping someone could see what I couldn't see myself. "Help me! It hurts!" I cried out, nearly mad with terror, tears filling my eyes. "Someone please! *Help me!*"

Chapter Three

I WOKE WITH a start the next morning in a somewhat familiar big, fluffy bed. Sunlight streamed in through the window, and the lacy curtains softly danced in the breeze. It took me a moment to realize where I was. My new bedroom, new house ... *last night.* The rush of memories made my heart thump in fright. I looked at my arm. And gasped. It was deeply bruised.

"You're fine, now."

A suited Mr. Marble sat in a maroon wing-backed leather chair tucked in the room's corner, fingers folded in his lap, one leg crossed over the other.

I bit my lip, trying to hold back the tears. "Apparently I'm not." I raised my bruised appendage to make the point. "What happened? What keeps happening to me?"

"I don't know."

"The hell you don't!" I pointed at him. "You seem to know everything. You knew who Will was, you know how he died, you know about tournaments, whatever the hell those are, so I'm pretty sure you know what's happening to me."

He rubbed his eyes and sighed. The he took a steady breath. "I ... probably handled this all wrong. I'm sorry. I've never done this before and I was just trying to follow Will's instructions. I swear, I wasn't trying to snow you or lie to you or make you angry. So. Let me start over. Please."

With a settling deep breath I scooted myself back to rest against the headboard.

He shifted a bit in his chair. "First, I genuinely don't know what happened last night. But we'll make a point of finding out. You say it's happened before?"

"Nightly, for over a week now." I looked at my arm. "But never like this. I always felt a grip, but never ..." God, I really don't want to go through that again.

"Same time?"

"What do you mean?"

"Does it always happen at the same time? At night?"

I nodded. "I guess. Around twelve thirty in the morning, yes." In all the emotional turmoil of yesterday I'd completely forgotten about it.

Mr. Marble walked to the bell cord and pulled it. He shoved his hands in his pants pocket. "We'll be ready tonight. I promise you." Someone knocked on the door. "Come in," Mr. Marble called.

Jeeves entered the room. "Yes, sir?"

"Twelve thirty. I don't care what they're working on now but get Smith and Wesson ready. And have Mama prepare that, um," he snapped his fingers, trying to remember, "*resilience* serum."

"As you wish, sir." Jeeves bowed and left.

I folded my arms angrily, then unfolded them since my wrist hurt. "So you *do* know something about what happened last night."

"No. I don't."

"Then what are Smith and Wesson getting ready for?"

He twisted his face, looking for an answer. Then he made his way to the window. "We work so hard to keep this world separate from human reality. I've never had to bring a normal into it before. I thought I needed to go slow, to ease you into it." He ran his hand through his hair. "I'm sorry, Mrs. Witherspoon, I truly am."

Bring a normal ...? *What in heaven's blazing trails is he talking about?* He looked at me. "Do you know why Will was a CPA?"

The change in topic stunned me into simply answering him. "He seemed to love what he did."

Mr. Marble gave a crooked smile, folded his arms and lean, casually against the wall. "Why didn't you two have kids?"

What did *that* have to do with anything? "I thought you were going to start explaining things."

"I am, I am. But I want you to look back on your life with him so I can put a few things into perspective. So? Why no kids?"

Okay, I'll play. "It wasn't a decision, yes or no. It just, well, never happened." Probably my failing. We had talked about them a number of times. But when I saw haggard, worn, unhappy people with crying, shrieking, arguing, miserable children I worried I'd be an awful parent. Will never pushed.

"Will was a CPA," Mr. Marble said, "because it was a decent paying job that only required him to work three months out of the year. He carefully selected clients to ensure that. That way he'd have time for the manor. For us."

"So all his business trips ...?"

"Any moment Will wasn't with you he was here. Trust me when I tell you there was only one thing in the world Will loved." He jutted his chin to me. "You."

Before I could react another knock came from my door. "Come in," we said in unison.

Jeeves floated in carrying his silver tray. I swear that guy walked on a cloud. "Beg my pardon, sir and madam, but I have brought you something to eat." He set the tray down, bowed to each of us, then left.

The scent of coffee forced me off the bed and I made a beeline to the tray. I poured a cup for myself and gave him a "You, too?" look.

"Please." As I poured he asked, "How do you like Mama's cooking?"

"Ah. Mrs. White. She's 'Mama'?"

"Yes," he said, taking the piping cup. "Will was never a proper sort. We all just use first names. Or nick names."

"Since none of you have *real* names." He narrowed his eyes. "Smith, Wesson, Black, White, Wilson, Marble ... it couldn't be more obvious."

"Oh, I assure you, those are real names. Everyone here has confirming ids, passports, and documents. Yes, sirree bob." He gave a wink. "As their lawyer, I can guarantee that."

"So you conjured the names for them?" It wasn't really a question.

He set his coffee cup down and shook a finger at me. "Remember that word, Mrs. Witherspoon. Conjured. It's going to have a whole new meaning for you." He pulled the small drop leaf table away from the wall and raised the sides until they clicked into place. He offered me a chair, then scooted the large wing-back—apparently much lighter than it looked—across from me. Without speaking he served up breakfast: buckwheat pancakes stuffed with fat, juicy blueberries, Steen's cane syrup, and a side of grapefruit segments sprinkled with candied ginger. He talked, stealing a bite or two when he could.

"Will didn't want to have kids," he said. "I mean, he did. He would have loved to have a family, he would have loved to call you not just his wife but the mother of his children. But he was scared. Scared for their lives. So, he thought, best not to have any."

"Scared of what?"

"Let's talk about Will's passing for a moment. Did you see him before he died? Did he say anything? Do anything?"

"You always seem to know everything. I'm surprised you have to ask."

"Humor me."

I had pushed the memory far away. Thinking about it brought me too much pain.

It started with a phone call. As soon as I heard the "unknown caller" ringtone, I knew. Don't ask me how, I just did. I knew something terrible had happened. I answered. The NOPD called to tell me there had been an accident. What happened next is a blur of images—rushing around to find my motorcycle keys, zipping to Touro Hospital, frantically finding his room, then ... then it's all very clear and focused. A nurse leads me to his bedside. She tries to sound positive but I can tell she's lying. She leaves us alone, surrounded by machines, tubes, and noise. I'll never forget the sound of the heart monitor.

Will's face was bloodied. One eye was swollen shut, black and blue. His bottom lip split, like an over ripe tomato. A white sheet covered the rest of him so I never saw the extent of his injures. I thank my lucky stars for that now. I'm glad my memories of him are mostly perfect.

His one eye looked at me as I neared the bed. I think he tried to smile. "Winks," he whispered.

"Oh, God ... *Will*."

As I neared his bedside, running, something happened. His good eye went wide. Before I knew it he grabbed my arm, the left one, just above the wrist. He said something I couldn't understand then ...

The heart monitor went flat, he closed his eye, and his hand went limp, dropping off the side of the bed. Nurses rushed in. Someone led me out of the room. From the doorway I heard terse instructions, then "Clear!" His body jumped.

"But it didn't work," I told Mr. Marble, as I went through the memory with him. "Will died." I hadn't told anyone that story before.

While I spoke Mr. Marble was able to finished his breakfast. My own half-eaten pancakes didn't look appetizing anymore. I pushed my plate away.

"Where?" he asked quietly.

"At Touro," I answer.

"No," he shook his head. "Where did he touch you?"

Without thinking I wrapped the fingers of my right hand around my left forearm. Where my dying husband last touched me, *right* over the bruises.

Why hadn't I noticed that before? I clearly could see his hand holding my arm, I clearly could feel that icy, excruciating pressure from last night. More frighteningly, the bruises I bore from last night's ordeal were all but gone. All but vanished.

"If you finish your breakfast they'll be gone entirely," Mr. Marble said, clearly sensing my distress. "One of Mama's talents. Good food for a healthy body." He poured us both more coffee. "And no, by the way. I didn't know the details about his dying. Thank you for sharing them with me. I know that was hard." He set the pot down, sat back, and crossed his legs at the knees. "We miss him here very much, but I can only imagine your pain. I knew Will well. He wouldn't have wanted you in perpetual mourning. It's time to start healing, Mrs. Witherspoon. Time to take the next step. His death will bring you a new life. For your sake, for all our sakes, you should embrace it."

"Then tell me why I need to."

"Let's start at the beginning, shall we?"

"Like, this house? Will's other life?"

"No, no, no. The very beginning. Like when the universe *exploded* into existence." He dramatically used his arms and hand in an expansive movement to emphasize his point. Very much like a stage magician. The Amazing Zingo? Mysterious Mr. Mustafa?

Theatrics aside, *are you kidding me?* The dawn of time? "I'm guessing this is going to take some time then," I sighed and sat back. Without thought my fingers pinched a bite of pancake from my plate.

"The universe comprises five pieces, Mrs. Witherspoon. Matter, space, good, evil, and the energy that binds them all. Five." He held up a spread hand. "And everything, *everything*, is composed of those five elements. You. Me. This house. That chair. The sun. The moon. Everything!"

I nodded, uncertain of his point. "Let's assume I understand."

"It's imperative you understand. Matter, space, energy—these things are neutral, but good and evil? That's where challenge comes in. That's where *choice* comes in." He took a sip of coffee and sighed audibly, quite like a Folger's commercial. "Over countless eons stars formed, galaxies formed, planets formed. Living creatures arose." He leaned forward. "Good and Evil manifested."

I took another bite, unsure of where he was going with this, but glued to his every word.

"Space, matter, and energy combined over time in a myriad of ways to create a myriad of things. The concepts of Good and Evil, however, loom as distant entities. They just hum in the background, like cosmic vibrations. Until you draw on them. Then they feed you."

"Feed you?"

"For example," he sank into his chair, which warmly creaked, "consider a woman standing in a grocery line. And consider a second woman who cuts in front of her. Let's not dwell on the second woman's actions, but only the first's reaction. She's been challenged. Will she accept this? Will she confront it? If she confronts it, will it be with words and understanding, or will it escalate to pushing and shoving. All of that is determined by how much anger—and therefore Evil—or acceptance—and therefore Good—she draws from."

I took another bite of pancake. "Not that I'm not fascinated, or anything," I said, chewing. "But how does this involve me? Or Will?"

He wagged his finger. "Before I get to Will and this house and you, Mrs. Witherspoon, there's one more bit of history you need to know. It's the most interesting part." I gave an uninterested nod. "While all of mankind is created from matter, space, and energy, not all of these are in equal amounts. That's obvious, of course, that a mouse contains a smaller amount of matter while an elephant a greater amount. A little known fact, however, is that some creatures contain a greater quantity of *energy*." I could tell this part excited him by the small smile that ran across his face. "Now, in the common mouse or elephant, this usually makes little difference. Those creatures are bound by their smaller minds and simple needs of survival, so it has nearly no impact. But in humans, madam, this is *big*." He rubbed his hands together. "This is *bigger* than big. Imagine," he said animatedly, "if you can tap into the energy that binds you, the very energy that binds everything, then you have complete access. To everything!"

"I'm not following," I said with a raised eyebrow.

"You can change matter. And space. And energy. Some can move items with a thought. Some can fly. Some can—"

"Wait, wait!" I held up my hand. "Are you talking about magic?"

He winced at the word. Then looked out the window. The late spring day was heating up, and the once comfortable breeze that nudged its way into the room had retreated. The air became still.

He spoke. "DC Comics call them *super powers*. Harry Potter calls it *magic*. We... we like to just call them *talents*."

"Are you telling me Will was *talented?*"

He gave a small smile, although his wet eyes did not escape me. "Will was very, *very talented*."

I scoffed, a little insulted. "Please. There's no such thing as magic, Mr. Marble."

To my surprise he responded with a light laugh. "Smith and Wesson tell me that all the time." He focused. "Now, there's more to hear before we get to Will and his talents. Let's assume it's all true, for the sake of moving this along, although I can see by your expression you don't buy any of this. Let's assume that some people are created with more energy than others. And they can tap into it. What else is there in that energy?"

I felt a bit like a student. "You're asking me?"

"Yes. Name the five elements that came out of creation."

"Matter, space ... ah, Good and Evil." He waited. "And the energy that binds them."

"Exactly."

Like a student being pressed in a quiz I concluded: "So if a person can manipulate matter and space, then they can manipulate Evil and Good."

He let the words linger in the air for several moments, letting them sink into my mind. Finally, he said, "They like to think so." He cleared his throat as he stood, walked to the headboard, and pulled the bell cord. "Have you ever known an addict?" he asked me. "Alcohol, or drugs, or even gambling?"

"No. Not personally, I mean. Why?"

"Take alcohol. For most people it's just alcohol. Something interesting to drink. Something to do socially. Something to enjoy periodically. Most people can decide when and where and how much. But an alcoholic loses control." Jeeves knocked on the door and floated in, padded softly to the table, and cleaned up. "The alcoholic doesn't have control. The alcohol does. It may take him a lifetime to realize that. And along they way, he may hurt people. In extreme cases, he may even kill someone." Without speaking Jeeves left, closing the door behind him.

"What you're saying then is that people with talents who would tap into Good and Evil can get corrupted by them. Addicted."

"Very well put."

Something gnawed at me. "Are you telling me Will ... was Evil?"

"Um," he stammered, "let's not discuss specifics just yet—"

"No. Answer me that. Was Will evil?"

"You don't even believe in any of this. Besides, that's isn't—"

"Answer. Me."

Mr. Marble scratched his head as he flopped back into the chair. "In the end, no. Ever since you'd known him, no. But. There was a time when he ... *explored* the darker side."

I folded my arms and sat back, and I casually looked down. At my arm. Then my eyes went wide. They were *gone*. The bruises had completely vanished. I looked at the door that Jeeves left through, then turned to Mr. Marble. "Mrs. White! She's feeding me magical food!"

He winced again, then nearly yelled. "Mrs. Witherspoon, please, don't use the word *magic*. It has one of two connotations these days; either some hack producing rabbits from a hat on a stage, or innocent people being burned at the stake." Then he relaxed. "One of Mama's *talents* is creating perfect meals. Not just in flavor, but in what you *need*. You don't have to tell her what you have a taste for, she knows what you *need* to eat. And when."

"Is everyone here *talented*?"

He stood abruptly, ignoring the question, and held out a beckoning hand. "It's time to take a walk, Mrs. Witherspoon. You'll want to see the rest of the place." When I failed to move quickly enough he urged, "You *need* to see the rest of the place."

We walked the long hallway of the second floor while Mr. Marble spoke. "Unlike the rest of your staff I don't live here. I do have a room, however," he nodded to a door we passed. "I stay on occasion when I'm needed. When Will needed me."

"Their rooms aren't here?" I asked, sweeping my hand at the hallway. There were eight doors, including Mr. Marble's and mine.

"No. Their rooms are in the back. In the slave's quarters. Modernized," he quickly added, "I assure you."

Back in the living room, the scene of last night's house meeting and its aftermath, Mr. Marble rambled on about the history of the mansion. "Right here," he pointed to a spot in front of the gaping fireplace, "that's where T. T. Witherspoon sat when he signed the freedom forms. That's what he called them, anyway. Three hundred and seventeen of them."

"Freedom forms?"

"The official emancipation documents that stated basically, 'you are free' to each of his slaves. One by one they stood in front of him and took their documents. Then he offered them employment, almost in the same breath."

I knew very little of the dark past of New Orleans and the Civil War. "Was that common?"

Mr. Marble shrugged. "Don't know. But T. T. knew he needed people to keep the plantation running. He fixed up the slaves quarters and turned them into decent housing, and hired as many he could."

"You seem proud of that," I said. "Some southerners wave the Confederate flag and go into a diatribe about how the war was about state's rights."

"Personally, I think of the war as a struggle for *human* rights, which always trumps state's rights. But then again," he said, "*I'm from Boston.*"

The last words came out in that high-pitched grating texture with an overdone Bostonian accent. Over the last day I hadn't noticed how completely it had disappeared. Then it occurred to me. I pointed a finger at him, eyes wide. "Is that one of you talents, Mr. Marble? That irritating voice?"

He gave a stupid grin. "Why Mrs. Witherspoon, I'm sure I don't know what you're talking about."

"Oh, you most certainly do," cackled Mrs. Black, as she joined us. Her long braided grey hair wrapped over the top of her head in a coiffure crown. She looked at me. "It's called the *power of persuasion.*"

He rolled his eyes and sighed. "I like to call it *the voice of reason.*"

"It's a passive gift," she explained, "but that doesn't mean it's harmless. Quite the opposite. It can be very dangerous in the wrong hands." She looked Mr. Marble up and down when she said "wrong hands", assessing him. To me she said, "Do you think you signed that document because you wanted to? *He*," she jutted her pointy chin, "made you."

What? "You *made* me?"

He defensively raised his hands. "I, er, well ... okay, yes. I did. Butbutbut ..." he said as I folded my arms, glaring, "it's what Will wanted me to do."

"Will wanted you to manipulate me?" I accused.

He pursed his lips. "Will wanted you to sign that document and stay here, at least until you completed your first tournament." He hissed at Mrs. Black, "And you know that." Mr. Marble shook his head. "I'm sorry, Mrs.Witherspoon, but I work for Will. I am both legally and morally obligated to keep my agreement with him, to safely get you through your first tournament. After that, my employment is strictly your call."

"So when this stupid tournament thing is done I can fire you?" Kinda looking forward to it now.

"Yes." He looked at Mrs. Black. "Feel free to fire the entire staff, if you wish."

"You need to treat her like an adult," she retorted. "Tell her the truth. About everything."

"I am!" he defended. "But you can't expect that she'll simply embrace it. So, I'm giving her the tour and explaining our world as I go."

"Does she know about the security yet? Or the information network?"

"No," he and I said at the same time.

He continued. "Those things aren't important right now."

"Huh," Mrs. Black threw her head back, disagreeing. "They aren't important *to you*, I see. You need to tell her. Just get it over with.

Like ripping off a fingernail."

Good gravy! Did she really mean to say that? My own fingers curled protectively.

As Mr. Marble opened his mouth to argue, she turned to me. With a poking finger she said, "Will's dead, child. If he passed his talents onto you, you need to learn how to use them, and right quick!" She spun on her heals and stormed out of the room, and called, "There! All done. Now *get on with it!*"

I exhaled in relief as she stormed out. "I don't think I like her."

"No one likes her."

For some reason being told I had *talent*, which only yesterday would have sent me packing, now left me dazed and confused. I looked at my healed forearm. "Is this one of my talents?"

"Nope. That's definitely Mama's cooking." He tilted his head. "You're starting to believe."

I shrugged. "I liked to say you were all out of your minds, however," I tapped my arm, where that grip has tormented me for the last few nights, "maybe I'm nuts, too."

He put a hand behind my back and gestured into the foyer. "Let's continue, shall we?" He led me into the back of the house, through a game room, complete with everything from an antique skittles board to modern Playstation and Wii consoles. Through a grand arch of sliding door panels we reached the sitting room, and beyond it the sun room, gloriously lit from the abundant sunshine. We sat opposite one another in clamshell-shaped white rattan chairs beneath a wicker ceiling fan whose revolutions stirred my brunette hair.

"Here's what I do know about last night," he started. "Usually we're better prepared for interplanal visitors. But we were so distracted by your presence that by the time the lights dimmed we were caught off guard."

"You saw the lights go brown?"

"Of course." He looked so frank. With a dismissive wave he said, "In this house that happens two or three times a month. Although, it's usually due to the old wiring. Anyway, by the time anyone could see what was happening it was over."

"Wait. Inter*whatta* visitors?"

"Inter*planal*. Like, between planes of existence."

"Do you mean ghosts?"

He wagged his head, "Well, not necessarily. Yes, that can be a plane that crosses over, and we've had some of those visitors here, but they tend to be a quiet bunch. I'm talking about other planes." He could see I wasn't following. "This is a toughie. No one gets it the first time round. Think of it like this. Do you watch Star Trek at all?"

"The original, TNG, DS9, or Voyager?"

"Ah. That's a yes, then. When they visit other worlds, how do they get there?"

"They beam down onto the planet." That, at least, I knew.

"And if the people on the planet don't know they're coming, having people just show up can, well, can frighten the bejeezus out of folks. That's kind of what's happening here. Another plane of reality is 'beaming' down here."

"That really wasn't the part I was having trouble understanding. It was the interplanal part."

"Think of the visitors as from different ships. Different planets, even. In reality, they come from somewhere equally challenging to get to. Different dimensions, different realities, whatever." He settled into his chair. "In short, something is coming unannounced, and that's never a good sign. Especially since it hurt you."

I looked at my arm, seeing Will's finger there as he passed. "You don't think it's Will, do you?"

"No. Not possible. He would never hurt you. That I'd bet my soul on." He noticed me caress my arm. "The location is just a coincidence. Possibly a sensitivity, since it's the last place he touched you."

"What do we do?"

"This time we'll be ready. Those of us who can see visitors will amp up those talents. They take a minute or two to kick in fully. Then we'll try to communicate with them, find out what they really want. If they persist, we go to war."

"Whoa. War?"

"That's the rule. No one invades a house unannounced without consequences. Even lesser houses know that rule."

I rubbed my face trying to wrap my head around this new life. "Lesser houses?"

"Mrs. Witherspoon, you were attacked last night. You said you'd been attacked for nearly a week. No one hurts a member of our house. We will start by assuming it's a misunderstanding, given that you weren't officially a member of the house until yesterday, and we'll go from there."

The thought of going through this yet again rattled me. I shuddered. I may have even whimpered.

"Hey," Mr. Marble said as he leaned forward and took my hand. "This time you're not alone. We'll all be there."

I nodded. "What should I be doing until then?"

"Unpack." He held up his hand in the air, and ticked off his fingers as he counted, "Three, two, one."

Jeeves entered the room. "Madam and sir. The lorry has arrived."

"We say 'truck' here, Jeeves," Mr. Marble said. "The *truck* has arrived."

"Beg your pardon, sir."

"What truck?" I asked.

Jeeves answered, "The lorry full of your clothes. But there is another matter, sir, madam, we have a guest. The Colonel from the Magnolia House is waiting in the foyer. Shall I bring him in?"

"My clothes? Wait, there's a truck with all of my clothes? Here?"

Mr. Marble ignored me. "No, I'll go talk to him." He turned to me, "I had them brought here. Everything else from the house I put in storage."

"Everything else?" Crap, this was moving way too fast for me. "But I wanted to go back—"

"Besides your clothes there was nothing there you needed. Bedding, towels, dishes, appliances, furniture. Everything is here already."

"But I might want to use some of my own things!"

He stood. "I'm sure you do. And you will. But right now we have a great many things to concentrate on and going through your trinkets and treasures isn't one of them. Not today. Today you unpack. Today you organize your clothes, take a good long bath, and start getting to know this house."

I exhaled deeply as I dropped my head backwards. My eyes spied a cobweb on the ceiling, complete with eerie black spider. "Look," I said, turning my face back downward, "can we get a real maid service in here? And an exterminator? There are roaches and spiders and webs all over the place."

Both Jeeves and Mr. Marble looked up. Mr. Marble started to say something, stuttering to find words, then Jeeves interrupted. "Perhaps, sir, she should meet the rest of the staff first, if you don't mind my suggesting."

"Nope. That's a good idea, Jeeves." He slapped the butler on the back as he left. "Have at it." As he just got out of earshot he called, "See you this evening, Mrs. Witherspoon."

Jeeves stood like stone, eye narrowed. "Ah," he said after a moment. "I'm beginning to see my folly." He looked at me. "May I get you anything, madam?"

"No. I'm fine."

"Very well. May I have a seat?" I gestured to the now empty

chair across from me. Jeeves took it, sitting properly, knees together and palms poised on his lap. He looked thoughtful, for a moment, then spoke. "Long before electronic devices, long before intercoms, long before security systems, and much longer than the internet has been around we've had a sophisticated communications and security capability." That sounded cool. "We even have a spy network, should we need it."

Okay, not so cool. "We spy on people?"

"Not just people, and not without cause, madam. Other houses, typically."

"Other *houses*?"

"Other talented houses."

"There are other talented houses? Here in New Orleans?"

"In New Orleans alone there are three. Fifteen in total on this plane."

Wars, spying ... none of this was sounding like "living the good life." I dismissed my worries for the moment and waved my hand, "When do I meet the staff?"

"The chief of communications sits next to you as we speak."

I looked to my right, following his oh-so-proper gesture. A big, brown roach was on the arm of my chair. I shrieked, jumping up as fast as my body would allow, visibly shuddering.

"See?" said a tinny, small voice with a French accent. "This is unacceptable! How can I work with someone so *bourgeois*, so ... so small minded!"

"Now, please, Hercule," Jeeves said. "Proper introductions are in order." He cleared his throat. "Mrs. Witherspoon, please meet Hercule Poirot, your chief of communications."

I couldn't move. My wide eyes stayed glued onto the small creature that danced left-and-right as my hands pressed hard across my mouth. My heart thumped loudly in my chest. Yes. I am that frightened of roaches.

Jeeves ignored me. "Hercule, please meet Mrs. Witherspoon, your new employer."

The roach stopped moving and, I kid you not, stood upright and bowed toward me. "*Madame.* I am pleased to make your acquaintance."

I said nothing. I did nothing. "Madam?" Jeeves said quietly.

I pointed a shaky finger. "Did ... did the cockroach just talk?"

"Indeed," Jeeves said.

"*Oui!* Of course! Stupid girl." he said, irritated. "Shall I dance for you like I would my brothers, hm? Maybe you'd rather communicate that way?"

It scurried a little closer. I scurried a step backwards.

"Madam, I assure you, he's harmless," Jeeves said. "He won't bite. And he doesn't sting. Save, of course, for his tongue."

Jeeves and I stared at the little insect, me with my hands still glued to my face.

"Well?" Hercule said. "Well? You have nothing to say, hm? You've just met a talking *cafard* and you have nothing to say. Women! Why is it always the same with them?" He started to scamper off. "By the way," he said back at me, disappointed, "you throw like a syphilitic baboon."

"Wait," I said. I took a breath, then another. A talking cockroach. Maybe ... I can do this. "That's cute. Er," I stammered.

He stopped, scurried his way back to the edge of the arm, and sat up, one leg crossed over the other. The other four "arms" folded in front of him. "What is so cute, *madame?*"

I took an unsteady step towards it. Him. Whatever. "*Cafard.* I like that better than 'roach'."

"Of course you do. Everything is better in French, *n'est-ce pas?*"

"And your name is Hercule?"

"*Oui.*"

"Hercule Poirot?"

"*Oui.*"

"Like the Agatha Christie character?" I turned to Jeeves. "Why does everyone in this house have a pseudonym?"

"That is my name! I had it first," one arm poked into his little chest, while the other pair remained folded. "It is hardly my fault that silly woman lacked the creativity to come up with a new name for her imbecile detective."

I knelt down for a close look, a bit more courageous. "You knew Agatha Christie? That would make you, what, a hundred years old?"

"I'm much, much older, *madame*."

"I didn't think roaches lived that long."

"They don't," he said. "But talented *cafard* do."

"You see, Hercule is a familiar," Jeeves said. "He guides those new to their gifts. He joined our household," he cleared his throat, "I mean, *your* household once Miss Christie established herself as a prominent author."

"Just before the second great war," Hercule said proudly.

"Then you raised Will?" I asked him.

He hung his little head. "*Oui.*"

"I miss him a great deal myself," I said.

"No, no, *madame*. You misunderstand. I failed Will. Something I deeply regret." He shook his head and got on all sixes. "Perhaps we will talk about it some other time, *oui*? You have much to do." He started to crawl away.

"Hercule," I called. He stopped, and turned to face me. "I'm sorry. About the shoe. But, I ... this ... is gonna take me a little time, I'm afraid."

"*Je comprends*, perhaps it's best if I only come when you call, *madame*." He continued as he moved out of sight. "That way you can adequately prepare yourself for my *hideous* appearance ..." He said something more, complaining about women and their inability to see past the exterior until his little voice disappeared. I looked to Jeeves for guidance.

"Please, do not fret. Hercule isn't happy if he isn't insulting someone."

I folded my arms, trying not to show how creeped out I was, while looking at the last place I saw the *cafard*. "Chief of communications?"

"Yes, madam."

"How does that work?"

"You simply speak out what you want or who you want to see. The roach network, as we call them, makes it happen."

"Here. In the house?"

"Anywhere in New Orleans. There are a good many roaches in the city. While only one of them talks, they all will understand you. Communication among them is almost instantaneous. It's a roach thing," he flitted his hand in the air, maybe a little creeped out himself. "Now. Are you ready to meet the chief of security?" Jeeves asked.

"I don't know. I'm a little weirded out."

"That is understandable, madam. Annabelle? Are you present?"

"I am," said a distant voice. Feminine. And small, like Hercule's. "Perhaps now is not the best time. Mr. Jeeves." I looked around trying to find the source of the voice.

"What news of the guest?" he asked.

"The Colonel came to visit Will, sir. At the moment we stand ready."

I looked around trying to locate to source of the sound. "Will?" I asked, puzzled. "What do you mean, to visit Will?"

Jeeves looked up at the spider on the ceiling. *You've got to be kidding me!*

The voice came from above. From the spider. "This house has denied that anything has happened to Will. It was safer that way."

Safer? I stepped out from under the web, my skin crawling.

"How ... safer?"

The spider picked her way out of the web and pirouetted down a fine gossamer thread as she spoke. "It isn't uncommon for houses to boast the death of their champion in an effort to draw out enemies. When Will passed away, my lady, we let it appear that that was the case." She dangled gracefully roughly a foot in front of me. "Then we spread rumors that he was still alive. A tactical decision on my part."

"The house supported her decision, madam. Without its champion, the house is weak and vulnerable."

"Against who?" I asked, shifting my weight from foot to foot. Maybe I backed up a bit, too. All the creepy crawlies I most dread are part of the house staff. Ew!

"We never know who exactly, madam" Jeeves explained. "But we stay on the ready."

Magic. Champions. Tournaments ... "That's why all the cobwebs."

"Yes. We have scouts positioned in every room for safety," the spider said.

"There are spiders in every room of the house?"

"Yes. And battalions in the attic at the ready. They have been prepped for this evening, in case things go badly. I must ask, my lady, by any chance do you know how to fight? Some martial arts, perhaps?"

Trucks with my clothes. Selling my house. Talking bugs. Talents. Spying. *War* ...

That was *it*. My brain overloaded with terror and panic. *I ran.*

"Madam?" Jeeves called after me. "Madam! Please wait!"

I ran all the way to the front door. A spider lowered to block me. I batted at it and hollered, "Get out of my way!" as I grabbed the handle and threw the door wide open.

I ran.

Past Mr. Marble, who shook hands with some elderly gentleman. Past the moving truck and the two brawny men unloading wheeled racks of clothing. Down the white horseshoe driveway. Between the two houses, onto the sidewalk, I ran. Blindly racing into the street, narrowly colliding with an oncoming taxi. He honked. *I ran.* Hard. As far and as fast as my terrified legs would carry me.

Chapter Four

I GLANCED AT my watch again. It was a little after ten at night. Which was just a few minutes later than the last time I looked. I sat on a bench in Audubon park. Officially, the park was now closed. But I and a few transients lagged behind. None of us really had anywhere to go.

I had spent the day wandering up and down many of the sidewalks between the river and St. Charles. With each step my utter terror gave way to sadness, then regret, and lastly what I can only describe as numbness of the soul. Eventually my fatigued feet wore out and ached for relief. Around sunset I planted myself on the bench and hadn't moved since.

My eyes spied the roach that danced at my feet. Just like I had been doing to every one of their creepy contingent I leaned down to it and yelled, "Leave me alone!" It acted as they all did today, running into some shelter to hide. And those around me acted more cautious, avoiding the crazy lady in baggy clothes who yelled at roaches.

I weighed out my options. I could take whatever money I had left and buy a train ticket up north. The City of New Orleans still ran up to Chicago. Never been. Could be neat.

Then I looked at my arm. The sensation was definitely more severe in the manor. Maybe leaving was the right thing to do—

maybe just getting out of the city would end this unearthly torment.

But maybe it wouldn't.

God, what if this never ends?

Deeply lost in my thoughts I didn't see him. A man, possibly homeless, had walked along the blacktop trail that separated me from the duck pond. My eyes raised up to him as he closed in. *On me.* His eyes bore into me, intentional and hating. I sat upright as he neared. My legs moved on their own, without commands from my mind. I stood and jumped over the bench, keeping it between him and me. He raised his hand. *Oh, God, he has a gun.*

My heart leapt into my mouth as I inhaled deeply, eyes wide. Instinctively, I held up my hands, which is stupid, I know, because they're not gonna stop a speeding bullet. But I did it anyway. Anything to try to survive.

Nothing happened for a moment. Then a long moment. Then the muzzle of the barrel brightly flashed and the bullet softly emerged, its black silhouette surrounded by a halo of gunfire brilliance. It slowly made its way to me. Slowly. *Very* slowly. In fact, I lowered my hands and easily stepped out of its way, watching as the small projectile drifted by me, much like Jeeves simply drifts through the mansion.

I looked back at my assailant. He still looked at the bullet, not me, staring at where his target once stood. Dumbfounded, I watched him as he watched the distant blackness. I watched as his eyes slowly widened, and he, in slow motion, started to look around. I wasn't waiting until he found me. I ran at him, and just before reaching him, I did a cartwheel and brought my airborne feet back toward the earth by way of his knee.

What I didn't tell the spider was that Will and I had been avid attendees of the local Capoeira school for the last fifteen years. I began to suspect that he insisted on attending because he knew what might come for me. I didn't have time to dwell on that thought as I twisted in mid air. But … I hadn't attended the class since Will's death so I was out of practice, and the new, lighter me misjudged the effort. I intended to knock his legs out from under him, thinking then I'd take his gun. Instead, I hit with such speed his leg buckled in a way the knee joint was never meant to move.

The loud crack zipped the world into alignment.

Everything started to move at normal speed again. I didn't think about it as his agonized scream filled the air, abusing my poor ears. He dropped the gun, and I kicked it away, under the bench.

"Hey, lady!" someone yelled as they ran up the walking path. A young black man clad in a worn Army jacket. "Lady, are you all right? How'd you do that? Damn, you moved so fast!" As he approached I noticed another man, this one in blue uniform, badge and all, following.

"I … don't …" I wrapped my arms around me, not knowing what to do or say. How could I possibly explain what just happened? Not that I surround myself with firearms, but I'd never seen a gun malfunction that way before. Despite my attacker's now nonthreatening activity—that of writhing in agony on the ground— the image of that man's eyes boring into my own scorched my memory. Who was he? Was I his intended victim? Or just in the wrong place at the wrong time?

The cop joined us and knelt by the wailing man's side. He made me and the Army guy sit on the bench and wait while he attended my assailant. With a small radio thingy on his shoulder he called for assistance and an ambulance.

The gunman ceased his caterwauling long enough to point at me. "She did this to me! She attacked me!"

The man next to me spoke up in my defense. "That's not true, officer, I saw the whole thing. That man took a shot at her first. Then, damn, you shoulda seen her, she moved like lightning and did that!" he pointed at his own knee for affect. "Like with Kung Fu or something," While he spoke I noticed the name "A. Jones" on the label stitched onto his worn coat.

"Just sit there and shut up," the officer replied.

So he did. And so did I. After a moment I quietly thanked the seated man for his help. "You're welcome," he softly said.

Over the next hour the area filled with pulsing lights, emergency vehicles of every shape and color, police officers, firemen, and EMTs. From somewhere came a stretcher, and after questions and IVs and bandages and orders the gunman was toted off. He looked almost princely, surrounded by servants and aids while I sat mute on a hard bench in the dark of night. Not sure the jerk deserved any of it.

But having that time was a relief. Even though I didn't have a scratch on me I couldn't keep the emotional tension at bay. A complete stranger just tried to kill me. My adrenaline throbbed through me with every heart beat and my mind sprinted with the images over and over. *I looked up, his eyes bore into my soul, he raised his hand…*

Chatter brought me back to the moment. The first officer spoke to a couple of non-uniformed individuals, a man and a woman, both of whom looked like they had some wonderful activity planned for this evening, but *no*, they had to be here. Us benched folks could overhear the conversation.

"And why were you here?" the new woman asked. I could hear her southern accent.

"This is my last round, ma'am." Hm. A superior officer. Detective, perhaps. "Just as the park closes I chase out all the stragglers and homeless folk."

"What did you see?" she asked. Her silent partner stood at her side. In the lamplight I could only make out blond, spiky hair. With hands in his pockets he looked over the scene. Eventually, they landed on me.

"First, I heard a gunshot. Then ran in its direction. This guy was ahead of me," he pointed to Mr. Jones at my side, "and she was standing near the guy on the ground," he pointed at me. "By the time I got here, Mr. Cruise was on the floor screaming. I made them sit then called an ambulance."

"Mr. *Cruise?*" the suited partner asked. His accent was *not* Southern. It was English.

"Yeah. *Tom* Cruise," the cop nodded. "I'm no detective but I'm betting that's not his real name."

Seemed to be the world I lived in, now.

"Thank you, officer." She gave some order to her spiky-haired partner, who continued to speak with the officer. As they walked off she came to us. "I'm Detective Duplantier. And you are?"

Before I could utter a word my defender spoke. "My name is Tony Jones. And this here lady was shot at. I saw the whole damn thing." He sounded angry.

Detective Duplantier turned to me and said, "And you are?"

"Winki Witherspoon."

She cocked her head. "Is that a nickname?"

"No."

"Winki!" Tony Jones said. "That's cool. I like that. Winki."

"Mr. Jones," Detective Duplantier said as she reached out and grabbed a random uniformed cop walking by, "*this* man will take your statement. Over there," he pointed. The cop, without argument, nodded and gestured for the young man to follow. All the while she looked at me.

Finally she asked. "Are you all right, ma'am?"

"Yes. I'm fine."

"Good," she smiled. "Maybe you can tell me what happened?"

I shrugged. "I was sitting here, minding my own business when, out of nowhere—"

"That's enough, Mrs. Witherspoon," said a voice. That grating, Bostonian voice. I looked over my shoulder, and coming up from the dark park was Mr. Marble.

Detective Duplantier took an annoyed breath. "Sir, I'm conducting an interview."

"Is she under arrest?" Mr. Marble asked.

She ignored him and turned to me. "Ma'am, do you know this man?"

"I'm her lawyer," Mr. Marble said, as I opened my mouth to answer. "Nathan Marble," he said, handing the lady detective his business card. "This is my client, Mrs. Witherspoon."

Detective Duplantier looked at the card, looked at the man, then looked at me. "Is this your lawyer?"

I gave a heavy sigh. "Yes."

"Did you call him?"

"No."

"Yes," Mr. Marble said, correcting me. "A while ago. We were supposed to meet here this evening."

"It's eleven thirty at night, sir. The park's been closed for over an hour."

"I'm running late." He turned to me. "Are you ready to go, Mrs. Witherspoon?"

"Hey, hey," Detective Duplantier stepped between us. "We just have a few questions."

"Is she under arrest?" Mr. Marble asked again, more grating this time.

She didn't answer, but turned to me. "Please. I won't take up much of your time."

"Tell you what," Mr. Marble said, "why don't you call my office and we will happily come down to the station and talk to you. Tomorrow. First thing in the morning." He turned to me, and swept with his hand. "Mrs. Witherspoon? Please, come with me."

She looked at her watch, prompting me to check mine, too. 11:32. PM. Roughly an hour before pumpkin time. And while I didn't really want to go back to the mansion, I also really didn't want to go through another unexplained and painful *experience* while at a police station; that could possibly end me up in the loony bin. I stood up from the bench and, albeit reluctantly, followed Mr. Marble through the drapes of Spanish moss.

"Mrs. Witherspoon," the detective called after me. She dashed up. "Please, just a few questions, and we won't have to meet tomorrow."

I halted Mr. Marble and turned back. "Let me just do this," I muttered softly. He gave a sigh, but stopped.

"In your words, what happened here tonight?"

"I sat in the park until it closed. Then this man came towards me. I'd never seen him before in my life, and I didn't notice him until he was very close. Unprovoked, and without saying anything to me, he raised his gun, fired, and missed. Before he could take another shot I knocked him down and kicked the gun away. I sincerely didn't mean to hurt him, just disarm him. By the way, it's under the bench," I nodded at the place I'd been sitting for a good part of the night. "Then the officer arrived."

"Wait, the gun? The gun is still here? No one bagged it?" She looked back at the sergeant, who inspected the bench.

"Everyone was way too concerned with the injured man, apparently. Meanwhile neither me nor Mr. Jones were worth talking to before you showed up." I started to walk away. "Good night, detective."

"Can I get get your address or number to contact you?"

"I believe my lawyer gave you everything you need for that," I said without turning to face her.

"Let me give you my card, then," she said, jogging to meet us. As she handed it to me he added, "In case you need to get a hold of me or my partner." Mr. Marble reached out for the card; the detective yanked it out of his range. She made a point of giving it to me.

I thanked her and added, "Good night." This time as we left Detective Duplantier didn't follow. I heard her yelling at the others as to why no one thought about the gun that started the incident. We turned off the walking path and headed for his car on a dead end street. It chirped as we approached.

"Are you all right?" he asked me, genuinely.

"That's the third time I've been asked that," I huffed in an I-don't-want-to-talk-about-it tone, which he seemed to understand. In silence he walked me opened the door, and we drove off.

St. Charles takes on a different feel after the sun goes down. It becomes eerie. Unnerving. *Almost supernatural.* I blame the enormous oak trees that line the street. Their heavy crooked branches reach outward making a canopy over the old road. In daylight they appear protective and comforting as if Mother Nature herself sheltered the historic street. Bejeweled with throws from yesteryear's Mardi Gras parades the bulbous branches appear adorned as sunlight twinkles off the colorful beads. Even their roots, which burst from the earth bulging and maiming the curbs and sidewalk amuse and challenge daytime pedestrians.

At night, however, the mood changes. The canopy chokes any useful beams from the streetlights above. The gnarled branches create a claustrophobic tunnel that closes in around you to take you far, far away. As streetcars pass their headlight reflects off the beads giving the branches a thousand blinking, watching eyes. The rooted wooded flesh almost purposely protrude to trip and tangle the inattentive passersby. In my current state of mind, with my heart still fluttering from the evening's event, I felt the fear of the dark. And of the trees.

It stayed with me, the anxiety. The memory. The man. *The gun.* Me. He was coming towards me. It wasn't a mistake, it wasn't a trick of the eye. He was going to kill me.

I pushed the memory to the back of my mind when I realized

that I had no idea where I was going. Had I been alone when the nice detective asked for my address I wouldn't have been able to answer her, since I honestly didn't know it.

Note to self: Find out where I live.

I paid attention this time, unlike the drive this morning. I recognized a great many streets and mansions since Will and I walked almost every inch of New Orleans historic areas. So how was it that I didn't know where this place was?

"That's part of its...*charm*," Mr. Marble said. "The manor goes unnoticed unless we want someone to find it."

I was certain I hadn't said anything out loud. "Is mind-reading one of your talents, Mr. Marble?"

"Well," he said, tilting his head, "not *mind reading*, in an 'I'm invading your privacy' kind of way. It's more like I'm perceptive of singular and strong thoughts, as if you were throwing them at me. A *thought catcher* I think is a better term."

He turned into the narrow driveway that I did recognize. The tires crunched over the crushed white gravel loop which was quite brilliant, even at night. I asked. "All thoughts? Whether you want them or not?"

"Yes," he said. "Well, the strong thoughts. When I came into the talent it was pretty rough. I felt like everyone was screaming things at me. Took a bit of mental discipline to push the torrent down, and exist above it. Like a little dinghy on the ocean. Sometimes it's calm, sometimes it's turbulent. Sometimes I go for a swim, see what people are thinking. And sometimes...sometimes I can't bail the water out fast enough."

"Hm." This time he didn't follow the gravel to the front door. He pulled off a little spur along the side of the house to a small doorway, covered by a small, green-striped awning. As I opened my car door, I said, "Maybe they aren't talents at all. Maybe they're burdens."

"Like many things in life the interpretation depends on whether you're a 'glass half-empty' or a 'glass half-full' kind of person."

How about a "half-empty or full, the glass has poison" kind of person.

The side door opened and Jeeves welcomed us home.

Chapter Five

I CONVINCED MR. Marble that I had time to shower before my *ordeal* began (which I did after arguing with the spider in the corner that I expected full and complete privacy in the bathroom—it dejectedly slank away). Feeling a bit more human and refreshed I threw on another overly spacious pair of jeans and t-shirt, pushed the past into the past, and trotted down the staircase to join the folks, the house staff, in dining room.

It looked just like…

When you were a kid did you ever participate in a séance? You know, sitting in a circle, holding hands, in a room lit only by candles, and a selected individual "calling the dead"? I recalled us kids using tarot cards and the selected individual wearing a turban. But my memories are fuzzy, and I might be confusing those incidents with old Johnny Carson reruns.

The room positively glowed by candlelight. Not only did we corner the market on these wax products but judging by the thick bee's wax scent they'd been burning for a quite a while. Everyone sat around the table chit chatting—Mr. Marble, Jeeves, Mama, Mrs. Black, Mr. Smith, and Mr. Wesson.

Mama sat at the head of the table, her hair wrapped in a brightly colored scarf or bandana. In front of her was—I kid you not—a God's honest crystal ball. As she bantered with those around her, her hands remained in soft, swirling motion, caressing the clear bowling-ball in front of her. Every now and again she turned her attention to the globe and peered into the thing, squinting hard, as if searching the interior for some speck of dust or micro flaw.

Mr. Marble stood when I entered the room. He gestured to the seat next to him, the other head of the table. I noticed a delicate china tea cup filled with a greenish hot liquid. "Please," Mama said when she noticed me notice it, "That's for you. Drink it, child. It will help with the sensation tonight. You should feel little pain when that damned thing comes for you."

My spine shuttered at the words "damned thing comes for you." Without more instruction, I smelled the brew. Minty. I timidly sipped, expecting the worst. Nope, minty. Pleasant even. I drank it as quickly as the heat allowed while taking in the rest of the crew.

Everyone looked calm, as if they gathered tonight to play Yahtzee. Jeeves and Mrs. Black sat next to each other on my left side, separated from me by Mr. Marble. They chatted casually about the day. Apparently they had to deal with an unruly delivery man—their words, not mine. Seated on my right were the gentlemen Mr. Smith and Mr. Wesson. They wore lab coats, of course. They, too, were engaged in conversation, although I never heard Mr. Wesson say anything.

"You want to test the interspersal rate first thing tomorrow?" Wesson nodded. "Good. I think we should start at roughly fifteen kilowatts." Wesson shook his head, and pointed to his electric data pad. "I don't think that's going to affect our prediction." Wesson scribbled something with a stylus. Smith squealed a laugh, like a child, while nodding. "That would be kind of cool. Okay. Let's try it."

While watching the interaction of the two I noticed something large behind them. It looked like a painting set on the floor and covered with a drop cloth.

"That's how we'll catch them," Mr. Marble said to me.

"What is it?"

"A mirror. But imbued with special properties. If we can't negotiate with the visitor we'll have them look in the mirror."

"Then what happens?" I sipped my tea.

"Then they get trapped in the mirror. And they can never hurt you or breach the house again. So," he said moving a little closer, "once we remove the cover, *don't* look in the mirror, understood?"

I nodded as if I understood. But I didn't. I hope he didn't notice my gulp.

Mama suddenly sat more erect. "Everyone to their places," she said.

Jeeves and Mrs. Black stood and blew out half of the candles, turning the gaily illuminated room into a chamber of dancing shadows amidst the dark.

"Child," she said to me, "place your forearms on the table. Be comfortable."

My voice cracked, "That's a joke, right?" Clearing my throat, I did as she asked.

Mr. Marble put a calming hand on mine. "It's going to be fine, you'll see. You've got a powerful house behind you this time."

"You've done this before, I take it."

"Many times."

"Yeah," I licked my lips. "This is my first." Out of my peripheral vision I saw something move above me. I nearly screamed when I looked up. The entire ceiling pulsated with the movements of thousands, possibly millions, of spiders.

Patting my hand, Mr. Marble said, "That's our army. *Your* army, Mrs. Witherspoon."

"We call it Plan C," said the tiny voice, as one of the arachnids slowly lowered to over the table. I assumed it was Annabelle.

"The spiders are Plan C?" I could barely squeak out the words from disgust and a sensation commonly called *the willies*.

"Yes, my lady. Plan A is discussion and negotiation," she said.

"And plan B is the mirror," Mr. Marble said, and waved a graceful hand to the covered object across the room.

I added, "So the last effort is a spider attack?" Boy, gotta tell ya, that's something I really hoped I didn't see. I had enough fodder to feed my nightmares from the haps already.

"You'd be amazed how effective they are," Mr. Marble said.

"It's time," Mama announced. She looked at Annabelle and said, "Thank you and your kind. Please, arachnid, ready your troops."

"Indeed," she said, effortlessly hoisting her way to the ceiling. I watched as she met with the multitude of other wiggling and jiggling spiders, when, in a wavelike motion across the surface they all stopped. The stillness was unsettling. I forced myself not to visibly shudder.

"Everyone hold hands," Mama said. I watched everyone put hands on the table and take hold; Wesson to Smith, Smith to Mama, Mama to Mrs. Black, Mrs. Black to Jeeves, Jeeves to Mr. Marble, he and I were already connected. I reached out to Mr. Wesson and once we clutched I felt a surge, ever so slight but definitely perceptible, of electric energy. It zinged through me.

I must have reacted so Mr. Smith chuckled. "Yeah. Kind of freaky the first time. It won't hurt you. It's just a residual affect of the energy made from the surrounding—" I heard a thunk under the table. "Ow!" He shot a look at Mr. Wesson, then said, "Another time, maybe."

The room got quiet. Only the sound of a distant ticking from the grandfather clock persisted. Everyone around me closed their eyes, bowed their heads slightly, and breathed. I did the same, hoping that would ease my fiery nerves.

And it happened. This time nothing around me reacted, no dimming lights, no popping noise. Only sensation. Something cold grabbed my arm, causing me to inhale in surprise. With wide eyes I looked at my arm, then at the people around me. I gasped a second time.

Mr. Marble's eyes were open, staring at some point in front of me. Through the dim candlelight I could see his eyes were bright green, positively glowing; not just the iris, the *entire* eye. Mrs. Black's eyes looked identical, bright, and green, but vastly bigger because of her glasses. Jeeves's face had changed to a more drawn and gaunt, with a greyish pallor of a corpse. His eyes remained closed, but he turned his head as if straining to hear some distance whisper. Mama's eyes, wide and focused, stayed fixated on her crystal ball. The geeks Smith and Wesson watched everyone, their gazes darting from person to person, but not with any kind of worry or angst, just engrossed.

"Help me!" Mama yelled out, just as Mrs. Black and Mr. Marble stood.

"What am I seeing?" Mrs. Black nearly gasped. "Dear lord! It's…it's…"

"Can't be," Mr. Marble said. "It's a trick!"

"Help … *me!*" Mama cried out again, eyes closed, yet her mind seemed to be focused on the ball.

Mr. Smith leaned close to me and whispered a quick explanation. "Mama speaks for the visitors so we all can hear, but Jeeves can really hear them. Marble and Black can only see them."

Mama cried out, "Winki, please, *please* …"

"It does sound like him, sir," Jeeves said, twisting to hear … whatever.

I, on the other hand, neither heard nor saw anything. Then I felt … something. Almost a trembling sensation, desperate. *Familiar.* "Will?" I whispered. "Is that you?"

"Winki!" Mama cried out, pained. "Please Winki … you're the only one who can stop this."

"It's him," Mrs. Black said. "It's Will!"

"Can't be. Ready the mirror," Mr. Marble ordered Smith and Wesson. With jumps, they dashed immediately to the covered piece of glass. One held it upright as the other gathered the drape. I only watched them out of the corner of my eye, all the while focusing on *whatever* they saw before me.

"No!" Mrs. Black said. "Stop, Nathan. It's Will!"

"It's a trick," Mr. Marble argued back. "Jeeves, I need your help."

"Indeed," Jeeves said as he stood. He and Mr. Marble held up their hands, as if pushing something heavy across the table and away from them.

"No!" Mrs. Black hollered as she slammed an open hand on the table. "You'll condemn him. He'll be stuck there forever!"

Off the hands of the two men formed what I can only described as a shield of light. It was hot white, yet translucent, as I could just make out their hands behind it. It curved like a lens about both men as they grimace in effort, shoving an immobile and invisible object towards the mirror. Sparks flew in all directions. Something fought back.

"Please, don't do this," Mrs. Black wailed. "It's *Will!*"

I wanted to argue. I wanted to be a part of whatever was going on. I couldn't see what they saw. I couldn't hear what they heard. I barely could feel it anymore. The grip lightened, the icy fingers ease and slowly let go. Then utterly disappeared.

Mr. Marble grunted, "Now!" just as Jeeves clapped his hands together just once, and the sound of thunder filled my ears. In that painful and bright moment I turned my head to catch a glimpse of the mirror. Mr. Wesson saw me look. He held up his lab coat, expanding it like a kite, to keep my vision from the glass.

Jeeves clapped his hands a second time. From his palms emanated a vibration, like the shimmer you see off hot pavement, only focused and flushing outwards from his hands to the mirror. A sudden eruption of wind filled the room. Something touched me, *fingers* washed through my long brown hair, and something soft brushed my lips. The wind tousled the window dressings, whipped all garments madly, and blew out all of the candles.

"*Go! Go! Go!*" I heard Mr. Marble yell out into the wind and then…

The entire house plunged into inky darkness and still silence.

After a several moments Mr. Marble asked, "Is everyone okay?"

I heard the frantic rustling as small glows illuminated the room. People rushed about relighting some candles. No longer blocked from my view I gazed at the mirror held between Mr. Smith and Mr. Wesson. Now a painting. *Of Will.*

I slowly rose from my chair, drawn the to perfect portrait that sat on the floor. With a hand outstretched I knelt slowly, letting my fingers caress the canvas where his cheeks were drawn. His lovely lips showing the slightest of smiles. Then my vision blurred, betraying me from seeing more of him. I fought the brimming wells in my eyes. A photograph would not have been a more perfect likeness.

"Mrs. Witherspoon!"

I jerked to face the voice. Apparently it had been calling my name for some time. The entire room was staring at me.

"Are you all right?" Mr. Marble asked. All eyes, returned to normal, bore into me. With the back of my hand I wiped my tears as I stood to face them. Mr. Marble had the strangest look of worry on his brow. Mrs. Black and Mrs. White exchanged glances. Mr. Smith cleared his throat while Mr. Wesson folded one arm beneath the other that thoughtfully stroked his chin.

Jeeves, asked me again. "Madam. Do you feel quite all right?"

Perplexed by their concern I turned my head to look again at my husband's portrait … and something moved on my shoulder. I startled, then ran my hand over my head of hair, holding out my hair

—my long *white* hair!

I shrieked at the sight, dashing to the mirror that hung over the fireplace. Yes. White hair. I screamed at them. "*What have you done to me?*" I didn't wait for an answer. In fact, I didn't even want to come back to this stupid house in the first place. "All of you, leave me alone!"

I stormed into the foyer with Mr. Marble at my heals. "*Wait! Please, stop—*"

I hurried towards the front door. I reached out for the handle when that damned cockroach raced up and into my view. I reacted to it the way I react to all roaches. With a gasp, and a jerk, and a stumble backwards. Right into Mr. Marble, who was still, at the moment, racing towards me. The impact sent us both sprawling, me ungracefully tumbling to the floor. Mr. Marble at least caught himself before he hit the deck.

"No!" I hollered, "I'm done. I want out of this place!" I backed up crablike on my hands and feet, scooting into the foyer. "I don't want anything to do with you people!" Mr. Marble opened his mouth to speak, but I wouldn't let him. "I don't understand any of this, and I don't want to. Look at my hair!" I held it out for the growing audience to see. "I've been *changed* and bugs are *talking* to me and people are *shooting* at me and you people are *totally* weird and all I want to do is go back to my old life and just *miss my husband.*" Bawling, I put a hand over my eyes, then buried my face into my drawn up knees. "I just want to go home," I whimpered. Nearby a sheet of wallpaper crumbled to the floor.

After several well deserved personal moments of silence I heard Mr. Marble move. Then I felt a soft hand on my shoulder. "We can't make you stay," he whispered.

"No. We must!" That was the roach.

"Hercule—" Mr. Marble scolded.

"Ask her!" Hercule demanded. "Ask her what happened tonight!"

"Why?" Mr. Marble cocked his head. "What happened?" He turned to me as I looked up. "What happened tonight?"

Now that was funny. "You're asking me?" I spat, wiping my cheeks. "How the hell do I know!"

Undaunted, he looked at Hercule. "What happened tonight?"

The little *cafard* let out a chuckle. "She's a *gardien du temps.*"

I had no idea what the roach said, but Mr. Marble jerked his head. In fact, my audience all gasped as they looked at each other. "Are you sure?" one of them asked.

"*Oui*. She slowed down time. That is how she stayed alive, *mon ami.*" Hercule made his way off the door and toward the two of us on the floor. Mr. Marble held out a hand and Hercule climbed up into the meat of his palm. "We saw the whole thing. She moved faster than the bullet."

Mr. Marble looked up at me. "Is that true?"

I sniffed. "I don't know. I freaked out when this guy held up his gun then the bullet came out moving slowly. So, yeah, I stepped aside. I thought something was wrong with his gun."

Heads turned to each other, as if everyone needed explanation.

Everyone except the labcoats. One by one we all looked at them. Mr. Wesson scribbled something on his pad while Mr. Smith watched over his shoulder, which wasn't hard for Mr. Smith to do since he was over a foot taller than his partner. "Yeah," Mr. Smith nodded, then waved a finger to point. "That calculation over there. With the gravity constant. Assuming she has good bone density. Carry the four. Say roughly four hundred meters-per-second." For some reason I was fascinated by how the two worked, tilting my head. Maybe I just needed a distraction. "Ha!" Mr. Smith stood upright nodding his head. He held out a hand and Mr. Wesson, rolling his eyes, rifled through his pants pocket handed him some money. Then he looked around and his proud victory smile faded into the realization that he was being watched. "Oh," he cleared his throat, "we just had a friendly wager. Mr. Wesson believed that the Hercule was wrong, and that Mrs. Witherspoon didn't slow time but rather attained super human speeds, allowing her to move out of the way. But we just proved that if she moved as fast as the bullet her brain would have been mashed in her skull and liquified." He proudly rocked back and forth on his toes. "So, she didn't move faster but rather slowed down the environment around her, ergo, *timekeeper*. Which is *soooo* much cooler!" He beamed and gave me a small bow. "Congratulations."

I think I can speak for the whole room when I say we were speechless.

Mama broke the silence. "How can that be? Will had no such talent."

Then Mrs. Black. "She's right. He was supposed to pass on his talents. That's what you told us." With that the room erupted into accusations. Mr. Marble stood to address them while fingers pointed and tempers flared. "You told us she'd be just like him!" "You wouldn't listen to me!" "Now we can't even summon him to speak!" "You condemned him into that painting!" "Admit it, you have no idea *what you're doing!*"

I watched the poor man take the onslaught of heated, almost hateful, accusations as I slowly regained my feet. As he defended himself against the continuing barrage I wandered back into the dining room. I knelt in front of the painting. But not a painting, somehow. Too realistic. But not a photo, either. I reached out again to touch the face on the canvas. Blue eyes that twinkled, blond wisps of hair that arched over each eyebrow. The image was from Will's waist up. And only that. There was no background to speak of, only black.

I numbed to it all; the heated yelling in the foyer, the logical arguments in my mind, and the tumultuous emotions in my soul. Probably as a result of my own exhaustion.

"I'm sorry, *madame*," Hercule said from somewhere.

"Is it really him? Is that really Will?"

He hesitated. "*Oui.* And *no.* Will is dead. There is nothing anyone can do to change that. But his essence, his spirit, or what some may even call a soul, that, *ma chére.* That is what is in the painting."

I sat crossed legged in front of the picture. "I don't understand. I'm so tired of not understanding."

"Would it help to know we don't either?" He took my failure to answer to correctly indicate "no." He sighed, "Okay, I'm coming into view now. Try not to, as you say, *freak out.*" The *cafard* scampered up and over the portrait—I could hear his clicking footsteps—and stopped on the ornately carved and gilded frame. "There." He sat upright and crossed one leg over the other and braced himself with his four "arms". "Where should I start? There's so much even I, the great Hercule, do not understand. For starters, I have no idea why your hair has turned white. It is quite, um, how shall I say, striking." I ran my hand over my head and softly took hold of the ends, inspecting them. He continued. "We told you we'd protect you this night from whatever has been attacking you. And now we all know that it was Will. Why would he attack you? Why would he harm you, let alone scare you? We all knew how much he loved you." I bit my lip as I stared at the picture. "We all believed that he imbued you before he passed. We all assumed, perhaps erroneously so, that that meant he passed on his talents. Now you've come into one of your talents and it's *gardien du temps*, a *chronométeur*, something Will was not."

"What does *gardien du temps* mean?"

"Ah, *pardon.* It means 'guardian of time'. A timekeeper. It is the name of someone who can, without the aid of a tool, control the passage of time."

"Control time? Like a time traveler?"

"No, *ma chére.* Only slow it. Perhaps even with practice stop it. We all travel forward in time, never backwards." He gave a sigh. "Ah, if we could only travel behind ourselves. Undo mistakes we made.

Perhaps save the ones we loved, no?"

"If only," I said with a sniff. I ran my fingers across the empty background behind Will. "Where is he?"

"In the painting. Was that not clear?" He sounded short with my question.

With open hands I gestured, "Where is that? There's nothing behind him. What is the painting about?"

"Now I understand." He switched his crossed legs while one of his arms stroked an antennae. "Let me see if I can explain this, but I must warn you, you're not going to like what you hear. You see, the painting is literally a painting. The essence of the subject, in this case, Will, is caught or trapped onto the canvas. This technique is used for the enemies of the house, and has been for centuries. We have a gallery full of those who have trespassed here. I'm very sorry Will is now among them." In an almost remorseful voice he added, "He never deserved that."

The answer didn't explain much to me but I let it go for now. I touched the sweet face I'd known for years. Imprisoned? "Can he see me?"

"I do not know. We don't know what those imprisoned experience. Until now I can honestly say no one ever cared." He paced a bit, back and forth, across the frame. His movements were jerky, almost uncontrolled, just like every other cockroach I'd ever seen. Then took the same spot, crossed his little legs again, and said, "I cannot possibly know what you might be feeling at this moment, *madame*. But I beg you not to leave this house. Not only are you coming into your talents, which takes time and concentration to hone and use safely, but we no longer know what those talents will be. We don't know how to prepare you for what's to come because we, too, do not know."

"I don't want any of this," I whined. Yes, whined. "Why can't I live a normal life?"

"Is that what you think you've been doing these last six months? Living? No! Sitting on a sofa for endless days is not living. That is waiting. That is wasting away. That is rotting. Let me ask this. If Will could see you would he be happy for you? Would he be content that his passing led to this misery? Is his memory being honored by the doing of nothing?"

The bug crossed the line. "How do you know what's best for me?" I yelled at the bug. "How do you know that nothing isn't exactly what I need to do. I don't expect a cockroach to know anything about mourning!"

I hoped to insult, but he didn't take the bait. "Mourning?" he asked, calmly. "Is that what you think you've been doing? No, *madame*. You have not been mourning. You have been dying." The words took me by surprise. I sat upright a little. "Look around you. At this house. What do you see? Do you see the decay? Do you see the ruin? The faded colors, the chipped paint, the worn carpets. Even the lovely bougainvilleas that used to bloom constantly are dead."

"Of course I see that," I muttered.

"That is how you are. The house is that way because *you* are that way." I furrowed my brow. "The house is tied to you."

"The *house*," and I couldn't believe I was having this argument, "only met me yesterday."

"No. It's known you for the last six months. It was tied to Will. When he died he passed that tie to you. We, all of use who have lived here, have watched this place crumble around us. Just as you have crumbled. That is how I know." He gave a small chuckle. "At least that is something I know." He took a deep breath and sung out a long sigh. "So I ask again, please do not leave here. You're still sad and lost. Overwhelmed, even. But we can guide you. We can show you this amazing new life you've yet to learn anything about. Don't dismiss it so quickly. With time will come the healing. Try only to be patient. Take a deep breath. Let time pass."

"If only that were possible," Mr. Marble said from the grand entry into the dining room. "The tournament is next month."

"Damned the tournament!" Hercule spat. "We cannot go now!"

"We *have* to go."

"How can we expect her to fight at a time like this?" the *cafard* yelled. *Fight?* "Do you know how to train a *gardien du temps?* Does anyone in this house? Of course not! None of us have that talent. We don't know how she triggered it. We don't know how long she can sustain it. We don't even know if it's defensible. Why? Because we weren't expecting it! No. We must pull out of the tournament this year."

"*Pull out?* Do you hear the words…what do you think will happen if we don't show up?" Mr. Marble's cheeks had gone red. "We'd spend our lives doing exactly what we did tonight for endless days. Oh, wait," Mr. Marble snapped his fingers, "that's okay with you because you don't do anything during these confrontations, do you! Never mind that the rest of us are exhausted. In fact, where were you this evening?"

"I was…Er…engaging the little grey cells."

"*Hiding.* It's what you do best during the gatherings, isn't it?"

"Enough!" I yelled, standing up, my head turning between the two arguing, um, creatures. "That's enough." I hiked up my baggy jeans.

Mr. Marble put a hand behind his neck, bent his head in a number of directions. "I apologize, Mrs. Witherspoon. It's late and I'm a little on edge right now."

I folded my arms. "Call back the movers who were here today. Have them take everything they brought in back out."

The two, um, creatures protested at the same time, then argued with each other about who said what to make me want to leave.

I hushed them both then addressed Mr. Marble. "Have them

drop off all the clothes at a charity. None of the stuff fits me anymore so there's not point it keeping it here. And I'm going to need an advance on my stipend for this month to buy new clothes." I pushed pass him on my way up the stairs. "Now if you'll both excuse me, not that I'm planning on getting a good night's sleep, but I'm off to go try." I grumbled to myself as I lumbered up the steps. "We can all continue this argument in the morning."

Chapter Six

I DAMN NEAR had a heart attack as I walked passed my bedroom mirror in the morning, startled by the white hair figure that I glimpsed out of the corner of my eye. I stopped to explore the change, running my hands through the tangled coif and pushing it out of my eyes. White. White as white. Not blonde or grey, but *white*. It felt different. Thinner. Brittle. I tossed my head to determine if it suited me. I gave a small grin at the sight. I had to admit that I felt surprisingly upbeat considering that I was nearly shot then condemned the soul of my husband to a painting.

Of course that crushing realization brought me humbly back into reality. That, and the knock on my door. I looked down; still in last nights sagging clothes.

Another knock was followed by the gentle English voice. "Madam, are you awake?"

I glanced at my watch. It was nearly nine in the morning. "Come in, Jeeves," I answered.

The door opened and Jeeves, carrying a tray—presumably breakfast judging by the carafe, a covered plate, and the wafts of coffee—practically floated into the room and put the tray on my small table by the window. I took a seat there as he poured some coffee and handed me the cup. "Thank you," I said.

"Pleased to be of service."

He lifted the shiny silver lid from the plate to reveal poached eggs with asparagus and some mushroomy sauce on what he assured me was a whole wheat English muffin. "Wow!" I remarked. "Mama knows all my favorites." Just the sight of it made my stomach audibly rumble.

"Indeed, madam."

I was about to dig in with I noticed that he did not dismiss himself. "Is there something more?"

"Several items, I dare say." He nodded. "Master Will used me as a kind of secretary. As such every morning while he ate I let him know what needed to be done, who he had to meet, where he needed to be, that sort of thing. He called it his morning report. If you'd rather not have my services—"

"No, no," I stammered. "Please. Report away." I picked up my fork and inspected my food while he talked.

"To start, I was instructed to inform you about your wardrobe." Arrangements to have it all taken away, I hoped. "With the exception of what you are currently wearing, Mrs. Black has taken the liberty of modifying your clothing. You should find the rest of it fits you, now."

"Really? Like abracadabra and poof! The clothes fit me?" I giggled in amazement. "How cool is that!"

"Hm," he said, almost insulted. "My thoughts exactly."

"I can't wait to try something on. I'll be sure to thank her."

He cleared his throat. "Then there is the matter of the painting."

Will. "What about it?" I took a bite of food and chewed thoughtfully.

"We were going to put it with the other paintings but I thought it better to ask you what you'd like to do with it."

"With the other paintings?" I repeat. "In the gallery?" Which I had yet to see myself but I was certain would be a walk through a veritable house of horrors. "I don't think Will should be there."

"Nor did I." I was curious who did.

I look about my room. Condemned or not I wanted him nearby. If he could see me, maybe—

Jeeves cleared his throat. "I don't believe that is wise, madam."

"What is?"

"You're thinking of putting him here in your room."

My eyebrows lifted. "You read minds, too?"

"One doesn't have to read your mind to know what you were thinking." I gave him a scowl as I pushed another bite of food at my face. He leaned in a bit. "I would have had that thought as well," he explained. "But it is not a healthy one."

I nodded and took a sip of coffee. Maybe he's right. "I think I'd like it to be in the dining room. Over the fireplace."

"Very good, madam. I shall let the house know." By that I wondered if he meant the staff or literally *the house*. "Lastly, Mr. Smith and Mr. Wesson would like to know when you can join them."

"Join them?" I asked.

"In the cellar." I sat perplexed, my head tilted. "To explore your talent." Still not getting it. "To prepare for the tournament." Ah!

"Someone still has to explain that to me," I huffed, taking another bite. "I can be there after I finish breakfast," I said.

"I will inform them that you'll join them at ten thirty. That is all for me, madam. Is there anything I can do for you?"

I shook my head. But just as Jeeves was leaving I stopped him. "Wait. Just one thing, maybe," I added after a little thought.

"Yes, madam?"

"You probably need to be back here around ten thirty. I have no idea how to find the basement."

"As you wish." The door softly clicked behind him.

~ ~ * ~ ~

As promised my clothes fit me. Perfectly. Jeeves led me to the basement and we passed Ms. Black who busied herself with dusting in the living room. Or, rather, one of the living rooms. I thanked her immensely and we continued through the maze of a mansion, passed the dining room (where Will hung handsomely over the grand fireplace—apparently things happen fast around here) round one corner, then another, until we got to an unassuming door. Down the creaky bit of staircase that spilled into the large cavern of a room stuffed with colorful boxes. *Yes, I do remember this now.* "The Amazing Zingo" and "The Mysterious Mr. Moustafa."

Mr. Smith stood reading a computer monitor over Mr. Wesson's shoulder, and nearly jumped when he saw me out of the corner of his eye. He beamed. "Mrs. Witherspoon!" Then he checked his watch. "And right on time. Very unlike your late husband." He gathered up a clipboard and pen, and gestured for me to take one of the laboratory stools, while Jeeves quietly slipped back up the stairs.

"Well ... now ... um," he started as he flipped through pages on the metal board in his hand.

"Ok, I'll start," I snipped impatiently. "What the hell is a tournament?"

He softly tossed the board onto a desk. "What do *you* think a tournament is?"

"Sounds like a medieval thing. Where a bunch of knights get together and joust."

He chuckled. "It's something like that. A bunch of competitors from the talented community are summoned once a year for the tournament. They show off their abilities a bit, then compete— sometimes alone, sometimes against other competitors—before a crowd and a counsel. Eventually eliminations are made, and one is left as the victor." He turned to Mr. Wesson who joined us. "I think that sums it up pretty well, how about you?"

Mr. Wesson enthusiastically nodded.

"Each house volunteers their best champion. For Gateway Manor that's been Master Will." I nodded, not really needing those dots connected. "Now, of course, like the knights of old, you get to bring with you some tools. But instead of armor and maces, you have, well," his thumb jutted between him and Mr. Wesson. "Us."

"You are my tools." I bit my lip to hold back the smile.

"We *make* you tools. Hell, we have hundreds of great weapons and tricks and protections that we've developed for over the last twenty years or so. An entire arsenal at Will's disposal." Mr. Smith positively glowed with pride while telling me this. "It made him damned near invincible. He won the tournament eight years in a row. So we were very excited when he heard he'd passed those talents onto you ... until the spectrograph ..." He stopped, licked his lips, then continued. "Well, you don't have the same energy signature as Will. It differs in wavelength, amplitude, and modulation," he saw my eyes glaze over, "which just means to say that your energy manifests differently from Will's. Which means that none of the tools we've developed for *him* will work for you."

I held up a hand to stop him. "Let me see if I understand this. You all are convinced I have magic talents."

Mr. Wesson exhaled in irritation while Mr. Smith explained. "There is no such thing as magic."

"Fine. Whatever. But you're saying my talents are different than Will's?"

"Close. Your *signature* is different than Will's. How you tap into the energy around you and use it, that's what's different. As a result, we've concluded, your abilities are different."

"And the tools you already have are for *his* abilities."

Again Mr. Wesson exhaled. But Mr. Smith smiled unabashed. "The tools we have work for a particular energy signature. Will's. That's what activates them. You can't use them. Heck, no one else in the world can." I folded my arms while scowling. "Okay, think of it this way." He looked skywards, then snapped his fingers. "Think of it in terms of uniqueness. Like a fingerprint. Or, let's say, DNA. His DNA activated and manipulated the tools we made but yours won't. Moreover, we, knowing his DNA, could in turn create tools and weapons specifically for his DNA."

"Doesn't that mean you can modify those tools to work for me?"

His hands gesticulated wildly. "Yes, that's exactly what I'm trying to tell you! See?" He said to his partner. "I told you she'd get it. All we need to do is monitor and analyze your own particular energy signature." He grabbed his clip board from the desk, and Mr. Wesson sat upright with his pad, holding it like a camera. They sat still, then Mr. Wesson lowered his pad. The two looked at each other. "So, we're ready to begin. Whenever you are."

"Begin?"

"Yes," he waved a "come on" motion with his hand. "You may begin."

"Begin what?"

"The sooner we have your energy signature the sooner we can start work on converting Will's arsenal."

"I got that. What am I supposed to do?"

"Ah," he laughed, finally understanding. "Whatever you did last night." They prepared themselves again.

"What did I do last night?"

"The ... the time thing. Do that!"

"I have no idea how to do that. I've never done *that* before. I'm not sure there's even a *that* to do!"

The two looked at me dumbfounded. Mr. Wesson scribbled something and showed it to Mr. Smith. "Try to provoke a trigger?" he nodded thoughtfully. "I don't know if that's a good idea. Jeeves has issues with real guns in the house. Maybe we should wait for Nathan." Mr. Wesson scribbled again. "Now that just might work. But we'll definitely have to wait for Nathan. We can turn her over to the spiders until he gets here——"

Before I had any time to react——no matter how polite those eight-legged critters are there's *no way* I'd be "turned over to the spiders"——someone cleared their throat. The three of us looked towards the entry.

"I beg your pardon madam and sirs," Jeeves said but looked at me, "but there is a guest waiting for you upstairs. I told him you were busy but he was insistent."

"So long as he doesn't have eight legs ..." I muttered, stuck on spiders.

"No madam. This policeman sports but two."

The two scientists stood at the word. "Police? Are in the manor?" Mr. Smith quivered. With worry in his voice he said, "Don't tell them we're here, and don't bring them downstairs!"

He fear was almost comical. Almost.

"That's fine, Jeeves," I said. "Lead the way."

"And Jeeves?" Mr Smith called after us. "Tell Nathan we need him for some hypnosis."

Hypnosis? Good lord! As we passed Will's portrait I called to him, "What on earth did you get me into?"

Jeeves remained unfazed by my outburst, strolling rhythmically through the mansion and lead me to yet another living room (that made three, I believe). Our "guest" had his back to me as he looked over titles of leather spines that decorated a large wooden bookcase. I recognized the spiky hair. Detective Duplantier's partner, I believed. *What was his name?* I couldn't remember if we'd been introduced.

When he heard us enter he spun around, shoving his hands into his pant pockets. Something struck me about the motion, how he moved his hands, but I couldn't quite see it. I passed off the feeling and took a good look at him now, given the more robust light. Yes, quite tall and lanky as I recalled, and spiky blond hair. His face was lamentably long, his nose a bit hawkish, and his complexion a pasty pink. Ruddy cheeks fleshed his face. The tan suit he wore looked overly large, reminding me of David Byrne. Then I realized, as intently as I was staring at him he was staring at me.

He cocked his head to the side. "Interesting color selection, ma'am. Not sure it suits you." His British accent was thicker than I remembered. It sounded like he called me "Mom".

"Color?" I started. "Ah," I said, running my hand through my hair. "I ... felt like I needed a change."

He gave a nod, then in a fluid movement, retrieved a leather wallet from his breast pocket, opened it to show me his credentials, then returned it to its home. "We weren't properly introduced," he said all the while. "I'm Detective Sergeant Frost."

I looked around. "Where's your partner?"

"Detective Duplantier is filling out paperwork. A burden for us all but, given my foreigner status, I'm spared the drudgery." He swept a hand to the small sitting area; two burgundy leather club chairs that posted themselves in the center of the room, tilted just so to acknowledge each other. "Shall we?"

"I'm not sure I should be talking to you without my lawyer present."

"It's convenient then that I came to do all the talking."

I hesitated unsure, then turned to Jeeves. "Perhaps some tea for our English visitor?"

"As you wish, madam." I noticed Jeeves gave the young Brit a quick and disapproving eye.

We sat. "So how did a detective sergeant come to work for the New Orleans Police Department?"

"A sort of exchange program. One of us here, one of yours there. An attempt to share and discuss ideas on criminology and techniques, I suppose."

"How are you liking it? New Orleans, I mean. Quite a departure from ...?" I openly gestured for him to finish the statement.

"London, ma'am. I find it blistery and mucilaginous."

I let the comment go, hoping not to tip my hand that I had no idea what "mucilaginous" was. "How long have you been here?"

"Eight months."

"Then you have no idea just how *blistery* and *mucilaginous* it can be." Jeeves drifted into the room carrying a silver tray with pot, cups, and the works. "But by mid-August you will."

We sat quietly as Jeeves poured perfect cups, prepared our teas, and presented them. The Detective Sergeant took his and in that motion I realized what had bothered me earlier. His hands were gloved. A very delicate, light tan in color, with small holes for breathability, but gloved nevertheless.

"But I didn't come to talk about the weather," D. S. Frost said after a sip. He delicately put his cup aside. "I came to tell you about Mr. Tom Cruise."

I wanted to laugh at the name, except the guy did try to kill me. "Still sticking to that title, eh?"

"Yes. And I'm afraid we'll not get another out of him now. You see, that's the paperwork Detective Duplantier is working on at this moment. Her report on Mr. Cruise. He's dead."

I slumped back a bit into my chair, staring off into the distance, but seeing that man's face. Those eyes, that stare ... the raised gun. "I wish I could tell you I was sorry," I said out loud, "but after what he did to me last night ..." Then I realized why he was here. "You think I killed him?"

"Oh, no, ma'am. That would be quite impossible. He was taken to the hospital for his knee injury, and was under surveillance until his surgery, which was scheduled for early this morning. When the nurse went into his room to do a routine bed check, he was found dead. The guard posted outside his room swears no one entered the room except for credentialed doctors and nurses, and none of them spent any prolonged time with him. Protocol, you understand; no one goes in and out of the room unescorted by a police officer. Unless you used *magic* for vengeance, I don't see how you could have done it. And we all know," he spoke as he gracefully picked up his cup, took a sip, and poised it and its saucer on his lap, "there's no such thing as magic." I didn't like the way his pale blue-green eyes looked at me. Slightly accusing. I swallowed. "I just thought you might be a bit relieved to know."

I let a beat pass. "How, if you don't mind me asking?"

"How what, ma'am?"

"How did he die?"

A quick smile fluttered across his mouth. "He's scheduled for autopsy this afternoon. Therefore, I will have to get back to you on that."

"I'm assuming that you couldn't tell me anyway."

"Seemed like natural causes, at a glance. No trauma, no signs of struggle, no obvious bruises or ligatures. We believed he was only his thirties, so a simple heart failure isn't likely, either. Quite a puzzle." He gave a deep sigh. "Mrs. Witherspoon, I want to tell you ..." He twisted his mouth a bit. "I haven't been entirely honest, ma'am. My partner is, in fact, doing paperwork but I'm here without her knowledge. I feel I should warn you." I swallowed. "You see, she and I are of two camps at the moment. While she believes that you are just a victim of last night's circumstance, being in the wrong place at the wrong time, I do not. I believe Mr. Cruise did, indeed, try to harm you. Possibly kill you."

The dark memory rushed to me with such clarity that my heart started to pound. "Why? Who am I to this guy?" I refused to say *Tom Cruise*.

"Under normal circumstances I would ask you that, but I've told you I'm only here to share information. So, that is all I will do."

"Can you tell me what makes you think differently? Why aren't I a victim of circumstance?"

To this he sat back, switched which leg he hand crossed tightly over the other, and sighed. "Nothing concrete, just a hunch. Compound your experience with your husband's death—"

"Will? He was in a motorcycle accident."

He sat upright a bit. "I was under the impression you knew. I pulled his file, Mrs. Witherspoon, also on a hunch. While it was closed as an accident there were great many questions left unanswered. The pictures taken at the scene showed skid marks from Mr. Witherspoon's motorcycle started on a straightaway, almost a full mile before the point of impact. It appears your husband lost control of his vehicle a good deal sooner than the corner where he collided with the oncoming car."

I bit my lip, hiding my sorrow. "I'm not sure that changes anything."

"The skid patterns were quite particular. They're indicative of a failed machine, say a flat tire or mechanical problem, and typically show loss of control. But that's what's so odd about it. At the speed we estimate he was traveling, nearly sixty miles per hour, that would mean he knew something was wrong with his motorcycle almost a full minute before he was killed. Surely he would have slowed down, or pulled over to inspect the bike. Wouldn't you?"

I never rode a motorcycle before I met Will. He volunteered his time at the Motorcycle Safety Foundation teaching folks how to ride. Like me. Will, after a number of dates, convinced me to try it out, promising me I wouldn't get hurt. I've never ridden anything but a motorbike since. "Will was meticulous about his bike and his safety," I said, my eyes focused on my teacup. "If he thought anything was wrong he would have stopped."

The Detective Sergeant took another sip. "Forensics went over his motorcycle with a fine tooth comb. They found nothing wrong with his bike, nothing that is except for the beating it took during the accident." He took a sip. "Sadly, given the remoteness of the road he was on, there were no cameras so we don't know exactly what happened. But it appears something went wrong, he drove on until he turned the corner and ... Just ..." He stopped, seeing my mournful appearance. "I'm assuming you've read the driver's testimony." I shook my head *no*. "He said he couldn't avoid hitting your husband. No matter what he did Will reacted ... adjusted the bike to come straight at him."

"Are you suggesting Will killed himself?"

"That was the initial claim. Until the Witherspoon estate asked for an investigation, which discovered the skid marks a mile earlier. That led to the case resolution as an accident." He let a beat pass, perhaps waiting for me to say something. But the sour pain in my stomach scarcely allowed me to breathe. "I've seen your husbands driving record. I know he was an advanced rider. So I believe something happened, something he couldn't control." He shook his head. "Again, it's just a gut feeling on my part. Your husband died under mysterious circumstances, then you are shot at under mysterious circumstances ... Something just isn't right." I could tell he was trying to console me, but I was lost in wave after wave of fear, anger, and grief. He whispered, "I thought you knew since your lawyer, Mr. Marble, knew."

"Mr. Marble?" I asked. Or squeaked.

"He's the one who insisted on the investigation. I'm very sorry to bring such bad news, especially after last night. I just wanted to ... please, take care of yourself." With that he finished his tea and stood.

I wiped my eyes, trying to be proper and offer a goodbye, when he cleared his throat. "I hate to be the bearer of more bad news, ma'am, but—" I looked up to follow his gaze, which went somewhere behind me. "Your home has roaches."

Yup, there it was on the wall behind me, his little tentacles dancing back and forth in a hyper swishing motion. Hercule, no doubt. At least the distraction brought me back into the present.

"This is Louisiana, sergeant. The cockroach is the state bird," I wanly, smiled. I offered my hand to him. "Thank you for stopping by."

He hesitated for a moment, then offered a gloved one, and we shook. "I'll see myself out," he nodded, then left.

When I was alone—except for Hercule and the spider in the corner, of course—I wrapped my arms around myself, suddenly cold. I turned to Hercule. "Did you know?"

The little *cafard* scampered left, right, and up and down. Then stopped. "No."

"Did Will kill himself?" I asked, not really wanting an answer.

"Of course not! *Mon Dieu!* What kind of question is that?" he raged. As he left my view he ranted. "You were married to him for how many years? How can you possibly think such a thing! Stupid woman ..."

"He didn't mean that," said a voice from up in the corner. It wasn't Annabelle, it sounded different from hers. Not sure how to tell the spiders apart. "He's just upset, my lady. Once everyone hears of this we'll all be. Please forgive him."

"So no one knew?"

"If Hercule didn't you can be assured no one did."

Except Nathan Marble. I nodded, upset myself. "Thank you," I said to the spider as I left the room and wandered back into the dining room. I stood, looking up at the face I thought I knew for years. Those handsome, tranquil eyes looked back at me.

"Jesus, Will, what the hell is going on?"

Chapter Seven

I SPENT THE next couple of hours wandering around my new "home", trying to get sense of foreboding off my back. Will's death and the shooting last night ... could they be connected? Was I in danger? I let my feet move me, as if the motion of walking could lead me away from the deep pit in my stomach. If only.

I purposely got lost in the house and the exploration; one room led to another room, which led to a hallway with several doors, each of which were other rooms that led to other rooms. Occasionally I'd recognize a room, leave it, only to enter a completely new room. Living rooms, waiting rooms, receiving rooms, dining rooms, a couple of staircases, a library—I only found one of those.

Then my nose led me to the kitchen, where Mama busied herself. Smelled like seafood gumbo, or crawfish étouffée, either of which were fine by me. She moved about the kitchen like a whirling dervish, stirring and chopping one moment, tasting and collecting various spices and seasonings the next. She'd get something, stop over the pot, sniff a bit, then shake-shake-shake, and off she'd go to the next pot. In between she'd assembled poboys with plump white baguettes of French bread, layering the split loaves with spreads, meats, veggies, and cheeses. It looked more like construction work than cooking. Then off she spun to another pot. Dizzying to watch.

I quietly slipped out the back door that, with the aid of a few rickety wooden steps, led to the driveway, the one we used last night. Service entry, I supposed. I stood there, surveying the grounds, calculating my next move. I crunched my way over the white driveway—now that I see it in true light I realized it wasn't gravel at all but crushed seashells—and eyed the large garden just on the other side. A brief thought to explore crossed my mind ... another time, perhaps. I continued around to the front and trotted up the big, grand staircase to the covered porch.

I hadn't notice the swing before, though I had just thought the porch would be perfect with one. Its wooden body, wide enough for two people, was suspended by shiny chains. Looked brand new. I sat, safely in the shade, and enjoyed the near brume of fragrance from the crowded jasmine vines that dripped over the patio's edge. My favorite. The more I sat there inhaling, the more pungent, sweet, and secure it became. A gentle breeze caressed me, and my eyes closed to take it all in. Every tense muscle in my body relaxed. I could see why Will loved the place.

Wait a moment ... *what jasmine vines?* I dashed out from under the porch and back into the driveway to look over the place. There they were, jasmine plants. Long, twisting vines over the building; up the sides and onto the roof. Looking absolutely thick and green and lush ... Wasn't that all dead just yesterday, when I first arrived?

I put my hands on my hips just as a car drove up behind me. Mr. Marble got out. "Ah, Mrs. Witherspoon. How are you today?" Then he looked at the building behind me. "Jasmine, huh? Nice touch." He swept his arm to the door. "Shall we go inside?"

"But I don't—"

Jeeves opened the door as we approached Mr. Marble hustled me inside, changing the subject. "You have lots to do yet today, am I right? I spoke with Smith and Wesson and they are onto something. Jeeves, where did you set us up?"

"I have prepared the sitting room, sir." As he spoke he was

relieving Mr. Marble of his jacket and suitcase.

"Perfect. Good idea, good idea," Mr. Marble rubbed his hands together.

"However," Jeeves continued, "I believe Mrs. White will insisted she be fed first."

"Lunch? Lunch is good. Better to do this on a full stomach," Mr. Marble agreed. "Starving myself. After you, Mrs. Witherspoon."

While I picked at the poboy presented me with homemade chips and peanut coleslaw, I watched him. By now, if Hercule and the spiders spread my conversation with D.S. Frost, everyone knew that Mr. Marble hadn't been entirely honest about Will's death. The others came and went; Mrs. Black did a little tidying up in the room, Mrs. White served a bit of this and that, and Jeeves diligently stood dang near motionless in the corner of the room. Just under a spider. But none of them mentioned it. Keeping up appearances, I gathered. I followed their lead. For now.

I washed down my sandwich with Jeeve's special recipe for Mint Juleps. A potent concoction. It definitely left me with a spinning head and heavy feet. When we were finished, Mr. Marble stood and announced he was ready to begin.

The full belly and tipsy head did their job putting me into a napping frame of mind. Which worked well with Mr. Marble's attempt to hypnotize me. I'm not sure why I went along with it; I'd never been hypnotized before and couldn't say it was on my bucket list, but I wasn't in an arguing mood. Bluntly put, julep-induced-dullness aside, I felt emotionally numb. They could have told me to jump off the roof and I'm pretty sure I would have done it.

I lay on a worn green velvet settee with a buttoned harlequin design with my feet propped on a gold lamé pillow. Jeeves closed the drapes while Mr. Smith lit a few candles. The quiet Mr. Wesson sat in a staunch leather chair, one leg crossed over the other, with his faithful pad in his lap. Mr. Marble knelt next to me and spoke in the softest, calmest voice I'd ever heard.

"Mrs. Witherspoon ... I want to ask your permission to call you Winki, may I do that?" I nodded, eyes already closed. As he spoke the words I felt myself sink heavily into the sofa. It was damned comfortable. "Thank you. Winki, I want you to follow the sound of my voice ..."

I can't say that I recall any "words" after that. I just remember being back in Audubon park. It was dark, pleasant breeze, Spanish moss swayed in the lamp light, and the soft scent of mold and mildew rose from the grassy floor. But I wasn't the one seated on the park bench. I stood next to Mr. Marble on the sidelines, watching the sad woman in baggy clothes who sat alone on the park bench ... watching me.

"Do you seen anything?" the soft voice asked.

"I see myself."

"Good. Do you see anyone else?"

"No." Then I saw the me of my mind. Her attention was drawn to us. No, *behind* us. I spun around to see ... *him*.

"Ah," Mr. Marble said. "So that's what he looks like. Now pay attention, Winki. Don't look at him. Look at you. Watch yourself. What do you do next?"

It was hard to turn away from that man's face but I forced myself. I saw me, the fear growing in my eyes. I saw me stand. The memory of the man walked by us, through Mr. Marble but I stayed with her ... I mean, me. She drew a deep breath, and raised her hands defensively, and ...

"What the hell is that?" Mr. Smith stepped out from behind a tree, notepad in hand. The scene completely froze, as if someone had pushed the *pause* button on the memory. Mr. Smith went towards the yester-me and pointed at my palms. "Do you guys see that?"

Both my hands were defensively raised, palms facing Mr. Tom Cruise. One of them was ablaze with light. Mr. Marble and I joined

Mr. Smith, trying to take a closer look. On the palm of my right hand was a brilliant illumination. Mr. Smith took a knee in front of it, and examined it with a pen. "It's some kind of writing." As he scribbled his own drawing of the ... whatever it was, both Mr. Marble and I knelt in front of the light. It was so intensely bright we couldn't look at it directly.

Mr. Marble gave a sigh. He turned to me, the real me. "Look at your hands, Winki."

I did, turning the palms upward. Neither of them had such a symbol on them now.

"Did you feel it? When it happened, did you feel anything in your hand?"

I thought about it. I looked at the woman's eyes. I felt fear. I felt confusion and disbelief. But nothing physical. Certainly nothing in my hands. "No," I finally said.

With that I woke up on the settee as Jeeves opened the curtains. "I don't understand," I said as I struggled to sit upright. "What does that mean?"

"It means," Mr. Marble sighed, "that you didn't use your own power. Someone gave it to you."

For a moment I felt relieved. Maybe they were all wrong about me. Maybe I'm not who they think I am. And maybe that's a good thing.

"Not necessarily," Mr. Smith interjected while he watched Mr. Wesson furiously type on his tablet. "We think she may have just gotten an energy boost."

Just like that my little glimmer of hope disappeared.

"What do you mean, *energy boost?*"

"Give us a minute," he said, watching over Mr. Wesson's shoulder. The little man poked and tapped away, his attention shifting from the screen in front of him to the scribble Mr. Smith made presented on his right. Then he froze, and raised his head a bit.

Mr. Smith did the same. Then Mr. Smith burst into laughter. "That's amazing! Fantastic! We can do that, too!"

"Do what?" Mr. Marble asked impatiently.

"Oh. Sorry," Mr. Smith said. "That symbol is from a lost logographic language. Like Kanji or hieroglypics. It doesn't translate into a specific word, but it's something like 'power'. Not like solar or electric, more like, 'infuse' or 'intake'." He could see we weren't getting whatever meaning he was trying to convey. "The symbol allowed Mrs. Witherspoon to tap into her ability without having her own power to do so. Like a cosmic outlet, so to speak. Something she just plugged right into."

"You mean she *can* manipulate time?" Mr. Marble said.

"Oh yeah! She might be able to do it on her own now."

"And how," I said, "would I do that?"

Mr. Marble turned to me. "That is a good question, but it's not the important one."

"What's the important question?" Because the "how" sounded pretty important to me.

He looked at Smith and Wesson, and me. "Who? Who gave you the *cosmic outlet?*"

The room fell ominously silent for several moments as I, and everyone else, pondered the question. Then Mr. Smith spoke. "Nah. We're with her. How can she do that now? But based on this we now have a better read on her signature. Heck, we can try to create our own cosmic outlet." He waved me towards him. "C'mon, Mrs. Witherspoon. We have real work to do."

As I left the room I watched Mr. Marble's face. His eyes, cast to the floor, puzzled, and his mouth twisted a bit, chewing on the inside of his cheek. I haven't known any of these people for very long, but I got the sense that Mr. Marble always knew everything. At this moment even he was in the dark. I rather liked that.

"Mr. Marble," I said. "One of the detectives stopped by this morning."

His eye darted up to mine. "You spoke to them? Without me here?"

"Don't worry," I said and nodded to the *cafard* on the wall. "Hercule will tell you all about it."

Chapter Eight

I FOLLOWED MR. Smith, who followed Mr. Wesson, down into the basement. I wondered as I carefully trotted down the narrow and dank staircase if the concept of being *below sea level* would ever feel comfortable. New Orleans barely sits on high ground, surrounded by formidable levies. Anything below that is, well, under water.

I gulped at the thought as Mr. Smith spoke. "Annabelle? Are you here?"

"Yes, sir," came a small and distant voice.

"Good. I think we're ready for Mrs. Witherspoon to start some combat training."

I stopped in my tracks. "This morning you wanted to work on my talents. What happened to that idea?" I was curious to know how they work myself. If I really had any *talent* at all.

Without turning to address me he answered, "This morning we wanted to see your energy signature. Now we have that. We can move right onto phase two. Training."

"But I'm fairly certain I haven't mastered phase one."

"You won't need to."

I muttered, mostly to myself, "I beg to disagree."

Mr. Smith waved a dismissive hand, and led me through another door and into a large, padded room. Again I stopped in my tracks. Two unnerving thoughts hit my head simultaneously. The first was my trust in these people; what's one to think when blindly lead into a padded room? The second was *where the heck did this come from?* I felt certain it wasn't here this morning.

Mr. Smith stepped aside and swept his arm grandly into the space. "*This* is the training room." Dingy white stuffed naugahyde with matching buttons covered the walls, grey-blue fluffy mats covered the floor, and even the ceiling looked puffy and soft. Along one wall stood dummies, nearly a dozen of them, all made of different materials like straw or wood or plastic, and all of them hung by their necks in a gruesome display. Opposite them squatted racks of equipment you'd find in some dark ages museum; shields and garments and weapons, some of them shiny and glitteringly new, others dull and scratched or broken. Along the back wall sat three targets mounted on bales of hay. And just steps in front of me was a long, wooden table that, end to end, displayed a variety of weapons, a representational subset of those along the wall.

"Take a good look, my lady," Annabelle said, as she floated down onto the table in front of me. "Do you see anything you like?"

"Not like," Mr. Smith corrected. "Does anything speak to you? Not literally, of course. That would be weird." Yeah. Unlike talking bugs *that* would be weird. "Just ... well, you'll figure it out."

I walked the length of the table looking at the selections. I reached out to touch one of them, a bit shy of what might happen. But nothing. Encouraged I walked the table length again, letting my hand drag softly over each item. A rapier, a scimitar, a bow and quiver (I stopped there to look at it—I always wanted to learn how to shoot one), a wooden club, a musket, and—

My hand lurched out for the object before I truly saw it. *A hammer.* Not your typical construction job type. This was more like a mallet but entirely silver. Its large metal head reflected brilliantly in the light of the room. Exquisite scroll designs embellished the head and handle. I picked it up. Surprisingly light for its size.

"Wow," Mr. Smith said. "I wasn't expecting that. Good choice, Annabelle." To me he said, "The hammer was one of her selections."

"I told you," Annabelle replied, "it's all about simplicity. My lady, close your eyes for a moment." I did. "Describe the hammer to me."

Describe it without seeing it. I started from memory. "Large and silver," then I felt it. *I felt the thing.* It vibrated in my hand. Warm. Deep. Oddly comforting. And profoundly familiar. "I know this hammer." Then I opened my eyes. "How is that possible?"

Mr. Smith shook his head. "Don't ask questions, just go with it. Keep your eyes closed. What else? Do you hear anything? See anything?"

Again with my eyes closed I thought about the hammer. How if felt in my hands. I moved my arm, lifting it into the air and for some reason an image of Mr. Marble focused in my mind. A great—for lack of a better word—*rage* came over me. I screamed out, and brought the hammer down hard on the table.

Behind closed eyes I could see the blinding flash. The floor bounced a bit as the victim table shattered, sending splinters in every direction. The labcoats, who turned away, slowly twisted back to face the small plume of dust as it settled. The table all but disintegrated.

Annabelle hung from a swaying thread. Both Mr. Smith and Mr. Wesson gawked at the brittle remnants on the floor. I, too, stared at the mess thinking it had to be some kind of trick.

"I believe," Annabelle said after some warranted silence, "we have found her favorite."

"That ... Was ...," Mr. Smith said, eyes wide with fear, then he suddenly burst into laughter, "AWESOME!" He jumped up and down like a child skipping rope. "Oh, man! Oh, man! Oh, man! We're back in business, baby!" He and Mr. Wesson did a chest bump.

I looked at the hammer in my hand, feeling nothing now except its hefty weight, while Mr. Wesson joined in the jumping fest.

Annabelle's web swayed to the hammer head and she landed upon it. "Are you all right?" she asked, correctly reading my awe and worry.

"I don't know. Was that supposed to happen?"

"Yes. And no. You are more powerful that we anticipated. In some ways that is good news. This house will be defended."

"Defended? What do you mean—?"

"However, if we cannot teach you to hone your power, or control it, or focus it properly you might hurt yourself. Or someone around you. You may even kill someone."

Oo. Didn't like the sound of that. "Why do I always feel behind the curve here? I don't know how I did what I did last night, I don't know how I did what I did with this hammer. *I don't know what the hell is going on!*"

"It's time for a break." We all looked behind us at the voice in the doorway. Mr. Marble.

"A break?" Mr. Smith exclaimed. "We just got started!"

Cool and calm he sidled up, hands in pockets, eyes on the rubble before us. "And by the look of things you're well along." Mr. Smith and Mr. Wesson both folded their arms, impatiently. "Guys, you know her energy signature, you know her favorite weapon, and you know, because Will's told us many times, she's quite capable in the ... um ..." he waved his hand, "What's the name of that martial art again?"

"Capoeira," Annabelle and I said in unison.

"Yeah. That. So we're ahead of the game right now."

"She doesn't know what she's going to face at the tournament!"

"Yes, some intensive practice is in order and we'll do that in a moment. But right now I need Mrs. Witherspoon. Fifteen minutes. Half hour, tops." He turned to me. "Would you please come with me?"

Hammer still in hand I started to follow him.

"Ah, no. Leave that here."

As if he knew what image provoked the wreckage at our feet—ah, of course. *Thought catcher.*

~ ~ * ~ ~

Mr. Marble sat behind an unnecessarily large desk in a wood-paneled room way too big to be labeled an "office", opening a bank of drawers on one side, then rifling through the drawers on the other. As he did so he spoke. "So you're mad at me. And I understand why. I didn't tell everyone about Will's investigation for a very good reason." He glanced up at me. "I know Will didn't kill himself. It is an absolute impossibility. So when the law firm got wind that was going to be the police's conclusion, I insisted they do a better job. You see ... ah!" He pulled out a file, slammed the drawer, and slapped it on his desk. "You see, everyone in this house loved Will. I mean, not just liked him, but *loved* him. They would die a thousand deaths for him, and happily follow him into hell. *That* kind of love. And we were all shattered by his death, as you were. So, to have any of them hear that Will took his own life, even if they didn't believe it, it would have hurt this house in unfathomable ways." He flicked through several pieces of paper. "So I never told them. I'm only hoping now that we're all far enough along in our healing that the mere thought of suicide won't have a lasting effect." He focused on a page, lifting it out of the file, and read it.

"I'm sorry you found out the way you did," he said as he walked along a paneled wall, stopping at a gruesome painting, fraught with flying red beasts donning twisted horns and a bleeding knight defending himself. He swung open the painting on cleverly hidden hinges, exposing a safe with a keypad on its face. He punched in some numbers. "I've followed Will's wishes to the letter T, Mrs. Witherspoon, in how to handle your admittance, shall we say, to the manor. We argued about it for months leading up to his death." The safe beeped when its metal door swung wide. He reached inside. "Looking back on all that I swear .... it was as if he knew his death was imminent. Anyway, it was his idea to wait six months before bringing you here. Which I did. And it was his idea to wait until showing you this until after the tournament." He closed the safe and handed me the item he'd removed. It was a DVD. "But I feel that after the shooting last night, and the matter of the painting, and now this mystery of who's given you a power boost, I think a little leeway is acceptable. Besides. What's he gonna do now? Sue me?" He gestured to a console behind me; a TV and a DVD player. "The remote's on the coffee table."

I looked at the thin jewel case in my hand and the rainbow reflecting disc it held. "What is this?"

As he backed out of the room, sliding the large pocket doors shut, he answered, "Don't know. Pop it in and see."

I turned it over and back. No writing, no description. A DVD could only mean one thing, right? I took a deep breath before I knelt in front the electronics. Power on, disc in, and plopped onto the overstuffed leather brown sofa in front of the sixty inch flat screen. I took a settling breath, unsure of how I'd react if I saw him again, and hit *play*.

My heart lept. I smiled, bittersweetly. Pixie shape of his face, soft pink lips, dashing blue eyes, and blonde bangs that arched perfectly over each eyebrow. I'd know that face anywhere. *Will*.

"Hi, Winks." He sweetly smiled. *God, I miss him.* "If you're watching this then, well, then I've passed on. I've had this feeling that I will leave this earth with unfinished business so I thought I should leave you a personal note. By now you're in the Gateway Manor. And I'm sorry, I'm so, so, sorry I never showed it to you. I swear that decision wasn't mine. But I do stick by it. You didn't know it but that's how I protected you. That's how I could give you the wonderful years of innocence you needed before ..." He hung his head, and took a deep breath. "Before you take the reins. Before you fight the good fight.

"I've instructed Nathan Marble to wait until after your first tournament until showing you this recording, but knowing him, you're watching it just days after moving in. Probably made some joke about my not being able to sue him." Will chuckled. "He's a hard man, Winks. But he's a good man. Trust him. If you don't trust anyone else you ever meet in the rest of your life, *trust him.*" I gave a small frown, uncertain of my own feeling towards Mr. Marble. But "trust" wasn't one of them.

Will shifted in his seat a bit. "Now I've taken great lengths to be alone for this recording, which in this house is a challenge. I'd like you to do the same. Pause it here if you need to, but make sure you're alone. No people, no roaches, and no spiders."

No denying any of it now. The acknowledgment of spiders and roaches—this home, this life, it was really all Will. I hit the pause button and looked upwards at the ceiling. The large room had not one but two posted spider scouts. "Okay, guys ... or gals, you heard the man. This is for my ears only." Without argument the little arachnids scampered towards the double door and disappeared into the jamb. "Any roaches? *Cafards?* Out." I paused. "Please," I softly said. Somewhere Hercule sighed. I heard little feet tapping out a retreat, but I never saw the guy.

I sat down, nervous. Like I was about to watch a horror movie. I took a deep breath and hit *play*.

Will gave me his crooked smile. "It's a lot to take in, I know. I had my whole life to prepare me for the tournaments, and you're only getting a short amount of time. I have the utmost faith in you, Winks. You're gonna knock 'em dead. And I mean that literally.

"There's so much I need to tell you. But I can't just give you all the information right now. You won't understand it. And I don't want to confuse you, and I really don't want to scare you. So I'm leaving you key pieces of information in the form of these," he waved a DVD. "In each I'm going to tell you what you need to know and then how to find the next one. These will be riddles." I moaned. "Don't give me that!"

"I hate riddles!"

"That's exactly why I'm doing this." I was a bit taken by his direct answer, as if he were here in the room. "You'll have to pool your resources, get to know those around you, gather the talents and information you'll need in a calm and controlled manner. You'll do great. I know you'll find all the DVDs in the end. And just like this one I'd like to watch them in complete secrecy. Got it?"

"Yes."

"Good. Now, you don't know it but the beginning will be the hardest part for you. And I don't mean your level of aggravation, I mean," he swirled a finger about him, "the path and destiny of this house. If you haven't figured it out yet, it's yours. The house. It is yours. Not merely ownership, it is a reflection of you. It's a living thing, Winks. Freaky, I know. And I was raised in this place. But you two are tied together now. That is, if I managed to set this all up right ... which I think I did ..." He shook his head coming back to the task at hand. "Anyway, if you are happy, the house will be, too. If you are hurt, the house will be, too. It will moan. You may even hear it talk occasionally. Don't panic. Just listen. It will only talk to you when it has something important to say. It is very, very old, Winks, and very powerful. Give it a chance, and it will heal you. Soothe you. It will be more than a home.

"It's called the Gateway Manor for a reason. It swings both ways. If the energy its tied to is good and noble, then so will be the house. If the energy is evil and dark," he paused, "so will be the house. The energy is you. And that's why your formative years here are so imperative. Like that stupid Star Wars movie, the dark side is very powerful, very fast, and very *easy*. You'll taste it, if you haven't already. The ferociousness of your own rage." I shivered at the irony of him saying that just moments after I went Conan on a table. "Once you start down that path the steps forward are so much easier than the steps back." His eyes began to glass. He dropped his head so I couldn't see him wipe his eye. His sadness made my own throat ache.

He cleared his throat and took a drink of water. With a deep inhale he continued. "You're going to hear stories about me, Winks. Some are total lies and fabrications but ... some of them ... I'm deeply ashamed that some are true. I won't say which ones, and I'm begging you not to endeavor to find out. Just know I've made horrible, horrible mistakes in my life that I'd give anything and *everything* to undo them. But that's not how life works. You have to make whatever amends you can and ... take all the lumps you're owed." He took a deep, shaky breath. "And since I've traveled that path I'm telling you as a voice of experience you *do not want to go down it. Please*, be patient. You're about to go on this amazing journey and see mind-blowing things and do incredible feats of good and benevolence. God, I envy you, I really, really do. You're a clean slate. So new and shiny," I smiled at the Firefly reference. "Don't let impatience and intolerance and fear and doubt and worry bog you down and wear you out." He smiled. "You're going to have a blast if you just, well, accept it all. Don't worry about the details, that's what Smith and Wesson are for. Don't fret about the logistics, that's what Nathan's for. You don't need to worry about daily routines, or meals, or anything. You have the best staff in all of creation working for you, and they'll take care of all the crap, I promise. All you *have* to do, Winki ... is have fun." He laughed out loud and he grabbed the camera with his hands, is if cupping my face. "Have fun. Have a blast. Have an absolute ball! Don't look for explanations in anything, just ... sit back in awe. Ride the wave, Winki. Open your heart and love and give ..." He gave a small shake if his head. "Like I don't know who I'm talking to. You are the most amazing woman I've ever met but patience and acceptance are not your strong suits."

"No. They're not."

"So ... from beyond the grave," he said with a Bela Lugosi accent while waving dramatic hands, "I will work one last magic spell."

"There's no such thing as magic," I said out of reflex.

"Bah. Don't let them tell you otherwise. The dead man can confess: It's magic. Now," he said, sitting more upright, he waved his hands in front of the screen, "when I clap my hands together you're going to change, Winks. You're going to become like a leaf on the wind, floating in whatever direction the breeze takes you, going wherever you may end up. You will become a witness. Acceptance and bliss will walk with you. You ready?"

"No." Okay, maybe.

"Here it goes." He rubbed his palms together. "One. Two. *Three.*" He clapped exactly once. My ears popped. Painfully so. I put my hands on the sides of my face, and opened my jaw to ease the discomfort. That worked. The soreness abated.

"What in tarnation was that?" I asked, a bit angrily.

"When did you start using words like *tarnation?*" My jaw dropped. I've never used the word "tarnation" in my life. "I know," he exclaimed. "Freaky isn't it! You'll get use to it. I promise."

"This ... this isn't real, is it?" I stammered.

"No. It's a recording. I just know you. I know exactly what you're going to say." I wrapped my arms around myself. "I love you, Winki. I love you a thousand times. And I know, *I know*," he grimaced, "that if the roles were reversed and something happened to you and I was left behind, I know I'd die. I couldn't live a day on this stupid planet if you weren't there to help me make sense of it. To give me purpose. But you're stronger than me, by," he spread his arms wide, "*mega* factors. You're kinder, and gentler, and wiser, which is why I know, I *know* ... You're gonna do great."

I had to admit I did feel different. Calmer. *Accepting.*

"Now, you ready for your first clue?"

I gagged, sticking my tongue out and crossing my eyes.

He laughed. "I dare you to do that to Nathan one of these days." Will shifted in his seat and cleared his throat, and I prepared myself for some long dissertation. I sat upright, too. Then he said, "Never on a Sunday." Then stopped.

I waited. He didn't' say or do anything. Impatiently, I asked, "What?"

"Never on a Sunday."

"Never on a Sunday?" I parroted. "That's it?"

"That's it."

"Could you be more obscure?"

"These aren't supposed to be easy. Trust me, I had a harder time coming up with them than you're going to have to solve them." I moaned in protest. "Quit your moaning! Besides, this will give us a longer time to spend together. Something to look forward to."

I couldn't help but smile. Then if faded. "Except you're not really here, are you."

He leaned forward. "Winki. I'm in the dining room."

My heart skipped a beat. "How can you possibly know—"

"I will always be in the dining room." I got up to run there. "Don't leave yet," he said, sitting back. I whirled to face him ... I mean the TV. "That's just a preview of what's on the next DVD. Now you're all curious, aren't you?"

"How ... can you possibly know?"

"I'm a dead man, Winki." He lifted his remote and fluttered his eyebrows. "The dead know everything."

The screen went black.

I stood there like a statue, heavy and laden to the floor, both in body and heart. *I wanted so much more.* Just moments ago I lost all the worry and angst and fear ...

The screen popped back on. "Oh. And I always get the last word." Then off.

That was an inside joke of ours. I started to giggle, then laugh. Then laugh heartily, like a crazy person at a zoo kind of thing. My feet buckled beneath me and still I laughed. I rolled on the floor and still I laughed. For the first time in long, dreary months, I laughed! It felt so good. I felt so light! I felt ... ready.

I took a few giggle breaths as I regained a vertical position, removed my DVD from the player, and lovingly put it in the jewel case. I kissed it.

I stopped in the doorway and inspected the wood that made the frame. I put my hand on it. I closed my eyes and listened. I didn't hear anything. I looked at the hallway ahead of me. The floor's carpet was worn to the floor boards in patches, the dull wallpaper blistered and peeling, the plaster ceiling cracked and uneven. Even the small light fixture was crooked with some bulbs burnt out. "I'm sorry," I said to the house, caressing the jamb. "I'm sorry if I've done this to you."

Wood popped across from me as the house settled.

"I'll fix it. I promise." Now I was ready. I was really ready. "Let the games begin."

Chapter Nine

AFTER TUCKING THE DVD in a dresser drawer I trotted to the basement (which I found all on my own, thank you very much). The dummies had been moved. Now they stood in the middle of the training room in a perfect row, each one behind another. Bounding them were two thin red lines, like a little dummy runway.

"There you are! Just in time." Mr. Smith said. "We just set up your first lesson." He gestured to the dummies. "We call it *the gauntlet.*"

I took a look at it again. "Kind of ominous. Why don't we just call it *the row of dummies.*"

"*The guantlet* sounds cooler. Here's what you're going to do." He handed me the hammer. "You need to walk down the little path without touching a dummy or a dummy touching you."

I noticed then the dummies hung by a good six feet of rope (was the ceiling that high just a few minutes ago?), which would make them swing. I walked up to the first one and stared at how it was suspended. Then down at the floor. The little path was only three feet wide, if that, and the dummy occupied most of it. "How do you suggest I do that?" I said, as I leaned over the look at the remaining crowd of hanged men.

Something beeped loudly, startling me. I turned to see Mr. Wesson at some computer console. He looked up at me, and wagged his finger in a "no-no" fashion.

"The tape on the floor is for your benefit," Mr. Smith said. "We've rigged up a laser plane to form your walls, or boundary. If you break the bounding planes, the alarm goes off."

"And that's bad."

"It's just an alarm. Later, it will be electrified."

"Wait—*what?*"

"It won't harm you, just sting a little bit. Trust me, it's nothing compared to what you'll experience at the tournament."

"This just keeps getting better and better," I said as I twirled the hammer in my hand. "So if I can't go around the dummies how do I get by them?"

"Oh!" he laughed out loud, "you can use *the hammer*, of course. The hammer can touch the dummies, but you can't. They have sensors as well, so we'll know."

"Let me guess. It's just an alarm and later—"

"Later they will be electrified."

You can do this, Winki. Will said so. I closed my eyes and tried to feel the hammer again, as I did earlier. Almost immediately it responded. It felt lighter, softer somehow. I raised my hand to swing at the first dummy.

BEEP!

"I didn't even hit him!"

"You broke the plane," Mr. Smith said. "Try again."

"Can you explain why that's important? I can understand avoiding the dummies part, but not the runway part."

"Hammers take a great deal of space to wield," Annabelle said from somewhere. "It's easier to be successful when you're in a cavernous room. But in many battles space will be limited. Low ceilings, narrow hallways. You'll be asked to do battle in a number of environments. It's not enough to use the weapon well. It must be of use to you at all times."

"Will's favorite weapon was the bow," Mr. Smith offered. "We use to stick him in tiny boxes where he couldn't even draw back his arm."

I tried to imagine that. Will was claustrophobic.

"If you can get comfortable using the weapon in the most cramped spaces, you will have greater success overall," Annabelle added. "Please, my lady. Try again."

I closed my eyes again and felt the hammer. It wanted to be swung wide, it wanted to be swung with might, I could just ... tell. Clearly I couldn't use it the way it would choose. I looked at the dummy and told the hammer to contain itself. Without thinking my hand shifted on the handle, buttoning up my grip closer to the head. With a quick upper-cut I jabbed at the first dummy. It swung out and away. I quickly spun and socked the second dummy in the stomach. As it moved I felt a sense of accomplishment—

BEEP!

I was thrown to the floor when the first dummy, returning from its pendulum motion, knocked me sideways.

With a roar I slammed my hand on the floor. "This is impossible!"

"No," Annabelle said, "not impossible. Don't think about it. Don't put your mind on the task at hand." She daintily twirled down into view. "You feel it, don't you? The power of the hammer?"

"I think so. I feel something." I looked at the shiny hammer. "But it wants big broad strokes."

"That is when it's most powerful, as demonstrated by the table. Give it the constraints. Give it the rules. It will do as you ask. Remember, when you two are joined it becomes a part of you, like any other limb."

"How does that help? I still have to move my limbs."

"When you practice your Capoeira what do you experience? Do you think about moving each limb or do you simply react to the situation?"

The little spider had a point. There were times at practice I experienced an *otherworldliness*; when I thought of nothing and witnessed myself simply doing. I returned to the start of the dummy line and closed my eyes. Without thinking the hammer moved from my right hand to my left. Then my body moved. I jutted, clipped, thrusted, punched, and spun my way down the line until, without realizing it, there were no more dummies. I turned towards my silent observers. The sound of twisting and swinging rope filled the room.

Mr. Wesson scribbled something on a pad.

"All right," Mr. Smith said. "Let's light it up."

"Wait, you mean we're gonna electrify this thing *today*?"

"Why wait? You were flawless. Go on, Mr. Wesson. Turn it on."

I shook my head. So, this is what it was going to be like, eh.

~ ~ * ~ ~

I held my shoulder as I limped my way up the staircase. I'd spent nearly three hours with the dummies. While that one performance may have been "flawless" the other seventy-two were excruciating. "A little sting," I muttered, cresting the stairs, "I'll give that guy a *little sting*."

My intention was to shower before dinner, which was supposed to be served in just fifteen minutes. It took me a good ten of those just to get this far.

I winced as I kicked off my shoes and started to remove my clothes, then froze when I saw the roach. "That had better be you, Hercule."

"*Oui*."

Like one of those dummies I fell backwards onto the bed.

"You need no modesty in front of the Great Poirot, *madame*. I have seen it all."

"And yet, I choose modesty." I moaned as I rubbed my face. "Did you want something?"

"Only to help."

"Unless you're going to tell me that Mama's got some kind of pain killer in the food I don't think you can do much."

"She does. But you won't need that." He came down from the wall and crawled up the side of the bed. When he reached me he said, "Did Will not tell you in his silly DVD?"

"Tell me what?"

"You're home. This is where you are strongest."

"Yeah. So."

"So, this is where you can tap into your strength." With a massive effort I rose onto my elbows and looked down at the bug. "You feel weak, yes?"

"Sure. That's a word." Sore. Tired. A little pissed off. Those were good words, too.

"Then tap into the house, *madame*." With another effort I scooted myself upright so that my feet would touch the floor. "Close your eyes and think of the house. Think of what it has endured over the years. Everything from heartbreaks to hurricanes. All the tournaments and the wars. And still it endures."

As he spoke images appeared in my head. I saw Will. A very young version, perhaps ten in age. He was running around the house with a toy airplane in his hand, imitating jet noises as the object swooped and dove over chairs, lamps and vases. One vase wasn't lucky, however. It was knocked to the floor and shattered. Out of nowhere Jeeves appeared. "Master Will, are you all right?" Will nodded, but worry and angst filled the room. "It's a small matter," Jeeves consoled, "don't fret—"

"WHAT'S ALL THE NOISE?" Will ran behind Jeeves to escape the shadow. I couldn't see it. But it loomed closer to the small boy. Jeeves tried to explain, but the shadow focused on Will ... it took him by his thin arm ... Will screamed apologies as he was pulled out of my mind ...

I gasped as I snapped back into my bedroom. "What was that?" I panted.

"Will's father," Hercule said.

"Was he evil?"

Hercule hesitated. "No. But he loved to ride that knife edge between all things good and all things pain. Will, I'm afraid, suffered his wrath more frequently than he should have. *Pauver enfant.*"

"He never told me any of that. He told me his dad had died when he was very young. That he had no real memories of him."

"Hm. Wishful thinking, perhaps."

"Why did I see that?" I asked angered. "What was the point?"

"Go back. You stopped it before the vision was finished. Let it take you."

"I don't want to see him get hurt. Wait ... you saw it too?"

"I saw it long ago. Go back," he encouraged. "There's more to see."

With a bit of prejudice I planted my bare feet firmly on the floor. "I don't want to see him get hurt," I said into the air.

The vision reappeared. Will, now bruised and limping, shuffled his way through the house. He held his shoulder much like I had done just moments before. *His arm was broken.* He headed for the hearth in the dining room. He bravely stood in front of the mantle, and with his good arm he put his broken hand on the mantle, whimpering as he did so. Then he placed his other hand next to it. He closed his eyes and said, "*S'il vous plaît, prends mon mal.*" As he stood there, right before my eyes, his arm moved. He grimaced as it popped back into place. His bruises faded. His cuts healed. When complete he stood erect. "*Merci,*" he said, then dashed off, as if nothing had happened.

"There is nothing special about the fireplace," Hercule called as I stood and left the room.

"There was for him." And that was enough for me. I went to the mantle and looked up at the gorgeous face that looked down at me. I put my hands where I witnessed him put his. I wouldn't insult the house with my French. "Please," I said. "Take my pain."

Unlike what I saw Will experience, which looked painful, a warmth washed over me. It felt like, well, love. It was soft and sweet and had the scent of jasmine and mint. It felt kind and thankful. Frankly, if felt wonderful.

"Whoa," I whispered as I took my hands from the mantle. "Thank you! *That was incredible.*" I shrugged, moving my once stiff shoulders from side to side. My legs, renewed with energy, dashed up the stairs.

"Okay, that was pretty cool. Thank you," I said to the *cafard* as I stripped, too happy for modesty, and made for the shower.

"*De rien.* "

Within a few minutes I was back in the dining room, fork at the ready and tummy on the growl. I didn't bother to dry my hair other than wring it with a towel, so the occasional drip chilled me from my back. It felt invigorating. The world did.

I ate alone. The food had been set out in preparation; spicy crawfish etouffee, steamy collard greens, golden biscuits with butter and honey, a salad, some wine, all of it enough for a small army. But I solely occupied the room. Not sure if I liked that. I could hear the others in the kitchen, chatting and laughing, but no one joined me. I don't know what the protocol was, here. Did staff and employers ever socialize? If I asked them to join me was that an insult? If I joined them was that an insult?

Not entirely alone. Me and the portrait. I sat on the table side, so I could face the lovely face. I decided to use this solitude for reflection. It had been a long day, starting with the visit from the Detective Sergeant Frost in the morning and the news of my assailant's death. Not to mention the news of Will's own investigation. Then the hypnosis and the light symbol that appeared on my hand. Mr. Marble asked who put it there. Someone nearby? Seemed to make sense; if someone wanted to help me they would have needed to be there to know exactly when. Not Tom Cruise, surely. Then ...

"Oh my gosh!" I burst. "Tony Jones!"

Chapter Ten

"TONY JONES?" MR. Marble repeated over the phone.

"Yes," I answered. I pulled back the bed covers with my cell phone on speaker, propped on the dresser. "His camo jacket read A. Jones, but he said his name was Tony."

"So," he paused as I heard him scribble, "*Anthony* Jones. Um, Mrs. Witherspoon, who is this person?"

"He was at the shooting last night. I just now remembered that."

"Why don't I remember him?"

I searched the ceiling as I recalled the night in question. Mr. Jones had been escorted away for interrogation before Mr. Marble showed up, and we ended the hypnosis before Mr. Jones showed up. I also went through my suspicions about the cosmic outlet. "Seems to me whoever gave me the energy had to be there to know I needed help. Since he was close by, maybe it was him. Doesn't that make sense?"

"Yes ... er, possibly. I mean it isn't necessarily true; energy can be mysterious. Someone could have given you the ability in case you needed it, and it wasn't until you were threatened that you used it. But," he said, "since we know nothing at the moment there's no harm in having a talk with Mr. Jones." He cleared his throat. "And how was the rest of your day?"

I looked at the small clock on my dresser. It read nearly

midnight. "I guess it went well."

"According to Smith and Wesson things went *very* well. They were very impressed. The staff is feeling a bit relieved right now. You should be proud of yourself."

Something about the words left me ill at ease. Like he didn't really mean them. "I suppose. It's late and I'm guessing there's more training tomorrow so I'll let you go. I just wanted to give you that name."

"Sure, sure. You have a good night. I'll see you sometime tomorrow. Bye bye."

I hung up my cell. Something in my head poked my thoughts, something about his voice. He didn't really sound interested in the story at all, did he? Or maybe he was trying to convince me not to worry my pretty little head about some veteran who happened to be in the park that night. Or maybe I'm only *thinking* that because he could manipulate my thoughts from over the phone. My mouth twisted at the twists.

But my body demanded sleep to prepare for another exhausting day. I let out a large and gaping yawn, opened the window, turned out my light, and crawled into the wonderfully soft bed.

No icy grip woke me. No pop of lights, no strange pain. Just blissful deep sleep. I hadn't had anything of the sort in months.

~ ~ * ~ ~

Ever since Will's clap on the DVD I felt remarkably light. Happy. And this morning was no exception. I woke at the crack of dawn, refreshed and invigorated, quickly dressed, ran a brush through my white hair (still startling to see in the mirror) and bounded down the stairs. I was relieved to have the house to myself. I walked around it, exploring again, touching each wall, inspecting each piece of furniture, brushing the myriad of objects and decorations with my fingertips. Will's house. *My* house. My healing house. I felt I owed it.

I returned to the dining room and placed my hands, palms flat, on the mantle. I didn't know what I intended. I just thought if I could communicate with the house, show it that I thought of it as amazing, and beautiful, and nurturing. I wanted to give it an offering of gratitude.

I closed my eyes and imagined it, the place in its magnificence. Staring in the room I occupied I saw the paneling as lustrous and gleaming, the crystal chandelier twinkling in brilliance, the hardwood renewed, and the carpet atop it rich in color.

I moved into the entry where the enormous chandelier cast lovely small rainbows from its faceted shards. The wall paper, back on the walls, vivid in its green and gold stripes.

From there I "walked" up the wooden staircase, watching while each tread transformed below my feet; like pebbles tossed into a pond, each footstep started a ripple of healthy, dark wood that spread across the step. As my hand dragged up the bannister it, too, took on a deeply waxed sheen.

I move through the hallway, down the next set of stairs, into the living room ... rooms, the sun room, the game room, and I flung open doors, finding myself in rooms I'd never seen before lost in the depths of this changing (yes, that's the word, always moving, always providing, changing house), and in each, I watched as walls, floors, rugs, and windows transformed. And shined.

I found myself in the kitchen, not sure how I got there, not sure it really mattered. *Oh, look, Mama was there, kneading some dough (what a quaint thing to imagine!).* As she worked the world around her altered; the cabinet doors, some of which kiltered on worn hinges, adjust themselves with small pops, then burst in new finishes. To my surprise Mama looked up, somewhat startled. She turned to face the cabinets behind her ... and shrieked.

I heard that.

I jumped back away from the fireplace, never having left the room really. My own jaw dropped, as I backed away from the mantle. The perfect, brand new mantle.

Great gobs of peanut butter ... this is really happening?

Mrs. White ran into the room, eyes wider than her normal eye-popping self. She stopped in her tracks, and spun in a circle taking in the room. It was perfect. Like the day the Witherspoon family first moved in.

I, too, stared wide eyed at the shiny new room.

"Child!" Mama said, raising a wooden spoon at me. "You need to warn folks when you're gonna do things like that!"

"I'm sorry," I stammered, wrestling for words. "I thought I was alone." *I had no idea this would happen.*

She waved her scolding spoon. "You shouldn't go changing a kitchen when someone's workin' in it!"

I took a guarded step away from her.

A herd of worried and woken people raced down the grand staircase. Some of them stopped and marveled. Others ran into the dining room. "What's going on? Are we under attack?"

"No, we're not under attack," Mama dismissed, pointing her angry implement at me. "But little Miss Thing over there decided to show off!"

"I wasn't showing off," I defended. "I didn't know anyone else was up." *And did I mention I had no idea any of this would happen?*

"Got to admit," Mr. Smith said, standing in blue-striped pajamas. "This is pretty awesome!" Mr. Wesson, in red-striped pajamas, nodded vigorously.

Jeeves gave a reassuring pat on Mama's shoulder. "Calm yourself, Mable. She didn't mean any harm, I'm certain." His voice recalled my vision of Will, when he tried to calm Will's father. I pushed the memory aside.

"I'm ... sorry," I said. I just wanted to show appreciation, not literally change the place. And I certainly didn't want to panic the household. Moreover, Mama's reaction was, well, more confrontational that I expected to deal with until I stumbled into the basement. Embarrassment flushed my cheeks. "Excuse me." And I left.

I walked down the seashell driveway and onto the street. I headed for St. Charles and the streetcars that would take me to breakfast salvation. Despite the mostly blue skies above me a single cloud, swollen and dark grey, sprinkled down on me. That seemed to match my mood.

I knew a great breakfast place called Coulis not far away. There I ordered the Eggs Benicio—a N'awlins twist on Eggs Benedict—and drummed my fingers on the table in boredom as I waited. An elderly gentleman nearby read the Picayune. I apparently bothered him enough that he handed me part of his paper. I thanked him and flipped through some of the pages, skimming the headlines.

The plate hit the table, and that wonderful scent of cheddar biscuit and pulled pork hit my nose. My stomach roared in anticipation. I wolfed the first few bites. I looked at my plate a little disappointed. Don't get me wrong, the food was delicious. But my body could sense the change. I suppose little in the culinary world could compete with magic—okay, *talented*—cooking.

I thought about my last visit here, months ago. I was with Will. One of our last meals out, as I recall. But that didn't sadden me. Quite the opposite. I felt happy about it. Thankful, really. Thankful that I got to spend whatever time I could with that wonderful man. My spirits lifted as I ate, moving between the explosion of flavors in my mouth to the shouting of words on the pages of the paper and back again.

My fork clattered on the plate as it fell from my fingers. I read it again:

NOPD confirmed the discovery of a body in Mid-City late last night. The man was identified as Mr. Anthony Jones. Jones, age 30, died from unknown causes.

"Ma'am?"

I read the full article several times while forcing the contents of my stomach to stay in its place, but it offered no details; no why, no how, no specific when ... and no who.

"Ma'am?" someone said. "Everything okay?"

"Uh," I swallowed. "Yeah. Sorry."

Leaving a twenty on the table, I stood quickly and stormed back to the manor. Interestingly, I returned in the same state as I left the place, with my mood dark and my mind busy. The weather too remained unchanged, as if that one stormy cloud wasn't satisfied unless it could get me a bit soggy.

Anthony Jones was found dead. The only other person at the shooting, the only possible person with some explanation. I wondered how "late last night" he was found. Had I spoken to Nathan Marble before then? And "unknown causes"? That's what D.S. Frost said about Mr. Tom Cruise, that his death was unknown. Almost magical. I hated the thought that entered my head ... *did Nathan Marble kill these men?*

In a haze of thought I reached for the doorknob, which opened on its own. Jeeves stood there. "Welcome back, Mrs. Witherspoon."

"Thank you," I said out of reflex, my mind fretting over Mr. Jones. I walked by him and towards the stairs.

"Mr. Smith and Mr. Wesson are waiting for you in the training room," he said.

"Yeah. Okay. Tell them I'll be right down." I didn't stop stride. *Did I just get that poor man killed?*

"Mrs. Witherspoon?"

"What?" I snapped as I faced him. I hadn't realized that Mrs. Black and Mrs. White stood at his side. Before the silence got awkward I cleared my throat. "I'm sorry. My mind's somewhere else. What's up?" I attempted a cheerful voice at the end.

"I feel," Jeeves said, giving a little bow to the ladies in his company, "*we* owe you an apology for the events this morning."

"No," I said. "It must have been terrifying. I completely understand." I headed up the stairs. "No apology necessary."

I got it, that he thought my listlessness was carried over from this morning. Not my real problem. *If you don't trust anyone else you ever meet in the rest of your life, trust him.* That's what Will said. What if he was wrong? What if Nathan Marble had fooled him all these years.

No. It's coincidence. Had to be. Why would Mr. Marble kill a man immediately after I mentioned him. It would only cast aspersions, call his loyalty into question, make me doubt him ... like now.

I don't know how long I stood at my bedroom door thinking with one hand poised on the knob, the other on the panel. Jeeves cleared his throat. He stood at the top of the stairs.

"Is everything all right, madam?"

Call his loyalty into question. "Jeeves, how well do you know Mr. Marble?"

His eyebrows shot up. "I do say ... Let's see. I've known Mr. Marble for over," his eyes looked upward, "twenty years now. Ever since Master Will hired him as his lawyer."

"Hm." I opened the door. "I'm just going to put on some sweats and I'll be right down."

"Before you put on another set of clothes Mrs. Black would like to take your measurements."

"Measurements?"

"For a fitting."

"A fitting?"

"For your armor."

"*Armor?*"

He paused. "Yes."

Armor! Good gravy. "Sure," I rolled my eyes. "Send her up."

~ ~ * ~ ~

"Not just any armor," Mr. Smith explained after I recounted the whole standing-on-a-chair-while-every-section-of-arm-leg-torso-and-head-were-measured ordeal. Took almost an hour! "Think of it as protective clothing. It isn't metal, like the olden days, or even kevlar. It will be a leather, most likely, but with its own energy signature that will blend with yours. That will offer more protection than, you know, clothes."

"Magic armor," I said bluntly.

He winced. "Just ... armor. Shall we begin?" In the center stood a boxing ring but in the shape of a pentagon; raised padded flooring, ropes around the perimeter—the whole kit and caboodle. "This session is one-to-one combat," he explained. "We're going to watch your Capoeira abilities."

"You mean your going to test them?"

"Of sorts."

"Who am I fighting?"

As if on cue Mr. Wesson, clad in an off-white *gi*, strolled into the room and hopped up onto the ring. In a warm up maneuver he jumped up and down repeatedly, like boxers do. Wrapped around his waist twisted a black belt.

"Wow!" I admired.

Mr. Smith scoffed. "Please. That's a Halloween costume. It's the spider you'll be fighting."

As I neared Annabelle slid down her translucent thread and landed on Mr. Wesson's shoulder. She made her way to his neck and disappeared in his curly coif. He stiffened, eyes wide and body rigid, then ... *wham*, he jumped into a disconcertingly confident martial arts stance; crouching, legs wide, arms raised defensively. In that Matrix fashion, he waved his fingers for me to approach.

I gave a sideways glance at Mr. Smith. "I take it he's done this before?" Not sure I ever want the spider to take over my body.

"Hundreds of times. He's in great shape, just has no talent. The spider has tons of talent. Together, they make a formidable pair. They put Will through his paces for years."

"I'm not going to hurt him by accident?"

"Mrs. Witherspoon," he giggled, "you're just going to try your best to stay off the mat."

Three painful and humbling hours later I hobbled up the narrow basement staircase and limped my way to the fireplace. I repeated my plea for relief, and the house thankfully complied. Dang, the spider was awesome. I don't know much about Karate or whatever she used but I'm guessing she's studied for years. She had moves I didn't know the human body could make. All in all I didn't fair too badly. I managed to get her on the mat a couple of times. Maybe once for every fifteen I wound up on the floor.

Lunch awaited. Toasted cheese sandwiches, all warm and melty, and piping tomato soup. I heartily ate while mentally replaying my recent sparring. With a spider. I smirked at the craziness of it all. It almost took away my frustration and anger over Tony Jones. Almost.

Out of the corner of my eye I saw Jeeves heading toward the front door. He opened it, and Mr. Marble stepped inside. I didn't hear him knock. Must have been distracted.

I eavesdropped on their conversation. "Whoa!" Mr. Marble remarked. "What happened in here?"

"The mistress of the house spruced it up," Jeeves answered flatly.

"Spruced? You call this *spruced?* In one day?"

"No, sir. According to those who witnessed the transformation, she did it in one minute." Silence. "I didn't see it myself. I was still asleep, sadly. But apparently it was quite startling."

"Jeeves," he lowered his voice, I assumed so no one could hear, but I still did. "Are you telling me she fixed up the entire manor, after six months of decay and neglect, in *one minute?*"

"That is exactly what I'm saying, sir."

By the silence I took it that the transformation wasn't common. I couldn't help but smile. For some reason I truly enjoy flapping the unflappable Mr. Marble.

"Is ...?" he seemed at a loss for words. "Is she okay?"

"You can ask her yourself. She's taking lunch in the dining room as we speak. Care to join her?"

"Yeah. Sure. Sounds great."

Hm. Didn't sound to me like he was quite as worried about my well being as he wanted Jeeves to think he was. Then again, I did just flap him.

When Jeeves announced him I turned and acted surprised. "Mr. Marble. Good to see you."

"You, too, Mrs. Witherspoon. I, uh," he took a seat, "hear you've been busy." He filled a bowl with soup. "The place looks, well, amazing really."

"Thank you."

"It hasn't looked this good for years."

"I owed it," I murmured though a mouthful of cheesy sandwich. "It healed me so I felt it was only fair to heal it."

"It healed you? Well, that's ... That's quite a thing. I'm glad you two have bonded so quickly." He ate a bit, then asked. "How, uh ... how did you know it could heal you?"

I ignored the question. "By the way, did you ever get a hold of that man I told you about? Tony Jones?"

"Uh," he hesitated. "No. No, I didn't." I felt a vibration up my spine. Or maybe the floor shifted beneath my feet. I had the distinct impression I had just been lied to. "Just haven't gotten to it yet, sorry. The office was a little crazy this morning," he half-heartily laughed. "I will though, before the day is over. I promise."

I kept the punch line to myself. I just couldn't shake the feeling that he knew more about Mr. Jones than he was telling me. But accusing him of lying wouldn't be useful. Even less useful would be accusing him of murder. Besides, he was a lawyer. Lying is in their nature, no?

We made idle chit-chat throughout lunch. Just as Nathan finished wiping his mouth, Jeeves rushed by. "You might want to wait a moment, sir. We have a visitor."

We followed him as he reached for the manor entrance. Standing just outside were Detective Duplantier and Detective Sergeant Frost, the latter with his gloved hand poised to knock. They looked shocked that the door opened.

"How does he do that?" I leaned over to Mr. Marble.

"He's got a knack," he softly answered. "Knows when folks are coming and going. One of the many reasons he's an excellent butler." He stepped forward, "Ah, Detectives. Nice to see you again. How may we be of service?"

"May we come in?" Detective Duplantier asked. D. S. Frost's head spun up and down. I don't know what he was looking at. Or for.

"Depends. If you're here to arrest my client or search the manor then I'd like to see the warrants first."

They looked at each other. "We just have a few questions, sir," she answered in a soft Southern drawl.

"Then by all means. Come on in."

As Jeeves led us all into the library D.S. Frost asked, "*Should* we be arresting your client or searching the manor?"

"Not for any reason I know of," Mr. Marble answered without missing a beat. "But I've never been quite as creative as the local law enforcement is at finding reasons to accuse the innocent."

"You're only creative at finding reasons to get them back on the streets, and all for a small but tidy profit," he parried.

"Touché," Mr. Marble exclaimed, taking none of the dialog personally.

The four of us sat almost simultaneously. "So," Mr. Marble started. "What questions do you have for Mrs. Witherspoon?" He settled back into the sofa, crossing one leg over the other.

They turned their eyes on me. Detective Duplantier handed me a photograph. "Have you ever seen this man, Mrs. Witherspoon?"

I looked at the black and white photo. Male, Caucasian, older than me, I'd guess, maybe mid-fifties judging by the salt and pepper hair and the lines on his unfamiliar face.

"No. I'm sorry, I have no idea who that is. Should I?" I handed the photo to Mr. Marble, a move that made D.S. Frost's mouth twist.

Mr. Marble's eyebrows shot up. "I do," he said. "He's a client of my company. Not mine, specifically, but I've seen him in the office. A mister ... Um ..." He snapped his fingers a couple of times, eyes clenched. "Ah! Mr. Redding, I believe." He handed back the photo and D.S. Frost pocketed it. "Why? Who is he to you?"

"Just a person of interest at the moment," Detective Duplantier said. "Eye witnesses put him at the location of Mr. Cruise's murder. We just want to talk to him."

"Murder?" Mr. Marble snapped. "I heard Tom Cruise had died but this is the first I've heard about murder."

"You aren't on our list of need-to-know contacts," D.S. Frost coyly explained.

The detective held up her hand, cutting him off. "We got the forensic report back just this morning, sir. Looks like Mr. Cruise was poisoned. We're testing a second victim now but at first glance it appears he died the same way. So it would be greatly helpful if we know where to find him and right now the only thing that both victims had in common was the shooting." She looked at me. "Your shooting."

"Who was the second victim?" my lawyer asked.

"Anthony Jones," she answered. My heart stopped beating when she said the name. I couldn't help but glance at Mr. Marble and he at me. She continued. "He was a witness questioned at your client's ordeal. Claimed in his account that she was attacked," she turned her focus back on me, "just like you said. We just found it odd that the only two other people involved with that shooting ended up murdered in a little over twenty-four hours after the event."

"Now, that does sound a little like an accusation," Mr. Marble said.

"No, sir," D.S. Frost said. "On the contrary. We're concerned for your client's well being." He shifted to address me. "We were hoping that maybe you saw this gentleman that night. Or could shed light on why both of these men were killed."

"For example," Detective Duplantier broke in, "did you ever get any copies or stationary from the Office Depot on St. Charles?" I shook my head. "That's where Mr. Cruise worked."

"But then you knew that, Mr. Marble," D.S. Frost coldly said. "He was, after all, your client."

If my heart didn't start beating soon I was going to pass out.

"What? I don't have any clients by the name of *Tom Cruise*."

The sergeant handed him a photo. "How about this man?"

Mr. Marble took the photo, which I didn't see. Fine by me—I don't care to ever see that man's face again. I did, however, see worry in Mr. Marble's eyes. "No. This is Collins, Todd Collins. *Forger*, as I recall. Served his time, five years, I think, out on parole, and, yes, I knew where he worked." He handed the photo back. "I had no idea that was the man who attacked Mrs. Witherspoon. But serve me the warrant and I'll happily hand you what files I have."

"A warrant?" the sergeant smiled. "Of course. Just like a lawyer to protect the rights of his dead client over his living one."

"Enough, sergeant." She turned to Mr. Marble. "Thank you for cooperating with us, sir. We'll have that warrant by this afternoon."

"I'll have the record prepared by then, how's that?" he offered.

With that hollow victory D.S. Frost looked around the room again, just as he had when he first came into the manor—head and neck craning in every direction. "Forgive me, but I don't recall the place looking quite so ... lovely when I was here last."

"Uh," Mr. Marble stammered, "we just had the place cleaned. Top down. It desperately needed it." He changing the subject, "I can have Mr. Redding's contact information by this afternoon, if that will help you folks," Mr. Marble offered. "We make it a policy to help our men, and women, in blue as much as we can." I had to suppress the reflex to roll my eyes. That probably sounded as over-the-top to them as it did to me.

"That would be lovely," she smiled and sang. "Thank you very much."

Once they left he shook his head. "I don't get that at all. Collins was a criminal but not a killer. I'm sorry. I had no idea I knew him. He looked, I don't know, *different* in your memory. Maybe your mind's eye saw him differently."

I folded my arms, unconvinced, but I just nodded. It hardly seemed the time to say, "I told you so." Besides. He looked genuinely surprised at the news of Jones's death.

"I gotta go," he said, checking his watch. "I want to have those documents ready for the detectives."

He left me, still wishing my heart would start beating.

Chapter Eleven

I RETREATED TO my bedroom thinking I'd catch a wink or two and let my belly digest before getting another foot thrust into it.

My bed happily accommodated. I stretched out on top, softly caressed by the jasmine scented breeze through my window, listening to the brush of fabric as the curtains swayed up, open, and out. But sleep eluded me. I stared at the ceiling, now perfect and shiny, and thought of Will. I recalled someone saying this wasn't his room. I hoisted myself onto my elbows suddenly curious why I wasn't put there in the first place. I mean, I was his wife. Why give me my own room?

I stood, bare feet planted on the new hardwood, and thought of Will. I asked if I could see his room. My mind filled with a vision; red walls, mahogany half-canopy bed, gold satin sheets, book cases, the scent of bergamot, frankincense, and leather. I felt Will course through my veins, and it made me desperate to be nearer to him. My feet moved on their own, out my own room, down the hallway a couple of doors. My hand reached for the doorknob. I opened it.

It looked just as it had in my vision. Every object, every fabric, even the smell. I quietly closed the door behind me and stood at the foot of the bed. I blinked and the room went dark—it took me a moment to understand I was seeing the past. My husband slept under a single bed sheet, his skin bluish in the pale moon light that lazed its way in through the window. He moved, turning over. Then sat up, and turned on the small lamp on his nightstand. Opening a drawer he took out a book. He scooched himself against the headboard, took out a pen hidden in the book's binding, and began to write. *A diary!*

I blinked, and in that moment I flew back to my time, standing at the foot of his bed. Hastily, I went to the same nightstand and opened the drawer. To my dismay the diary wasn't there.

I put my hands on the wall. "Do you know where it is?" Instantly I saw another scene. Daytime. Will removed the diary from his bedside and flipped through its pages as he walked to a small desk. He retrieved a folded piece of paper, putting it at the start of the journal. From a bookcase he pulled out an encyclopedia volume. I watched over his shoulder as he opened the large tome and placed his diary inside, in pages that had been cut away to make room for the journal. He kissed the new book. "This is for you, Winki," he said, and returned it to the gap on the shelf.

I blinked and dashed to the bookcase. I looked over the books. An old encyclopedia! I pulled out the book I'd seen Will use and, lo and behold, found the diary.

Gingerly, I pulled out note, sat in the chair by the window, and read.

Winks,

I'm hoping you read this letter first before reading my journal. If so I'm begging you not to read the book. My diary is my own. Those words are for me. Please, let them rest in peace. Burn the book if you must, but do not read the words here. It holds no answers for you.

What's important is this:

My death was no accident, and I would never leave you on my own accord. I have been betrayed.

Long ago I made a deal. I was young and stupid, and never realized the true consequence of the agreement. As time went on, however, the horror of my actions became clear to me. I bartered. I begged. I sacrificed. Yet my debtee would not be kind, nor release me from full payment. My mark was put on a list, and in time would come due. I have accepted that.

But someone close to me changed the order. Someone moved my mark to the top of the list. My name is next. I shudder to think about what's to come, the endless cold and dark. Know that I face my demise bravely, but not willingly.

I don't know why my mark was moved, why my death was hastened, but that isn't the real mystery—that payment was always due. The real mystery is who. Who pointed the finger and said, "Take him now?" Who had the kind of authority or influence over those who owned my soul? I do not have the time to discover the answer myself. They have made certain of that. But only those in this house knew I had such a debt. The traitor, then, is here, now.

I hesitate to tell you any of this. You will need to trust the people around you to succeed in your future. I don't want you to doubt them, or fear them. I cannot stress this enough—you need them, Winki. You need to work with them. Take everything they have to offer you!

But be cautious. If you are seen as a threat to them, your own life might be in grave danger.

I don't want you to spend your precious time trying to find my murderer. Not yet, anyway. Put the matter of my death aside for the moment. You now have the upper hand. Walk with them. Fight for them. And know ... someone is not the friend they claim to be.

My deepest love, always,

Winki,

> *Will*

I could barely read the last sentence through my blurry vision. My throat burned in soreness.

Outside, it began to pour.

~ ~ * ~ ~

After an hour or so of sitting on Will's bed I collected myself. I put the diary back in its hiding place, keeping the letter for my own. I hid it in my own room, then, like a man to the gallows, slogged my way down to the basement. Must keep up appearances. *Take everything they have to offer you!* Seemed like a good plan. For now.

"Mrs. Witherspoon!" the man in his white lab coat, Mr. Smith, called happily as I entered the room. "We have something for you." He gestured to a manikin clothed in leathers. "Your armor is ready." *Already?* There was a jacket, pants, boots, gloves and a helmet that reminded me of a Mexican wrestler. All were a light blue with white stripes and silver piping. Just gorgeous. It looked like a cross between motorcycle gear and a superhero's outfit.

It was a sight for my sore eyes. I smiled as I ran my hand over the silver threaded stitching. I rubbed the supple leather between my fingers. Way too light to be useful, I thought.

"Go ahead. Try it on." He and Mr. Wesson left me, calling, "let us know when you've dressed. We want to take it on a test run. We'll be upstairs."

I removed my sweats and donned the new gear. The fit was perfect. I went through some Capoeira motions, including spins and kicks. The leather didn't bind or impede or prohibit anything. In fact it felt better than my own clothes. Surely, this isn't the "armor" they spoke of. I called them back into the room.

Mr. Wesson whistled; thus far the only noise I've heard him make. "Have you taken a look at yourself?" Mr. Smith asked. He opened an armoire, one cluttered with weaponry, but on the inside of the door was a full length mirror. Curious myself I complied. I looked amazing, if I do say so myself. Feminine, yet tough. Winki, the super hero! My long white hair stuck out from under the leather cap of a helmet and poured down my shoulders. The whole works matched.

"One more thing," he said, as he approached me. On the right side of my pants dangled a leather loop. He slid the silver hammer into it. "Now. You're set. Keep that with you at all times while in the suit."

"This is all very cute," is said playing with my hair, "and I appreciate the outfit, I really do. But I wouldn't call it armor. A cool set of leathers, yes, but—"

As I turned to them my eye popped as I realized Mr. Wesson had shot an arrow at me. I gasped and instinctively held up my hands, just as I had at the shooting. It did no good. The arrow hit its target, which was me, right in the chest. Then bounced off me with a "tink". Like I was made of steel.

I angrily picked up the arrow. "What the hell?" I yelled at Mr. Wesson. "Why are you shooting at me!" I shook the arrow at him.

"To prove how it works. Not just any leather," Mr. Smith giggled. "We gave it an energy field, one that matches your own signature, amps it up a bit. Well," he tilted his head, "not matches. More like plays with. Well, not plays with, more like adds to."

And shooting an arrow at me was better than just saying that, *why?* Come to think of it, "Why couldn't I stop it, like the bullet?"

"Don't panic," Mr. Smith said as he cautiously took the arrow from me. "We're working on it, really. Let's focus on the positives. You got a hammer and you got armor. We're ahead of schedule! Now. Where were we ... ah! Let's put that new armor to some use."

The rest of the afternoon was spent going through a type of obstacle course, which covered the entire basement, not just the training room (how could there be this much space down here?). I had to get from point A to point B within a certain time. But as I jumped over barrels, ran across rickety bridges, climbed over fences, and dashed from cover to cover, Mr. Wesson shot various guns at me. Paint guns. On my new outfit! "That way we can tell if you've been hit," Mr. Smith had explained. "Don't worry. It cleans easily. We promise."

By six that evening Mr. Smith announced it was quitting time. Before he and Mr. Wesson began to dismantle the course he handed me some wet nap cleaners. "Wipe up with these?" he said.

"Me? I gotta clean up? The paint wasn't my idea!"

"It works best for you. It's your armor, your energy ... trust me on this."

I rolled my eyes but did as he suggested. I don't know if he was honest about why it worked, but it did. The paint just magically whisked off. Took mere seconds. The stuff in my hair, on the other hand ...

Someone raced into the room. Jeeves. Wow, didn't know he could move that quickly. "Hurry," he panted to the men in white lab coats. "She will be needed upstairs." They exchanged looks. "We've got incoming."

They turned to me. "You heard the man. Go!"

Following closely at Jeeves's heels I ran up the stairs and into the living room, the largest one. Jeeves stopped short and pointed to the center of the room. "Here," he said, as Mr. Smith and Mr. Wesson joined us. "They will come here."

An electric energy softly hummed just as he finished the words, then grew in intensity to a buzzing sound. The lights around us dimmed. The space in the center of the room moved, contracted, as all of the light got sucked into to the center. I tilted my head, trying to understand what I was seeing. A giant sphere of distortion appeared, as if collapsing everything in that space toward a point in the middle.

The ladies Black and White came racing in. "Oh lord!" Mama cried out, "it's started. They found out. Malador's coming!"

"Please," Jeeves silenced her. He'd changed; his face gaunt and his eyes glowed green. Just like they looked at the séance. He leaned to me and said quietly, "Do not let him touch you, madam."

A great wind exploded in the room, knocking over lamps and

baubles, throwing hung pictures to the floor. Then out they came. Little green men-like creatures, about half the size of a human, some thin, some pudgy, all clad in armor—the real stuff, not leather, like mine. Their skin was pocked with blisters and pus-filled sores. Their eyes were blood red, and their faces were mashed and twisted. They marched out from the distorted sphere in twos, turned away one another, and made a file on either side of the windy ball. About twenty or so had entered when—

"Here he comes!" Someone called. Judging by these guys I couldn't imagine what Malador must look like. I assumed a larger, meaner, uglier, or puss-ier version.

He stepped through. The bubbled vanished with a soft "puff".

And my jaw dropped.

Malador stood tall. His dark hair softly coiled from his head, and dripped luxuriously at his shoulders. His stunning brown eyes rivaled the color of chocolate. His chiseled face and prominent cheekbones were dusted with a dark shadow of beard. Perfect pink lips. Clear skinned. A man. A drop dead *gorgeous* man. The quintessential "tall, dark, and handsome."

He looked me up and down. "What do we have here?" he said, slowly pronouncing each word. Like that, the spell was broken. He just had to speak.

Long ago, before I met Will, I used to work in a bar, a divey little place in the heart of the French Quarter. Drunk locals, drunk football fans, and drunk tourists. Oh, yes, I'd been drooled over before, so I know my creeps. And I know how to handle them. I was secretly thankful he turned out to be a jerk.

"The missus, I presume?" he asked me. I said nothing. Just watched. "And aren't you just pretty as a picture," he stepped slowly closer to me. "I can see why Will bedded a common creature." His eyes roamed my body again as he licked his lips. "Perhaps not so common after all." And closer. "Yes, I think I may have to taste some of this for myself. My room. My bed. I can almost feel you writhing beneath me." Nearly two feet away now. "Begging for more. I guarantee you, fine lady, you've never had a rapture like the one I'll give you."

"Hey, pal, back off!" Mr. Smith said, and tried to come between us. Malador merely raised his hand in Smith's direction and Mr. Smith flew through the air, crashing hard against a wall behind him. He collapsed in a heap. Mr. Wesson rushed to his side.

It was the perfect distraction ... well, perfect for me. During his stalk I had worked my hand slowly to the hammer at my side and gripped it just beneath its head. Once Malador, satisfied with his humbling of Mr. Smith, turned back to me I let the rage fill me.

Hammer in hand, I gave him a hard uppercut.

The man flew nearly thirty feet and landed on his ass quite ungracefully. He stood, enraged. His face red with either hatred or embarrassment. He pointed at me. "TAKE HER!"

No. Not in my house.

I raised my hand. And everything slowed down, nearly to a stop. Well, it turned out, not everything. Just Malador and most of his minions. Two or three of them looked around, perplexed.

My staff, who'd readied themselves for a fight, armed with small swords and—bless Mrs. White's pea pickin' heart—a rolling pin, also looked perplexed, eyes darting from each other to the intruders and back.

"What on earth?" Mrs. Black said, crouched for battle. Her green eyes flitted from creature to creature, trying to determine which green statue she was supposed to fight.

Using my hammer, and just a little bit of anger, I popped each one of the greenies in their snoots, knocking them down like bowling pins. I eyed the unaffected critters, who scampered to the aid of those I batted, keeping their distance and tentative eyes on me.

I admit, the act felt too easy and a little unfair. But they did come here uninvited. I took my place in front of Malador and swung back ... No. Too easy. *Him I'll just embarrass.* I'd already made a big point.

I snapped my fingers. Time revved up and back to normal speed. Malador, who'd just finished his attack command, looked around to see his small army crippled and moaning all around him.

In one smooth move I put the hammer in its holster and folded my arms, never taking my eyes off of the intruder.

"In case it isn't clear, Mr. Malador, let me say this just once." I used an acrimonious tone. "*This* house. Is. Defended."

He didn't move, didn't blink. Then a small smiled drifted over his lovely lips. Malador took a step back, giving himself room for a deep sweeping and gallant bow.

"Forgive me, good lady. I can see you are a more worthy opponent than your husband."

I turned away, confidently exposing my back side. "Mr. Jeeves? I trust you can send them on their way."

"I'd be all too happy, madam." He clapped his hands once. The event began to recreated itself. As the room distorted I leaned casually against a table. "Mr. Malador. Feel free to visit in the future. But next time I fully expect you to use the front door."

He smirked as he reached from little green thing to little green thing, tossing them, one by one, unceremoniously into the sphere. When the room was cleared he headed for the sphere, but stopped and turned to me. "Mrs. Witherspoon, I sincerely look forward to meeting you again. At the tournament." He gave a small sweep with his hand, which seemed to summon a thousand tiny points of light. They gravitated and collected within his grasp. With a tiny fireworks-like pop the sparks arched to the floor leaving behind a prefect blood red rose between his fingers. His eyes on me he kissed the flower, then casually tossed it at my feet. In a second gracious bow he backed up and, "poof" he and the sphere were gone.

"Woooo hoo hoo!—Ow ow ow ..."

We all looked at Mr. Smith, doubled over, holding his head.

"Come now," Mama said, "let me have a look. That's just a little bump. Wesson, help me get him to the kitchen. Don't worry, I'll get you all patched up."

While the three slowly made their way out of the room I reached down to pick up the rose. "No!" Hercule called out from somewhere. "Do not touch it!"

Jeeves pulled a handkerchief from his pocket and tossed in down to cover the rose. He then picked it up himself. "I will take care of this, madam," and left.

That final warning finished me. My adrenaline rush faded. Or reality hit me. My body quaked with fear. Before I passed out or lost my stomach I sank into the sofa.

I sat there trembling violently. "Oh, my!" Mrs. Black worried. "Are you all right? Can I get you something?" She took a seat on the sofa next to me, putting a kind hand on my shoulder. "You were fantastic, dear. You did Master Will proud."

"I ... I don't know how I did it. Any of it."

She chuckled. "You did it very well."

"No, I mean ..." I took a deep, settling breath. My queasiness ebbed enough for me to sit upright. "Earlier, not just hours ago, I couldn't stop Mr. Wesson from shooting at me with an arrow. Or a hundred different guns! So why did this work?"

She had no words to offer. Finally, Hercule, who appeared on the armrest next to me, said, "Because you needed it to."

I gave a sign. "That's not helpful."

"It is true!" Hercule said, as he danced left, then right, then back again. "You didn't see Mr. Wesson as a real threat, therefore your powers did not work. Malador is clearly a threat, hence your ability to stop him."

Jeeves came back into the room and made a beeline for the

portable bar in the corner. He mixed up some ingredients and stirred vigorously. He handed me a crystal goblet filled with a yellowish drink. "I can say, madam, that this is not unusual. When each of us came into our talents we felt a sense of panic and confusion."

Mrs. Black agreed. "We all ask the same questions. Why now? Why today? Why did it work this time but not the last? We've", she waved a finger between her and Jeeves, "not only experienced it, but we've seen it many times."

"In short, *madame*, it happens when you need it to," Hercule added. "For now you just have to trust that."

I finished the drink in a big gulp. I would much rather control the power than have the power control me.

Chapter Twelve

"Malador?" Mr. Marble coughed as he spat out his drink. "Was *here?*" We all sat around the large dining room table for dinner, enjoying the pizzas Mama had made. Well, the others enjoyed. My appetite was on vacation, still reeling from my meet with Malador. Apparently, unlike the last few meals, we all eat pizza together.

"You shoulda seen her, boss," a bandaged Mr. Smith said. "She was awesome!" Mr. Wesson gave a single, determined nod of agreement. "Used her hammer! Slowed time! We all saw it!" He giggled with glee.

Jeeves gave Mr. Marble a napkin for his small mess. "Thank you," he said to the lanky butler, who'd begun eating.

"I must admit," Hercule added from his post on the wall, "she was almost flawless."

"Almost?" Mr. Smith challenged. "What more did you want her to do?"

"Killing him comes to mind."

Mr. Marble regained his normal, calm demeanor. Picking up a piece of 'za he asked, "So, what happened?"

The gang told their stories. They laughed, they shouted, they hooted, and they praised. Only Mr. Wesson and myself remained silent, but even he showed his enthusiasm with jubilant raps on the table, or loud applause.

"He left something?" Mr. Marble said at the end.

"Yes, sir," Jeeves answered. "A rose."

"Did you destroy it?"

Jeeves finished chewing. "Sadly, no. It seems indestructible."

"Don't like that," Mr. Marble muttered. "Show it to me after dinner." Then he turned to me. "How are you, Mrs. Witherspoon?"

"Not as excited as everyone else."

"And why's that?"

"I feel overwhelmed, I suppose. Who is he? *What* is he? And what were those ugly green things."

With a furrowed brow Mr. Marble turned to Jeeves. Jeeves explained, "The goblins, sir."

"Goblins?" I echoed.

"Goblins," Mr. Smith said. "The minions of the dark side."

"Minions? Why don't I have *minions?*" I asked. Mr. Wesson gave me a light smack on my arm, then gestured to himself. "You. You're my minions?"

"We call ourselves 'staff'," Mrs. Black said. "Sounds better."

"Pays better, too," Mr. Smith muffled through a full mouth.

Mr. Marble wiped his mouth and took a sip of soda. He got comfortable in his chair. "Malador is the head of another house, Ravenswood, here in New Orleans. If you recall I told you there were three." I nodded. "Ravenswood Manor, the Magnolia House, and us," he used his fingers, flicking them out as one-two-three. "Ravenswood is the dark house, as you might have guessed. Magnolia is the light house."

"We are always at war with one of them," Hercule chimed in.

"Why is that?" I asked.

"Because we're the Gateway house," Mr. Marble said, as if I hadn't been paying attention. "We—"

"Swing both ways, I've got that part," I impatiently said.

"But you clearly don't understand. You see, most houses have their own energy, light or dark, tending to good or evil. And those born in those houses get that energy. The houses themselves can never be changed."

"But the Gateway Manor works in reverse, *madame*" Hercule added. "It gets its energy from the champion of the house. It can be either light or dark."

Mr. Marble continued. "When Gateway's been light, the dark house attacks in hopes to persuade the champion. Or kill them, if need be. And when it's been dark, Magnolia House does the same. Each of those houses tries to win Gateway."

"Which is why," Mr. Smith said with his mouthful, "we're always under attack."

"Do either of them come to our aid?" I asked.

"Funny. Never seems to be the case," Mr. Marble sighed.

"That's why you don't want me to touch the rose," I snapped my fingers. "You think it's some attempt to persuade me?"

"Persuade. Infect. Whatever," Mr. Marble nodded. He took another slice. "Never underestimate Malador. He's always got his own agenda." He ate a couple bites as the others told stories of Malador's last attack several month ago, quite soon after Will's death. They managed to defeat him, and convince him that Will "just wasn't home that night."

"Which was not uncommon," Annabelle said, as she pirouetted onto the table. "Will didn't live here full time, as you know. But we didn't want the community to know he was dead. We would have been very vulnerable."

"As for *what* Malador is," Mr. Marble swallowed, "he's an incubus."

"A *what*abus?" I asked.

"An incubus. A demon that feasts on, er, sexual energy."

I raised my eyebrows. "Feasts?" Then I realized, "A demon? He looked like a man to me."

"*Was* a man. Then made a deal with the dark lords. Now a demon."

Dark lords? Someone really needed to explain this hierarchy to me.

"You didn't ...," Mr. Marble cleared his throat, "*feel* anything for him, did you?"

"I thought he was handsome. Until he talked. Then I realized he was dumber than a bag of hammers." That tickled Mr. Smith. He offered me a high-five, which I took.

"Yes. Feasts," Mr. Marble didn't seem amused. "He seduces and feasts. Once he touches you, you're his. You're doomed. He feasts until his victims are either dead, which is the best case scenario—"

"That's the best case scenario?" I worried.

"Or a quivering mass of babbling insanity." Okay, that might be worse. "I've seen it. Don't touch him. Don't touch anything he gives you."

"The armor will protect—" Mr. Smith started.

"No!" Mr. Marble dismissed. "Just. Don't. Touch."

Got it. Noooo touchie.

"Now, please join me in the smoking room," he stood, and helped me out of my chair. Odd, but I agreed.

Curious which of the many rooms received the title "the smoking room" I followed Mr. Marble through the maze that was the house. We settled in a room I hadn't explored yet. Very masculine in feel. Maps adorned the walls, old books sat stacked on various tables and consoles. Brown leather chairs and sofa with bright brass tacks outlining their backs and arms. It smelled of tobacco, the real deal, from a pipe, not a cigarette.

Stuffy, in other words.

Once I entered the room Mr. Marble slid the pocket doors shut behind me. I noticed the *cafard* scamper under the door to join us as Mr. Marble poured himself a snifter. He offered me one.

I declined. But I thought to ask. "Mr. Marble? Does the phrase 'never on a Sunday' mean anything to you?"

He closed one eye, thinking. "It's a song, right." Then he sang, "Never ever on a Sunday, a Sunday, a Sunday, no, that will never do." He cocked his head. "Why?"

"I came across it recently in a riddle. That's all."

"Hm. Hercule," he said, "are we alone?"

"*Oui.* I have already dismissed the scout."

That made me look around the room. Yup, no spider.

He nodded, "Good. We have something we need to talk about." He sniffed his brandy. "This attack today. This isn't good news."

I shrugged as we sat. "I agree. I'm not happy about being attacked."

"No. I mean ... As you know we've been keeping Will's death quiet. In fact, only those in this house knew Will was even married. That was done to protect you, frankly. While his love for you was very strong, it wasn't his strength. Someone could get to him through you."

"Through me?"

"Should someone threaten you, or kidnap, or ... whatever. They could make Will do what he otherwise wouldn't. I know he'd move the moon save you if he had to."

"And if they got to Will, *madame*, they could get to the house."

I thought about why they were telling me this, recalling the conversation, albeit short, that Malador and I had. "Malador knew," I realized. "He called me 'the missus'."

"*Oui.*" He sounded so proud.

"Someone in this house told him," I concluded.

Mr. Marble raised a hand. "That's a jump. It could have been innocent. They could have told someone else and word got around. Let's not assume you were betrayed. However, to attack right now, when you're still new, still learning, still vulnerable, well—"

"Yes," Hercule cut him off. "You were betrayed."

Mr. Marble frowned, then took a drink. He didn't argue this time.

My eyes were glued to Mr. Marble. *I was betrayed*, Will wrote. And now, so was I.

My lawyer rubbed his eyes. "For the first time in years I don't know what to do."

"We do what we've been doing," Hercule said as he scampered his way up to the arm of Mr. Marble's seat. "She continues her training. She readies herself for the tournament."

"This house was attacked!"

"And she did an outstanding job of defending it, *oui?* They won't attack again anytime soon. Now, we have some time. Now, we must move forward."

Mr. Marble stood and began to pace. "Malador knows she can manipulate time. Next time he'll have a solution. Next time he'll come prepared."

The little roach danced, to and fro, then said, "Nathan, what does he really know now? Yes, she is a *gardien du temps*. But what else?"

"She wields Thor's Hammer." *Thor's Hammer!?*

"*Oui.* And what else?"

Mr. Marble slammed his drink down. "Isn't that enough?"

Hercule laughed. "*Mon ami*, think about it." A nearby clock ticked off a few seconds. "He now knows what we know. And what do we know?"

Mr. Marble thoughtfully licked his lips. "She has different talents than Will."

"*Oui?*"

"So Malador's old arsenal against us is useless. He needs time to defend himself against her talents. And even if someone in the house told him what talents she has ..."

Hercule finished the thought. "Malador has no idea what all of her talents are. Because we do not. No one does."

"I don't get it," I said, feeling a bit thick. "What difference does that make?"

Hercule explained. "You embarrassed him. He thought you'd be a pushover and you were not. He will not come unprepared but he does not want to repeat such an outcome. So he will wait. I don't expect he'll attack again until after the tournament."

"Something to look forward to," I growled.

The man smiled. "Thank you, Hercule. I don't know about you, Mrs. Witherspoon, but I feel better." Nope, not so much. He swirled his drink in the glass, then threw it down the back of his throat. He winced as he swallowed, then checked his watch. "Ouch. I gotta get going. I told my wife I'd be home by nine."

"Wife? I had no idea," I said. For some reason it never occurred to me that he had a life outside of this house. He was here so danged often.

"Yep," he said as he took out his cell phone. "Wife. Two kids. And a dog. Here." He handed me his phone. Happy family pics. I flicked through them. "That's Michelle, and my sons, Richard and Andrew. Rich is nine. Andy's five. Oh, and that's Soup."

"Soup?"

"The dog. Got him last year. His name's Soup." I handed him his phone with a cocked eyebrow. "Never let a four year old name the dog." He shoved the cell in his pocket and waved, dashing out the door.

I turned to face Hercule. Tough to have a serious conversation with a cockroach. "What do you think?" I asked.

"I would have to agree. Never let a four year old name the dog."

"I mean about the house. Did someone betray it? Us?" I swallowed. "Me?"

He danced a bit. Maybe that was how he thinks, with his legs. "*Ma chére*, some people are happy when they hear what they need to hear. Others are happy when they hear the truth. I do not know you well enough to say which is the case for you. So I ask. What do you wish to hear?"

I pinched the bridge of my nose. "I don't think I'm best served with a lie."

"Malador and Will used to be the best of friends. In hindsight, perhaps useful; we all know how to defend ourselves against him."

"I know. I mean, I'd gotten the impression Will wasn't always ... the kind man I knew."

"This house, everyone here, served him then. I mistake," he said in broken English as he sat upright in his back legs. "Not Smith and Wesson. They came after he converted."

"Converted?"

"To the light side."

I swallowed. *To* the light side. So, *from* the dark. My husband had been at some point *evil*. "Why did he convert?"

"He wasn't given a choice. Magnolia House attacked, captured him, and took him to the Light Lords. There he was converted."

"You make it sound like he was brainwashed."

"My point, *ma chére*, is that it is possible, perhaps likely, that someone in the house wants to return to those days. Yes." He dashed down the sofa and disappeared behind a book-ladened table. "I believe we have been betrayed."

~ ~ * ~ ~

I woke to the guttural rumble of distant thunder. I sat upright, alone in the dark. Well, except for the spider in my room. I needed to know. I wanted to see it.

I donned my robe, then padded with bare feet down the staircase and dashed to the dining room. A brief flash of lightning lit up my husband's face. That small smile. Those dashing eyes.

I place my hands below him on the mantle. "Show me that day."

"Here they come!" someone yelled. I spun around, startled by the unfamiliar voice. It was a man I've never met. "Will! Get your ass in here!" Already the sphere-like portal was forming in the room. It was daytime, and this was not a room I recognized.

"I'm ready. Keep your shirt on," he yelled as he trotted into the room. Great gracious ... *it really was him.* Younger, though, so very young, maybe just into his teens, but not innocent. His face, which I'd only seen as kind and sweet, sneered cold and angry. A thin mustache penciled over his upper lip. His cheeks were ruddy with rage, and dark circles swirled below his eyes. From a glance you could see the darkness inside him. I had to look away. Maybe this wasn't such a good idea. Maybe I didn't want to see this side of him.

Both of them wore outfits. *Armor.* Black leather clad each of the young men. Will's outfit sported angry red designs with a skull-like face on his chest. The other man's was equally scary, but bright yellow, like an angry bee. Will held a crossbow. The other a halberd.

Others joined them. I recognized them; Jeeves, Mrs. White, and Mrs. Black. Younger, each of them, but not by much. All of them bore hot-tempered looks in their eyes.

The sphere exploded as an army of men rushed into the room, weapons raised and battle cries abounded. It took courage to stand in the middle of the battle, even though I wasn't really there. I felt the warriors run through me, and weapons swished over head. The house was outnumbered. Wave after wave of warriors came through the portal until dozens of them surrounded each of the household members.

My own, albeit short, training came to mind as I watched the two men. Will fired his weapon, then used it in hand to hand battle as he spun, jumped, kicked, and whacked his attackers. Several times an attacker's arm would reach out and Will used the bow to block, tangling the arm, only to twist and snap it neatly. He'd raise the crossbow; with a red flash it loaded on its own. He'd fire it again and repeat his defense.

The other man was masterful with the halberd. In the small room he effectively used it as a spear, an ax, and a staff, all the while avoiding thrusting and prodding weapons.

What training I had came into focus. *Using your favorite in a small space.* I could see now why that was needed. The two men were amazing.

Mrs. White let out a call to the air around her, and green, poisonous flumes seeped from her fingers and shot like arrows down the throats of some of the men. They fell immediately, immobile. Or dead.

Mrs. Black called out, "Spiders!" and they rained down on the masses, crawling into the clothing, covering faces and bodies. I shuddered at the sight. It worked. Most of the intruders busied themselves with brushing off the bugs, which made them easy prey for those defending the house.

Jeeves, simple daggers in each hand, moved in a sweeping motion that reminded me of a windmill, cutting and slicing anything near him, and moving onto the next without waiting for the first victim to fall. It was beautiful. And terrifying.

They were winning. The house would remain—

"Edward!" Will called to the other, "Behind you!"

That forced me to look. I saw Edward, the man in yellow, as the sword ran through him from behind. The blade's protruding tip dripped with his blood as he sank to his knees.

"*No!*" Will screamed as he ran towards the man.

"Master Will," Jeeves tried to grab him, "you cannot help your brother now. Please! Stop!"

Brother? Will had a brother?

Men grabbed and held Will steadfast by his arms, preventing the crazed man from seeing his dying brother. He screamed his brother's name over and over. *I will never get rid of that sound.*

"Let him go," someone said. An elderly man with brilliant white hair. His clothing looked like a leather version of General Lee's attire. He looked familiar to me, but I couldn't place him.

Will ran to his brother's side, dropping to his knees. Edward looked up at him, and the fighting in the room subsided. Everyone watched the gut wrenching display as Will cradled his brother in his arms, buried his face in Edward's hair, and wept, "Don't leave me. Please, don't go."

The wounded man coughed, spitting blood down his cheek and chin. He looked up at Will. "We ... have ... lost ..." His eye closed, and his body went limp.

"No no no no," Will wept as he futilely shook the man back to consciousness. I wiped my own teared eyes.

"Master Will," said the white-haired man in charge, his voice big, noble, and full of honor. "You are now the champion of this house. And you are captured." He put his sword under Will's chin. He gave a smirk, and unnecessarily chided, "I'll give you a choice, boy. You can either come with us for conversion or," he pressed the sword forward, cutting Will beneath his jaw, "I'll run this through you now." Will grimaced as it bit into his flesh. The armed man leaned closer and hissed. "Go on, *you filthy bastard*, give me justification to end your miserable life."

I know that scar. When asked Will passed it off as a "consequence of childhood stupidity", then laughed, "Never climb trees during a hurricane."

Gagging, hot tears streaking his reddened face, Will slowly raised his hands.

Two men unkindly grabbed him and hoisted him to his feet. The elder man ordered one of his men to form a portal. As the bubble emerged he looked over Edward's body, brutally removing the sword from the dead man's gut. "Take him, too."

"No!" Will screamed. "Let him be buried. He's owed his peace," Will pleaded. "With honors. With our ancestors."

The white-haired man spun around and kicked Will square in the stomach. The two men who held him kept him upright as Will's legs gave way; one grabbed his hair, pulling his head mercilessly backward.

"To the victor goes the spoils, boy," the elder said. "I'll do with his miserable carcass what I wish. I owe him nothing."

Will was shackled, neck, hands, and feet, then led, dragged like a dog, harshly through the portal. Soldiers aided each other as they dragged and limped into the hot sphere center. The elder man turned to the Gateway staff, all of them deflated more than battered, before stepping through himself and proclaimed, "I spare your lives as I understand you are victims of this damned house and its damned curse. But I warn you all. Do not think your new master can be saved. *He* is *mine*."

He stepped through the portal and, "poof".

I stood there, alone in the dark, when a great flash lit up the dining room, followed by a raucous roll of thunder.

What I had just seen ... by the stars! Those were the *good guys?* The white house?

I let go of the mantel, curling my fingers as if they'd just been burned. I looked up at the man looking down on me. So obviously kind. So completely gentle.

"Heart of Hades, Will, what did you get me into?"

Chapter Thirteen

THE NEXT WEEK settled into a grueling schedule. Up early. Eat Breakfast. Undergo an exhausting round of torture, beatings, gauntlets, obstacle courses, and fights that the men in lab coats insisted on calling "training." Lunch. Another exhausting round of torture, beatings ... yadda yadda yadda. We added a "break," where Jeeves rescued me around four in the afternoon for a "spot of tea and biscuits"—I'd grown partial to that. More sparring. Then dinner. Then I got to collapse. Even being helped by the house and Mama's awesome food didn't completely remove the mental exhaustion.

One thing was added to my regimen, something Mr. Smith called "talent practice." Having seen my time-slowing talent for themselves, the two lab coats came up with a number of tests and trials, everything from "catch the arrow" to "save the puppy," a picture of a cute doggy they'd shoot at and I was supposed to rescue. I figured it out, to some degree. If I could convince myself ,"No ... not in my house," I could do it, reliably. The convincing was the trick. Hard to care about a puppy picture, even though it was admittedly darned cute.

The last couple of days, after all the work, practice, and activity, I heaped myself onto a puffy sofa in the game room and watched TV. My life almost felt, well, normal. I at least had a routine to hold onto.

The tournament was still two weeks out. No one would give me specifics other than "Just keep doing what we tell you and you'll do fine." I couldn't help but envision knights in shining armor, jousting on horseback. I had no idea how to ride a horse. Or joust, come to think of it.

I kept my visions to myself, not sharing with anyone that I saw that battle that ended the life of one brother and changed another. It haunted me constantly. Those were the good guys. If the bad guys did anything similar, if they attacked in numbers that large, how on earth would I defend this place? *No, Winks, you need to focus.* Get through this stupid tournament. Then I'd have time to deal with the rest of it.

But the rest of it wouldn't leave me alone. Mr. Smith, Mr. Wesson, and I had just begun one morning when Jeeves came in to announce a visitor. "That D.S. Frost, madam, he wishes to speak to you."

When I joined the detective in the entryway I asked, "Where's your partner?" Jeeves didn't bother putting him in a room, perhaps hoping the detective would keep his visit brief.

He shook my hand with his butter-soft glove. "She sent me to get your answer, ma'am." Swear, it sounds like he calls me *mom.*

I tilted my head. "Answer?"

D.S. Frost raised his eyebrows. "He did tell you, didn't he? Mr. Marble?"

"I'm not recalling anything."

"About posting guards outside your home. For your protection." He nodded. "Did he tell you about Mr. Redding?"

"The man in the photograph. Did you find him?" I was hoping for some good news.

"Yes." *Excellent.* "He's dead, ma'am." *Okay, not excellent.* "He was poisoned in the same manner as Mr. Cruise and Mr. Jones. We told your lawyer that several days ago and offered, under the circumstances, a guard to be posted outside. He said he'd talk to you about it."

I folded my arms, suddenly chilled. "No. He never mentioned it."

He cleared his throat. "It's not my place, ma'am, and I do apologize for being forward, but in my experience lawyers are often over protective of their clients. I'm beginning to think your Mr. Marble doesn't have your best interests at heart."

"Hm." That came from behind me. Startled, I turned to see Mama hurrying her way back to the kitchen.

"Yeah, me, too," I said to the detective.

"If you feel you're in danger we can help you."

If only you could. "Thank you, sergeant."

His mouth twisted, searching for another argument, I think. But he nodded, and handed me his card. "In case you lost the last one. Please don't hesitate to call."

"I promise you, I won't." My mind raced. "Sergeant, I'm sure you can't tell me the details, but how was Mr. Cruise poisoned? When we first spoke about his death it was a mystery to you."

His eyes looked deep into mine, trying to find something. "Very well, but you didn't hear it from me. Mr. Redding. He posed as a doctor, entered Mr. Cruise's room with our guard, all to swap out an IV drip. The bag contained the poison that killed Mr. Cruise."

"Not magic, then," I winked.

"Would seem that way, yes. It was most unfortunate that when we caught up with Mr. Redding he was already dead himself. We don't know why he killed Mr. Cruise. Nor Mr. Jones. Nor his connection with either of the dead men. We don't even know how he forged the hospital credentials he used, which, according to the guard, looked perfectly official. And I cannot say more, at this time." The Sergeant looked at his feet for a moment. "Ma'am, this will seem a complete change of topic, but I was wondering. I recently got my motorcycle license here in Louisiana, but I'm unfamiliar with the roads. I'm assuming you know the better ones to ride. Perhaps we could do a bit of touring, if you have some time?"

"That would be great." I genuinely meant it. It had been months since I've ridden a bike at all. In fact, getting out of this stuffy house sounded beyond wonderful.

"Good," he smiled. "You have my number. Just ring me."

I watched him walk to his car and disappear into the greenery surrounding the narrow driveway. I made a straight line for Mrs. "Mama" White.

I found her tending several steaming pots on the stove, diligently stirring one. "Come in, child," she cooed before I was sure she could see me. "I cannot leave this roux. You'll have to come here."

"What are you making now?" I really didn't care. But I thought idle conversation was a good way to start.

"Gumbo. For lunch." She smiled at me kindly. "You have a question for me." Then she held a finger to her lips and looked up with her eyes. I looked up, too. A spider.

"Yes, um ..."

"You want to know where I keep the potatoes?"

No. Okay, that was weird enough I got curious. "Sure. Where do we keep the potatoes?"

She gave a low chuckle. "Clearly you haven't read the will. It's all there. All the little cracks and crevices of the house. All the little *details*," she looked up at me, "about what goes where. What to do in some emergency? Worth reading, I think."

I nodded slowly, not entirely certain of what I needed to do. "That's sage advice. I will take the time." I nodded. "And read the will. Thank you, Mama."

"My pleasure, child."

~ ~ * ~ ~

After dinner I made my way to Mr. Marble's grand office. I didn't have my own copy of the will, at least not in my hot little hands, but I believed one was kept in the safe behind the demon picture. I asked the house to show me Mr. Marble opening the safe last—and immediately stood over his shoulder as he did—then emulated the combination he used. It popped open with a satisfying click.

I heartily thanked my house. How many times have I heard the phrase, "if these walls could talk." Mine sorta do. Gotta admit, bonding with the house had become a highlight in my life.

I sat behind the big desk. The vast acreage of its top made it easy to spread out and leaf through the two-inch thick document.

After reading the first two pages, I laughed at myself. Really? Who was I kidding. *I'm reading this book of legalese in hopes of finding, I don't know, where the potatoes are?* This is why people have lawyers. I felt a great deal more dislike for Mr. Marble at that moment.

I heard Mama's voice. *"What to do in some emergency?"* I thumbed through the index. Nope, nothing there that specifically said "emergency." I did notice, however, a section on survivorship. I flipped to that part of the document and read it. And I read it again. A painful twist in my stomach caused my heart to stop beating. After Will died the house would pass to me, his wife. If, during the two years I'm required to live here, something should happen to me, then house is awarded to ... wait for it ... the executor of the estate. *Mr. Nathan Marble.*

The "DVD Will" told me to trust Mr. Marble above everyone else. The "letter Will" told me someone close betrayed him.

"DVD Will" told me to float through all this like a leaf on the wind, carefree. "Letter Will" told me to watch with open eyes.

I don't know who to trust. Including *which Will.*

~ ~ * ~ ~

That night I laid on my stomach, sprawled on my bed with a laptop in front of me while googling the phrase "never on a Sunday." I decided not to dwell on my sinking feel about Mr. Marble and distract myself with the curious words Will left me, only for the umpteenth time in these last few weeks, but maybe I'd get lucky today. I hoped that the new DVD would contain better information about Mr. Marble and what actions I should take. But mostly, I just wanted to see his face again.

Never on a Sunday. A movie, which we never saw. A song, which we never sang. Drinking, having sex, swearing, working, eating no meat —these were things some cultures never do on Sundays. But neither Will nor I were part of any of them. In my disappointment, I dozed off.

Frantic pounding on my door startled me right off the bed. "Madam! Madam!"

"Jeeves?" I croaked, clumsily regaining some composure. I glanced at the clock on my mantle. Good gravy, it was three in the morning.

He pounded again. Then I panicked. *Malador was back?* "Madam! Please!"

I could hear others running around outside my door. I think Mr. Smith called out, "Get that new comm device ..." as he ran down the hall.

I opened the door. "Madam," Jeeves said, looking frantic. "He needs your help."

"Who?" I said, running my hand through my unkempt hair.

"That detective. D.S. Frost. If you don't help him he will die tonight."

Okay. Not something I want. "How do you know?"

"There isn't time to explain." His voice full of worry.

Not sure why Jeeves was so upset, but, hey. "What do you want me to do?"

"Don your armor and meet me at the base of the stairs. Hurry, madam! Time is of the essence!"

Jeeves always struck me as a man under control. I did as directed merely because he seemed so ... *Un*-Jeeves.

Fully dressed I ran down the staircase and met the fretting man, wringing his hands in worry. "Please, follow me, madam." He spoke as we walked quickly. "I'm not supposed to show this to you. It was to be a gift from Mr. Marble and the staff once we returned from the tournament. But under the circumstance, I feel I have no choice." Jeeves led me to a door I hadn't yet explored. The garage. And smack dab in the middle of it was—bless the gods—my Ducati! I almost didn't recognize it due to the fancy baby blue paint job. Matched my armor.

Mr. Smith stood next to it. "You like?"

"You have no idea," I smiled.

Mr. Smith handed me a new helmet (baby blue, with white lightning bolts) and the keys. "There's a headset already in the helmet," he said. "We'll be in constant communication. We should be able to get you in and out of there quickly." He nodded to Mr. Wesson, who waved a tablet, map already displayed. A small blinking light showed our location. "The bike's lojacked. We'll know where you are every moment."

"So where am I going?" I looked at Jeeves, putting on my helmet.

His eyes were glowing green, his face gaunt and frighteningly skull-like. Mr. Smith pushed the button on the wall and the garage door opened. A portal was already forming on the other side. Ah.

I lit her up and revved the engine.

"Can you hear me?" Mr. Smith's voice said in my ear.

"Loud and clear."

"Good. I'll give you a go. Hang on." I didn't look back, just toward the morphing sphere just thirty feet in front of me. Never been through a portal before. I swallowed, not knowing what to expect. I revved the engine again, and my duck just purred beneath me. Familiar. The only thing familiar in my life at the moment, and that thought comforted. I nodded that I was ready.

"We'll drop you on Elysian Fields, heading south. Get ready to make a right turn. You'll be heading for Treme." I nodded again, making a mental note of the location in my mind. I knew the area, but not really well. "*Go!*"

I popped the clutch and squealed out of the garage. And into the void. I felt a tingling sensation as the world converged and melted around me, and instantly, I was squealing my tires on the pavement of Elysian Fields, and right in front of a car, no less. He honked in aggravation. *Hey, pal, you don't know the half of it.* I sped up and out of his way.

"You guys there?" I asked.

"Yeah," Mr. Smith said. "Get ready to take a right."

"On?" A street name would help.

"Now!"

Great. A one way, and going the wrong way. I didn't argue. I turned, my alert-o-meter on full. Thankfully, given the time of night, no traffic to dodge.

"Go three blocks," my co-pilot said, "then stop and wait."

One. Two. Three. I pulled over and waited. "What should I be looking for—" Then I saw it before I finished the question, bright flashes of light. A man came running around the corner followed closely by a posse of men, shooting carelessly, chasing after him. "I think I found him," I reported. I revved up the bike and headed toward the fleeing man. I spun to a stop, blocking his path.

In the dim glow of the street lights I could see his face, eyes wide, chest heaving for air. Looked like he'd been running for a while. And when he saw me he stopped, thinking I was foe. I waved him to join me. In my mind I thought with a Schwarzenegger accent, "Come with me if you want to live."

More flashes, and this time I heard the pops of gunfire over my engine hum. D.S. Frost grimaced as he jolted forward and grabbed his shoulder. Damn it. I raised my face shield. "Get on!" I screamed at him.

He was already moving by that point, hobbling his way to me. I heard him grunt and he straddled the bike. As he wrapped his arms around my abdomen, I popped the clutch, and we tore back down the one way. "Got him," I reported. "Where am I heading?"

"Back the way you came," Mr. Smith answered. "We'll have a portal ready."

I reached Elysian Fields, ready to turn left. Two police cars, blue lights ablaze, were heading for me. I turned right, admittedly, without stopping for the sign. I'm certain they were responding to the incident already, so when they saw a fast motorcycle fleeing the scene, one of them followed me. "Uh, guys. I have company."

"We see you. Just a sec."

The cop behind me sped up. As I crossed Galvez, now running red lights, his siren screamed for me to stop. My passenger's grip tightened around my waist as he pressed his body against my back. I could feel him trembling. And I was running out of road. Elysian Fields ended at the Mississippi River.

"Got it!" Mr. Smith said. "Get ready for a right turn. We're taking you into the French Quarter."

"Bad idea. Lots of people, lousy streets—"

"Turn. *Now!*"

I decelerated quickly, and banked her round the corner onto Royal. My pursuer couldn't make the turn as quickly, which gave me some time, I thought. But this was a very popular area called Marigny, and these few blocks were chock full of bars, music, and people. Tonight was no different. I swerved around drunk patrons strolling what are normally quiet streets. I didn't hurt anyone, but my pace slowed. When I finally got to the Esplanade, I had not one but two cars on my tail.

Of course my light was red. I slowed, but zigged my way across to the neutral ground, then zagged my way into the Quarter.

"Right on Ursulines. Hurry!"

I zipped down Royal, quieter on this side of the Esplanade thankfully, then made a tight banked turn. And there it was. Salvation. *My portal.*

I knew it was a bad idea, coming into the French Quarter; these are some of the oldest and worst kept streets in New Orleans. But hoping for this to end I accelerated again, nosing the Duck forward.

A shadow flashed in front of me. I swerved to avoid hitting the black cat that made an ill-timed dash across the road, but the damned dark hid the tire-eater of a pothole, and I hit it sideways. It dipped my front tire, twisting it. We were already sideways and airborne when we entered the portal, and the three of us—me, D.S. Frost, and the Duck—slid across the garage floor, smacking hard against the back wall. A rain of tools, paint cans, and debris fell on us.

The helpful arms of Smith and Wesson came out of nowhere, hoisting me to standing while the rest were bent over the unconscious man. Dammit, he had no helmet. My spirits fell as I realized I failed to help him at all; how was being in a motorcycle accident helpful? As if being shot wasn't enough.

The Duck continued to moan as its back tire still spun free, now on its side and scraped to all hell. I shut it off. Then watched the others hover over the poor man on the floor.

"Can we move him?" Jeeves asked Mama.

D.S. Frost ended up on his back, his head lolled to the side. Mama's gentle hands cupped the sergeant's face, then slowly made their way down his neck, over his shoulders, and onto his shoulder blades, delicate fingers moving along the way. With one hand she reached carefully, so as not to move him, under his back, making her way down his spine. "No broken bones along the spinal cord," she said with that Jamaican accent. "Yes, we can get him into the house."

Smith, Wesson, and Jeeves lifted the limp body. I noticed blood on the floor beneath him. One of his gloved hands was torn open, exposing a deep gash across the meat of his palm. I looked around. His hand must have caught a falling saw blade. The round serrated disk lay bloodied near the motorcycle.

Once the crowd left I gave the motorcycle a look-over. My new cool bike. With a sigh I heaved her erect. The front tire was trashed. "Sorry, girl," I said as I turned out the garage lights and followed the trail of blood drips through the house.

They had the poor man reclined on a settee in the library. Mama was already at work with some stitching on his hand. As I approached Jeeves stopped me. "Madam, you should try to get some rest, yet."

I leaned out to look at our guest. "Shouldn't we get a doctor? He might have banged his head. He wasn't wearing a helmet."

"Please," Jeeves said. "You did your part. Let us do ours."

"I saw him get shot, for Pete's sake," I pressed. "We should call an ambulance."

"Madam. We got him into this. We will get him out, I assure you." Not particularly happy with that result there wasn't much more I could do. I knew better than to argue with what I didn't truly understand. I nodded and left. "And madam? Thank you. He owes you his life."

I gave a wave with my helmet tucked under one arm, topped the stairs with a wide-mouth yawn, and made my way to my room. As I undressed I realized that I suffered no injury from the crash, not even a bruise. My armor looked pristine, save for some of the sergeant's blood on the shoulder.

Chapter Fourteen

THE SOUNDS OF raised voices rudely penetrated a surreal dream of horses and jousting. The shouting came from Mr. Marble. I threw on clothes and dashed down the stairs.

"What the hell is wrong with you?" Mr. Marble hollered. "You realize we're just days from tournament, don't you? But you sent her out into a gunfight?"

"I beg your forgiveness, Mr. Marble," Jeeves softly said. "I merely thought—"

"*Thought?* Really! You actually used your brain here—"

And that was all I allowed. "Enough!" I screamed at Mr. Marble. "Jeeves, please get me some breakfast. Go." The butler bowed and left the two of us.

Mr. Marble opened his mouth, but I wouldn't let him say a word. "No. It's done and over and no amount of ranting will change what's happened. So, enough." He looked thoughtful, then tried to speak again. I pointed an accusing finger, "I may be the newbie in this house but it is *my house.* And under no circumstances will you, nor anyone, belittle, denigrate, or criticize my staff. Is that understood? They work for me, not you."

He let a beat pass as he ruddy complexion faded. Then he nodded. "I'm sorry."

"You owe Jeeves the apology, not me."

Pursing his lips he twisted his face. "I will be sure to apologize to him next time I see him, ma'am."

"Good. Now, have you seen him yet? The detective? How is he?"

"He's up and about," Mr. Marble lead with his head for me to follow him. "Already having some breakfast." He leaned in to speak quietly. "Mama healed him best she could and Mrs. Black repaired his clothes a bit. I was hoping we could just pass this all off as a dream but the bullet wound was significant. As was the damage to his hand. We stopped the bleeding and hastened repairs but the scars remain. We need a story."

"I was taking a late night ride, saw the gunfire—which is true—only to realize that I recognized the sergeant and tried to help out."

"And you didn't take him to a hospital... because...?"

Oo. Got me there. I thought a moment and snapped my fingers. "I didn't know he needed a hospital. I was just trying to get him to safety."

"And the high speed chase with the police...was...?"

"I... uh... okay, that's a toughie. Does he remember it? Maybe we can pass that part off as a dream. I mean, that would make no sense, racing carelessly through New Orleans with a cop on my bike."

"Hm," he nodded, rocking back and forth on his heals. "Let's see what he does remember."

We entered the dining room as D.S. Frost buttered some toast. His right hand, ungloved, had a nasty, red scar that coiled from his palm to the back of his hand. It looked painful. The scarlet color from the scar contrasted with his natural-beyond-pale skin tone—the boy needed a good tan, if you asked me. I assumed his glove became tatters in the accident. I decided against mentioning it, even as Mrs. Black handed him another one. He thanked her as he donned it gingerly.

Mama had prepared him a traditional English breakfast. Eggs, bacon and sausage, toast, and jam, but he'd only eaten the toast.

Coffee scent filled the air. I poured myself a cup as I sat across from the guest.

"You're up early," I sipped. Mr. Marble sat next to me.

"Sadly so," he said, delicately spreading strawberry jam. "My shoulder still hurts a good bit. I found a deep slumber elusive." He ate as if it were just another day. A good sign, I thought. "I don't recall the events clearly of what happened last night." Hm. While I felt relief from the words I couldn't shake the feeling he offered them rather than the truth. "I remember partaking of a very late supper, I remember the inebriated patrons heated words that turned into fisticuffs, and the next thing I know I was chased into the street by an angry mob of hooligans. Not at all how I planned my evening. After that it's all vague. And I certainly don't remember," he said looking around, "how I got here. But I suspect I owe you thanks."

I raised my cup to hide my exhale. *No jail time for me. Yet.*

"Anything to help the boys in blue," Mr. Marble said, disingenuously. I frowned at the words behind my coffee.

D.S. Frost, being clever, saw my reaction and didn't let it go. "Mr. Marble. Did you get a chance to talk to your client about a guard on her house?" Good man.

"I, uh... no. I mean, as you can see, she can take good care of herself."

"Indeed." The detective gave me an "I tried" look, with a small shrug of his shoulders. Then winced a little.

"I'm fine in this house," I said, not so much to aid Mr. Marble but to assure D.S. Frost. Probably out of guilt. "I don't leave very often. Last night was just a fluke."

Note to self: Why did Jeeves send me out last night?

"Fortunate for me, so it would seem."

Jeeves, who'd been standing staunch-still in the corner gave a small step forward, his cue he had an announcement. "Detective," he addressed the man, "I took the liberty of calling you a cab. It will arrive momentarily. They've been instructed to take you wherever you desire."

Just as he stopped speaking a car honked from outside.

"Ah," D.S. Frost said, pushing back his chair. Using his teeth to hold his toast he struggled to put on his jacket. Jeeves assisted, but his eyes grimaced as he maneuvered his wounded arm into a sleeve. I dropped my gaze in guilt.

Once he was out the door it dawned on me he that, for a detective, he had little interest in the details of the evening. I muttered as I scratched my head, "How ... convenient."

Mr. Marble turned to me. "Of course I didn't mention it to you," he defended out of the blue. I blinked, not followed his thought. "Why bother? We could never have a guard sit outside the house, not with what all going on in here. What if Smith and Wesson blow up the place? What if Malador comes back? What if the roaches hold their convention here?" *Roaches? Hold conventions? In* my *house?* I raised a protesting finger but he cut me off. "Look, Mrs. Witherspoon, I have one job. *One job,*" he said rubbing his face, "and that's to get you safely *to* and *through* the tournament. That is what Will wanted me to do and, by the astral planes, that is what I intend to do. You're safe in this house," uh, *except for the explosions, attacks, and... RoachCon,* "which is why I was livid when I was told they sent you out last night but fine —" He held up his hands before I could say anything, "You're right. It's done and over. But that didn't make my one job easier, did it? Now. If you'll excuse me I need to get to the office."

~ ~ * ~ ~

The house had been a-buzz last few days. People were packing and organizing and stacking things in the middle of the living room, and by "things" I mean tents, sleeping bags, camping cooktops with pots and pans, duffle bags and backpacks in all shapes and sizes, and everything else one might need for a camp out.

This left me with a very ill feeling. I hated camping.

Bashing in goblin heads I'm prepared for. Bathing in a stream, not so much.

I only realized this morning that the big day landed on the summer solstice. Just one of the many reasons I judge myself to be a couple of apples shy of a bushel. I hadn't realized how it correlated with Will's annual "Tax Conference" that took place this time of year. Of course he was always gone for just a few days, and from what I know the tournament takes a couple of weeks. I'm sure it would all make sense soon.

On the big day we gathered in the living room; Mr. Smith, Mr. Wesson, Mama, Jeeves, Mr. Marble, and myself. Smith and Wesson wore their usual attire of white lab coats. The rest of us donned crushed velvet robes, blood red in color, with ample sleeves and cowled necks that we hiked up over our heads like hoods. A little cult-ish, if you asked me. But no one did.

The house keeper Mrs. Black didn't don a robe. "Aren't you going?" I asked her.

"You're only allowed five in your party," she said. I counted only four red robes. "You'll get a healer once you're there. Besides, someone needs to hold down the fort. That's me. And the spiders."

A healer? Wait, no spiders? "Annabelle? You're not coming either?"

"No, my lady. My work is done. Yours is just beginning. Be safe and farewell."

Mr. Marble wore something that made him stand out, a thick and gaudy gold necklace dotted with hefty fleurs-de-lis that draped over his shoulders and onto his chest. "Let us join hands." I hadn't done this since the séance. Just as it had then, when the circle was complete a small electric pulse ran through me. Seems like years ago since ... since we put Will in a mirror.

"Firstly," Mr. Marble said, "This has been a miserably hard year for everyone here. So I'd like to start with a moment of silence to honor our fallen loved one. God, Will, you are missed." I clenched my eyes hard, trying to keep the battalion of tears at bay. Mr. Marble's words were so heartfelt my own heart broke standing there.

"Secondly, I want to give all of you my gratitude for getting us here. Because just a few months ago even I didn't think we'd make it. I bow to you." He did. We stood there ... well, they stood there, I just followed suit.

"Lastly, I want you to know that there are no pretenses now. They know. They know we have a new champion coming. They think we're weak. But I know and you know, we stand strong!"

"We stand strong!" everyone responded. Except me, of course. And all eyes turned to me.

"Ah. I see I'm supposed to give some rousing words of encouragement."

Mr. Marble gave a small shake of his head. "It's not required—"

"No no. I mean, I'm ... I'm just not good at public speaking is all. But that doesn't mean I don't recognize the efforts and hard work, not to mention patience and blind faith, all of you have put into the unknown that is me. Looking back on when you all first met me, well, I have a much greater understanding of your hesitation. So thank you. All of you. I will do my best not to let you down."

"You won't," Jeeves encouraged. "Because together we stand strong."

"We stand strong!" Everyone echoed.

"We stand strong," I nodded.

Mr. Marble broke the circle. "Jeeves, if you please."

The butler closed his eyes, and his face changed into that gaunt and sullen appearance. He clapped. In the middle of the room, behind our small group, a portal quickly formed.

"Hercule?" Mr. Marble called out.

"I'm coming, I'm coming ..." said a small distant French voice. "Look down, *madame*." The little *cafard* was at my feet.

"Technically, he's your familiar," Mr. Marble said. "He needs to come with you. Will used to let him ride his shoulder, but he'll go into your pocket, if you'd rather."

"*Oui.* There is nothing more I enjoy than traveling in a pocket, like a piece of lint."

I rolled my eyes and tapped my shoulder. "All you had to do was ask."

Once he scampered his way on to my shoulder he took a prideful seat. "*Allons-y!*"

"Good luck!" called the spider from the corner. "We'll keep the house safe while you're away!"

Two by two we stepped through; Smith and Wesson, then Mama and Jeeves. Mr. Marble gave a polite gesture to the orb. I took a deep breath, and we walked through the portal.

Chapter Fifteen

LIKE THE NIGHT of my ride, I felt a tingling sensation, sort of a buzzing, throughout my body as I stepped through the portal. The room melted, swirling around me, and collapsed while another expanded, swirling its parts into perfection.

I'm assuming perfection. I don't know where we ended up. It was nowhere I'd ever been before. *Forget Kansas, Dorothy, we're not on planet Earth.* We stepped out onto a hilltop, and followed a switch-back trail carved into the rocky and steep hillside. It gave me quite a vantage point.

As far as my eyes could see the land was scorched and barren. A few enormous trees dotted the landscape; gnarled, twisted and completely devoid of life. A distinctive shimmer of heat surrounded me yet I felt no warmth. No rivers or streams. No life. The black of the earth contrasted to the hot orange glow of the sky. No sun to create it, and oddly uniform in color. No clouds, just brilliant orange.

In the distance I could see other portals form, swirling spheres, and other groups emerge, all wearing red robes. We all headed in the same direction, to the only feature on the horizon amidst the scatter of barren trees. A castle. At least I thought it was a castle … black as the earth around it, backlit by the bright sky. But asymmetric and twisted, with spires that jutted from odd angles. Wrong angles. Parts of it looked to defy gravity.

"Long ago," Hercule said, "there was chaos. Good and evil energies fought for domination on every plane. Until one day the lords both light and dark, whom we call the elders, created this place. *La Citadelle.*"

"Now we just fight here," I offered.

"*Oui.*"

"Why? I mean, what's in it for the good and evil energies?"

"The same as before. When a good force wins the tournament, then there is more good energy in the world. Only obtaining it here requires less killing. Well, there is the killing, just less death. Well, there is the death, it's just less permanent."

"Wait, are you saying I'm going to die here?"

"Oh, *san doute.* Do not despair, *ma chére.* You are not being singled out. Every champion will, I assure you. But you will return home, safe and sound. That is the promise of the elders. Once you step into *La Citadelle,* you will step out."

I gulped as I looked around.

"You have more questions? Go on. Ask the Great Hercule. I'm feeling benevolent at the moment."

"Oh, thank you, great cockroach." I pointed at some of the other parties. As we drew nearer to the Citadel it was becoming apparent they weren't all, well, human. Some of them were too hunched, others lumbered more than walked. But their robes hid who—or what—they were. "I don't get this. There are fifteen houses on our plane, right." I did get that small bit of knowledge before leaving home. "But there are hundreds of people here. Or … *beings.*"

"Five planes in total, fifteen houses each. Seventy-five in total come to battle. The rest only to watch."

"To watch, huh." *How do I get that gig?*

Hercule continued. "This is a special place made where all planes can exist. Otherwise, we wouldn't all be able to breathe each other's atmospheres let alone fight."

"Different planets?" I asked.

"Different *planes*. All earth, just various layers, various rules, various creatures."

"We all battle each other, all seventy-five of us, and only one will leave the supreme winner."

"*Oui.*"

"But if only one house wins, won't that only affect the plane of that house?"

"Ah, *bon!* Good question. It will affect that plane, the home plane, the most, *oui*, but it will affect all planes to some degree, *comprends-tu?*"

"I'm starting to."

I noticed that the groups formed several queues, one of which we ambled into. The group ahead of us were very large, nearly three feet taller than us. I couldn't make out their forms from their red shrouds. But I thought I saw a tentacle.

I turned away, embarrassed by my lack of knowledge. Spread luxuriously between our line and the next stood a tree. Unlike the other trees, this one was alive. Its branches brimmed with healthy clusters of leaves, its trunk smooth and whimsically curved. Bright dots of red peaked out from beneath its foliage canopy.

"Is that a cherry tree?" I asked, dumbfounded.

"*Oui.* It is said to be a gift from Lidomyr himself, er, the founder of the white house of Prague. Legend says that as long as the tournaments thrive so shall the tree."

"Our Prague? Of our plane?"

"*Oui.*"

We shuffled forward again—this started to feel like a trip to Disneyland.

I turned to the rest of my party. The white lab coats of Smith and Wesson starkly contrasted to the red cloaks of everyone else. "You guys look so—"

"I know," Mr. Smith interjected before I could finish.

"You're only allowed five in a party," Mr. Marble said. "But you can have an entourage. Look around, there are a few others."

We slowly moved forward as party by party were being admitted into the Citadel. I motioned to Mr. Marble. "Not that I'm jealous of the fancy bling," I said as I weighed his necklace with my hand, "but why do you get the jewelry?"

"I'm your orator. I do all the speaking, manage your calendar, and introductions. This," he swept his hand over the bangle, "is a clear identifier. If they want to talk to you, they need to talk to me first."

"And the rest of us dress the same?"

"In case of an ambush. If someone wants to harm the champion of a party, they can't tell who that is."

Wow, I liked this less and less.

The big guys were up next.

"In case you are asked," Mr. Marble explained, "I am the Orator, Mama is your Chef", she gave a little curtsy, "and Jeeves is your Keeper of Arms."

"Arms?" I scoffed. "Plural? I carry a hammer. Count 'em. One."

"And your armor," he added, defensively.

"Oh. Wait, was I supposed to bring that?" Five heads snapped towards me with ten popping eyes. Even the *cafard* gasped. I raised my hands, and twisted them to display blue gloves. "Wow. You people are jumpy. Not to mention gullible."

Us next. Mr. Marble walked to the front, and gave a deep bow to the ... *thing* before us. "Gateway Manor, New Orleans, Midland Plane." I tried not to gawk at the ... *thing* that was a combination of black cloud and skeleton, with shining purple eyes.

The ... *thing* looked into a crystal ball, waving his bone hand—no, not boney, *bone*—then stood erect. It waved its bone hand, which cracked a bit as it did so, gesturing to the large gape of an entrance. In a gravel voice it rasped, "Welcome, House of Gateway. Proceed to the Obsidian Tower."

Mr. Marble bowed and led us into the castle. Awed by the creature I barely noticed the massive doors propped open so all the travelers could enter.

"Um," I cleared my throat and whispered to my shoulder, "what was that?"

"Bone Wraith," Hercule answered. "Guards of the Citadel and inhabitants of the Phantom Plane. You will meet them in battle. But don't worry. I'll teach you how to fight them."

As we walked the black hallways, dimly lit with torch sconces, I heard the words again, "Obsidian Tower?" I asked.

"There are several towers. Obsidian, Coal, Ebony, Onyx, and Slate—"

I interrupted him with a burst of laughter. "Really? Black. It's all black. No one thought of red, or blue, or, I don't know, peridot? Even numbers would have been clearer. Tower One, Tower Two."

"I ... never really thought about it before," Hercule said.

Mr. Marble lead us through a maze of stone hallways. We passed an occasional group, all with robed hoods covering faces. At last we headed for a pair of towering wooden doors that opened as we arrived. Behind them stood a stout man dressed in a velvet robe like ours, only emerald in color. His thick grey hair swept from his face and dangled down his back in a ponytail. When he saw Mr. Marble, his grey bearded face broadened into a glorious smile that puffed his rosy cheeks and made his blue eyes twinkle. His arms opened wide. "Nathan, my boy!", his voice boomed, "Come in! Come in!"

We entered a round cavernous room, filled with clusters of sofas and seating, tables and chairs, and in the center of it all blazed a warm fire. Not warm in heat, just in mood; comforting. I was drawn to it. Several beings stood around it, hands and claws spread to the flame. The stone walls supported sconces like those in the hallways. Between them was a gallery of portraits; landscapes, still lifes, a creature or two.

"How are you, Jeff," Nathan said to the jolly fat man.

"I'm very well, thank you. I'm so, so sorry about Will. He was truly a wonderful man. We all miss him, here."

Mr. Marble nodded. "Let me introduce you to someone. Winki?" I pulled myself from the fire to join them. "Winki, this is Jeffrey, Master of the Obsidian Tower. This," he said to the man, "is our new Champion. Winki Witherspoon. Will's wife."

I offered a gloved hand, but Jeff just gave a humble bow. "Welcome to the Obsidian Tower, Champion. If there is anything you need, please feel free to ask me." In a somber voice he added, "And let me offer my sincerest condolences."

I nodded a thank you.

He turned to Mr. Marble. "Nathan, your suite is ready; number seven at the top of the stairs. You can get your party settled but I recommend visiting the Chancellor quickly," he leaned in and whispered, "He has set aside the better healers for you."

"Ah. Jeeves, you're in charge. Collect our things, set up the room, and get ready for the ball. Mrs. Witherspoon?" I gave a small hop to show my enthusiasm. "Please, follow me."

Back into the cave-like tunnels of the Citadel Mr. Marble led me, and my *cafard* passenger, to another tower. This one looked more business like. The walls were the same, black, sconces, portraits here and there, and fire in the center, but modern desks outlined the space, complete with phones, monitors, computers, and ergonomic chairs. I stopped stunned at the view. I felt like I had walked into the dot-com of hell. The beings weren't all humans. *Good gravy, is that an octopus?*

A goblin woman, dressed smartly in a nice suit, looked up at Mr. Marble from behind her desk. "Title?" she asked. While small and green, she didn't sport all the blisters and boils that Malador's henchmen had.

"Gateway Manor. New Orleans, Midland Plane," he answered.

She typed in the her computer. "Mr. Marble?" she asked. He nodded. "Chancellor's expecting you. Straight back, double doors, can't miss it."

"Thank you," he bowed. She stood and did the same.

As we walked I said to Hercule, "Not all goblins are evil, I take it."

"Not all of anything is evil."

"I thought goblins were the henchmen of the dark lords. Kinda implies 'evil.'" I used air quotes.

"It kinda implies dark lords pay better." Oh yeah, just mocked by a roach.

Mr. Marble rapped on the door with his fist. "Enter," came the call from the other side. He lifted the large handle, and pushed hard against the heavy wooden entry.

"Mr. Marble, so good to see you, dear man. And this must be your new Champion?"

The Chancellor stood as we entered. Thin and frail—and ancient—he took shaky steps towards us with the aid of a cane. His back hunched just slightly. His face shaved clean but age spots and wrinkles covered his cheeks. His sallow eyes looked alert despite that one was brown and the other milky.

"This is Winki Witherspoon," Mr. Marble said. "Will's wife."

"Yes, I've heard. How do you do, madam? Welcome to your first tournament."

"Thank you, sir."

"Emily? Bring them in," he said to his left. That's when I noticed the small desk where a young lady in her early twenties sat behind a monitor.

"Yes, uncle."

"Emily is my new assistant. My brother's youngest. She has promise, but don't tell her I told you that. You know kids these days."

"I can hear you, uncle."

I couldn't see the walls of this tiny room since bookshelves, clogged with books, covered them. The only contrasting feature was the door Emily opened.

Three cloaked individuals softly padded their way into the center of the room. They stood in a row, heads down. Unlike the crisp and colorful cloaks I'd seen thus far theirs were dull, brown, tattered, and patched. The only adornment was a rope bound around their waists like belts. Fully draped I could not see faces. Nor hands. Nor species, for that matter.

The Chancellor asked me, "Do you know who these people are?"

"No, sir."

"*These* are healers. They will ensure your safety during the tournament. I'm going to ask them if one of them will aid you in your quest, but I must tell you, that is improbable. They know you are new, and therefore, statistically speaking, not likely to succeed. But if none volunteer, one will be selected for you. Please do not feel rejected if they do not want to work for you. Healers are known to seek glory."

"It's saving face," Hercule whispered to me. "If they volunteer and you don't do well, they look like fools. A champion's success can depend on how quickly they are healed."

"What about Mama?" I asked.

He chuckled. "Mama isn't a healer. She's more of an ... *herbologist*, one who can heighten the healing properties in food. Masterful at it, too, *n'est-ce pas?* But you'll need someone faster. Much faster."

Meanwhile, the Chancellor turned to the row. "This is Winki Witherspoon, champion of Gateway Manor, New Orleans, Midland Plane. Do any of you choose to aid her?"

No one moved for a moment. Then two stepped forward, almost simultaneously. One looked at the other, and the other bowed with a "she's all yours" gesture, and stepped back.

"Well," the Chancellor said shocked, "your house's reputation remains intact. This one will serve you well." He picked up blue sash from his desk. "Please step forward," he said to me, "and raise your arm." I did, and so did the healer, each of us facing the other. The Chancellor loosely wrapped the sash over my arm and then his. I took that time to look into the shroud, but the large hood kept me from seeing his face. The Chancellor spoke. "I bind you now, healer, to the needs and purpose of this champion, Winki Witherspoon."

A little surge of energy ran through me. I gave and smile, "Oh!" I looked at the shrouded figure. "You realize in some cultures we're married now."

"It is done," the unamused Chancellor said. "This creature is now yours to do with as you see fit," he said as he unwrapped us. Mine? Seemed a bit ... slavish, if you asked me. "Just sign for him with the front desk on your way out. And, Nathan," he put a kind hand on Mr. Marble's shoulder, "I'm genuinely sorry for your loss. Both of you," he nodded to me. "And you, Monsieur Poirot."

"Thank you," I said. It seemed clear I was going to get a lot of that, apologies and constant reminders of my husband's passing. I knew they meant well, but it still hurt a little, each and every time.

We all made our way, the healer walking subserviently behind us, back to the Obsidian Tower and to our suite. Jeeves greeted us after we crested the sixteen flights of stairs to get "home." He showed the healer to his cot, which unceremoniously occupied a dark corner of the main room.

But what a room! Kitchen and hearth occupied most of it with a hefty long table in the center, bounded by equally hefty benches. Opposite the entry gaped a window devoid of glass. It allowed us the positively lovely view of black, rocky, barren landscape and clear, featureless orange sky. Spiraling upwards in one corner was another staircase that looked more like a tree than architecture.

Mama busied herself with unpacking our cases. Funny, I didn't know how the equipment got here, since we certainly didn't bring it. I gave a sigh. I felt like I learned a million new things every day, but I still knew nothing.

"You and Mr. Marble have rooms upstairs," Hercule broke my self pity. "And it's time you changed."

"Changed?"

"*Oui*. Tonight is the opening ceremony and dinner. The tournament starts tomorrow."

Jeeves joined me as he spoke. "You're gown is ready for you in your room. Mrs. Black prepared it before we left so it should fit you perfectly. She also gave me instructions as to how to style your hair. Just call if you need anything, madam."

Gowns? Fittings? Hair? I came ready to fight ...

Will, what did you get me into?

Chapter Sixteen

JUST FOUR OF us—dressed to the nines—were allowed at the opening ceremonies, which was an elaborate dinner in elaborate dress. What better way to meet those we were about to bludgeon. The four were Mr. Marble, Mama, Jeeves, and myself. My entourage, including my healer, had to remain in our suite. Hercule managed to accompany me tucked into the folds of my skirt. Somewhere. We stood together waiting for our, or rather, *my* introduction. Groups were announced in order of their standings from the previous year. As the defending house, we were announced last.

"Are you ready, madam?" Jeeves asked.

I nodded. The grand door opened with a boom. "May I present," said a loud and full voice, "Mrs. Witherspoon, Champion of Gateway Manor, New Orleans, Midland Plane."

The small train dragging behind me made a swishing noise as I walked. Mrs. Black had created a glorious baby blue gown, decorated with intricate paisleys stitched from white thread and small silver studs: A mandarin collar, a small teardrop opening on my chest, then long, twinkling sleeves ended in points of fabric on the tops of my hands needing an irritating elastic piece to keep it in place. Tight through the bodice, the ruched fabric flared into a skirt; the pleats in front hit just above the knees, but lengthened behind me into the train. Surprisingly comfortable silver pumps adorned my feet. As promised Jeeves fastened up my stark white hair with a matching silver hair comb. The outfit looked stunning. I didn't know if I'd ever looked more beautiful. Now, however, with a roomful of eyes on me, I wished I were invisible.

The Chancellor's table sat on a riser in the center of the room. Seated with him were two men and two women, none of whom I knew as they weren't announced to us.

I led the party into the room, as protocol dictated. What I hadn't been prepared for was the view beyond the table. A huge portrait of Will stared at me from the far wall. Its likeness was uncanny, he almost looked alive. He wore a black leather suit decorated with silver lightning bolt designs on his rib cage. A quiver slung over his shoulder. His folded arms held a thick, silver bow. I almost stumbled when I saw it. Mr. Marble gently took hold of my elbow to steady me. "I'm sorry, Mrs. Witherspoon," he whispered to me. "I forgot to tell you about the picture. Just address the Chancellor, and I'll tell you why he's there."

After a deep, calming breath I walked up to the Chancellor, gave my bow. The five stood abreast and bowed in return. Then our *maître d'*—a goblin in a *tux*—seated us.

Once we reached our table the entire room stood.

The Chancellor addressed the room in a booming voice, which shocked me; he had seemed so frail in his office. "Greetings one and all to the opening ceremonies of this year's tournament. Before we begin I'd like you all to raise a glass and join me in a toast." The room rustled as every person and creature raised some glass into the air. "Firstly, to our fallen champion, William Rutherford Witherspoon." Everyone turned to the portrait on the wall. "Never has there been a more ruthless yet diplomatic warrior among us. May he rest in peace."

"In peace," the room echoes as glasses were lifted, then imbibed. A chill ran down my spine. Before I could regain my composure he continued.

"Secondly, to those he left behind, his party, his friends, and his beautiful widow," the room rustled again as everyone turned to face ... *me*. I swallowed the hard, painful lump forming in my throat. "We solemnly salute you." Glasses again raised, and again all drank. All but me. I only hung my head, licked my lips, and clenched my fists—It was that or run.

"Please be seated," the Chancellor said. Thank the stars. I don't think I could have stood there much longer.

Mr. Marble leaned to me and in a hushed voice whispered, "The winner of last year's tournament get their portrait displayed in the Great Hall." Sounded like he, too, was a bit emotional. I looked up and noticed his glassy eyes. "That way everyone is reminded of who they ultimately must beat. Will's portrait's hung there for eight years now." He took a sip of water. "This will be the last year it will ever be displayed." He cleared his throat and sat a little taller. "Now, can someone pass me the bread?"

Averting my eyes from the haunted image of my late husband I looked at the other tables around us. Specifically the patrons, no longer hidden by draping robes.

Next to us sat a group of goblins; green, but stocky and better built than the ones Malador brought to my home. Beyond that I couldn't recognize, well, anything. I munched on a piece of bread, ogling the room around us.

Mr. Marble waved his butterknife like a wand over the room. "I know we haven't truly educated you on all of this," he said, "so be patient, just a little longer. We decided that we'd focus on the fighting part of the tournament and not a lot of the details about who and what you'll fight. As you go along, we'll tell you what you need to know."

"As I go along?" My eyes were drawn to a group of hulking...I'm gonna go with lobsters. In chainmail.

"*Ma chére*," Hercule said once he'd climbed his way to my shoulder top, "I will not let you enter any confrontation without complete knowledge of your enemy's strengths and weaknesses. This I promise you." He gave a little bow.

"That is the advantage," Jeeves added, "of having Mr. Smith and Mr. Wesson with us. They'll watch your competitors before you compete and return with suggestions on what to expect, and how to best be victorious."

"My point is," Mr. Marble said to me, "once this is all over and we're back at home, safe and sound, we'll start a real, *proper* education. The kind Will received as he grew up in the manor. We'll explain the planes and the houses, and the history, and who comes from where, and how the current allies came to be ...?" He waved his hand broadly. "But we felt ..." he nodded his head, thinking, "*all* of us felt that you wouldn't have the time, nor the attention, to take it all in this year. So we focused on battles in these few weeks. I apologize for that, for making decisions for you without your input. I'm sure you're tired of it, but it really was the best plan of action."

Jeeves, who sat next to me on my left, leaned over. "Madam, if I might suggest, don't look around." *Too late, Jeeves.* "And should something come up to greet you, just convince yourself it's a costume of some kind, or a trick, like they use in movies. What's the term? C-G-I? Some of the participants can seem rather unworldly." He tapped the back of my hand, gently. "Best not to dwell."

I took his advice. As I buttered my own roll rows of waiters and waitresses—some human, some goblin, some floaty-cloudy-skeleton things—marched single file into the room from several different doorways around the room, each of them carrying silver platters high in the air, all covered with large bell shaped, jewel encrusted, domes. Once all the servers reached their tables they simultaneously removed the lids and served the parties. We received soup. I glanced around—hard not to look—and I gathered that not everyone received the same thing.

"When will I know?" I asked the table. "Who I'm fighting, I mean."

"Tonight," Mr. Marble nodded. "After dinner the orators from the tables are called up to receive your schedule. Times of battles, opponents, any restrictions—"

"Restrictions?" I sat upright.

"Every now and again you'll be told no bladed weapons or no shields, stuff like that."

"As Master Will liked to say," Jeeves said holding a spoon delicately, "Any opportunity for the mages to screw with you." He nodded at the table in the center.

I couldn't help but laugh at that. While that sounded so much like something Will would say, I think I was most tickled by hearing a refined English gentleman use the phrase "screw with you."

A white-haired gentleman approached the table. My smile faded immediately. It was the man from my vision, the man who attacked and chained Will like an animal. Once I saw him in living color I realized where I'd seen him before. He'd come to visit on the day I arrived at the manor—it was him I ran past on my way out.

The man bowed to the table. "House of Gateway, I greet you in peace."

"In peace," the table answered. All but me, that is. I just stared, a small fire raging in my stomach.

Mr. Marble stood and shook the man's hand. "Colonel, may I introduce you to Mrs. Winki Witherspoon. Mrs. Witherspoon, this is Colonel Cleveland Mustard, House of Magnolia, New Orleans."

The name did put a damper on my growing rage. "Colonel ... Mustard," as I stood I gave a false smile. "Of course it is."

"The Colonel and Will were good friends for, what, the better of twenty years?"

The man nodded. "Abouts." He offered his hand. I looked at Mr.

Marble for guidance, and he gave a reassuring nod, so I took it. Begrudgingly. "Very fine to meet you, madam," the Colonel cooed. He had a well-spoke, Southern refinement to his voice. Slow, deliberate, enunciations.

"Indeed," I said, then sat, rather rudely.

Mr. Marble smoothly changed the topic. "I didn't recognize one of your party. Where's TJ this year? Your, um," he snapped his fingers, "your valet."

"You didn't hear?" the Colonel said, jutting his head upright. "TJ was murdered. Poisoned, as the police tell it, but I haven't the foggiest idea how. He was discovered in Mid-City, just a few weeks ago."

"I'm ... I'm so sorry, Colonel. I had no idea."

TJ ... T ... J ... Tony Jones ... "I'm sorry," I interrupted, "but was his name Anthony Jones?" I asked as I hid my trembling hands in my lap. "A young black gentleman? Ex-military?"

"Why, yes," the Colonel answered, his brow furrowed. "Did you know him?"

I had my table's attention. "I only met him once," I said as I shot Mr. Marble with my eyes. "I'm sorry for your loss."

"Indeed, a tragedy," the elder man nodded, "but also cause for continued concern. We retraced his whereabouts and determined he was poisoned, right in our home."

"You're saying he was killed *in the house?*" Jeeves asked. His voice wavered. I saw worry in his face. "How is that possible? The house protects. It would have fought or alerted you if its own were in danger."

"Poison" I thought outloud, "could be administered discreetly enough that the house wouldn't know, right?"

"It still implies," Mr. Marble solemnly said, "that the provider was considered a friend. An enemy wouldn't have gotten into the house."

"You mean there's a traitor," I put bluntly.

"'Traitor' is such a strong word, madam," the Colonel huffed. "But ..."

"Go on," Mr. Marble encouraged.

"I know during the opening ceremonies such news isn't good for the spirit. However, we were able to conduct our own *autopsy*, shall we say, to determine what kind of poison was used. Knowing how long it took to do its deed, he was definitely at home. Fact was, this time of year, he rarely left. He'd only gone to visit an ailing relative for an hour or two. Never got there. We all know Magnolia House only allows persons of certain energies within its walls."

"He means," Jeeves translated, "white or light energies. Good energy. No one dark or evil can enter."

"So someone like Malador couldn't have done it," I said, showing that I was catching on. "Even through a portal?"

"Again, the house would have alerted."

"Yes," the Colonel said. "Which is the pity." He turned to Mr. Marble. "There is a wolf among us dressed as a sheep. This news does not bear well for either of our houses."

"We will keep vigilant, good Colonel" Mama said with that island voice, "and informed. Between us we will find and remove any *wolves*."

With that the Colonel gave a small bow. "Pleasure to meet you, madam, and best of luck during the games."

"Bite me," I answered. But it came out as, "And you."

As Mr. Marble sat the next round of food arrived, in the same manner as the appetizers that came before; rows of waiters, silver trays, fancy domes, and a simultaneous presentation.

"So," he said, "what was that about? You were just a tad rude to the Colonel."

"Really," I said, turning to him. "That's what you want to talk about? I told you his name. I said the man who helped me was Tony Jones, and you—"

He held up his hands to stop my diatribe. "You honestly believe I knew that was *the* Tony Jones? That there's only one 'Tony Jones' in all of New Orleans? You don't think I feel terrible that it was him?"

"TJ?" Jeeves asked. "*He* was the man at the park when you were assaulted? Why on earth would he have been there?"

"He must be the one," Mama said, lugubriously. "He gave our champion the ability to tap into what she could not tap into alone." She pointed to her palm, recalling the white symbol we saw there under hypnosis.

"The cosmic outlet," I whispered.

"It would be my guess," she continued, "he was there to protect you."

"How would he know who I was? *I* didn't know who I was."

"The white houses always know their kind, child."

At that moment something grabbed my ankle, something shockingly cold and clammy. I screamed, and pushed myself away from the table. Clinging to my leg was a defenseless frog.

My shriek got the room's attention and nearly everyone turned to us to see what was the commotion. Meanwhile, someone kept apologizing. "Sorry ... sorry!" I heard, but my vision was on my little assailant.

"Must this happen every year!" Mama cursed, as she slammed her palms on the table.

"Sorry! Little fella got away from me," the goblin said as he knelt in front of me, and removed the sticky amphibian. Then, in front of me—and to my absolute horror—he popped the whole bugger into his mouth. And chewed. "Sorry," he said again through full teeth.

Without thinking I moaned as I covered my eyes, unwilling to watch further. When I did, the room erupted in amused laughter.

Wave after wave of distinctly different emotions washed over me while I stood there with my face buried in my hands and laughter filling the hall; first horror, then disgust, then embarrassment, then nausea, then great embarrassment, then finally my own amusement. That gave way to hilarity. Even I could see the foolish woman they laughed at. When I removed my hands I was laughing hysterically myself. I mean, seriously, what kind of champion would I, no, *could* I possibly be?

When the room realized I, too, was entertained, they applauded, and cheered, and clinked their glasses, even the goblins tabled next door. Thankfully, they then turned back to their own parties.

As I sat, wiping my the laughing tears from my eyes, Jeeves put a kind hand on my shoulder. "Madam, are you sure you're all right?"

I nodded. "I'm fine. Why didn't any of you tell me goblins eat frogs?" I managed, as my giggling receded.

Mama stabbed at her plate. "Mostly because we think it's disgusting."

"That's the only thing they eat," Mr. Marble said, looking over his shoulder at the indulging goblin table next to us. He visibly shuddered. "Gotta be fresh, too."

"Doesn't mean they can't be constrained," Jeeves said. "My sincere apologies, madam."

I had to laugh. If they didn't think I was a push over before, I'm guessing everyone, or every*thing*, thought so now.

When all of the meals were ended, and the used plates and utensils cleaned away, the Chancellor clinked his glass to get the room's attention. We all turned to face him.

"If I may have your attention, please," the frail man bellowed, "the time has come to cover this year's rules."

"This year?" I whispered to Hercule.

"*Oui*. They change every year and are only announced at opening ceremonies. That way no one house will have any particular advantages."

I nodded as the Chancellor continued. "Firstly, the use of proxies is suspended for this year's events." That seemed to upset some people, judging by the low grumble that coursed through the room.

"A Proxy is ...?" I whispered to Hercule.

"A proxy is a substitute. It is someone you select to suffer in your stead."

"What?"

"You battle, and any injury you gain is suffered by your proxy. Very important if you don't have a good healer."

The Chancellor continued. "As a result, competitors of the second stage will only need a First Fall to win. Neither blood nor injury will be necessary."

"Hm," Hercule danced on my shoulder. "Seems fair enough."

"However, competitors of the third stage will need either First Blood or expiration to win. Only in the fourth and final stages of battles will competitors need to be the last man standing for victory."

Jeeves mused out loud, "A kinder, gentler tournament this year." The table laughed. I swallowed. Nothing about the phrase "last man standing" sounded kind or gentle.

"There will be no restrictions this year on weapons or talents," the Chancellor said, "however, during the second stage competitors will only be allowed to use one of each."

"Handy," I said. "That's all I got." My table chuckled at my little joke, thankfully.

"It's almost as if they tailored this year just for you," Mr. Marble said.

"Really?" I asked.

"Odds are. We are the defending champions, and now we're starting over. It's not uncommon for them to show some leniency."

The Chancellor continued. "If there are any questions orators are encouraged to ask when they pick up their champion's assignments. Now." He picked up a scroll from his table, unrolled it, and began to read. "House of Gateway, please come forward."

Mr. Marble stood and approached the center table. I took a good look at the mages then. Two women, one fat and jovial looking with a natural smile on her lips. Her short brown hair paged about her face. The other woman thin, and proud, sitting painfully rigid. Her hair, swept up on atop her head, was fiery red. The other two men looked middle age. One was completely unremarkable, you wouldn't look at him twice if you passed him on the street. Normal height, normal build, receding hairline of mousy brown, thick black frames on his glasses, and pudgy facial features. The other, however, looked hawkish. Black hair, black eyes, and drawn cheekbones with a beak-like nose. He reminded me of the villain candyman from *Chitty Chitty Bang Bang*, the one who catches children for the Queen.

When Mr. Marble arrived at the table he gave the mages a great bow. With one hand he accepted a scroll, and the other he shook the Chancellor's hand. Then he returned to us.

"House of Ravenswood," the Chancellor called.

"Ravenswood ... Isn't that ...?"

"*Oui, ma chére,*" Hercule said. "Malador's house."

"These are in order of winners from last year?"

"*Oui.*"

"So the final battle was between Will and Malador."

"*Oui.*"

As he took his seat Mr. Marble unrolled the scroll. I watched Ravenswood's orator take their scroll, and followed him into the crowd as he returned to his seat. But I couldn't see the other people at his table, including Malador. I doubted we'd meet this year, as none of us expected me to make it to the final round. I hoped I wouldn't. I beat him once, but now he knows my talent. I don't think I'll get so lucky next time.

He heaved a deep and heavy sigh, "So much for ease," and passed it to Mama, who passed it to Jeeves.

"Esmeralda!" Jeeves exclaimed. "*And* the Arch Lich?"

Mr. Marble shook his head. "Smith and Wesson are going to

freak."

Then (finally!) the parchment came to me, a page filled with a list of unpronounceable names. I handed it back to Mr. Marble, uninterested, and resumed my meal. It suddenly had the feel of a last supper.

Chapter Seventeen

AS MY PARTY and I returned to our suite my good nature waned. My anger toward Mr. Marble over TJ swelled.

"I'm sorry," he said for the hundredth time, as I kicked off my shoes and plopped my silver gowned body into a stiff wooden chair. "I don't know what more to say. But I need to know what's your problem with the Colonel."

"I have no problem with Colonel Mustard," I said, mockingly. And I muttered, "In the *library* with the *lead pipe.*" I couldn't resist.

"Mrs. Witherspoon. His house is very powerful and our ally."

"Really?" I said, as he took off his tuxedo jacket and undid his bowtie. "And where was our ally when Malador attacked us just a few days ago?" Before he could answer I seethed, "Or you, for that matter."

That deflated him. He hung his head and clasped his hands in his lap. Since we'd been sniping at each other for the last hour, when he stopped talking the room fell quiet. Only the popping of firewood from our grand hearth spoke.

Mr. Smith and Mr. Wesson, who'd been playing a game of cards when we came in, softly put them down. No one moved.

"I saw him," I finally said, barely able to get the words out. My mind filled with the image of that boy sliced under his jaw, and kicked savagely in his stomach. "I saw him the day he came and took

Will away in chains. The day the house fell. The day his brother, Edward, was killed." Still no one moved. A thick anticipation hung in the air. "I never even knew he had a brother."

After a moment or two Mama started some cleaning, washing the plates from the dinner my entourage ate while we were at the ceremonies. The soft clanking of her busywork helped break the cloud that hung above us all.

Mr. Marble softly spoke. "I know you're angry. And I know you're angry at me, and that's fine ... if it will help motivate you over the next few days. But I think you should know, Mrs. Witherspoon, that the Colonel showed remarkable restraint on that day." I raised hot eyes to him. "What the house didn't show you, because the house didn't see, was what Will did to that man's family. But instead of killing Will and taking revenge, he made Will an ally."

His family? *Will, what the hell did you do?*

"You're going to hear stories about me, Winks. Some are total lies and fabrications but ... I'm deeply ashamed that some are true." I bit my lip recalling the words. I wanted to ask. I wanted to press. *No, Winki. It's best if you don't know. At least for now.*

Again the room fell silent. Mama had finished her chores. She stacked the two bowls and set them aside. Wait ... only two?

"Who didn't eat?" I asked Mr. Smith. He waved a finger at the shadow of a man sitting on the cot in the dark corner. "Wasn't he hungry?"

He shrugged. "Don't know."

"Did you ask him?"

"Why would we do that? He's a healer."

With emphasis I asked, "Do they eat?"

He gave me the strangest look, as if I'd just poured gravy on a snowman. "I guess."

After I rolled my eyes I went to the shrouded figure. I stood in front of him, and he hung his head deeper, making sure I couldn't see his face. "Are you hungry?" The man nodded, just once. "There," I said to Mr. Smith. "Was that so hard? Mama, please give me a bowl." She filled a shallow bowl with red beans and rice she'd made, and added a slice of buttered bread on top. I handed the bowl to the figure, who took it with his oversized sleeves. Possibly with hands, but I couldn't tell. Maybe he's not a man, or a woman, maybe just human shaped.

"We tend not to socialize with them. Healers are ... different," Mr. Marble said. "Don't get attached."

"What do you mean, *different*?"

"He's here to do a job. Next year he'll do that job for someone else."

"We treat them like spies," Mama huffed. "Anything he finds out about you he's likely to tell his next employer. Keep them at arms length, child."

I'd had enough. Between the news of Tony Jones, and Colonel Mustard, my possibly murderous late husband, and now this ... I'll be damned if anyone here to help me wouldn't be treated with respect. Or fed!

"Fine. Keep him away from the secrets and whatever else you feel you need to protect, but for chrisake, you will feed him. Is that clear?"

I stormed up to my room, stamping out every step, and slammed the door. In my own cloud of frustration I took off my clothes and collapsed in the stiff bed.

~ ~ * ~ ~

A small bell rang from the doorway as I walked into my favorite ice cream store on Prytania. They have the most unusual flavors there—eight different flavors of chocolate alone.

The woman at the counter asked, "Can I get you anything?"

I checked my pockets. My empty pockets. *Damned Mr. Marble.* "I don't have any money."

"That's okay," she said, then nodded across the room. "He's buying."

I turned to see ... *Will!*

I felt such relief to see that beautiful boy of mine. "Will? Is that really you?"

Occupying a seat in a booth he took a lump of ice cream from a paper cup and sucked it off his plastic spoon. "Hey, Winks. Long time, no see."

I took the seat opposite him. Somehow I knew it wasn't real, it wasn't the man himself. But it felt so comfortable, so familiar; that soft blonde hair, those gentle blue eyes. It felt wonderful just to be seated with him. "You're dead, aren't you?"

"Yeah. You know that."

I twisted my head in thought. "You know, in all this time I can't remember having a dream about you before. In over six months, nothing. Not one."

"It wasn't possible before," he casually said, and took another bite from his frozen treat. "I forgot how awesome this stuff was," he said with a full mouth, pointing his spoon at the cup. "Thank you for bringing me here."

"I ... Didn't?" *I don't think so.*

"Do you know where you are?"

I looked around. Checkered floor, red plastic table tops, pink walls decorated with children's drawings—I'd know the place anywhere. "The Creole Creamery."

He shook his head, with a small smile. "You know better than that."

"The word I'm looking for is 'hell'."

With a twisted frown, "Winks."

With a huff I said, "The tournament."

"Let me give you one word of advice. *Lighten up.*"

"That's two words," I pointed out.

He took another bite. "I was never good with math."

"You were an accountant."

Will winked at me. "Smile, Winki."

"How can I? I'm so out of my league. You left such big shoes to fill!" I took a shaky breath, looking into those dashing eyes. "I miss you so much. And you're everywhere. And I didn't get to be a part of it. Any of it!"

"I know. And I'm so sorry. But this is your time, Winki. This is your world, now. You're powerful, so very strong, you don't even know. But I do. And it will come, all of it, will come to you. Just laugh. Just open up and laugh, Winki. Like you did today, with the frogs. You handled that brilliantly."

I wasn't listening. I wanted ... "I have so much to tell you. To ask you."

"Like?"

"I think Nathan can't be trusted. I've got this feeling that he's the one who betrayed you, and he's trying to kill me."

"*Nathan?* Winks, please. There's not a mean synapse in that man's brain. You'll never meet a more honest and fair guy in your life. And he's a lawyer—what does *that* tell you."

"Tells me to run away as fast as I can."

He paused. "Fair point. Never mind that. Please, Winki. Trust him. Every step of the way."

Again, not listening. "Where's the DVD?" I asked abruptly.

With repeated strikes he scraped the last of his ice cream from his cup, licked his spoon. "You're on your own, there." Will chucked the cup across the room. When it clunked into an empty trash can ... I woke up.

Sat up, with a startled inhale, feeling surprisingly fresh and alert. I'd go as far as to say happy, even.

My bed lay beneath the open arch of a window. I scooted closer to it to take in the view. The sky still blazed orange, looking unchanged. The black landscape spread as far as my eyes could see. Nothing moving. No wind or breeze. The only living thing I could see, or recognize, was the lush cherry tree just a few hundred feet away. I wondered what time it was. I wondered if there was a sun at all, or rotation, or moon, or night ... such an *unearthly* place.

Refreshed after a quick bath I donned my super suit complete with hammer nestled against my hip and trotted downstairs, just as wafts of biscuits and gravy made its way to my nose.

"You're looking chipper," Mr. Marble remarked.

"Ready for a new day," I said. Mama cooked, Jeeves assisted her, and everyone else already sat at the Paul Bunyan-esque table. All but the healer, who sat in exactly the same spot on his cot in exactly the same manner. As I passed him I said, "Please tell me you laid down to sleep." He nodded, once. "Good. If you're hungry take a seat. The table's big enough for everyone."

"Uh, Mrs. Witherspoon," Mr. Marble protested, "we were going to go over the schedule today and talk about strategies."

"And he won't hear that from *way* over here?" I grandly swept a gesture to his cot just five feet away. "Please," I said the the healer, "come eat."

He hesitated, but stood and took a space on the end, as small as he possible could. I sat opposite him.

Once we all had plates Mr. Marble talked. "Today is the first day of the second stage, where the battles begin. As you know you only need to knock down your competitors, so these should be quick. Keep them quick. Don't waste a lot of energy."

"We recommend a one-two punch thing," Mr. Smith said. "Slow 'em down, knock 'em out. And move on."

I leaned to the healer. "You getting all this? Very technique-y."

"Each battle begins with a coin toss," Mr. Marble ignored me.

"Given you're the winning house, the others will all get to call it. Winners choose who moves first."

"First?" I echoed.

"Yeah. These battles are a they-go-then-you-go style."

"Wait, so if they win the toss and they come at me with an ax, I'm supposed to just, what, stand there and take it?"

"Course not!" Mr. Smith giggled. "That would be silly!"

"You can duck, or dodge, but you cannot use your talent or your weapon against it."

"I can't block with my hammer?"

"No, you can. You just can't take his knees out. Keep in mind they only need a first fall, too. They won't be trying to cut your head off, not yet, anyway." I honestly believed he was trying to by encouraging. He took a sip of coffee. "Also, some victory yield prizes. Awards. Everyone can get them."

"Prizes?" I said, "Oo, I like prizes." I perked up.

"Sometimes they're weapons, sometimes they're potions, and sometimes they're talents."

"I can get talents?"

"They will only work here, in the rings of the Citadel, and they'll only work for the duration of the tournament. But, yes, you can get talents. Keep in mind they aren't particularly special, like your own. They are generic, and anyone can get them. You may be in a battle with someone having the same talent, or someone who had that talent years before and knows how to overcome it. At this point, however, anything is better than just the one."

My interest piqued. "Weapons? Potions?" *Don't tell me this isn't magic.*

"Weapons can range from small knives to maces to single-shot pistols. Anything, really. And potions can do things like grant you more energy, or resist your opponent's talent."

"Sometimes you can get *poisons*," Mr. Smith fiendishly said. "We really like poisons." Mr. Wesson nodded enthusiastically.

"As you get more experience the prizes get better, but they come less frequently. Now, let's talk about Herithon."

"Herithon? Is that a talent?"

"Your first battle. This morning."

And so it begins…

Chapter Eighteen

THANKS TO THE intense training from Mr. Smith and Mr. Wesson, stepping into the ring, even for the first time, felt commonplace. It looked just like the one that appeared at home; five-sided, padded, and raised. There were two exceptions; the bleachers that surrounded it for any spectators, and the huge scoreboard that hung above it.

We arrived early. Mr. Marble, bedecked in robe and necklace, led me into the ring while my healer brought up the rear. I gazed up at the illuminated board.

"I know. Shiny," my orator said. "There's just a couple of things you need to pay attention to right now. One is your opponents talents, which is listed just under the name."

My opponent's name was *Grob*, which I cunningly deduced since it wasn't *Winki Witherspoon*. He (or she) possessed one talent: doorman, which meant they could make portals.

"The other is your level. That't the number that you strive to get as high as you can. It doesn't matter much for these bouts, but the higher the level, the stronger the opponent. If theirs is much higher than yours, even with your talent, you're going to have a hard time winning."

Both Grob and I ranked as level 1, the absolute lowest. By Mr. Marble's logic, I should have no problem.

"Lastly, see the light above the names? When it's your move, it will go on. If you move when the light is over his name, you'll get penalized. Trust me, you don't want that."

My opponent, a goblin, led by his orator entered the room, looking just as mean and muscled as any I'd seen. I swallowed.

"He's new, too, Winki. This is his first battle." He faced me. "Since we're the defending house, everyone else will get to call the coin toss."

I nodded. I must have looked apprehensive.

"I promise you, this will be quick and easy. Your talent will make these first few battles trivial."

I nodded again, more assured.

An ethereal voice from nowhere spoke. "Call the toss."

The goblin grunted, "Heads."

From above a coin fell to the mat. The goblin and I peered forward. It displayed a dragon's head. "Heads it is," said the voice. Although, I had no idea how the voice saw the coin.

Our orators and healers left the ring. We stared at each other from the ropes.

"Begin," said the voice.

The goblin charged at me with a knife, which I deftly dodged (my thanks and eternal gratitude to Annabelle). At my turn, I held up my hand and thought, "No." The goblin slowed.

I stood there, confused for a moment. I looked at Mr. Marble. *Now what? Do I wait until he slowly attacks me?*

"Assist!" Mr. Marble called upwards.

"Granted."

He pointed up at the board. The light over my name was illuminated.

Confused, I said, "But it's his turn."

"He can't take his turn since you slowed him to a crawl. It's your move."

I shrugged. Now I understood why he felt these would be trivial. "Got it."

Mr. Marble waved, indicating our time out was over.

"Continue," said the voice.

Throughout my time out, Grob ran across the ring in slow motion. Using my trusty hammer, I knocked his feet out from under him. Slowly he tumbled to the mat, arms stretching outward while, bit by bit, his face expanded in shock. I spun my hammer in my hand a couple of times before putting it back in it's holster, and Grob still hadn't hit the floor.

I folded my arms as we all waited. As soon as the first part of him touched the floor, he sped up into real time.

"Winner, House of Gateway," announced the voice.

"I told you so," Mr. Marble smiled. "Right this way."

And so went the next three battles, all of them against goblins.

I received small rewards for my victories; a small knife, a leather shield, and an energy potion, should a battle go on for some length and I needed a pick-me-up. Trinkets, really. The items were delivered to our suite while we breaked for lunch.

But the three battles benefited me. I ranked at level four.

After lunch the battles continued. I was allowed to use my new leather shield, since it didn't qualify as either a weapon or a talent. Even though it was petite, I found it useful right off the bat.

My opponent was a wraith—I was secretly happy to fight something new—more of a cloud than a creature. I tried to read its name, but it contained way too many consonants for me to pronounce. I was pretty confident it began with the letter "R", although it was backwards on the board. He ranked a level 14, much higher than me.

"R" drifted onto the platform as a cohesive gloom and loomed there until we began. It won the coin toss. And it used its talent, called *bind*, first. It was successful—it bound my feet to the floor. I couldn't move them.

I did my usual, slowing him down, which meant "R" missed his turn, but my feet didn't release, so I, too, missed a turn. I thought about throwing my hammer, but what would it hit? "R" was a cloud. Moreover, I'd be without a weapon.

"R" rushed at me. With my feet still stuck my attempt to duck failed. I saw a quick glint, then felt a blade slice through my arm. I cried out in response to the bright pain, and desperately tried to keep my balance as I held my bloodied bicep. He quickly retreated out of my way. *How the hell was I going to fight like this?*

"Assist!" Mr. Marble called out.

"Granted," said a voice from somewhere.

Mr. Marble climbed into the ring and approached me, my feet still immobile.

"Because it's ranked so much higher over you, your talent has less of an affect on him than his does on you. Which is why he can move, and you can't."

"Great. So I'm a sitting duck."

"For the moment. But keep in mind that once he moves, he's moved. You don't have to wait for him to move away. Strike immediately."

I nodded, and he left the ring. He raised his arm.

"Continue," said the voice.

Again it came at me. Without waiting to see the weapon, once "R" neared I squatted down and raised my shield. I heard it tear just above my hand. I immediately yelled, "*No!*" and raised my hand. Timidly, I stood. The wraith loomed there, softly billowing as it started to drift away.

It didn't matter that I couldn't take a step. I didn't need to, given it was in reach. Uncertain of how a hammer would affect a cloud, I gave it my all, swinging it like a bat.

It went right through the wraith, separating it into two puffy parts. Then it fell, like sand, to the floor.

"Game over. Winner, House of Gateway."

Relieved, I grabbed my gaping wound and turned to my bench. My healer already stood in front of me. Wow, he moved fast. He raised a cloaked hand and put it on my wound. His garb prevented me from watching what, exactly, he did. But it felt like his stuck his fingers into the cut. In other words, excruciating.

"Hey," I exclaimed, grabbing his arm.

"Take it easy," Mr. Marble said. "It will only last a moment."

Thankfully, that was true. When the healer removed his hand by arm felt fine. Even the armor had been repaired.

I inspected the work, then nodded to the healer and jested, "I forgive you."

He bowed a bit.

"Can you always assist me?" I asked Mr. Marble.

"Only up to level fifteen. Then you're on your own. It's going to get more complex," he said. "Those numbers are going to change, and mean a great deal more in the next stages of battle. Make sure you pay attention. Even your own talents will change and get stronger."

"How cool is that!"

"One of the prizes you can receive is a boost to your own talent. It's called a gonzo, and it comes in the form of an amulet."

"A *gonzo*? You've got to be kidding me!" I saw the wraith reform after a visit by his ... its healer. "Just a sec," I told my group, then ran up to meet "R". It backed away slowly as I approached, looking nervous ... if that was possible for a cloud.

I raised my hands in a friendly manner. "I just wanted to thank you. For the bout. That's an awesome talent." With a hand on my heart I bowed in front of him. It. Whatever.

The mist churned and swirled, forming itself into a human shape. And bowed back. "Until next time," I said and waved as I left.

~ ~ * ~ ~

I had some time before my next bout. Mr. Marble told me I should join Smith and Wesson who were watching some of the advanced attendees. Without argument I did so, only to notice I had a shadow, my healer. "You can go back to the room," I told him. He stood motionless.

"No," Mr. Marble said, having overheard my comment from down the hall. "Where ever you go, he goes. From now on he's attached to you."

My healer and I found Smith and Wesson at the battle between Esmeralda and a lich, one of the lobster-looking creatures. The battle was in full swing when we took seats, my healer seated behind me.

Esmeralda gave me the willies. After only five seconds of viewing I hated her. A human, who walked proud and insulted everyone. Bright red hair, fair skin, and stunning green eyes. Beautiful to look at. But, like Malador, loathsome to listen to. She smiled wickedly at her competitor. Her weapon was her own fingernails. She used them ferociously, swiping her hands across the lich's body, cutting through both his chainmail and his thick shell. Black lich blood covered the ring floor in spatters as it suffered a torment by a thousand shallow cuts.

She swiped at the lich, again, this time cutting off a tentacle. "Oh, dear me," she callously said, "did I do that?" Sent shivers down my spine.

His body was a golden-brown color, almost obscured by his blood. He maneuvered upon six pointed legs. His arms, massive and muscled, were covered in spiky protuberances; one, a claw, and the other, a three-fingered hand. His bulbous plating, I gathered, was his own skin, a kind of exoskeleton. From the top of his head protruded six tentacles ... well, five now.

The lich staggered, heaving from the bout. He raised his dagger and tried to lunge at her. Esmeralda dodged it, and used her talent to turned him to stone. With his momentum it looked like the end, the stone lich plummeting to the floor. But Esmeralda stopped him, stood him upright. "No, no, my dear ... not yet. I'm having so much fun," the words dripped from her mouth like honey.

A goblin took a seat next to me, bulky with pocks all over his skin. "She's such a twit," he leaned to me. "I like to watch her bouts just on the off chance she loses."

"Doesn't happen often, I take it."

"Nope."

"Wait a minute," I read the board, "this is *that* Esmeralda," I said to Mr. Smith, seated on my other side. "She's on my list."

"My condolences," muttered the eavesdropping goblin.

Mr. Smith nodded solemnly. "We've been watching her all day. Trying to find a weakness." Mr. Wesson nudged him and tapped on his tablet. "So far, all we've got is her shitty personality."

All this woman had to do was knock her opponent down. But she was playing. She was having fun. She was torturing the poor thing. I rooted for the golden lich.

"Why doesn't he just give up?" I asked. "He could just sit down, right?"

"He's a lich. They fight to the death, regardless."

"Who is she? I mean, where does she come from?"

"Esmeralda is the Queen of the Diamond Realm, Radiant Plane. They don't have houses there, more like serfdoms. Dark energy, in case you didn't guess that. And a succubus."

"A feminine incubus," I whispered.

"Malador's sister," Mr. Smith said.

"Get out!" I exclaimed.

"Every year it would come down to Will fighting one or the other of them for the title. It alternated so perfectly that we," Mr. Smith gestured between himself and Mr. Wesson, "were sure they rigged that somehow. But we could never figure out how."

Another tentacle was lost. The lich shrieked in pain, a sound that made most of the attendees cover their ears. Including me. "How did Will defeat her?"

"His strategy was to keep her as far away from him as possible. Will was a master of the bow. He could injure her from a distance. Hey, you remember that one year," he nudged Mr. Wesson, "when Will shot an arrow threw her foot? Pinned her there at one end of the ring. The bitch couldn't move," he recalled with glee. "That was awesome."

The lich stumbled when he tried to strike a blow, but Esmeralda caught him, propped him upright. "Really, dear, this is how you want to go out?" She shoved her fingers under one of his plates. The tortured creature tried to move away, flailing and shrieking, but her grip held fast. My teeth ached at the sound.

"Enough," said the faceless voice. "Penalty, Diamond Realm." A lightning bolt from the ceiling struck at Esmeralda. She gripped the ropes of the ring, bearing it. When it was over she smiled up the sky, licked her red lips, and asked, "Was it good for you?"

I gagged. The people in earshot around me chuckled, including, I think, my healer. That made Esmarelda look. I smiled and waved my fingers.

"Are you crazy?" Mr. Smith snapped, "What are you doing?"

"She's on my list so I'm guessing I'm on hers. No point in going into my battle with warm feelings." She was the first trial of my stage three battles. The *first blood* battles. I wondered what strategy she'd use then.

While locked on my eyes she raised her lich-bloodied fingers to her mouth and sucked the black ooze off. My stomach roiled in nausea. I blew her a kiss and winked. Her eyes widened as her body stood erect. *Did I really get to her?* She turned to the lich and kicked him, knocking him down.

"Game over. Winner, Diamond Realm."

Esmeralda stormed out of the ring, rolling her long, green cape royally over her shoulders. Heading for the exit, her cape flew wide behind her, like a giant spiderweb.

Something touched me seductively, running their hand down my back. I sat up rigid and exhaled in frustration. "Dammit, Malador." I didn't even have to look. "I was hoping it was me she reacted to, but it was something you did, wasn't it?"

"No, no," the goblin next to me confirmed. "It was you." He stood and waved. "See you tomorrow!"

Malador gave a shallow laugh and waved, which faded when the goblin turned away. "Little imp," he said under his breath.

"I heard that!" the little green man called back.

"Wasn't anything I did. I was just sitting here," Malador said as I turned to him. He'd taken a seat next to my healer. I looked the man up and down myself. Black leathers with padded shoulders and some red design, like a crest on his chest. Matching boots and gauntlets. A red cape draped behind him. The high collar reached up to touch his chiseled jaw. His beard, perfectly groomed and trimmed, accentuated his striking cheekbones and big, brown eyes. His hair swept up off his face with a single tuft dangling over his brow. My eye lingered on his soft, pink lips. Why did he have to be so gorgeous?

"Admiring the view?" he looked me up and down. Which broke the spell.

"What?" I forced myself to look upwards, "What do you want?"

Wrong words. "What I *want* is a good long night with you, my dear. You, me, my bed, ... some chains—"

"Hey, pal, back off—" Mr. Smith came to my rescue.

I held him back with my arm. "No no," I smiled, "Allow me." I turned completely to face him. "Mr. Malador," having just watched his sister, the master of the sickeningly sweet smile, I tilted my head,

"I can honestly tell you that all the bats in hell will have evolved into men and received their doctorates long before I ever do a dance with you."

"Oh, I love it when they play hard to get," he leaned forward. "I think we should have dinner together. Are you busy this evening?"

"And why would I do that?"

"Because I have information that I think you will find interesting."

His attack on my house raced to my mind. "Let's assume that I believe you," I said. "Why would you share this information with me? I've got in on good authority you're not the sharing kind."

"You do me a favor, and I'll do you a favor." His eyes went right to my breasts. "And I do so need a favor."

"Remember the bats," I snarked.

He sighed and sat back, resting his elbows on the bleachers behind them. "I know a great many things, having fought here a great many years. Like how to defeat the red-haired witch, sister-of-mine. I want to see her lose, and if she lost to a junior warrior, such as yourself, it would bring humiliations galore. Might even prevent her from being in the sweet sixteen."

"Sweet sixteen?" *Like in basketball?*

"The final countdown?" With a large gesture he rolled his eyes, "Good gods, woman, you really need to hire competent people! How is it you don't know the sweet sixteen?"

Mr. Smith jumped in. "We were getting to it."

"Come dine with me," Malador said again. "No tricks, I swear. Bring your healer, if you like. Besides, I can hardly harm you here," he looked at Mr. Smith. "Do I speak truth?"

Mr. Smith twisted his face, trying to read the evil man. "Technically, all talents are stifled in the Citadel except in the ring," he said to me. "In theory, he can't infect you." Mr. Wesson vigorously shook his head, expressing great negativity.

"What time?" I asked.

"What time?" Malador echoed.

"What. Time. As in, when do you want me to show up for this dinner?" The questions stunned them all, including my healer who turned his shrouded head towards me.

With such swiftness as to stun me Malador swept up my hand, then bowed towards me, bring his lips dangerously close to my glove, his deep eyes boring into me. He slowly smiled. "Dinnertime." Then he released me, stood, and trotted down the stairs, his red cape swishing behind him. He never looked back.

"That," Mr. Smith pressed, "is such a bad idea."

"I know," I said, standing. "And yet." I and my healer left.

Chapter Nineteen

DESPITE THE CONSISTENCY of the Citadel's interior, dark, damp, and dreary, I had no problem finding Malador's lodging. I walked along the narrow, torch lit hallways, my healer padding silently behind me.

Apparently, every evening all attendees were invited to a dinner in the grand dining hall, where the opening banquet had been held. Hence, *dinnertime*. No one argued with me as I headed to my date. Mr. Marble strongly offered a "This is a bad idea." For once I agreed with him. But I had some questions. I still didn't know what happened to Will, exactly. Moreover, I still didn't know who tried to have me killed in the park. And I was tired of being stuck in neutral by my staff and Mr. Marble. So I felt compelled to go have dinner with my enemy. Besides, I brought my healer. What could possibly go wrong?

I walked the halls of the Citadel a full and qualified level seven—whatever that meant—knowing Malador was a level forty-two—whatever that meant. Thinking back on his attack and how a lowly level seven beat him bolstered my confidence. Still, I knew full well, should we meet again, he'd have the advantage.

Upon entering the common room we were greeted by the tower Master. It looked identical to ours; roaring fire, sets of tables, chairs, sofas, and settees, except that adorning their walls were pictures of liches, goblins, wraith and other creatures I had not yet laid eyes on.

While exchanging pleasantries with the Tower Master, Malador arrived. "Ah!" He called, entering the room, "You're here. Please, follow me." He waved.

I stopped, stunned. He'd changed his clothing. He wore a long sleeve t-shirt with the sleeves hiked halfway up his forearms, blue jeans, and tennis shoes. I still wore my leathers.

I did follow, keeping my eyes active, looking for any trap or ambush. He then stepped out of the way, leaning against the door jamb to his suite, and gestured for me to enter. "Ladies first."

"It's exactly like ours," I remarked, as my eyes swept over the room. I entered with caution, my healer behind me.

"They all are," Malador said. "That way there's no sense of favorship among the competitors. May I pour you some wine?"

My heart raced a bit, uncertain of what to expect. Wine, or a poison? Would he dare to kill me here?

"Sure," I said, albeit unsurely.

"Please, make yourself comfortable."

Five softly burning red tapered candles decorated the table in the center of the room. While Malador pulled a bottle of wine from a cupboard, I took a seat. My healer joined me, keeping a respectable distance.

"You can do better than that," he smiled, pulling the cork from the bottle. "I can't infect you here. Go on. Take off your helmet and gloves. Kick back. Live a little, woman."

Said the spider to the fly. But I did. I admit, freeing my hair from the leather hood always felt good. I shook out the white coif.

"Very nice," he smiled. "I hope you like red," Malador said pouring a glass. "I made us some pasta."

"You made?" I said. I didn't mean to mock him. "I mean, you don't have a cook that travels with you?"

He shook his head as he place the full glass in front of me. "You only can bring so many, and I don't like an entourage. I'd rather have a strategist than a cook."

I reached for my glass when my healer rudely snatched it away. He sniffed the wine, or at least I assumed since the hood hid his face from view, before taking a small sip. Beats passed. He set the wine down in front of me and nodded.

"He is supposed to do that," Malador said, seeing my bewilderment. "Honestly, woman, you need to hire a better staff. Yours are going to get you killed. Repeatedly."

"Says the man who's tried to kill me."

"No, no, my dear lady. I want to *turn* you. Killing you would just mean Gateway would find another champion, and I'd have to start all over. Do you know how long I've waited for Gateway to have a *woman* champion?" He set the bottle and himself down across from me. "I want you to walk by my side, dark and dark. We could do so many things, have so much fun together. But," he raised his hand to stop me, because I was gonna start protesting, "that is not why I asked you here this evening. I'll say no more." He took a sip from his own glass. "Hm. Needs to breathe a bit. Now, I need a favor and I have information. I am willing to trade. You do me the favor and I will give you information."

"Right to business, eh," I said.

"You'd rather dinner first?" He stood. "Very well." He opened a pot simmering on the stove and heaped pasta into bowls. He did this with his back to me, allowing me to indulge in the view. Malador didn't need padding on his shoulders. They were naturally broad. His body tapered to a narrow waist and tight fitting jeans. I forced myself to look away.

I cleared my throat. "What information to you have?"

He looked over his shoulder. "Favor first. Information second."

"How will I know I want it, or that it's worth the favor?"

"Fair point," he said turning to me with piping bowls of pasta. The noodles were coated in olive oil and garlic, and tossed with cooked broccoli and cauliflower. "I learned the recipe when I lived in Italy. Back then they didn't use tomatoes a lot. But that was back in the sixteenth century."

He must be pulling my leg. "How old are you?"

Malador chuckled. "That's one of the benefits of being dark, my dear. We age exceptionally well." He winked, then took a mouthful of food. Malador continued, "We lie, we cheat, we steal, and we kill when it suits us. So, we can manipulate all the games, including the aging one. Your lot, being all just and noble, have to play by the rules. You die young and we persevere." As he spoke I handed my healer the fork. He ate, chewed, waited a bit, then nodded, handing the fork back to me. I tried to ignore the mad man across the table, but the information was damned depressing.

"Now," he said, just after a sip of wine, "a favor. Sister-of-mine. I know her list and I know her skills. Therefore, I know she will likely lose three battles come stage three. And I want you to be the fourth."

"Why me?"

"As a junior warrior you should be a pushover for her. If she loses ..." he leaned close to me, "*badly* then not only will she be humiliated. She won't make the sweet sixteen." He sighed. "Please tell me you know what that is now."

"Yes. Stage three is a sorting and ranking of all the competitors. The best sixteen go on to stage four." While I spoke he didn't eat, he just watched me. And I him. His soft dark hair framed his handsome face. I cleared my throat, shifted my gaze back to my food and stabbed my noodles. "Moreover," I deduced, "you won't have to fight her."

"True. Not the point here, just an added benefit. You have to fight her anyways. You might as well win."

"If I'm all just and noble," I mocked the words he used, "how can I do that without cheating?"

"With ..." he excused himself from the table and returned with a shield. "This!" It was beautiful. Entirely white surface with an opalescent hue that shimmered in rainbow colors. Framed in gold with scrollwork and filigree the center of it bore a crest; I recognized it to be the one he wore on his armor. He set it down on the ample table.

"This is your house, isn't it?" I pointed to the decoration.

"Oh, yes. I have no problem with sister-of-mine knowing who aided you."

"And I can use this?"

"Shields aren't considered weapons, and there is no restrictions on gifts. Yes. You can use this. And keep your goody-two-shoes image unblemished."

I gave a hard look at the dazzling exterior. "How? I saw her nails cut through metal."

"That surface is all kedorite. Completely impenetrable. Her nails can't get through it, and in fact, it will, well, sting her a bit when she tries." He took a sip of wine and muttered, "Knowing her she'll probably enjoy that."

In the back of my mind I kept hearing Mr. Marble warn me not to touch anything Malador gave me. I stared at the dazzling item. "She is your sister. Why the bad blood? What do you want?"

To that he put his fork aside, and put his elbows on the table, his hands folded so his fingers could touch his chin. He licked his perfect lips. "I want you."

I rolled my eyes, and went back to my food.

"Hear me out. I want you. I want your house. Look at me, right now." I did. "If we had, say, bumped into each other at a coffee shop, me dressed much like this, and I started some idle conversation, I know ... *I know* I could have had you in my bed in three, four hours tops. That was my plan. Seduce you, take you, turn you. Very simple. I was just waiting for you to get out of that damned fortress of yours. And you would have been mine." I didn't want to admit it but he very well may have succeeded. The right face at the right time, feeling as lost and lonesome as I had ... I shuddered at my good fortune. "But sister-of-mine told me to just go get you. Attack. 'She'll be a pushover, don't wait, dear brother, just take her before she gains any strength of her own.'" He stuffed some pasta into his mouth.

I hung my head, nodding that I understood, quietly eating.

"No, you think you know how it turned out. I lost half my regiment that day. They quit following me. And three of my staffers walked out because of how weak, and unorganized, and *stupid I was!*"

He screamed those last words at me. Without looking down I reached for my hammer ... if he got any closer, I wouldn't hesitate.

But Malador sat back. "She used you to humiliate me. I want to use you to humiliate her. Turn about, fair play, yadda yadda yadda."

After several minutes of quiet I broke the silence and asked my healer, "Are you hungry?" He didn't move, but I couldn't imagine him not being so. "May I fetch him a bowl?" I asked Malador.

"The wretch?" He gave the healer a sneer. "If you must."

Having noticed where he got our bowls I retrieved one, filled it for my healer, and returned to my seat. "Okay, this is going to sound like another newbie question," I prefaced, "but why does everyone hate healers?"

Malador watched the shrouded man, who held his fork with his sleeves. "Everyone has different reasons." He closed his eyes and shook his head, which made his soft locks swing free. It caught my eye. "What you feel," he said, quietly, "is my natural charm, you know. No talent. Just me. I am gorgeous."

"Honestly, do these lines work on any woman—" Before I could finish he grabbed the back of my neck from across the table and pressed my lips into his. I struggled, taken by surprise at his swiftness, and tried to push myself away. My healer sprung at Malador with faster reflexes than mine, managing to separate me from the vice-like grip.

Malador smugly folded his arm across his chest and tilted his head. "Well?" he asked. "Anything?"

With the back of my hand I wiped my mouth, enraged that the first man to kiss me since my late husband was this bastard of a demon. I also felt utter humiliation at being waylaid so effectively—*idiot, you're in Malador's suite, for Pete's sake*—and bitter disappointment in myself; that after all this training I failed to use the hammer on my hip. Then I got it. I wasn't supposed to feel any of those things ... he was an incubus. I was supposed to be *enthralled* now, right?

Malador's eyes twinkled as, from somewhere, he held out a long, twinkling kitchen knife. "Give me your hand." My eyes fixed on the dazzling blade. "Come now, if you don't leave here with some story of how I cut you your house is going to think we ... did other things." I hesitated, then held up my ungloved hand. With a quick swipe Malador sliced my palm.

"Dammit," I hissed, pampering my bloodied appendage. My healer took my injured arm and, with my hand under his ample sleeve, healed me. I looked at my palm. Nothing was wrong with it at all. No visual evidence, no physical linger. It was all gone. "He can heal," I said, slowly putting it together, "in the Citadel. We have no talent now, but he does." I scowled. "You could have just said that, without the kiss-and-cut demonstration."

"They can heal anywhere," he continued. "They cannot be restricted and they cannot be resisted. They, alone, get to choose who lives and who dies. Which gives them the ultimate power. And everyone hates ultimate power when they don't have it themselves."

My healer wasn't eating. "They heal," I said. "Without them the tournament wouldn't be possible."

"They don't do it because its what they love to do. They do it because it's power. It's glory. You of all people should know—" His eyes grew wide and his mouth dropped. "They didn't tell you." He laughed. "And they call themselves the 'good house.'"

"Tell me what?"

"No, my dear. You'll have to ask them. About last year. About Will and Esmeralda. Ask them."

I really hated not knowing anything. But I pushed on. "Glad we got back to that. Let's say I take this fancy shield of yours and win—"

"Not win, *humiliate*. That part's important."

"Fine. What will you do for me?"

"I have information."

"Like?"

"Your part first, dear lady."

"I need something. How will I know this information is worth it? Even with your shield, assuming it works, I could be in for a slog of a fight." I finished my wine.

"You have to fight her anyway," he shrugged. Then sighed. "Fine. There's a traitor in your house."

"Yeah. That I know."

"I have a name." I froze at the words. "Someone told sister-of-mine that you were vulnerable. Someone told her you were ripe for the taking." *Someone wants me dead.*

"Why didn't *sister-of-yours* attack?"

"A number of reasons. Firstly, different planes, makes surprise attacks much more difficult. But I'm guessing, mostly, that she didn't have all the facts and knew it. So she threw little brother under the bus." He finished his wine, arching his head high to empty his glass. "You stop her, I give you a name. Deal?"

I wiped my mouth with a napkin. Why didn't this feel right?

Malador refilled our empty glasses. "Clearly you need another motivation. What do you say, healer, shall I tell her what you did last year?" My healer didn't move. "Him. Or some other guy. Never can tell. Their anonymity works in their favor. Never know who to blame, do we?" He slapped my healer on the arm, as if they were pals.

"What happened last year?" I pressed.

"Last year the gallant Master Will of Gateway House nearly didn't win. Sometime during stage three he stopped showing up for bouts, something of a no-no here. After a day, and much protesting by the Gateway staff, it was determined that he wasn't just slacking off. He'd gone missing. The next day, all events were suspended and a search ensued. He was found." His glee made my hands tremble. I dropped them below the table, out of his view. "One of the prizes offered here, one of the most coveted as a matter of fact, is an elixir called *Immortality*. It's like the Holy Grail. You drink it and you can't lose. No matter what's done you can't die. Oh, you still feel the pain, but you don't get any weakness and you can't be killed. Ultimately, your opponent either gives up, or you kill them. Anyway, last year sister-of-mine won that elixir. But, dear sis. She found a much more *entertaining* way to use it." He took a hearty sip of wine. My lungs ceased to work properly. "She subdued Will, force fed him to drink the potion, then ... she had fun. And you've seen what *fun* is to her. When they finally found your husband, tied spread eagle in the Ring of Champions, she'd had nearly two days with him. She cut and sliced, and disemboweled him. The elixir wouldn't let him die. He couldn't even pass out from the pain." He gave a sickening smile. "It took three healers to put Humpty Dumpty back together again. I have no idea what it did to his mind." He jutted a chin at my healer. "*That* led him to his demise. His trusted healer. I don't know how but I'd guess sis paid him well." He read my rage. "That is what sis does best. I use sex and seduction to get my victims. She uses pain, and she's a master of it. She will push and prod and turn you into a raging vengeful monster, and once you've taken that step, that first strike, you're *hers*. You're *ours*. *You are dark.*"

I twisted my lips to bite the inside of my cheek. "What did Will do to her? When they fought?"

"She was dismissed. They never fought. Probably saved his soul."

I'd had enough. Heart racing I stood, stumbling, and made my way out from behind the table with my healer behind me. I stopped when I passed the shield, letting my eyes gaze on the great plate. I took it.

"Good night, dear lady," he called as I stormed from the room. I slammed the door, as Malador's laughter faded behind me.

Chapter Twenty

"OF COURSE WE did not tell you," Hercule cried out as he scampered along the Citadel wall. He'd been with me the entire time, I discovered, hiding somewhere in the room. "We wanted to prevent this!" I raged on, heading back to my own suite. "*Madame*, you must listen to me. No good can come from this knowledge. Hatred? Rage? Revenge? That is what you feel, no? That is the path to the darkness!"

"No!" I spun to face the roach on the wall. "That's *not* what I feel." I pointed an accusing finger at him. "I feel lost. I feel left out! I feel like everyone around me knows everything and keeps it from me. Think about it. Everyone here knows what happened last year. *Everyone*. Malador. You. Him," I pointed to my healer. "It's bad enough that I don't know a halberd from an ax, or a wraith from a lich, but I have to deal with not knowing my house's history. That my husband was kidnapped and tortured right here, where all of you have *convinced* me was a safe and protected place. And all for what, sport? Entertainment? *That is what I feel.*" My rage quaked through me with such ferociousness that my legs couldn't hold my own weight. I collapsed on the wall behind me and sank to the floor. Sobbing.

They let me cry, sitting there on the floor, both Hercule and my healer. They patiently waited for me to catch my own breath.

Hercule made his way down the wall to the floor next to me. "We did not keep this from you to keep secrets from you, *ma chére*. We kept if from you to spare you this exactly. What you go through now. We all went through it. When we found him ..." The little bug sighed. "We all felt exactly like this. All wishing we were dark so we could tear that foul *pute* limb from limb with glee."

My memory went back a year ago. Every summer Will disappeared to go to some accountant convention, which I now know was the tournament. He did seem sadder when he came home last year. More serious. He spent more time with me in the days that followed, avoiding work and his office. The following months were much more intense. *Passionate.* I lost him that November.

I slid the shield closer, and took a hard look at the crest. A dragon design coiled over the face with three words below. *Tolle. Converte. Tormentum.* "Take, Turn, Torment," Hercule said. "Words Malador lives by."

"Will it work?" I asked.

"The shield? Most certainly."

"Can I humiliate her?"

"A fine line will be walked. But we don't do it for the nefarious Malador. I do not think we can trust his information. We do it to avenge Master Will! *Allons-y, ma chére.* I will lead you."

~ ~ * ~ ~

I let Hercule recount my dinner with Malador, and its conclusion. As he did so, I watched the others, hoping to spy the spy. But they remained elusive. Admittedly, unless they stood and confessed I probably couldn't have identified my traitor.

The room was quiet for several minutes until Mr. Marble asked Jeeves for my scroll. "Smith? Wesson?" he ordered, and the two lab coats stood. "Get me the competitor's standings at this moment. Also,

I assume there's a pool?"

"Um ... Er ..." Mr. Smith cleared his throat.

"I want to know stats, not how much you put in. Predictions. I want to know who are the favorites, and who are the dark horses." They didn't move. "Now!" The two men scurried out the door. Once gone he turned to the healer. "You. Get out."

"No no no," Hercule said before I could protest myself. "He must stay."

"Hercule, we're risking a lot here. We're doing it because of last year, and it isn't going to be ..." He lowered himself to the roach and whispered, "above board. He'll sell us out."

"The Great Hercule has a good feeling about this one."

Mama sniffed, "Does the Great Hercule want to share with the rest of us?"

"This one is protective of her for some reason." They all turned to the shrouded man sitting on the modest cot. "He came to her aid when Malador kissed her."

"Malador kissed her?" Jeeves exclaimed. Hercule had left that small detail out in his retelling.

Mr. Marble screamed at the healer. "Do you know her?" The healer didn't move. "Answer me!" He gave a slight bow. With that he lunged for the man's hood. The healer grabbed it, pulling it over his face even harder. The two men struggled.

"Enough!" Hercule cried out. "That is enough!"

I agreed, pulling Mr. Marble from the tan shroud. Mr. Marble scoffed as he turned away.

Hercule continued. "If I am right then his anonymity may save his life. If his face is seen, he is at great risk next year. No. Keep him concealed. And keep him close."

"And if you're wrong?" Mr. Marble said between clenched teeth. "And this is a game to betray us? Again?"

"We will deal with him but only then, *mon ami*." Mr. Marble's reddened face stared at the healer. "Let me put it to you this way, Nathan," Hercule continued. "It may be of great benefit if he knows in advance what types of injuries she will experience. I assume that is what we are thinking, *oui?*"

Mr. Marble ran a hand through his hair and exhaled as he took his seat. "Yeah."

"Are you ready for that, *ma chére?*" the *cafard* turned to me. "This path requires a bit more suffering. For the greater victory. You might be sabotaging your own overall status."

I sat quietly, contemplating my near future. I looked at my healer, the man who would make it possible. "Bring it on."

Chapter Twenty-One

STAGE TWO GOES on for five days, one of which was under my belt. I started the second with a new mission, one laid out by Hercule and Mr. Marble. As successful as I was yesterday, I needed to "fall apart" today. Crumble under pressure. Simply put, lose. I'd been given warning. If my opponent was truly dreadful, and losing would look obvious, then don't—go for the kill. Otherwise, trip, miss, fall off balance, do whatever I needed to throw the matches. None of us felt proud of that. But we all agreed it would make for a more spectacular finish. "Don't worry," Mr. Marble said to me, "we'll play for keeps in stage three. That's what will really matter."

As a result of my utter incompetence I didn't advance my standings at all on the second day. I remained a level seven. New rosters got handed out at night for the bouts the following day. Mr. Smith and Mr. Wesson took my list and, like they did the night before, gathered the new stats on my next opponents.

On the third day I was allowed and encouraged to beat the worst of the worst. "Anyone less than level seven you should solidly defeat," Mr. Marble told me. So I did. Easily, given the intense training I'd had.

It was on the third day that I first died. My opponent, a wraith, brought with him a scimitar. I won the coin toss and I used my talent —no getting around that, since I'd used that technique successfully the first day. But when I swung my hammer I didn't use full force. His cloud didn't completely separate, and he remained active for his turn. He bound me—seemed like all the wraiths had a "Bind" talent—my arms to my sides. When he went for me with his sword, I moved, albeit slowly. It went through my armor and me, like butter.

I'd never felt such pain before, so bright, so sharp, so ... complete. I dropped to my knees, staring at the hilt in my abdomen. It took everything from me, my heartbeat, my breath ... my life. Warm blood poured between my suit and my belly. I felt this cloud form around me, a dark shroud of my own. I hit the mat, eyes upward, trying to see, trying to focus on life. My healer came, I think. I saw his figure. I looked into his hood to see his face. Eyes of blue and green. But the blackness punched down, taking the last thing I had in life, my sight.

I woke with start, body arched, hand clutching at the floor, and my lungs screaming for merciful air. Only minutes passed, I was told. It felt longer. Deeper. It felt like breaking through a cement casing, like a butterfly out of a cocoon. Or so I gathered from snippets on Animal Planet.

Hands helped me stand on new, baby foal legs. My wonderful heart beat again, coursing hot blood through my fingers and toes. I laughed, observing my own hands. *I was alive!*

"Mrs. Witherspoon?" I knew that voice. Wait a moment ... "Can you hear me?"

I nodded. Ah. That was Mr. Marble. The fog on my mind was clearing ... tournament, scimitar,... *blue-green eyes of my healer.* I recalled that detail now. Kind. Gentle. Concerned. Still unrecognizable. "Yes," I answered, as I stood upright. A flurry of people left the room, and another flurry settled in for the next match.

Mr. Marble wrapped his arm around my waist, pushing me towards the ropes. With each step my strength returned. Once I reached the edge I pushed him away, able to stand and walk on my own. "I supposed that had to happen sooner or later," I grumbled.

"We had hoped later," he, too, grumbled.

I looked down. Blood stained my leathers, even though they'd been repaired by the healer's touch. "I have to go clean this," I said. "Mustn't look bad for the next fight."

I purposely left Mr. Marble perplexed as I made my way to the suite.

~ ~ * ~ ~

By the fifth and final day of stage two I had only advanced to a level nine. The Chancellor stopped by to wish me luck on the day, but I overheard him express disappointment in our house this year. Maybe he tried to motivate me, or just subtly tell us he was onto my failures. I'm not sure anyone would have guessed that the new kid on the block, the one replacing the old king of the block, would purposely throw fights.

But then not everyone was Esmeralda.

I won two bouts on the fifth day which squarely placed me at a level ten—we were shooting for somewhere between eight and fifteen, so I claimed victory.

Dinnertime. My entourage and I sat at our table in the grand hall enjoying, of all things, pizza. Surprisingly good pizza, considering we weren't on the plane known to have invented the stuff.

A shadow creeped up and loomed behind me. A shiver ran down my spine. I turned to see "Sister of Malador." I addressed her as so.

She extended a hand. "I don't believe we have been properly introduced. I am Esmeralda, Queen of Diamond Realm, Radiant Plane."

"Yes," I nodded, snubbing her handshake, "I know." I held up my pizza, hoping it would offer a reason I chose not to shake her hand. Fact was, I didn't want to touch her.

She raised one eyebrow, impatiently. I kicked Mr. Marble under the table. "Orator?"

"Ah. Esmeralda, let me introduce the champion of Gateway Manor, Midland Plane, Mrs. Winki Witherspoon."

I bowed, keeping my seat at the table. "Charmed," I said with my mouth full.

"We meet tomorrow, dear child," she said to me.

"I know."

"Your first battle in the next stage of combats. Are you excited?" She almost sang her words, in the most insincere song.

"Got goosebumps," I said, holding out my leather coated arm. "This whole thing is pretty freaky," I waved my pizza around to indicate the room.

"It can be overwhelming," she nodded. "Which is why I took the liberty of talking to the Chancellor, on your behalf, you see. I didn't get the impression that you were quite ready to advance into the big leagues, shall we say?"

I cast a quick glance at Mr. Marble. "I'm not getting your point."

"I don't think you're ready. You haven't quite shown competency in the stage two rounds, and quite frankly, those are the easiest. But I can't change the order of bouts either, so we must face each other." I nodded to make clear I followed the thought, even though I didn't. "He was quite amenable to changing our bouts rules, given that I, the senior competitor asked for them to be ... lightened. So. When we meet tomorrow it will be using the stage two rules. You should be most familiar with those, since you've used them the last five days."

I hoped my glee didn't show. I thought back to her combat with the lich, and how she tormented the poor thing until I provoked her to end it. First blood is first blood; end of game. But first fall can be prolonged. She can torture me for hours.

I played stupid. "Really?" I said, shocked. "Wow, I don't know what to say ... are you sure you're okay with that?"

"Oh. Quite."

"So we only get one talent and one weapon. And we take moves, like a game of checkers." She smiled, sneered almost, and nodded. "That would be awesome. Thank you," I stood, throwing down my pizza and wiping my hands on my armor, and extended one for a shake. "Thank you so much. See you tomorrow."

"Indeed." She didn't return the gesture. Just turned and left.

Once she was out of earshot I leaned to Mr. Marble. "She's winning the coin toss, I take it."

"Undoubtedly."

I played the bout out in my head. "She takes a swipe, I block, I slow her down—"

"She's very resistant," Mr. Smith said. "It's one of the reasons she's so successful. Slowing her down might not work."

"He's right, especially given your low rating," Mr. Marble nodded. "Once she's close you know what to do."

"Unless she opens with a talent," I said, then asked Mr. Smith, "What else does she have in her arsenal?"

"She's only used *stone* so far."

"I'll wager that's not all she has."

He shrugged. "Most talents from her plane all deal with fire, like summon it, quell it, throw it. We're not sure what she can or can't do, but during this tournament, she's used *stone* a good bit."

"How is 'stone' dealing with fire?" I asked.

He shrugged. "I'm guessing because it's totally resistant to fire."

I suddenly felt ill. "What if I've been set up? What if Malador gave me the shield that stops her nails but not her fire."

Hercule, who squatted just off my plate munching on a piece of crust answered. "That shield is what he claims it is. It was forged in the Aqua Plane. It was made, I believe, specifically to stop her."

Mr. Marble added, "Fire and Water Planes never really got along. Lots of history. Lots of bad blood." He waved his food. "Damn good pizza, though."

A little green man appeared at my right, timidly approaching our table. "Uh, are you Winki Witherspoon?" the goblin asked. I recognized him as the one who sat next to me at Esmeralda's bout days ago.

"I am. And you are?"

"Theodore."

I couldn't help but raise my eyebrows. I'd fought a number of goblins by now and they all had names like Herithon, Avonroo, and Grunuck. Not Theodore. "What can I do for you, Mr. Theodore?"

"I don't know if you remember me. I was with Malador when he came to your home a couple of weeks ago."

The attack. "I'm sad to say I was a bit preoccupied, what with defending the house and all. Sorry."

"Oh, I understand. Turns out it was a good thing for me. I got a better job somewhere else." He pointed across the room. "Gentilly Realm. Aqua Plane. I work for King Hector, now. Better pay. And a good dental plan."

"Well, good for you," I said, offering my fist. The little guy's eyes flew wide and he ducked. "No, no. I'm not hitting you. I'm offering what we call a *fist bump*. I make a fist, you do the same, and we bump them together. It's a type of handshake, but more a show of solidarity." I made a fist again. With reservation he did the same, then we bumped. He beamed in pride, which showed off his impressive smile.

"Wow!" Mr. Smith nodded at his smile. "That is a good dental plan."

"Like that?" He flashed his ivories. He pointed to one in particular. "Got that bad boy fixed just last week. Anyway, some of us goblins heard about your bout tomorrow with Queen Red Hair and, since you're not doing very well, we wanted you to have this." Nervously he looked left, and right. He came close to me and presented his palm. In it was a medallion of some kind, silver and delicately etched. "It's a gonzo. Very powerful. Belongs to the King himself. It doesn't affect your own talent, but it greatly lowers your opponent's resistance."

"Would it be allowed?" I asked Mr. Marble.

"It's not a weapon, nor a talent. It's just an amulet. Considered part of you attire."

"I would be honored," I said to Theodore.

He handed me the necklace and held up a fist. I bumped it. He started off, then turned and added, "By the way, you have a lovely home."

Hiding the necklace under the table, I gave it a closer look. "The enemy of my enemy," I whispered.

"And she has so many enemies," Hercule said with his little cheeks full of crust.

~ ~ * ~ ~

The start of the day involved a bit of pomp and hoopla, since the stage three bouts were coming. These were the real fights, the ones that not only establish your level but rank you in the overall standings. At the end of the fifth day the top sixteen would start the next stage; everyone else would become observers and audience.

My entourage, my party, my healer, and I arrived to our designated ring early. Not early enough. A crowd had already assembled on the bleachers around the ring. I'd been to a number of these now, none this well-attended. I felt butterflies in my stomach. I had counted on talents, and razor sharp nails, and possible fire balls, but not stage fright.

"It's a match like any other, she made sure of that," Mr. Marble encouraged.

I took a shaky breath. "Why are they all here?"

"Are you kidding? They're here for you, Winki. They want to see you kick her ass. Now, let's not disappoint, okay?'"

My hands trembled. The butterflies turned to ravens. "I really don't want to do this," I stammered.

My healer moved in front of me. Without words he put his hands on my face, cupping it. They were very warm to the touch. I couldn't resist putting my own hands over them. I closed my eyes, enjoying the contact. My stomach fell silent. My mind turned glacial. My heartbeat slowed and steadied, its rhythm subtly rocking my body as I stood there. He slowly let go, his fingers caressing my cheeks as they left my face. I felt grounded. Confident. He hid his hands quickly, covering them in the folds of his large sleeves.

He turned away, and I grabbed him by the arm, stopping him. "Thank you," I said. He nodded and took his seat ringside.

"Now," Mr. Marble said, "when she enters the ring and you hear the word, 'begin' what are you going to do?"

"I have the shield ready, so I'll—"

"No," he stopped me. "First I want you to see her. Look at her. I mean a hard look. What do you see?"

I remembered the lich. I remembered its suffering. I remembered her wicked indulgence in its pain. "That wretched woman," I answered.

Esmeralda entered the room, her green cape just touching the floor as it widely floated behind her. Mr. Marble took me by the shoulders and pointed me at the woman. He moved his lips close to my ear so only I could hear his soft whisper. "Here's what I want you to see. I want you to see Will tied to the floor of this very ring, arms and legs stretched wide. I want you to see the puddle of blood he lay in, the blood spray coating these bleachers. I want you to see his internal organs wrapped around the ropes. I want you to see his eyes wide with terror, and pain, and madness. I want you to see what I see. Each and every time I look at her." By the end he seethed through his teeth. It matched the seething in my soul.

His words put me in a trance. I watched her remove her cape and gracefully duck the rope as she climbed into the ring. She tilted her head, seeing the shield I had at my side. I raised it into position, ensuring she could see the crest. Esmeralda gave me a hot glare.

"Brother-of-yours sends his best," I said.

We took our places, the room went silent. I looked at the board. Her talent was listed as "Bind." Not my favorite. One last cast at the audience. I spied Malador along the back, with Colonel Mustard not far from him. It was standing room only.

She won the coin toss.

"Begin."

She took three steps toward me and swiped her claw-formed hand at me. I raised the shield, and with a *zing*, sparks flew in every direction. With an audible grunt she took a step back, clutching her hand.

I filled my head with that horrible image, my husband as her prisoner. I raised my hand. "No!" I screamed. I felt a strike of heat in my chest. The amulet hidden beneath my armor reacted.

Esmeralda stood there, nearly frozen in time. I waited just a moment, just so her gaze could catch up with my face, just so she could fully know what was to come. With a Pete Townsend maneuver I swung my hammer in a large circle that came upwards to her jaw. The impact felt true. And very satisfying. Esmeralda flew high into the air. Once she left the confines of the ring she snapped back into time, somewhere around twenty feet above ground, and her body limply tumbled like a despised rag doll tossed carelessly aside. She landed unconscious on some patrons in the bleachers behind her, who no more wanted her touching them than I did. Her face was smashed beyond recognition.

"Winner. House of Gateway."

The attendees of the room jumped to their feet. The roar of their cheering was so painful I had to cover my ears. All of my party ran onto the ring, stumbling and clapping, and I received a big group hug; a Smith, Wesson, Mrs. White, Jeeves, and Winki sandwich. All but Mr. Marble and my healer. When my staff moved away I made a point of hugging my healer. "Thank you!" I said. "I mean it. I couldn't have focused without your help." He returned my hug gently, as if I were made of glass, and lowered his head next to mine, in a receptive gesture. I noticed Mr. Marble raised his red robe's hood over his head. "You okay?" I asked.

He didn't answer for a moment as he watched Esmeralda's healer do his work. "It wasn't enough," he whispered. "It just wasn't enough."

He started to leave. "Mr. Marble?" He waited. "Is this really the ring they found him in?"

Without answering he stormed off. The roach appeared on my shoulder. "No, *madam*. It was not this ring."

I watched Mr. Marble until he disappeared into the crowd of people, now looking like spawning salmon, exit the room.

I went into the battle a lever ten. Esmeralda was a level forty-four. The victory should have been clear, but the disparity of her loss was so great it cost her rank. Which was the plan. She would have to win all of her battles in stage three to qualify for the next phase. And fight opponents vastly better than me.

We did want we had wanted to do. We took her out of the games. If I went home now, I should feel quite accomplished. Only trouble was ... I didn't.

Chapter Twenty-Two

AFTER THE WIN, and after a nap, I made my way to the next bout. Just me and my healer—Mr. Marble hadn't been seen since. But I felt better. I walked taller with a pep in my step.

"Champion! Champion!" called a voice from behind. It was my goblin ally.

"Theodore!" I called, glad to see him. "Dude, please call me Winki."

"I, er ... Goblins don't address their superiors by their common names."

"You did me a solid." I held out my fist, and he bumped it. "Please, call me Winki." I pulled the amulet out from under my leather jacket. "What's the protocol here ... shall I just give this back to you or do I need to see the King himself? I owe him thanks as well."

"That's why I'm here. He'd like dinner with you this evening, if," he gave a grand little bow, "you can spare the time."

"Of course. Tell King Hector of Gentilly Realm I'd be honored to take dinner with him this evening."

"Cool. You can keep if for the day, use it if you like." He scampered off. "See you then."

As I walked my mind drifted to the shrouded man behind me. He had confessed he knew me to Mr. Marble. In my curiosity I was piecing together an image of him.

Him, yes, definitely a human man. Caucasian, from just a slight glimpse of the hands that held my face. Tall and wiry build, almost waif-like, which I felt in the hug. Blue-green eyes, I'm almost certain of that. But that didn't describe anyone I knew. Or thought I knew.

I entered the ring for my next bout. Mr. Marble didn't rejoin us. His grief was clear. Hard not to feel sorry for him, as much as I disliked the man.

My opponent this time was a lich. Lich number four. That's what the board read: *Winki vs. Lich #4.* When he lumbered into the ring I recognized him as the lich Esmeralda tormented. Also listed on the board were his weapons, sword and poison—always something new to experience here—and his talents, *Blind, Choke,* and *Fear.* Now that we were allowed to beat the living snot out of each other we could bring everything and anything to the game.

"I can guess what Blind and Choke do," I said to Hercule on my shoulder, "But what's *Fear?*"

"*Fear* is exactly that. He can make you feel fear, a great deal of it. You cannot resist it, and because we took the low road to get here, you likely can't. It may stop you. Your heart will race, your hands will tremble, and you'll have to muddle through panic. It is a very powerful talent, *ma chére.*"

I took a deep, calming breath to steady my already raised heartbeat.

No coin tosses now. We would just come out fighting.

"Begin."

I took a wide legged stance, left hand out in front of me ready to block, and my right, hammer in hand, resting on the small of my back. I liked them to move first. I waited.

The lich crawled right up to me and stood there. I looked into the big, beady, black eyes. Was he waiting, too? He drew out his sword then ... tossed it out of the ring.

"Winner. House of Gateway."

"Wait. What?" I looked at him.

He growled, then lumbered out of the ring, retrieved his sword, and left the room.

"What?" I asked, spinning to my team.

Jeeves stood erect. "I can't tell if that is good news or bad."

"What?" I asked again. Demanded, really.

"It would seem," Hercule said, crawling his way up my torso to my shoulder, "we have been found out. The act of laying down one's weapon is an act of surrender."

"He gave up?" I asked. "We didn't even get to fight."

"Your competitors put it together. They know you kept yourself at a low rank to achieve some goal. Until this morning they did not know what. I believe they approve. So, knowing that you sacrificed your own standing to eliminate the witch, they are sacrificing battles, so you may regain some lost ground."

"It won't last, madam," Jeeves explained as we headed back to the suite. "Just a few will."

"It is refreshing, isn't it, child," Mama cooed, "to know even the dark ones have scruples."

Hm. *Dark ones have scruples.*

My next match wasn't until after the midday meal. They scheduled much more time for the stage three matches, and since mine took no time at all I headed back to my room.

Since I'd napped already—I admit, I didn't sleep well last night, worried about the meet with Esmeralda—I sat at the window, looking out into the bright orange vista and the black landscape below. My cockroach joined me, sitting on the sill.

"We are proud of you," he offered. I shifted my gaze to him. His shell covering was a rich brown color. I extended my hand and, with my index finger, stroked his back. I'd never touched him before. "You do not fear me any longer?"

"I never feared roaches. I just don't like them. They're unpredictable."

"Bah! You screamed when we first met." He did a small dance. "In what way, unpredictable?"

"When roaches see you they're just as likely to run towards you. Any rational creature should run *away*."

"Hm. Like a wolf?"

I laughed. "That's the point. Things to be afraid of come at you."

Below my window was the cherry tree. Its leaves splashed the only color you could see for miles, other than orange. "Why a cherry tree?" I asked. "Why not an oak or some other kind of tree?"

"Who knows. Perhaps it meant something to *la bohéme*."

Cherries. My dream of Will suddenly flashed in my head. We were at an ice cream store. *Will was eating ice cream.* "Oh. My. God!"

"What?" Hercule panicked, scuttling in every direction. "What is it?"

"He wasn't talking about the *day*. He was talking about the food. *Sundaes!*"

The *cafard* stopped. "You have lost the Great Hercule."

"*Never on a sundae.* Hercule, we never put cherries on our sundaes. Will hated maraschino cherries." I looked out the window. "It's in the tree. It's got to be in the tree."

I dashed to the door. Out of the corner of my eye Hercule raced beside then ahead of me. "No! No, *madame*! You cannot!" He managed to get to the doorknob before me. "Please! You cannot go outside. You are not protected there."

"It's in the tree. Will left something for me in the cherry tree."

"Perhaps so, but you cannot got out there. The protections of *la Citadelle* do not extend into the territory around it. You can be hurt there. Possibly killed."

"But I have to—"

"Do not think for a moment that, from now on, that rotting carcass of a woman won't be looking for something gruesome and torturous to do to you. I will not allow such an opportunity. No. You cannot leave *la Citadelle.*"

"The Citadel didn't save Will, did it?"

He flustered, looking for words, as he danced back and forth. With a sigh he said, "What? What is it you seek?"

"A DVD. Will left me a DVD."

"Fine. I will go and see if anything is there first. If so, we will all discuss how to proceed. I'm sure Nathan will happily—"

"No!" I stopped him. In a hushed tone I said, "No one else should know."

"But, why not, *ma chére?* The others can go out in secret and retrieve—"

Again I stopped him. "Someone betrayed Will, someone in this house. Someone, I'm confident, who is here, now." I knelt down to look at him. "Hercule, they killed Will. They tried to kill me, and when that failed, they killed everyone who was there in the park, anyone involved with my shooting." He didn't move. "Please don't tell anyone. I don't want them beating me to it." The words hit me hard. "I really need that DVD."

I bit my lip as I sat on the floor, my back against the door. My vision blurred. I felt Hercule crawl his way to my knee. With a sniff I wiped my eyes.

"I will go," he softly said. "I will look. I will tell no one."

"Thank you."

He scurried off across the floor, up and over the window sill, all the while muttering to himself, "Why this needs to be done now, Hercule wonders. Such a human thing, this impatience. We don't even have a DVD player with us, *pour l'amour de Dieu ...*"

The knock on the door startled me. "Madam?" Jeeves called from the other side, "your midday meal is ready."

"Lunch, Jeeves," I stood, wiping my face free of wet. "Those of us from the Midland Plane call it lunch."

~ ~ * ~ ~

I had four bouts on my schedule that afternoon. All of the, *all of them*, went the same way as the lich. My opponent bowed, or nodded, or smiled, then tossed his or her or its weapon out of the ring.

"Winner. House of Gateway."

The last man, Colonel Mustard, offered a warm handshake after the call. His dress amused me a bit. He looked like a leather version of a civil war re-enactor; high collar, blazing gold buttons, oversized gauntlets, and epaulets on each shoulder. His leather pants pouched over his thighs, tucking into his leather riding boots. "Well done, madam," he smiled.

"Oh, for the love of peanut butter. You know full well I did nothing."

"Ah, madam, but you did. And it is not only appreciated by those who fell to her before you, it was very, what is the word," he put a finger to his lips, "*satisfying*."

"Colonel," I said, "I, um, want to apologize about our first meeting. At opening ceremonies? I was misinformed as to your friendship with the house. I'm so sorry if I angered, or distressed you in any way."

He offered his hand, and I took it. He bowed, brushing the back of my hand with his mustache, then stood. "It is a hard and complicated world you and I live in. I understand, and accept your apology. But I must tell you it ends here." My eyebrows shot upward. "The gratis. Come tomorrow you'll be expected to come out swinging. There will be no holds barred." He leaned closer, "And I suspect you'll do just fine." He left with his own entourage, but just before reaching the door turned back and called, "Oh, and please give my best to Hector. He is a damned fine lad."

Chapter Twenty-Three

I HAD A stop to make before my dinner with King Hector. It was time to see if Malador would live up to his end of the bargain.

Shield in tow, I trotted through the dark Citadel halls hoping to catch Malador before he left for dinner. My healer kept pace behind me.

The door to his tower's common room swung open as he and his party were leaving. He scowled when he saw me.

"Malador," I offered his shield, "my house and I give you thanks."

He gave me a hard look, took the shield, and handed it to one of his party. He turned to walk away. I jumped in front of him, making it clear there was more to do.

"What do you want?" he asked in a dismissive voice.

"The name."

"Hardly. You didn't live up to your end of the bargain." He moved off.

Again, I moved into his path. "I disagree."

"I told you she needed to suffer."

"You told me she needed to be humiliated. And she was."

With two small and greased-lightning steps Malador moved deeply into my personal space. With equal speed my healer managed to get his shoulder in between us. He did nothing more, only proved his diligent and protective intention.

Malador looked the man up and down. Until that moment I hadn't seen the family resemblance, that desire to hate and hurt that permeated Esmeralda's eyes. It was there, now, in Malador's leer at my healer. "Well, look at you," he sang into the healer's ear. I could barely hear the words. "You're not a healer at all, just a puppy dog. I promise you," his voice chilled me, "I will find out who you are, and I will have you work for me next year." He gruffly gripped my healer's chin, over his cloak. My healer staggered a bit, trying to free himself as Malador hissed. "Won't you just love having to heal the man to tortures you all night long."

"Hey!" I shoved Malador off him. "The name!"

The sound of swords liberated from their sheaths filled my ears as his party armed themselves.

Malador caught himself against the hallway wall. He held up a hand, quelling his angered followers. He then erected his body, brushing off any dusk from the stone. He yanked slightly on his jacket, breaking it free of wrinkles. "If I were you," he said coldly, "I'd keep my eye on my lawyer." Then he turned and marched away, party behind him.

We both watched him as he turned the corner out of view. My healer hung his head. "Hey." I put a hand on his arm. "Are you all right?" He looked at my hand. "Did he hurt you?"

The hood shook *no*.

"That's not a real threat, right? He can't do that." The healer didn't move. "Surely you could request a new competitor to serve. Or protest? There must be some course of action you could take if you were abused." He shook his head. "Are you telling me you're just a ... a *slave* here?" He nodded once. I dropped my hand, shocked at the concept. "Thank you," I said. "But you don't have to protect me. You're here to heal me. Maybe it's best for us both if we stick to that."

As he bowed I turned and headed off. My head swam with bitter thoughts of slavery. *There was so much I didn't understand about this world.* I decided there and then to stop trying to figure out who he was. It might be best not to know. For his sake.

~ ~ * ~ ~

Good King Hector of the Gentilly House of the Aqua Plane was known for his jolly demeanor. Not by me, of course, as I knew no one. But when I came to his tower the air of the Citadel seemed charged with positive ions. It felt warmer here. I noticed my pace lightened with glee as I drew near the tower door. I knocked. "Winki!" exclaimed the goblin Theodore as he opened the door. "Come in, come in. Have a seat or look around. His royalness will be with you shortly."

"Thank you, Theodore."

By stepping over the threshold I was transported into another plane altogether. Not really, we remained in the Citadel, but this lot took it upon itself to own and redecorate its tower.

The sea-foam green walls—not the drab black covering the rest of the building—appeared to move, swaying like a soft current. The curve of the staircase looked like strands of sea weed frozen into helpful steps. A school of shiny, silver fish swam by. They stopped to inspect me. I reached out a timid hand to touch them. Before I could they scattered, quickly disappearing in one direction. "But how ...?" I stammered.

A jovial laugh answered. "Magic, my dear!" He entered the room, a large but powerful looking man. Half man from waist up, half seahorse below.

He swished up to me then floated at arms length. His brown eyes twinkled, his long silver hair flowed out and around him, as if we were under water.

"I don't know the protocol, King Hector," I said as I bowed. "So please don't be insulted if I'm supposed to curtsy, or something. I've never met a king before."

"Champion Winki! I have little use for protocol here. Please, do. Take a look around."

A sting ray floated by me, its wings slowly fluttering their motion. I put my hand out to feel the air around me. *Oh my goodness!* "Are we under water?"

"We are. You are in air. That is the power of the Citadel. Otherwise our planes could not intersect, and we could not gather together."

"You called it *magic*," I smiled. "I'm told there is no such thing."

"As a rule we keep such terms to ourselves."

He floated beside me as I paced about the room, my jaw dropped and my eyes wide. I reached out to touch a starfish lodged on a mantle. It felt prickly, just as it would in my world. "Fascinating." I looked at Theodore. "How is it goblins work for you? They seem more earth bound."

"Goblins are one of the few creatures who can happily exist in any plane."

"Absolutely amazing," I sang, dazzled. "This world is such a mystery to me."

"You are the mysterious one," he said. "The new power to the powerful House of Gateway. You've done an excellent job of keeping your talents secret. None of my spies could find them out. A good way to keep your enemies guessing, I suppose."

Suddenly, I was reminded I might not be in the company of friends.

"Hm," I mused, watching the jellyfish gape and maw. "What makes you think I don't only have the one?"

"Time guardian? Your only talent? It is much too strong. Typically, easier talents manifest sooner. Time control is one of the most difficult, most powerful. So, surely you have lesser powers, too. You are wise to keep them hidden."

That was an interesting piece of news.

"Speaking of hidden," I retrieved the amulet from under my jacket, freed the chain from around my neck, and held it out for the king. "Thank you, so very much."

He held it up, letting the silver coin spin and reflect bluish light. "I hoped it served you well."

"You didn't get to see?"

"My own first battle occurred while yours did. But I heard the story. I'll wager it will be told frequently over the next few weeks. Possibly years." He laughed. A hearty, jolly laugh. "Please. The food is ready. Let us sit and eat."

We did. After hours of talking, laughing, eating and drinking, the pleasant night gave way to my own fatigue. I said "goodnight" and "thank you" again, then made my way back to my suite.

Once I cleared the doorway of the Aqua Plane I noticed the cockroach on the wall.

"Hercule? Where have you been?"

"What do you mean, *madame*? I've been searching the tree," he crawled along the wall at eye height as I walked. "That is what you asked the Great Hercule to do, no? The menial task of searching—"

I didn't let him finish complaining. "That was hours ago."

"It is a big tree. I am but a little bug!"

Without further words we walked home, my healer behind us. Once in our lodging I chatted idly with my party about King Hector, but yawned, making it clear I wanted to end the day. My healer took his seat on the cot, and Hercule and I headed up the stairs.

I sat on my bed, propped up with pillows, and picked up the conversation there. "And? Did you find anything?" I asked in hushed tones.

He danced on the pillow next to me, left-and-right. Then

stopped. "Oui."

I punched the air. *I found it. I figured it out.* Now I just had to get it. "Will you help me?" I asked him.

"*Bien sûr.*"

"Tonight. After everyone else is asleep. I want to get the disk."

"I know this thing is important to you but leaving *la Citadelle* is very, very dangerous."

"You'll be my lookout. Warn me if I'm spotted, but I have to do this, Hercule. Just tell me where it is. It should be quick."

"It is inside the tree, itself. Master Will must have cut a hole. But the tree has healed a bit. You will need to bring something sharp to dig it out."

I'd put my knife on my nightstand. "I'll use this." I inspected the small blade as I took it from its sheath. Easy to conceal. It would be ideal.

"You met with Malador," he asked, changing the subject.

"Yes. I did."

"What did he say?"

I thought about it. I decided to keep the information to myself. "He told me what I wanted to hear."

"Does that mean you don't believe him?"

"That means nothing is clearer. At least not to me." I rested my head against the bed's headrest. "I don't know who to trust. I'm tired of being scared and angry. I'm hoping the DVD will have some answers." I closed my eyes. "I need answers."

"I fear to say that you might never find them. This world is complex. Light and dark doesn't always mean good or bad, or honest or dishonest."

"Like how we cheated to best Esmeralda?"

He chuckled. "Case in point, *oui.*"

My mind went back to my encounter with Malador, and his threat. "Tell me about the healers."

"What is it you want to know?"

"Who are they?"

"They are ... healers. I do not understand the question."

"Are they slaves here in the Citadel?"

"Ah! You want to know where they came from, their history, *n'est-ce pas?*"

"*Oui,*" I said.

He scurried onto the bed's footboard and sat upright, crossing one leg over the other. "Long long ago, long before anyone even conceived of *la Citadelle*, the planes warred for control over all planes, everhwhere. In the great war, the last war, a new faction emerged, changing the balance of everything. It was those we now call 'the healers'. They'd always been there, but it wasn't until the end, when they were neither on the side of good or evil but their own, that chaos ensued."

"What did they want?"

"What everyone wants. Power. They themselves are not moved or swayed by either good or evil. They felt that made them superior, they were above the pettiness of the warlords. That was their mistake. You are now very aware of the saying, no? The enemy of my enemy is my ally."

"So light and dark joined to suppress the healers."

"*Conquered* is a better word. They were slaughtered, and those who survived were enslaved. Forced to work for one side or the other."

"Slaughtered? They can't heal themselves?"

"The war was long ago, even before the Great Hercule. So I know not about how they heal, or how they were destroyed. But I do know that here, in *la Citadelle*, they have no choice. They are healed, and they must heal." So the threat was real. Malador could torture the healer, who would heal himself, only to be forced to heal his brutal master in turn. Hercule did a little thinking dance. "In a way they are partly responsible for this very fortress. Once light and dark joined forces, they found other common ground. *La Citadelle* was a good place to end the ongoing wars and keep the healers locked away."

"The healers are slaves, then."

"In modern times, only here. Only now. They are allowed to leave when the games are finished and live their normal lives in whatever plane they call home. But they are required by law to come here and serve during tournament, wearing the shabby robes to remind them of their place. Any healer that fails to show up is hunted down and executed."

"Sounds brutal."

"It is better than it was. Not long ago, once a child was determined to be a healer, they were swept away from their families and raised in squalor. The only time they ever saw light was during tournament. Now, healers must register and attend, but they can live wherever and however they choose, otherwise."

"Their anonymity ensures that."

"*Oui.* It is more important to them than to us. Some houses or realms have their own healers, those they've captured and enslaved. Once a healer is discovered he or she is at great risk."

Why, then, would a healer betray my husband and bring him to Esmarelda? What could he have gained? Sounds like the only thing a healer couldn't gain for themselves was ultimate freedom. It also seemed like the only thing no one else could or would grant them.

"I think it is time," Hercule said. "Let me make sure the others sleep. Stay here, *ma chére.*" He disappeared under the door.

I expected him to ask why I trusted him. Fact was I didn't. This would be his test. If the DVD was still there, and if he didn't betray me to Esmeralda or Malador, then I could confidently cross him off my list.

This night, I would know one way or another about the Great

Hercule Poirot.

Chapter Twenty-Four

I TIPTOED PASSED my sleeping healer with the *cafard* on my shoulder. The others slept tucked away in their little rooms. The perpetual light from outside had one advantage; it made it easy to get around in the night—there was no dark.

Carefully, I closed our suite's door and skulked through our tower's common area, then padded into the network of tunnels. I put Hercule on the wall. The process was painfully slow; he'd scurry out then back. "Is clear." I wanted to run through the place and out the doors. I wanted so much to hold the DVD in my hands.

The halls appeared empty and unguarded. Good, I thought as we rounded the last corner. The enormous double doors stood between me and the outside. A large piece of wood suspended in thick metal plates acted as a lock. I gave it a hard look, ensuring it didn't hide some alarm or trigger. Once satisfied I hoisted the beam upward and out of its cradle. Damn thing was heavier than it looked.

With a grunt, a quiet grunt, I managed to push the log aside. I opened the door just enough to slip through and raced to the cherry tree.

Hercule instructed me where to look. "On the side away from the pathway, away from the building, away from the portals. Will had hid it where no one would find it by accident." I dipped below the tree's outstretched arms, until I could touch the trunk. "That crack,"

Hercule said, "Just up. It's in there, *ma chére.*"

I could see it, the plastic jewel case just a half inch below the skin of the tree. I got out my knife and began to chip and chisel, trying not to harm the tree while freeing the disk inside. After what seemed like hours, with a little leverage from the knife tip I could push one end down; the other popped out just enough to pinch it free. "Gotcha," I whispered, and kissed the case. I tucked the media into my jacket. "*Allons-y!*" I said to Hercule.

With relief I headed back to the grand doors. Something moved. I stopped. The air began to move and contort. *A portal was forming.*

"You must hide," Hercule said. "Quickly!"

I looked around. With the exception of the cherry tree now too far behind me to reach in time there were no features. No rocks, no trees, not even a bush. Nothing to hide behind.

I raced to the door. My only hope of not being found out was to get back inside before whoever made the portal stepped through. My legs, trained to move quickly over the last few weeks, moved me swiftly past the portal and straight at the gate. I had never run so hard and fast in my life, forcing my oxygen starved thigh muscles to pump harder and harder. I was almost there. Just a few more steps—

With a boom the door shut solidly. *Dammit!* I heard the wooden bar shift back into place.

I grabbed my hammer and turned to face ...

"Well, well, well," Malador said, surrounded by a dozen goblins. "What do we have here?" He slowly walked towards me. "My bride-to-be out taking an evening stroll. Didn't that incompetent group tell you? You have no protection outside the Citadel."

My knife in one hand, my hammer in another, I watched him while my peripheral vision focused on the rest of them. He stalked closer.

"Are you afraid to face me alone?" I spat. "Needing a small army at your side?"

"I don't care about rules or honor or fairness, my love. I've told you all along. I want you. And now, *you're mine. Take her!*"

I tried to focus my rage. I held up my hand and to stop them with the talent, but ... *it didn't work!*

"Behind you!" Hercule cried out. Pain coursed through my legs, bringing me to the floor. A goblin cut me with his sword.

They came at me all at once. I struggled to my feet. I cut the one nearest me with my knife, then bashed the one behind me with the hammer. I spun low, ducking a blow from an ax while kicking the feet out of another. I managed to push the pain of my leg back into my mind while I popped a goblin with my elbow, then punched another with my fist. But they still came, slicing and battering. The height difference between us gave them an advantage. They focused on my legs and hips, bringing me to my knees a second time. Despite the my frantic struggling, they subdued me, arms outstretched, and forced me to kneel before the incubus. One of them had a handful of my white hair, pulling my head back mercilessly.

As he came towards me Malador took off his leather glove, pulling each finger one at a time. Hot tears of defeat streaked down my face as he moved in. *Don't let him touch you*, I heard Mr. Marble say. *Once he touches you, you're his.*

"Now, now," he said, reaching out. "Don't struggle. You'll learn to love me." His fingers delicately brushed my cheek and ...

Every cell, every nerve, every fiber of my being exploded with white, hot, intense desire. My nails and hair and skin and organs, crushed my senses into a myopic microscopic point of arousal. My loins shivered with ecstasy. The flush of lust blazed from the top of my head to my tiniest toe. I wanted this man, no ... I *needed* this man. *Touch me ... please!*

"See?" he said as petted my face, "it's not so bad."

Will. I tried to call out his name. I flooded my mind with his memory, his laughter, his taste, his spirit ... but this stroke, so soft, so delicate as to almost tickle, brushed my husband from my brain, like fine dust from an old book. My body quaked in anticipation. *Glorious anticipation.*

He moved closer, his lips just a breath from my own. I wanted it, dearly, to touch him ... to kiss him ... *I wanted* ... He stopped moving nearer. *Bloody hell*, he was making me come to him. *He was making me want him.*

A freezing flash of lightning coursed through me, chilling me to the bone and sharply breaking the trance. I was suddenly free, free of the desire, free of the want, free of the lust. My muddled mind searched for clarity. Some of the goblins that held me let go. Somewhere I heard a struggle. It took moments for my senses to return, and when my eyes could see, they witnessed Malador. Fighting my healer.

All goblin eyes watched the fight, too, which made them easy prey for me. I focused on a group, held up my hand and thought, "No! Not again." It only affected a couple, and I let loose on them, thumping left and right with my hammer.

"A portal!" a retreating goblin called. "Quickly!"

I kept at them as the portal shimmered its way into existence. Once the sphere formed, some of the goblins, those left standing, ran through.

My healer clearly had had some martial art training. Despite his cloak he had Malador bested, with roundhouse kicks and quick jabs. Malador could only raise his hands in protection, never getting an opportunity to strike. The leather-clad man clumsily fell to the ground and cowardly crawled backwards to get away from my shrouded savior, toward the portal. Once he found his feet beneath him he dashed for it.

My healer let him run away, relaxing his stance. He saw victory, and turned to me. But, I saw the bait and switch. "Behind you!" But it was too late. Just before Malador stepped into the void he threw a knife. My healer turned at my warning, then collapsed, the hilt sticking out from between his ribs.

"*No.*" I raced to the fallen man. Red blood seeped through his brown cloak. Without seeing it I knew the wound was mortal. "Come on," I said, pushing my panic aside, "Heal yourself. Just concentrate!"

Desperately he pointed to the door, his ample sleeve falling away. *The Citadel.* He needed to get to the Citadel to heal.

I looked at the door, which looked miles away, "Yes, I can get you there. Come on—" I stopped. *His hand.* I swallowed.

Forcing myself to concentrate I wrapped my arm around him and hoisted him to standing. He let out a muffled cry as he gripped his side. We hobbled to the opened door he'd left coming to my rescue.

Our feet had barely touched the hallway floor when a shrill sound surrounded us; so bright and sharp an alarm I winced in pain. He collapsed, trying to cover his ears. Looking out I saw dark figures, flying in the sky, making a beeline for us. I tried to close the door, but I couldn't do it quickly enough. Their bodies hit the door, squeezing through the gap. I recognized them. The guardians and protectors of the Citadel. The bone wraith.

"No, you don't understand," I called to them. "We're supposed to be here." Forcing the door wide, they swarmed on us like bees, biting and stinging, kicking, and tearing. We both frantically waved our arms. Within the Citadel walls, I could only fight, my talent suspended. I flashed my knife and hammer as quickly as I could, but there were hundreds. They moved too fast to see, let alone hit.

"Enough!" boomed a voice. The attack diminished immediately. The Chancellor walked down the hallway, the bone wraith lining the walls like ghostly soldiers as he passed them.

My healer remained a huddled mass on the floor. He struggled with the knife still lodged in his side. I put a hand on the hilt. He nodded, ready for me to proceed. "I'm sorry," I said, then I yanked it out of him. His body jerked as the blade separated from his body. He settled with an exhale in a restful, reclined position. I adjusted his cloak, keeping his face and limbs hidden.

"Champion Winki Witherspoon." I looked up at the Chancellor. "Please follow me." He sounded so serious.

My party and many other curious patrons had gathered from our commotion. I swallowed, slowly stood, and like a busted teenager, hung my head as I limped behind the principal. As I passed Jeeves I said, "Please make sure my healer is okay."

"Madam?" he nodded behind me.

I jumped in shock. My healer stood there. On his feet. As if nothing had happened. Without instruction, he knelt before me and started to repair the myriad of cuts on my body, from both the goblins and the wraith. The Chancellor watched and waited patiently as my healer did what healers do. The hall had filled with patrons awakened by our disturbance. I blushed as they watched the tender display, as cut by cut the cloaked man stuck his fingers into my wounds and made them disappear.

Lastly my healer stood. He delicately put his thumb on my lip. I didn't even know it had been split open. I jerked a bit from the initial sting. Seems healing has to hurt, first.

"Now, if you're quite finished," the Chancellor said, "both of you come with me."

I walked a fair distance behind the great mage as he and the bone wraith escorted us to his office, a display intended to shame me. But my mind remained fixated on my discovery, what I saw outside; The healer's hand. I saw the scar there, the one that wrapped around his thumb from his palm to the back. The one he got from the motorcycle accident.

My healer was Detective Sergeant Frost.

Chapter Twenty-Five

"THERE ARE STRICT rules," the Chancellor opened once we were seated, "about leaving the Citadel once the tournament has begun. I'm sorry, Champion Witherspoon. But you are disqualified from the tournament this year."

"Wait ... what? I didn't know that! No one told me."

"Ignorance is never a good excuse." I hung my head. "What could possibly have compelled you to venture out there?"

I was damned if I would tell him about the disk. "I ... Needed ..." *Think, Winki!* Then looked at my healer. *Really? This is the your choice?* "I didn't go there because I wanted to. I was told." I swallowed my pride. *Forgive me.* "My healer told me there was something in the tree I needed to see."

When I accused my healer the Chancellor's eyebrows shot up. "Your healer?"

The cloaked figure next to me turned his head. He had to be furious—he had just saved me.

I turned to him, facing the faceless glare. "He ... told me my husband put something in the tree for me." I implored the Chancellor. "It hasn't been a full year since Will's death. I'm still vulnerable to such ideas. Please. Punish me for my stupidity, but sending us packing will be a terrible blow to my team. They've worked so hard this year. And with so little."

The Chancellor's eyes bore into the healer, who'd hung his head. "Is this true?" he asked.

The healer sat in the chair like stone.

"I'm rather disappointed, number fourteen," the Chancellor said as he came around his desk to stand before us. "You had such potential." Without warning, the old man—this decrepit, frail, shaking, cane-using old man—slugged him, *hard* across the face. The healer sprawled to the floor.

I jumped, surprised, in my seat. The Chancellor grabbed him by the back of the neck. "Maybe forty lashes will loosen your tongue." *You did this, Winki. Now get him out of trouble.*

The Chancellor shoved him harder into the floor, then turned to me, wiping his hand with a kerchief, "I will have another healer sent to you."

"But—"

"We don't tolerate traitors, greed, or misconduct. He will be punished, I assure you. Severely."

I stood, angered. *Stick to it.* "Is that really necessary? After all, it wasn't you he betrayed. It was me. My house. I'd rather keep him." As the healer worked to find his hands and knees, I stood on him with one foot, pushing him into the floor. "My house and I would prefer to deal with him." To sell my rage I envisioned Malador under my foot. So much easier to hate that image. "Besides. Until now he's been an excellent healer."

The Chancellor didn't respond. *Come on. Buy it!* Then he slowly nodded. "Very well. Do with him as you please. Should you change your mind I would understand. The offer for another healer is still yours." He took out his spectacles and began to polish them. "I must warn you, Mrs. Witherspoon, you aren't as clever as you think."

I swallowed, my foot still on the healer's back.

"Your antics to defeat the House of Diamond were not subtle. And after this incident, even if there was treachery involved, you've made quite a fool of yourself and your house. I will look the other way this time, but if any of your party even sneeze in the wrong direction, I will, as you put it, send you packing."

I gruffly heaved my healer to standing. "I understand," I said.

He sat and pointed to the door. "You may go."

To maintain the deception I shoved the healer towards the door.

The Citadel halls were still empty. The day hadn't begun. Anyone who'd been roused by our disturbance had returned back to their towers.

We were halfway to the suite when I turned to my healer. He kept a much greater distance behind me now. When I stopped to face him, he didn't close the gap.

"I'm sorry," I said, hushedly. "I'm so, so, sorry. But I couldn't tell him the real reason why I'd gone outside." As I approached him he stepped away callously. From my jacket I retrieved the DVD. "This is why I was there. Will left this for me in the tree. I had to find it." His lack of reaction cut me. "I just don't know who to trust anymore. But now I know, *I know* I can trust you." Disappointed with myself, I added, "Even though you can't trust me. Here," I handed him the disk, "you take it. Keep it for me. Hide it somewhere only you know. I can't put it anywhere in my suite, not now. Not while there's a traitor sleeping there." Still no reaction. "One of them had to tell Malador I was outside." I licked my lips, and swallowed the wave of soreness in my throat. "One of them is trying to kill me."

Slowly, he reached up and with a sleeve-covered hand took the DVD. It disappeared into his cloak fluidly, like a sleight of hand magic trick.

"Thank you." I reached for his arm, but he pulled it away. "I don't expect you to forgive me for what I just did," I whispered. "Fact of the matter is I will never forgive myself."

I left him alone in the hallway. The shrouded figure so clear to me now, so obvious. I hated the fact that I knew who he was.

I didn't go to the suite. I took a seat on a sofa in the common room of our tower. I curled up into as tight a ball as I could be, trying to disappear from this dark world. Good? Evil? As far as I could tell there was no distinction.

~ ~ * ~ ~

The common door slamming shut woke me with a jolt. I sat upright. Mr. Marble looked at me, stunned. "Why are you there?" he asked.

"Where have you been?" I asked, sharply.

Taken by my words, he approached slowly. "Out. Walking." He collapsed on a chair opposite me. "Thinking."

I didn't know what kind of answer I was looking for, short of "betraying you to Malador." With a sigh I retook my reclined position.

"I don't blame you for your lack of trust," he said, looking at some point in space in front of him. "This is a hard, miserable world. Revenge and murder are lures to the dark. Cross those lines and suddenly, like magic, you're the very thing you hate. The playing field isn't level. They get to succumb. They get to kill. And torture," his eyes winced shut at the word, "then laugh as we stand by, unable do anything." He hid his eyes with his hand. "They get to cheat while we ..." I saw him swallow.

I was convinced his grief was genuine. "You've been walking since the Esmeralda bout?" He nodded. "Your feet must be tired."

He chuckled, thankfully.

Without waiting for him to recover I asked, "Who in this house wanted Will dead?"

"I don't know." He sank into the chair like a slouching teenager. "I would have told you everyone here would have walked through fire for him, or would have followed him back to the dark side, if need be."

"Malador told me you couldn't be trusted."

"I'm not surprised. Classic strategy. Keep you in doubt. You don't trust me, you don't trust the house, so you run to him. They win." He took a deep breath. "They always win."

The door opened again. Mr. Marble shot whoever a hot look. "Where the hell have you been?" I didn't bother to get up. I waited until they came into view.

My healer stopped when he realized I was on the sofa, and stood over me.

Mr. Marble pressed, "Well?"

"Back off, Nathan," I said. "He ran me an errand."

He sat upright. "You just called me 'Nathan.'"

I yawned. "'Mr. Marble' is getting cumbersome." My growling stomach moved me to my suited for breakfast.

But I heard him just before I left earshot. "Interesting. Not clear if you meant the name, or me."

Chapter Twenty-Six

APPARENTLY I HAD won a couple of new talents from yesterday's victories. Today, before my first real battle, I read the board's new listing.

Winki Witherspoon, House of Gateway
Level: 14
Life Points: 152
Talents: Bind, Life, Time-slowing
Weapons: Knife, Hammer

I laughed. "Reads like a personal add. They need to add 'Turn ons: walks along the beach and slow, deep kisses, Turn offs: Demon blood on her clothes.'"

Nathan and my healer both gave me odd looks. Ignoring them I said, "What's *Life*?"

"The potion you won," Nathan said. "When you drink from it you'll heal a bit, get back some life points."

"What about him?" I looked at the healer.

"Only after the bout ends. Until then you have to find a way to work through all the injuries you accumulate."

"And *Bind*," which I knew all too well. "How do I use that?"

"Just, I don't know, use it. Image now how you would call it. It will work. Here the talent simply needs to be summoned."

I looked at Nathan, raised my hand, and closed my fist tightly. With a shift his arms pressed hard against his body. "Yep," he squeaked, "that will do."

I opened my fingers; he almost collapsed.

My opponent entered the ring. A human, woman, someone I didn't know. I read the board:

Anya Slatkva, House of Shlyuz
Level: 32
Life Points: 294
Talents: Air, Lightning, Cleansing
Weapons: Mace, Bow

"*Air?*" I asked.

"She can suffocate you."

"*Lightning?*"

"Just what you think. You'll know when she's calling it. She need a lot of time to gather the energy. Stop her. If she manages it, you're done."

Certain I wasn't going to like the answer, "*Cleansing?*"

"Cleansing of the mind. You'll forget everything. Who you are, why you're here. You won't see it coming." He pronounced the word in perfect Russian. "Shlyuz. It means Gateway."

"Oh. Is it good or bad?"

"Really. Does it matter?"

"Competitors take your places," the voice called. No coin toss now. Just wait for the word.

"Come out swinging," Nathan said with an encouraging tap on the back.

Anya wore a silver suit of armor that made her look like the lady in the opera. She wasn't fat, but the suit, shiny, bulbous, complete with shield and a helmet with horns, struck my funny bone. Elmer Fudd-like. I couldn't help but laugh.

When we two women stood alone the voice said, "Begin."

I did what I always do, being the one trick pony. I held up my hand, "No!"

I felt it flow through me, solidly, unlike how it worked outside. But it had no affect. She was resistant. She raised her bow and fired.

That I could slow, and I stepped out of its way and rushed her, my shield and hammer ready. She blocked my hammer strike with her shield, the clank jarring me.

She swung her mace. I ducked, then spun a kick, making good contact with her feet. She came down in a heap. With my hammer I hit her hard on her chest plate. The boom of the contact rocked the small venue, but didn't do any damage. Anya sat upright quickly, squarely connecting with my forehead with her horned-headdress. I fell backwards, my head ringing.

I knew the recovery was taking too long but my skull felt thick and heavy, my vision blurry and strained. I got up on my hands and knees. She was talking. *She was summoning.*

Through my daze I patted the floor, trying to find my hammer. I found something and threw it at her. It was my leather shield. It was enough; she stopped chanting.

I awkwardly stood to face her. Tink! An arrow destined for my shoulder, bounced off me, like I was made of metal. "Thank you, Smith and Wesson," I said and rushed the woman again, scooping up my hammer on the way. My weapons were up close and personal. If I wanted to win, I'd have to stay in her face.

She swung her mace again, and I moved with it, letting it brush my back and used that momentum to spin me. I reached behind my back for my knife, and when I turned in her direction my arm swept wide, the blade prone.

I sliced her throat wide open.

With a sickening gurgle she drop to the floor and died.

"Game over. Winner, House of Gateway."

I couldn't move, however. I stood there and watched as her healer rushed to her side and did his work.

"You won!" Nathan said, giving me a hug. But I couldn't celebrate. "What's wrong. Healer, check her out."

"I'm fine. I just ... I've never killed another human before. Seems wrong."

We all heard her take that first breath, that gasp for glorious oxygen. I waited. I wanted to see her stand. I wanted to make sure I didn't genuinely harm her.

Her party tried to rush her off the ring. "Madam!" I called. They turned to me, anger and hatred in their eyes. She stepped forward. With an open palm I placed my hand on my chest and bowed to her. I don't know what made me do it. I just wanted her to know it wasn't personal.

She gave a curt but proud nod, then left.

"Okay, I lied, not fine," I said, as my head's pounding began to rattle my teeth. My healer put his hands on my head, his warm fingers nestled in my white locks. *Dammit, I wished I couldn't see his face.* But I clearly saw him, the sergeant in my mind's eye, holding my head.

The healer dropped his hands and backed up, as if I'd pushed him away.

"Hey, buddy, you okay?" Nathan asked him.

The cloaked figure stood there, slumped, clearly upset.

"Okay," I interjected. "Onwards and upwards."

~ ~ * ~ ~

The next three battles went well. For me, anyway, not so much for my opponents. My hand combat training had paid off in spades.

In most cases I couldn't use my talents on the competitors, but I was very successful at slowing their weapons. That rocked! My armor did a fantastic job of keeping off lighter weaponry, like arrows and small knives. And since mine required me to get within an arms length to use, I had a plethora of options once I got that close. My biggest problem was getting that close. With each battle it got harder to do.

Much like my own entourage of Smith and Wesson, other patrons had spies or party members to watch and learn from. As battles unfolded we all learned more about each other; our talents, our abilities, and our weapons. Not to mention any other tricks we may have.

During lunch back at the ranch Nathan told me I should be prepared for a miserable failure. One of my battles today was with the Arch Lich.

"I've battled liches before," I said.

"Not the Arch Lich."

"What's so different about the Arch Lich?"

"He's way bigger and way meaner."

Mr. Smith added, "And he's completely undefeated."

"Will had to beat him," I said.

"No. Will never beat him. No one has."

"How is that possible? If everyone lost to him why isn't he the grand champion?"

"Because he quits." I tilted my head. "Year after year," Nathan said, "he shows up, kicks everyone's ass, then quits and leaves the tournament."

"No one knows why, madam," Jeeves added.

"Don't you find that odd?" I asked, slurping on my own soup. "Why wouldn't he want to claim the full prize?"

"Clearly it isn't important to him," Nathan said.

"But coming here, year after year, and having a perfect record is? Why bother?"

"Maybe he feels it keeps him sharp," Jeeves said. "He is a lich. They don't always think straight."

I had a battle before him, which I won without much effort at all; the bone wraith I faced had no resistance to my talent, so I slowed him down and knocked him out of the park. Felt quite gratifying after the events the night before.

Then came the Arch Lich. Bigger than the other liches. His shiny jet black exoskeleton seemed thicker, too. He lumbered onto the floor of our ring, squeezing his large body between the ropes, and stood in front of me. He was a good four feet taller than I was.

Unlike the other liches, Archy—that's what I decided to call him —had not one but two lobster claws.

"Good to meet you, Archy," I said to lighten the mood. He wasn't impressed.

Nathan left with a forlorn look on his face, like he'd just taken his beloved dog to be put down. I let out a horse's sigh.

"Begin."

I opened with my favorite move and, as expected, it had no affect. He rushed at me. I spun with my hammer and connected solidly with his chest plate. The resonation shot back up my arm, and jolted my shoulder. I cried out as I dropped to my knees.

With one lobster claw he grabbed me at the neck. He raised me up. Wildly kicking and punching I fought with the air around me; the length of his claw was longer than my arms and legs. Then he added his second claw.

Archy began to squeeze. Panic gripped me when I realized ... he was cutting off my head. I screamed as the edges punched through the skin, then severed the muscles and tendons. I gasped for air as my windpipe got crushed. I heard the final snap of bone just before the strangest sensation of separation took hold. I couldn't feel my body any longer, nor my heartbeat, nor my lungs. My eyes, however, kept working, much to my distress. My head fell, and the world spun as it rolled like a bowling ball across the floor. The merciful dizziness plunged me into darkness.

Before me was a door. Curious, I opened it. It led to a white room, white from puffs of clouds and fog. A figure approached me, coming into focus through the soft billows. It was D. S. Frost. He wore one of his overly large suits. His hands were shoved into the pant pockets, which hiked up the buttoned jacket. His face, ruddy and flushed, emoted anger. Spikey blonde hair, blue-green eyes ...

"How did you know?" he snapped.

"Where ..." I turned and looked around. "Where am I?"

"*How did you know?*" I didn't understand the question. He came in close. "How did you know I was your healer?"

"Your hand," I defended, not liking his attitude. He pulled it out of his pocket and inspected it. "I recognized the scar."

He looked at his palm. "Damn that woman," he muttered. "If she'd let me alone I would have healed just fine."

"Where are we?" I pressed.

"In a place," he said, "in my mind." He turned his back to me, caressing his scarred hand. "I worked so hard, played by their rules, did everything expected of me—"

"What do you mean? What's wrong?"

"I'm doomed, ma'am." Even here it sounded like "mom." "If you figured it out it won't be long before he does."

"Who? What are you talking about?"

"I overheard you and your bug talking about healers. He painted you a rosy picture of our world." I didn't think there was anything rosy about it. "It's worse than that, far worse. We are the most hated race of beings anywhere on any plane at any time. We even hate each other. Hell, most of us hate ourselves. When I leave here, leave this miserable castle behind me, I'm *free*. I have a real life. I'm a cop. And I *love* what I do. I *love* my freedom."

"I don't understand."

"Because you're not listening. My anonymity is my freedom. Once I'm found out, once they know who to look for, I'm doomed. I become hunted." He frowned. "If caught I become a slave."

"I won't tell anyone, I swear—"

"That may not matter, whether you speak the words or not. If someone *thinks* you know all they have to do is get their healer to touch you. This," he swirled a hand in a circle, "is in my head. You speak no words yet we talk."

My throat really hurt. I touched it, twisting my head. "I have no reason to share this information with anyone. And why does my neck ache?"

"It's over for me," he moaned, not hearing or not caring. He ran his hands over the top of his head. "My life is over."

"No, it's not. Your secret is safe with me."

"Safe? Why should I trust you?" He pointed an accusing finger. "You were very quick to throw me to the wolves to save your own skin."

"I'm sorry, I'm so sorry about that. If it were only my skin I wouldn't have done it. Hell, I'd happily leave this place. But I worried if I told him I'd actually retrieved the disk, he'd want it. The story made it sound like I was only out there because of a tale you lured me with. I swear, I had no idea he would hurt you. It truly disgusts me how they treat you." My throat raged. I grimaced.

He looked at me with red eyes. "You don't realize how intimate this is, this contact. My fingers in your body, my mind connected to yours. This is a merging of two separate beings. More intense than friendship, or love, or even sex." He shook his head. "At least it is for me. That's the true burden of the healer. In order to heal I need to merge with you, to feel your flesh, to take your pain, to become an extension of you."

"I didn't know."

"Working with someone like you is ... *blissful*. Your mind is so innocent and pristine, and your heart so warm and unclouded. Underlying it all is this profound sadness that breaks my heart every time I have to push through it, and yet I suffer no discomfort or discontent. But imagine if I had to heal a creature as vile as Malador. God, I don't want to know what's in his mind, what horrible, malicious, agonizing thoughts fill his head. Or heart."

I cleared my sore throat. "How can he force you to heal him? You just, I don't know, *don't*."

"And suffer what your husband suffered?" I exhaled, deflated. "We have no choice." He scowled. "You don't know the half of what they can do. What they want to do." He ground at his eye with the palm of his hand. "Back in our world, if Malador … if *anyone* knows who I am, they'll make me disappear. No one would know. People go missing every day. But I'd be a captive," he swallowed, "a slave in some house, forced to serve, forced to suffer. Until I died."

"No." I took a step toward him, grabbing his arm. "I will never let that happen. He won't find out, certainly not through me, and if somehow he did I swear to you … I will come for you. I will find you." I winced, then coughed. "My throat!"

"I can't wait any longer. I need to heal you now." He put his warm hands around my neck in a strangle-type position. But I felt immediate relief. "Aren't you going to ask me?" he whispered.

I furrowed my brow.

"Where I put the disk?"

"No. Keep it safe for me."

He leaned forward bringing his forehead to mine. Warmth, and joy, and peace washed over me, and then …

My body arched as I took that first, deep breath, filling my lungs with as much air as they could possibly hold. I labored to lift myself onto my elbows.

"Why did that take so long?" Nathan demanded. "Is she all right?"

My healer nodded. "I'm fine," I agreed. With assistance I got to my feet, took a couple stabilizing breaths, rubbing my throat, then headed off for my next battle.

Chapter Twenty-Seven

STAGE THREE BEHIND us all the houses gathered for a ceremonial dinner in the grand hall. The final sixteen would be announced at the end of the meal, those lucky few who would go on the next three days. Even if we weren't in it, and I was certain we were not, all participants were expected to stay and watch.

I felt a bit depressed about that. Over the last few days I'd enjoyed my time in the ring more than out. In the ring the rules were clear; kill or be killed. The enemy stood before you, in 3D, sensor-round, technicolor. I could see them. Feel them. And I knew their intentions.

But out of the ring my shadowy world awaited. Enemies lingering, smiling at me, ready to stab me in the back. Their intentions unknown. When they'd strike was unknown. I had to constantly think, constantly be vigilant, constantly watch the words that I uttered. I shuddered at the thought of spending three more days without the distraction of the bouts.

Funny thing, now that I thought about it. The tournament took fourteen days time. Will only spent four days at his "conferences." Time must pass differently here. I didn't even bother to ask. I was tired of always having to ask.

The goblin table next to us managed their frogs better as the days went on. I watched them, just to keep my eyes off my own party.

Two talked together, then laughed, then did a fist bump. I smiled. I'd apparently had a minor impact on the goblin world.

My healer ate very little. Since our *encounter* he kept his distance, doing only what was required. I died a couple of times, only to be healed; I never got to share in his secret world again. His tattered brown cloak remained blood stained from Malador's knife. If there was any anonymity in the drabness of the robes the discoloration made clear to all he was my healer.

Just as desert got set before us the Chancellor clinked his glass, bringing the room to silence.

"As you all know," he boomed, "this night completes the third stage of this year's tournament. I'm honored to say it has so far been most successful. Before I announce the sweet sixteen we, the mages of the tournament, have decided that one of you deserves special recognition. One of you has, single-handedly, changed the tone and camaraderie of the tournament. This patron met each challenge with grace, honor, and regard, which in these times is refreshing, if not rare. In turn, her poise has become infectious. We have noticed other participants sharing in that same sense of sportsmanship.

"And so, will you please stand, raise your glasses, and join me in a toast." We all did. I looked around at the tables wondering who he was talking about. "Here is to you, Mrs. Winki Witherspoon."

My jaw dropped. *Me???* You've got to be kidding. "What did I do?" I quickly whispered to Nathan.

"Here, here!" many called. Flabbergasted I raised my glass back and gave a bow.

As we sat Nathan said, "Look around you. People are laughing. People go to other tables and talk just to talk, not to threaten or bluster. The games are fun this year."

"You always acknowledge your opponents after the bouts," Jeeves added. "Whether bested or victorious. No one ever did that before, madam."

I shrugged. "We only have to hate each other in the ring. Isn't that what the Citadel is for?" The table gave me quizzical looks. "I had dinner with a king who can only exist underwater while I stood on land in the very same room. That's amazing, isn't it?"

Jeeves gave a nod. "We've all just forgotten."

The Chancellor continued. "Now, here are the list of the eight dark house contenders, starting from the bottom."

He started to rattle off names. A good number of them I knew, now, having met in battle, most of whom I beat. I leaned to Nathan, "How did I beat the best of the best?"

"Your talent is extremely powerful. Once you build up your own resistance you'll be a top contender. If you'd won a resistance gonzo you likely would have made it into the finals."

The Chancellor continued. "House of Ravenswood, Malador." Malador stood up and trotted to the center table, his red cape wafting behind him. Once he received the scroll he gave a flamboyant bow to the table.

I rolled my eyes at the display. Nathan chuckled at my expression.

The head mage called out the last name, the number one ranking, "Realm of Cardamom, the Arch Lich."

"I love cardamom," I told my party. I apparently was alone in that. A murmur of disapproval bubbled across the room. Somewhere, someone even hissed. No one moved towards the Chancellor. I looked around, raising my head to see over the crowd to spy the lich. His table was empty.

"Since no one has stepped forward the realm has forfeited. All dark competitors move up one notch."

"Why the reaction?" I asked.

"Because everyone hates that the Arch Lich comes but never completes the tournament. Some claim his realm should just be eliminated from the games," Nathan explained.

"If he ever lost," Jeeves added, "he would be "

The Chancellor continued. "The added competitor to the dark challengers is Realm of Gentilly, King Hector."

"I like King Hector," I said with a quiet applause. He swished his way up to the table and took his scroll. Seems the biggest un-fans of Esmeralda were all on the dark side.

"Let us move onto the list of eight white houses. House of Magnolia, Colonel Mustard."

I bared my teeth with an "ouch" face. "That's my fault, isn't it. He gave up a better position to lose to me."

"Don't worry about the Colonel," Nathan said. "He'll be fine."

"I don't know," Mr. Smith said quietly as he leaned into the center of the table for us to hear. "Wasn't a good showing this year. I think the death of TJ hit the house harder than they want to admit."

"Who was TJ to the Colonel?" I asked.

"He called him his valet, but in reality TJ was his coach."

Suddenly, I felt grumpy. I'd almost forgotten that *that* part of my world—those deaths, that shooting—waited for me once we left here. I couldn't quiet the questions that bogged down my mind. The who, the why, the constant querying with no answers.

Someone touched my arm. My healer. "Yeah," I said, assuming I knew the question. "I'm fine."

~ ~ * ~ ~

I sat in the common room, alone, slouched in a comfy chair. I'd been doing this more frequently throughout the tournament, taking an hour or so to be alone before turning in. Too bad I couldn't just park my bed here. I'd rather that than sleeping in the company of people I didn't trust.

A few attendees from other houses were about, playing cards or reading books. I just stared into the constant fire that produced no heat, lost in my head.

"*Chére?*"

"Yes, Hercule," I droned without looking for him.

"We never spoke about that night."

"No. We didn't."

"You think I betrayed you?"

"Anything's possible."

"No!" he said, scampering into my view by crawling across my lap. "It is not possible! I am *un cafard*! I do not betray."

"What does being a roach have to do with anything."

"Familiars do not betray. Bugs do not betray. If you can trust no one else, the spiders and I will always protect you. We will always defend you." I didn't react. "We are incapable of deception! Ask anyone. You ... You there in that insipid blue suit. Tell her! Tell her about the sunken."

The once-reading-now-insulted man, inspected his wardrobe. "It's a fine suit."

"Trust me, it is time to ask for a raise. Tell her about the sunken," he demanded.

The man set down his book. "The sunken are the lowest talented creatures in any plane. Typically they abused or overused their abilities and, as a punishment, were *sunk* to the lowest level of existence."

"Bah," Hercule stamped. "Tell her of the mandate!"

The man rolled his eyes. I shrugged an apology. "Once you've been sunk you're freewill gets squashed. You can only serve one master. That has been described as a 'mandate of the sunken.' They are always loyal." He looked at Hercule. "And miserable to deal with."

"See? The blue monkey knows the truth!" The man shook his head, and resumed his book. "It is not possible for me to betray you. No!"

"Then who did? Someone served me up to Malador. Someone

told him where I'd be. You were the only one who knew."

"Even your lowly healer managed that, *ma chére.*" I looked at the man standing behind me. Valid point. "Obviously we were not as quiet to leave our suite as we believed."

"Tell me then, oh, Great Hercule, knower of all things." I whispered so only he could hear. "Who then? Who benefited by killing Will?"

"Only you."

"And who benefits by killing me?"

"No one!"

"Nathan does. He gets the house, he gets the money, he gets to be champion."

"Stop! Enough! Nathan is not the one. This I know." He danced back and forth, waving his antenna. "But I must admit, even I do not know who wanted to eliminate Will. I felt certain that everyone in the house would follow him back to the dark side, if they had to."

That was eerily familiar to the words Nathan used. I nearly mentioned it when the common room doors opened. The Chancellor and the four mages entered the quarters.

Everyone stood. I followed suit.

"Mrs. Witherspoon," the Chancellor addressed me. "Please fetch your party."

Oh, oh. Did someone sneeze? I did as requested, all of them had perplexed looks on their faces as we gathered in the common room. Mama quickly poured her red robe over her clothing while those from other houses quietly dismissed themselves.

"We've come with news," the Chancellor started. "Two of the final sixteen houses have forfeited, leaving two vacancies. I'm glad to say that the House of Gateway is now in the games." We glanced at each other, speechless. We never planned on making it this far.

"Are you certain?" Mama asked.

"Yes, quite. There was a poorer showing in the white side this year. As a result you were ranked ninth overall." A couple of the mages nodded.

Nathan frowned at the news. *I thought he'd be pleased. All I heard before coming here was how strong we had to be leaving in order to protect the house this coming year. This wasn't the reaction I expected. What now?*

"What team left to allow us to continue?" Jeeves asked.

"House of Sky, Orphelia," he said with an air of irritation. "Have the rules been explained to you, Mrs. Witherspoon?"

No. "Yes, sir."

"Good." He handed Nathan a scroll. "You are the first bout of the day. We look forward to seeing you then." They turned to leave.

"Wait," I said, "Um, sorry, but you said two teams forfeited?"

"Houses, Champion." *Houses, realms, teams, whatever.* "The other was Gentilly Realm. King Hector said he didn't feel well."

"So who made it in?" Nathan asked.

"Diamond Realm. Lady Esmeralda."

Crap!

As the door closed Nathan took a seat, and hid his face in his hands.

"Isn't this good news, sir?" Jeeves asked. Nathan didn't hear him. "Sir?"

"Yeah, yeah," he snapped up, "it's great news."

"Not for me," I moaned. "I have to fight that witch again."

"Nah, probably not. The bouts are single sided throughout the stage, whites battle whites, darks battle darks. It isn't until the final combat, stage 5, that light and dark battle."

"It's more fun that way," Mr. Smith said, with a smile on his face.

Sounding better. "So who do I fight?"

"The top seed. The highest ranking battle the lowest, the second highest battle the second lowest, and so on."

"Like March Madness!" Mr. Smith added

"Eight bouts tomorrow. The morning four are white, the afternoon four are black," Nathan said, then pointed, "and that means you. First bout, the lowest ranks fighting the best house." He left the room, saying, "Better get some rest, Mrs. Witherspoon. You're gonna have a big day."

The others followed him, leaving only me, my healer, and the *cafard* on the arm of the sofa.

Everyone seemed certain I wouldn't fight Esmeralda again. But the *convenience* of both her and me making it into the finals squeezed my stomach. I put my hand down, letting the little bug crawl onto my palm, then raised him to eye level. "What are we missing, oh, Great Hercule?"

"*Oui*," he said softly. "What, indeed."

Chapter Twenty-Eight

A FUNNY THING happened while walking through the dark, dank halls of the Citadel on my way to my first stage four battle. I was stopped by a goblin.

"Psssst."

The sound made all of us turn, but I recognized the little green creature hiding around a corner. Before I could say his name he held a finger to his lips to silence me, then waved for me to join him.

"Stay here," I commanded my group. "All of you," I specifically said to the healer, aka, my shadow. And went around the corner.

"Hey, what's up?"

"I wanted to warn you. Something's not right." I knelt down to see him, eye to eye. "My royalness didn't leave because he is unwell."

"Why then?"

"I don't know, he didn't tell us. Only that we were forfeiting. But I could tell." He looked around, over his shoulder, both up and down the hall, and came closer. "He's scared."

"Do you think he was threatened?"

"He's very powerful. I can't imagine a threat that would cause him to leave the tournament. But then again, I've only known him a short while. Since the red-haired witch and you are both in the finals, something seems ... just be careful."

"Thank you, Theodore." I offered a fist bump. Instead he

reached for my palm and opened it, then shook my hand. "Best to you," he said then he trotted away.

I watched him disappear but my mind wandered to the news. The king, who seemed pretty powerful indeed, was muscled out? While Esmeralda and I managed to get in. "Mr. Smith? Mr. Wesson?" I called from around the corner. The two lab coats joined me. "I have a job for you."

~ ~ * ~ ~

The small auditorium was packed. Made sense, since most of the attendees had become audience, but apparently they all wanted to watch my bout. The murmur of anticipation brought back my performance anxiety. I closed my eyes, recalling the peaceful place my healer exposed me to the last time I felt nervous, before my fight with Esmeralda. I took a few deep breaths, I focused on the large, cool and calm expanse.

"All right," Nathan said, pointing to the board. "What do you see?"

My competitor's name was Gareth, House of Tempest, Zephyr Plane. I hadn't fought anyone from that plane before. I must have said so out loud.

"He is very tricky," Nathan said. "Master of air. He can give you a lot of it or take it away."

"Air hardly seems scary," I said flippantly.

"One word," he said. "Tornado."

"Ah." I looked at the talents. *Typhoon* and *Vacuum*. "I don't suppose *vacuum* means 'cleaning?'"

"No. And notice how powerful it is. It can last minutes. Once you feel it you need to strike immediately. Humans don't do so well in a vacuum. But I've seen his *typhoon*, too. Beware them both."

"How do I fight that?"

Gareth entered the ring. Flew in, really. Human in appearance, but translucent, almost see through. White hair, white eyes, white clothes against his white skin. He moved fluidly, as if hovering and yet walking. I blinked a few times trying to process the information my eyes gave me.

"Quickly," Nathan answered. "Don't let this go on. End it fast." He gave a reassuring squeeze on my shoulder then left the ring.

He made it sound simple, but Gareth was the highest ranked of the white representatives. The *highest.* That alone made me feel like I'd already lost.

My healer moved close to me and stood facing me, standing nearly toe to toe. He leaned in, careful not to touch me, and whispered, "You already feel you've lost."

His voice sounded so quiet and soft I'm certain I wouldn't have recognized it if I hadn't already known who he was. I nodded, stunned by the fact that he spoke to me at all.

"The good are weak this year," he whispered. *Yes, I recall the Chancellor saying that.* "Gareth could never defeat Malador."

"Please exit the ring," the voice said. "Competitors, take your positions."

My healer backed away, face completely shrouded by his cloak. "You can see just fine in that, can't you," I accused as he left the ring.

"Begin."

I rushed him immediately, deciding not to even try my talent. The statistics on the board told me I had a fifty-fifty chance. I'd rather not wait. I didn't use any weapons, either, only me. At the last moment I did a cartwheel to connect with my feet. I should have hit him in the chest, squarely. I ended up on the ropes, almost embarrassingly tangled.

He'd moved. I didn't see it, I don't know how, but he stood on the opposite side of the ring. He swirled his hand, and a small cyclone emerged in the center. He thrust his hand at me, and the cyclone moved, swishing towards me. I raced out of its path but some flying dust or sand splashed in my eyes. The wind left the ring and vanished, or so I gathered, still unable to see.

I wiped my tearing eyes with an arm, while reaching for the small knife behind my back with the other. I threw it at him. The knife was true, flying without waver in his direction. But missed ... he vanished, into thin air.

I made a note to apologize to the poor woman who found it embedded in her shoulder.

I spun to see where he'd gone, my eyes squinting make out any image, when an icy grip came from behind me, long, freezing fingers wrapped around my throat. Sharp to the touch they stung as they tightened, taking my breath. With an elbow I smacked my assailant behind me, but hit only air. The touch, thankfully, had vanished.

I waited a moment, not moving. He'd vanished again. *Air is see-through, Winki!* My cursed eyes were useless.

Okay, you can't see him, I thought. On a whim I closed my eyes. And listened. Every nerve of my skin bristled with vigilance.

I felt a stir, ever so slightly. *Next to me! He stood next to me!* I turned away from him, to goad him into thinking I was lost, then, hammer in hand, spun and swung.

Blessed impact. I'd hit something.

He'd vanished, this time reappearing as far away in the ring as he could. He held his arm. Again he flicked his wrist in the air, again a cyclone appeared. He opened his hands wide and, to my horror, all his fingers had become small knives—yes, that I could see. He uttered some word as he gestured grandly to the cyclone, and all the knives flew into the wind and were lost from view.

Bloody hell! The wind headed for me, now loaded with knives. I stood tall, held out my hand. "No!" The wind and its cargo slowed to nearly motionless. I picked them all out of suspension, one by one, and with only my sense of sound, flung them at him as fast as I could move — left, then right, then behind, then over there ... I threw the knives. When I had tossed them all, only then did I look for Gareth.

I spied him, or some form, kneeling as he clutched the ropes for support. Four knives had found their mark.

Wait a minute ... I had earned *bind*. I made a clenched fist with my hand. He reacted, his body lurching towards the ropes, then falling on the floor.

I rushed, raising my hammer ...

"Game over. Winner, House of Gateway."

I knelt beside him as his healer put him back together. His white eyes focused on me.

"You are remarkable," he said, his voice only in my mind.

I helped him stand, his hand feeling light and cold, as if it didn't really exist somehow. I put my hand on my chest and bowed. "Thank you," I said to him. With a small breeze he vanished.

Nathan and my healer joined me, the latter looking me over for any wear and tear. "What was he?" I asked.

"An elemental," Nathan said. "Air, in form. Was a time when elements were the most formidable talents in the community."

"What happened?" I asked.

"Humanity. Come on. Let's go watch some of your upcoming challengers." He escorted me by my arm. "You know what this means now, yes?"

"No."

"You're going to leave here ranked in the low thirties. That's way better than any of us believed possible." He gave a smile. "You did good. You did real good."

Chapter Twenty-Nine

NATHAN, MY HEALER, and I watched the bout between the fourth and fifth ranked patrons, two realms of liches from the Phantom plane. Looking at a lich you'd never guess they could be considered "good." But Nathan explained to me that every plane has both good and evil influences. "Although," he pointed out hushedly as we watched the battle, "in the Phantom and Aqua planes white and dark aren't as clear cut as they are in the Midland, Zephyr, and Radiant planes. For example we think of lying or cheating or stealing as wrong, and therefore bad. But in the Phantom plane, it's only murder that separates them. Everything else is considered acceptable."

We watched the two liches battle as liches do. Swords flashed, shields clanged. Almost no talent was used as they were perfectly matched and neither could best the other. So, it was a game of exhaustion.

Nathan put his hand on mine and whispered in my ear. "Did he talk to you?"

He meant my healer. "Why do you ask?" I purposely didn't answer him.

"They aren't supposed to talk," he said. "You're getting too close. They are filthy, despicable creatures, lacking in morals and scruples, and can't be trusted under any circumstance."

No sooner had he ended the comment when Mr. Smith and Mr.

Wesson entered the room, looking around to find us. I waved my arm, drawing attention. They made their way.

"I beg you," Nathan ended, "please keep him away from you."

The two geeks sat in front of us. "Well?" I asked.

"You were right. But no one has any specifics—OO!" Mr. Smith said, reacting to the bout in front of us.

"Right about what?" Nathan asked.

"Theodore," I quietly explained, "told me King Hector didn't leave because he was sick. He said something scared him from the competition."

"So," Mr. Smith took over, "Mrs. Witherspoon asked us to find out why the House of Sky left. No one knows specifics but—ouch!— a few got the impression Orphelia had been threatened."

Nathan sat quiet for a long while as the liches sliced each other to shreds, splashing black lich blood in every direction. I thought I heard him say, "Huh," but I couldn't be sure.

The combat slogged on for another hour before one of them managed to run through the other, both gasping and heaving in exhaustion at that point. I think the one that lost felt grateful for the battle to finally end. Goodness knows the audience did.

~ ~ * ~ ~

We all sat around the large wooden table, healer included, eating our lunch, a jambalaya Mama prepared. Soul food, she called it. Keeping us grounded to our roots, the home we're here to fight for.

Hercule crawled about the table, eating the occasional crumb. I offered him his own portion of something, but he declined. Said it was better for him to eat on the run. "Moving keeps me thinking."

"About?" I prodded.

"A great many things. The deaths of those men at home. The betrayal that brought Malador to our house, and then again outside the Citadel."

"Wait," Nathan's head snapped up from his bowl, "What? You were outside the Citadel?"

"While you were on walkabout," I said. Then I threw Hercule a look of "you had to say something."

"How did you miss that?" Mr. Smith chuckled. "Alarms went off and everything!"

"Why?" Nathan ignored him. "Why in hell would ever make you go out there?"

My healer gave a small sigh, assuming I'd blame him again. No. Not again. "Will left something for me in the cherry tree. He told me so in the DVD you gave me. Hercule and I went to get it." How did he not know? If that was real, then he wasn't the one who sent Malador. I stared at his face, looking for a tell, looking for a lie.

"And the nefarious Malador lay in wait," Hercule embellished. "He ambushed us on our way back."

Nathan's eyes displayed concern. "Are you okay? What happened?"

"We fought." I ate. But the crowd around me waited for more. "I lost."

"What do you mean, *you lost?*" Nathan pressed.

"He overpowered me. If it weren't for my healer I ..."

"Did he touch you?" Nathan's voice was stern. I hesitated to answer. The rest of the room was deathly quiet. "Did. He. Touch. You?"

"Yes." I looked around at the table full of wide eyes. "My cheek." Before the silence could pop my ears I said, "But when the healer knocked him off me it was over. Like it never happened."

Angered, Nathan said, "You're telling me that, right now, you feel nothing for him?"

"Does a great deal of loathing count?"

He looked at the *cafard*, then back at me. "How is that possible?

His touch is persistent. An infection. Mrs. Witherspoon, you don't just get over it."

"As soon as it stopped it was over. I don't know what to tell you." I shrugged.

"Perhaps," Hercule offered, "we don't understand this plane as well as we thought? Perhaps the talents are stifled a bit more, *oui?*"

"All I know," I added, "was my talent totally sucked out there. I couldn't slow most anything down. That's why he was able to clean my clock so easily." I took a bite of food. "By the way," I said to Smith and Wesson, "when we get back we need to add a goblin exercise to my regimen. I had a hell of a time fighting a dozen creatures the size of munchkins."

Mr. Wesson took notes on his pad with Mr. Smith looking over his shoulder.

"I have it on good authority," Nathan muttered, "that all talents work fine out there. Only in the Citadel are talents stifled."

"Perhaps, something has changed?" Hercule asked.

Nathan abruptly, not to mention rudely, excused himself and left the room.

"What was *that* about?" Mr. Smith asked.

I put my hand on the table palm up. "Hercule, you're with me." I, for one, was going to find out what *that* was all about.

Keeping a safe distance behind Nathan we—I, Hercule, and my healer, who simply would not stay behind—followed him to the Chancellor's office.

He walked into the tower and right past the goblin secretary. "But wait! Sir! You can't go in there!"

Ignoring her he picked up his pace, nearly trotting to the large double doors of the Chancellor. First he tried the door, pushing it with his shoulder. Then he banged on it. "I know you're in there, Chancellor. Open up!"

I heard the secretary use the word, "security", and turned to see a pack of bone wraiths floating their way to us.

"Come on, Chauncey! Let me in!"

With a loud click the door unlatched and creaked open. Impatiently, he helped it along, pushing it hard and shoving his way into the room. We followed, but hovered just outside the door.

"How long have you known?" Nathan screamed at the frail man behind the desk.

The Chancellor's eyes hit several points in the room; he wasn't alone. I leaned in a bit to see two of the other mages with him; the doughy guy and candy-man. "You're treading on very thin ice, Nathan Marble."

"How long?" No one answered the question. "Magic isn't working outside in the Citadel plane," he pointed out a window. My eyebrows shot up at the word *magic*. "I want to know how long? How long did you sit here, keeping it quiet? Keeping it from the competitors? Knowing what it meant."

Enraged the Chancellor stood. "This is your last warning—!"

"The tree is dying," Nathan seethed. "The plane is eroding. No one is safe anymore. Not to mention the scheming and threatening of competitors to force them out of the tournament."

"Watch your tongue or I'll throw your house out!"

"You won't have to. We quit." Nathan folded his arms.

We quit!?

"How dare you, you insolent little punk—"

"Don't give me that crap. I've been around this rodeo way too long for your pomp and bluster to bother me. Fact is, it isn't safe anymore." He shook his head. "Look, I got a newbie that kicked her own ass to be here, worked like hell to make a strong showing, and she did it for no good reason. She did it because we *asked* her to. Now I can't be a good orator or guardian *or lawyer* if I know she's being put needlessly in harm's way." He turned to me, hiding in the doorway. "We did what we needed to do. I'm throwing in the towel.

You okay with that?"

Before I could answer the Chancellor came around his desk. "Nathan, please. Let's be reasonable. Let's just take a few breaths and cool our heads. The Citadel is safe."

Nathan gave a deep sigh. "For now. Maybe." He removed the garish necklace from around his neck and placed it on the Chancellor's desk. "The House of Gateway, New Orleans, Midland Plane forfeit. We don't need your approval or rating to know we can protect our house."

On his heals he turned to leave. When he reached me he looked over his shoulder and said, "I expect to see an assessment on the tree and the plane's integrity before the games next year. If not, not only will we *not* be present, but I will make sure every white house and white realm know the Citadel is no longer safe."

He stormed off with me and my healer flanking his wake.

"I don't understand," I said, my feet hastening to keep up. "What about the world? The plane? Weren't we in this to keep evil away?"

Nathan shook his head. "If evil wins this year it will be due to deceit and cheating, which will weaken its effects. We'll be able to combat that on our own plane as we need to."

"But Esmeralda made it to—"

"Not my problem," he huffed. "Not yours either. I told you before. My one job, my *only* job, is to get you safely through your first tournament. That's what I promised Will I'd do. Quitting now is the only way to do that. When we get home, feel free to fire me."

Quitting now also meant putting the plane in danger. I pursed my lips. Maybe this was the plan all along? Maybe I knew exactly who my traitor was.

Nathan Marble.

Chapter Thirty

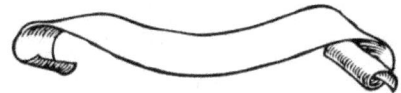

THREE HOURS LATER we were packed up and standing at the Citadel's threshold. My healer stopped at the massive beams of the door, unwilling to cross into the plane.

"This is where we part ways, I take it." He nodded. "Will you be safe?" He nodded. "Thank you. For all of your help." He nodded and I turned to catch up with the group.

The grumbling within my party hadn't stopped since Nathan told them the news. "We're just leaving? We've never given up before," Mr. Smith said.

"It's not giving up," Nathan said, for the hundredth time. "It's protecting our Champion." We shlepped our own gear—this time the task was ours—as we climbed the black path around the black rocks heading up the black hill. Nathan gave a final explanation. "Look, why do we come here?" Jeeves started to answer but Nathan stopped him, "We come here to protect our house. We come here to show the community we are not to be trifled with. That our modest manor in the Midland plane stands strong."

I raised my hand. "What about the part with good or bad vibrations affecting all of mankind or something?"

"Mrs. Witherspoon, you always cling to a simplistic view of the most complex realities. Yes. That happens, but that's not why *we* come here. The hard houses, the ones who have their energies tied to their champions, that's why *they* come here."

Not the explanation I'd heard before. "So, the weight of the world isn't on my shoulders?" I sarcastically asked.

Nathan sighed, just as we reached the top of our hill. "Mr. Jeeves, if you please."

Eyes glowing green, Jeeves started forming our exit.

"Mrs. Witherspoon, that's what Will felt like. And I think that helped put him in an early grave." He put two hands on my shoulders. "I've been an orator for over eighteen years now. I've never known this plane to be anything other than solid, and I've never know competitors bullying others to leave. And I'm not risking the life of our newest champion, my best friend's wife, just to stay and see how far you can go. You'll go far, I promise you. You've done what we asked. Time to go home." He sighed. "There's always next year."

"We are ready, sir," Jeeves announced.

"Mrs. White?" Nathan addressed her, "Please go through first and let the spiders know it's us before they assume we're under attack."

"*Allons-y!*" Hercule called, as we stepped out of the Citadel plane and into the living room.

I couldn't help but take a deep inhale through my nose. Hundreds of scents bombarded me; water, wood, jasmine, mildew, carpet ... I hadn't realized that the Citadel plane had absolutely no odors at all.

The others didn't seem to notice. They all started carrying the cases and luggage and boxes back to the corners of the house from whence they came. I took a moment to look at the place. The manor. *My house.* It felt good to be home.

"You have returned early?" a small but concerned voice asked from the corner.

"Annabelle! Good to see you," I said to the tiny figure in the web.

"Yes. We quit."

She jumped in her tangle. "You ... *quit?*"

"Nathan's idea. Apparently, something was rotten in the Citadel."

"Nathan? He didn't give a reason?"

"Annabelle, I've just been a passenger on this ride. I go where I'm told, I do what I'm told. I fight when I'm told. I'm tired of asking for explanations." The spider sat quiet. "Aren't you going to ask how we did? You worked so hard to get me ready."

"Sorry, my lady. How did you do?"

"I'm told since we abandoned it's unofficial and won't get recorded. But everyone knows—I achieved a level thirty-two."

"Congratulations," she said, giving a tiny bow in her web. Then she crawled across the ceiling and let herself gently down a thread in front of me. "Mrs. Black is running an errand," she said with some urgency. "We weren't expecting you back so soon. She has some news. We have discovered—"

"Ah, Annabelle!" Nathan said, joining me. "Did Mrs. Witherspoon tell you the good news? We're all very proud of her."

"Yes, sir. That is very good news, indeed," she said in her Disney voice, almost too sweet. It put my wits on guard.

Jeeves, who'd been busy helping Mama with the cooking, floated into the room. "Sir? Madam? We have a guest."

"Never a dull moment," I said as we followed Jeeves to the front door. He swung it wide just as D.S. Frost, who stood on the other side, held his hand poised to knock.

"That is truly remarkable, sir," the detective said to Jeeves.

"I know. Can I help you, detective?"

The sergeant looked past Jeeves, spying me and Nathan. "May I speak to the lady of the house?"

Jeeves stood aside. "Madam? Are you taking visitors at the moment?"

I suspected Nathan would want some assurances so I turned to him. He shrugged. "Are you arresting my client today?"

"No, sir. In fact, I've come bearing gifts." He retrieved from a pocket a rainbow reflecting DVD and waved it.

I nodded to Jeeves, and the detective stepped into the entryway, as Jeeves drifted out of view.

"And what is that?" Nathan asked.

"I found it on the internet," D.S. Frost said. "It's an informational video on motorcycle safety, and contains an assortment of clever bits of news. For example," he said as he handed the disk to me, "did you know that when you are being pursued by cars with flashy blue lights on top," he twirled his hand above his head in imitation, "that you are legally required to pull over and stop?"

We stared a moment as I searched his pale blue-green eyes for some clue as to what he was talking about. Oh! The chase! I'd completely forgotten about that—it happened, what, four or five weeks ago? "I, er" my mind raced for some answer. "You were shot and I panicked. I was taking you to a hospital."

"And yet I woke up here. I'm fairly certain that you passed two hospitals on the way."

"Uh," my lawyer started, "this is starting to feel like an interrogation." Nathan swept his arm behind the man, trying to usher him back outside.

"My visit is a courtesy call, Mr. Marble. I, myself, barely recall the incident, and while curious about the details I'm quite satisfied with the outcome. Detective Duplantier, on the other hand, is nothing but curious." As he spoke his gaze wandered between me and Nathan. Then he landed them on me. "She's coming within the hour. She will ask you to take a drive with her to the station for questioning."

He started to leave on his own. "Perhaps the two of you should —"

"Him! He's the one!"

We all spun in the direction of the voice. Mrs. Black pointed her finger at Nathan as she marched down the hallway. "Nathan Marble killed Master Will!"

Hearing someone vocalize the words I'd only heard in my head before made my blood boil. I took a step away from him, standing next to the sergeant.

Nathan, shook his head and smiled, "Mrs. Black, I don't know what—"

"Shut up, you filthy man! I have proof." The one thing I lacked. Feelings and hunches galore, but no proof. "That's where I was just now," she said handing me a piece of paper. "Making copies of this, just in case he manages to destroy the original."

"What is that?" He reached out. I shoved his hand away and took the parchment myself.

She stepped right into his face. "It's your contract. The one you made with the dark lords."

"What the hell are you talking about?" he defended. I inspected the document which did look like a contract, complete with wax seals and signatures. The paper felt heavy, yellow in color, and tattered edges. The name signed below read "Nathan Marble," and after reading some of his legal stuff, it looked authentic.

"It's a deal," she pushed. "It says you owe them one pure soul. You gave them Will, you bastard, didn't you!"

You gave them Will. I stopped hearing the arguments and the denials. I didn't see the crowd as they gathered around us. I became keenly aware of my heartbeat, elevated, loud, and pulsing with such massive throbs that I felt gallons of hot blood jetting through my veins. My eyes focused on the parchment, but I saw Will, in the bed ... at the hospital. *I heard the machines, I saw the nurses, someone yelled, "Clear!", his body jumped ...*

You bastard you bastard *you bastard, "You bastard!"*

I spun to face the traitor, that scheming, loathsome man who played the best friend, and hid behind his influential voice. I was going to kill him. I raised my gun.

"Whoa!" he cried out, raising his hands in the air. "Wait—"

Others moved away from him, leaving him mine. "You put him in the painting when you realized he hadn't crossed over. When you realized he could warn me about you."

"Winki," he slowly backed away, "I didn't know it was him, I swear."

"Then you had me targeted, didn't you. You had Mr. Cruise, or whatever is name was, try to kill me. You knew him! You put him up to it!"

"I did no such thing," he voice cracked in fear.

"But someone in Magnolia house realized I was vulnerable, so they sent TJ to help me. So you had him killed, too."

"Why?" He screamed. "Why would I do that?"

"Because both Cruise and TJ could identify you and warn me before you killed me."

"How?" He nearly tripped backing away, his hands visibly trembling. "How could I have poisoned—"

"With another client from your office, Mr. Redding. You had him take care of Cruise and TJ. And once he did his job, you killed him." He stumbled, moving backwards. "You ... want the return to the dark side!"

"Winki," he licked his lips. "I'm being set up. I'm being framed —"

"Shut up!" I hollered, out of my mind with rage. Seeing him tremble, seeing his eyes filled with fear, seeing that murderous man suffer—my heart pounded harder.

He couldn't back up anymore. His body pressed against the front door, pushing hard to get away from my weapon. "You still haven't told me why. For god's sake, why? Why am I dying today?"

"Because you want this," I gestured to the house. "All of it! You get the house, the talent, the money, and," I waved the document, "*the power.* And eliminating us from the tournament will make it easier for the dark side to conquer us." *Damned blurry vision! I want to see him suffer.*

"I would never make a deal with the dark lords, not ever," he screamed, tears filling his desperate eyes. "And I would *never* hurt Will!"

My eardrums nearly burst from the blood thrumming through their drums. "Why?" I shrieked, and quickly wiped my eyes, "Why should I believe you?" Kill him. *Kill him now!* I started to press the trigger, feeling its resistance against my finger. *Just a little more ....*

"Because Will was my brother!"

I froze. My heart stopped beating. All eyes fell on him. Small gasps from Jeeves and the ladies Black and White. One of them whispered, "Edward?"

I pushed my gun forward, trying to get back to the glorious hate. But it vanished.

As casual as crossing the street, D.S. Frost stepped in front of Nathan. His hands in his pants pockets, his unbuttoned jacket open, his eyes on me. "Mrs. Witherspoon. I've heard your reasons and, even as a law official, I couldn't agree more. This man needs to be punished. But before you shoot him in front of all these witnesses I have only one question for you." I swallowed. "Where did you get the gun?"

What a ridiculous question! What did he mean, where did I get ... I looked in my hand. I looked at the small but weighty pistol I held there. I felt its heft, its cold metal, its smooth wooden handle. I inspected the object. Where *did* I get the gun? "I ... I don't know." I lowered the object.

"Edward?" Jeeves stepped toward the slightly relieved man. "Is it really you? How can it be—?"

Mr. Smith burst into laughter. "*A conjurer!* Woo hoo! We're so gonna kick butt next year!"

"No!" Mama cried out and rushed towards me. She raised my hand, and pointed it at Nathan with my hand still on the trigger. Her vise-like clutch clamped down on me. Before I could react, before I could fight, I felt the subtle click, felt the device kick, felt the metal turn hot.

Nathan folded at the waist, gripping his abdomen, and collapsed on the floor. Blood oozed its way between his fingers.

"You stupid bitch," Mama pointed at me, backing away. "All you had to do was kill him! And you could have had *everything!*"

Mr. Smith and Mr. Wesson jumped on the cook, while Jeeves and Mrs. Black sank to their knees helping the shot man. "Call 9-1-1," Jeeves said to Frost, who was already on his cell.

Mrs. Black tenderly stroked Nathan's head, and he smiled up at her. "No time," he sputtered, then swallowed and choked. "Damn, it hurts."

Mama managed to get out of the grip of the two lab coats and ran back towards the kitchen.

"Spiders!" Mrs. Black hollered and pointed at the dashing woman. They came from everywhere, suddenly, the walls and ceilings filling in with black movement. Out of view I heard her scream, "Get off me! Get off me!"

I stood over Nathan. My brother-in-law. Family I didn't know I had. His skin turned sallow. His eyes lost focus as he looked around at nothing. "I would never hurt Will," he whispered. "I loved that man. Never ... I miss ..."

Quaking from my breaking heart I turned to the detective. My healer. I asked with only my eyes.

"Don't," he warned.

"Please. I'm so sorry, but I'm begging you." I put my hands together and pressed the index fingers at my lips. "Please, please help him. Please, heal him.'"

His face flushed will anger. "You told me ... you promised ..." He looked at the dying man on the floor.

"I know. And I meant it. But I just found out that I have family. I have a brother-in-law!" *I have a living relative of my husband.*

"Wait?" Mr. Smith joined us. "You're a healer?" He looked between us. "You're *her* healer?" D.S. Frost winced at the words. "Well? Get on with it! For pete's sake, you owe her. She saved your life!" He gestured between us. "*We* saved your life!"

"It doesn't work that way," he defended. "I don't get to choose who lives and who dies. Don't you see? I *can't* choose."

Jeeves stood, taking the sergeant by the arm. "Jack," he whimpered, "Edward was like a son to me. I raised him. I lost him once and it nearly killed me. I'm begging you, Jack, please, don't make me lose him again."

"You know better than anyone," he hissed. "It doesn't work that way."

"Just ask your mother. That's all I ask."

The lights had gone out. Nathan's body lied limp in Mrs. Black's loving cradle. "I'm sorry," she wept as she rocked him, "I'm sorry I doubted you."

The detective swallowed, wheels churning. The quiet could have killed us all. "Outside," he ordered. "Take him outside."

Mr. Smith, Mr. Wesson, and Jeeves hoisted the body up as Mrs. Black opened the front door. As the men laid Nathan on the green of the earth D.S. Frost quickly removed his shoes, his socks, and his gloves. He took a catcher's stance next to Nathan, squatting high on his toes, and touched the earth with his long fingers. He closed his eyes, and sat there motionless. It seemed to take an eternity.

"What's he doing?" I asked Jeeves in such a quiet voice I didn't think he could possibly hear me.

"Asking Mother Earth for permission to heal him."

Mother Earth? "How do you know that?"

"Because," Jeeves said, with a tearful swallow. "*He's* my son."

Mouth agape my eyes dashed between the two men. Once said it became so obvious. Both tall, thin, long in the face … "That's how you knew," I said. "The night you sent me to go save him. You knew he was in trouble because he was your son."

"I know when people need to come to our home," he said, his wet eyes on the healer. "It's especially strong with my own family."

With a saddened sigh the detective leaned forward. It took some effort but he managed to push his middle finger deeply into the bullet hole in Nathan's stomach. Seconds passed. I put my hand to my mouth, hoping to maintain some distance from tears that lingered.

"No," Frost said, to no one. "Not that way. Come to me. Follow my voice." He paused. "That's it." He gingerly removed his finger.

With a jolt that could have only come from a revived dead man Nathan gasped. Moaning he turned himself over onto the lawn, extending his arms, gripping the grass between his fingers. I knew that feeling. That sudden startle of life, followed by the glory of existence.

Painstakingly, Nathan trembled his way to his hands and knees, only to roll on his backside again. He began to giggle. Mrs. Black and Jeeves knelt beside him and helped him up to sitting. He took a few shaky breaths. Mrs. Black sweetly stroked his hair. "How did we not see?" she sang, then gave him a kiss on is cheek. "I've missed you so much."

The sergeant stood once he finished. He hung his head, eyes closed. His long face accentuated his obvious woe, the down-turned corners of his mouth.

Nathan eyes landed on the healer in front of him. "Thank you," he said.

Without words, and without a glance towards me, D.S. Frost gathered his shoes and socks, and turned away.

Chapter Thirty-One

DETECTIVE DUPLANTIER AND a team of police escorted Mama into a squad car. I never got a chance to talk to Mrs. White, to ask "Why?" Why betray Will? Why frame Mr. Marble? Why get me to kill him? The police kept us busy and away from *the perp*.

Each of us gave a statement on the attempt on Nathan's life. We all saw it; even D.S. Frost. Thank goodness we had a few minutes before Detective Duplantier's arrival to work out the details, like how Mama attacked Mr. Marble with a knife—yup, a bold faced lie. But you can't very well tell the police a shooting has happened without surrendering a gun. And this one was conjured, after all. No telling where it came from (although Smith and Wesson were dying to find out). Besides, her fingerprints were all over the kitchen knives. We simply laid one of them next to her unconscious body. Oh, and she must have tripped and hit her head or something, which is why she's laid there out like a light. Nope, no attacking spiders here. So, even though the lady detective stopped by to take me in, she left with a bigger fish to fry. I was off the hook.

For now.

D.S. Frost avoided looking at me the rest of the day. Even as the police made their way around the house, taking pictures and collecting evidence, he made a point of averting his eyes. He had warned me. He'd told me his freedom was in his anonymity, and not one hour after seeing him on this plane I outed him. He left with his partner, without a word to me.

Nathan and I sat opposite each other in the smaller living room with overstuffed leather sofas that faced each other. Jeeves brought us the tea I asked for. Mint. My mind needed soothing. "I have a thousand questions," I told my newly discovered brother-in-law, "too many to know where to start."

He held up a hand. "I promised Will I would never tell you about his dark side," he said. "So don't ask me."

Not that I wanted to know. Not yet, anyway. "Can you tell me how you survived the attack, the one when you were kids? I saw you die. I saw the Colonel kill you."

He took a moment to collect his thoughts, sat back deeply in the chair, and crossed one leg over the other. "I wasn't supposed to survive," he said, then whispered, "I wanted to die. I was going to betray him, betray my own house." He grimaced. "You see, Will crossed one line too many for me. I knew why he wanted to be dark, I knew that the vengeance against our father bore heavy on his soul. So I followed him. Even though I was the older brother, even though I was the champion of the house, I followed him. And for a while it was fine. Fun, even. But it started to deepen in him. He didn't just use the power, he craved it. More and more." He took a shaky sigh. "I just couldn't let my little brother turn out so … black hearted. So, I went to the light lords and threw myself on their mercy, prostrating myself spreadeagle on their floor. I wanted to save our souls. His soul." He stirred his tea with his shiny silver spoon. "They said they'd help but the payment was that Will needed to be converted, and I was to forfeit my life. I agreed. I planned the attack with the Colonel. The attack on Gateway Manor."

He looked up, and I followed his gaze. Jeeves and Mrs. Black tried to duck out of view behind the large pocket door frame. "Come on in," he said to them. "You should hear this, too. I betrayed the house, not just Will."

The two timidly entered the room. Mrs. Black quickly took a seat, stiff-backed and alert; Jeeves remained standing.

My eyes watched Mrs. Black. She seems so happy, like her long lost son had finally returned home. In a way, he had. "How did we not see you all this time?" she asked. "It's so obvious now." She reached out and tenderly stroked his face. "Edward."

"No," he corrected. "*Nathan.* I went to Boston, where I got my law degree and had some work done." He indicated his face, turning it left and right. "The Light Lords also gave me this," he pulled a medallion from under his shirt and displayed it dangling on the chain, which he removed. "A gonzo. Makes you see the face you're told to see. So, when Will introduced me as his lawyer from Boston, that's what all of you saw. All those years ago." He held her hand. "Edward is dead. Has been for a long time."

"How is it the house doesn't recognize you?" I asked. "You were its champion. I saw that in the vision."

"When I died," he said, "that energy, *my* energy, passed with my life. When I was brought back in Magnolia Mansion it was with that house's energy, light energy. Gateway didn't recognize it. The next time I stepped into the manor I did so as a complete stranger. That was the hardest part, I think." He cocked his head. "When my own home didn't know me."

"Back to the story," he cleared his throat. "I knew that as wicked as Will had become he'd mourn my death. And I was happy to give it in exchange for Will's soul. But the next thing I knew I woke up in Magnolia. The Colonel had me healed. I've never known why." He shrugged. "Anyway, by the time I woke Will was already gone, taken to the conversion. I was a prisoner, of sorts, in Magnolia House while Will was ..."

"Getting converted?" I finished. I didn't want to hear what word he searched for. The impression I got already frightened me.

"Getting converted. He was gone for three weeks. He told me later it was over two years for him. Will never ever told me what actually happened to him during that time, but he had a clear understanding of what he needed to do with the rest of his life. He knew he'd find true love, and he knew they'd live in utter happiness their entire marriage. Then, just after the last tournament, he *knew* he had to put his affairs in order. I mean, it scared me how sure he was of things to come." He visible shivered, then drank a hearty gulp of tea.

"Mrs. Witherspoon, there are two ways you become evil, or dark, in the talented world. The first is to commit some act of evil; murder, torture, whatever, which is what I did. In that case no *formal* contract exists, but an unwritten one does. The second way is to join the Dark Lords by way of a contract. That's … that's what Will did. He sought their help to …" He stopped himself. "It doesn't matter. And as I've said, I promised him not to tell you. As a result, when I died my soul was supposed to go, well, wherever damned souls go. However, in saving my life, the Colonel saved my soul. And the Dark Lords don't like losing souls." He cleared his throat. "That's why I had to go underground, change my name, my appearance. Even though they ultimately released me, they have ways of making you pay."

Nathan grew dark. "Once Will completed his conversion the Colonel and the Light Lords escorted us to the castle, Malevolence Tower, home of the Dark Lords. They spoke on our behalf, like lawyers," he chuckled, but the gloom quickly came back. "The Colonel helped negotiate our release from our contracts. Tried to." I could barely hear the last words, he said them so quietly.

Nathan didn't talk for several moment. His eyes were distant, fixed on a random point on the floor. I saw him swallow a couple of times. My own hands began to shake. *What more needed to be said?*

He finally spoke. "I went into these negotiations thinking they'd keep me and let him go. I mean, given his cleansed soul, the Dark

Lords could no longer use him as a servant or warrior. But they had a formal contract with Will, one they saw no need to break. Despite that Will's soul now brimmed with good and light energy, he could still be useful as sustenance. Nourishment." He cocked his head. "We were perplexed. We had no idea what they were saying, even the Light Lords asked for clarification. To demonstrate, they took him. He just vanished in front of us. He was gone only for a few seconds but when he came back ..." he clenched his eye and rolled his lips over his teeth, "When he came back he was screaming mad, out of his mind. Worse than what we witnessed at the tournament last year. He crawled on hands and knees to me and grabbed my legs, and quaked so badly he nearly knocked me over. He bawled into my thigh. Broke my heart, my kid brother, wailing from so much pain. 'What did you bastards do to him?' I hollered. They said only two words that struck me to the core. They said, *We fed.*"

I noticed Jeeves rock back on his heels, and Mrs. Black wring her hands. Both hung their heads. Before I could press for details—*because surely right now my husband isn't in horrific agony*—Nathan continued.

"That was the deal. I go free, and Will becomes food for the Dark Ones. I said no. I wanted the original deal, take both our souls and we would both serve. But Will, still shaking from the experience, found his feet and stood. 'I want time,' he ordered to the dark ones. 'Give me time in the Midland Plane. Time to live. Time to undo the horrors I've done.' They didn't answer. 'Come on, you loathsome wretches! What have you got to lose? In fact, think of what you'll gain. Give me time, give me years to purify my soul, and I can feed you for *eons.*' I thought he'd lost his mind. Not only would he suffer for an eternity but that kind of light energy feeding the dark side could greatly shift the balance between light and dark. But before I could argue, before I could say he doesn't speak for the both of us, they said the word. *Done.*"

I clenched my eyes at the word. Will's deal. The one he knew would someday come due. An eternity of agony. *He didn't deserve it. I knew the man he'd become.*

Nathan couldn't sit any longer. Pacing the room he rambled, "So that was the deal. I got this brand new life with no strings attached and his name was put on the list, his destiny sealed to an eternity of suffering that I can't even begin to imagine." He pace quickened, his mood darkened. "How many nights since he died have I had that nightmare, reliving that experience over and over? Often I hate to go to sleep. I mean, day after day, I get happiness and, now that he's died he's passed over into the void and those monsters—" Nathan stopped cold.

We all looked at the frozen man, "Once he died his soul ... Passed ... Over ..." Now we looked at each other. "Sonofabitch—*He ran!*"

Nathan raced out of the room at such a speed that he smacked into the hallway wall, misjudging the turn. That didn't stop him. We three ran behind him, trying to keep up.

"Nathan?" Mrs. Black called. "Where are you going?"

Through a myriad of rooms we followed him until we caught up with the crazed man. In the dining room. He stood, arms wide, facing the painting. Will's painting.

Will was in the painting. His small smile spoke volumes. For the first time I knew, *I knew*, Will was in the painting.

"You fabulous son of a bitch!" he laughed at the to the portrait and clapped his hands. "Bravo! You did it. You screwed them!" He punched the air. "*You*," he pointed at me. "You saved his soul. You saved his damned soul," he rushed to me and gave me a bear hug. "You gave him a happy life and then you saved his soul. He always said that, too. Whenever he talked about you he said, 'Someday she's going to save my soul.' I thought it was a figure of speech." The ecstatic, babbling man grabbed my face with two hands and kissed my forehead. "He ran to you, Winki. He ran from them to you and you came to us and we ... Thank you." He held me again. "Thank you, thank you, *thank you.*"

"But I didn't ... do anything." I could barely get the words out, he held me to tightly.

"Think about it, Winki. You told me he touched you at the hospital. He didn't imbue you then. He just attached himself to you, like a tether. Tied himself and this house to you. So he could find you. So when you came to the house we could save him. We could put him someplace the Dark Lords couldn't get to him." He clasped my hands in his. "That's probably why the first few months after his death were so painful for you. Technically, he was right there beside you all that time. It wasn't until the night of the séance, the night we put Will in the mirror, that you came into your own power. I can see it so clearly now—I don't know how I missed it before. His last act before he left this plane, before he was put into the mirror, was to imbue you. You know exactly when it happened." He reached for my head and ran his fingers through my hair, bring some out so I could see. "He changed you." My white hair interlaced between his fingers. My *white* hair.

I recalled that night, the torrential wind that tossed the room. I felt fingers run through my hair. A tender brush on my lips. I hadn't known then—I felt my husband's touch for the last time.

"So I didn't have my own talent at the park," I mused out loud. "Someone else helped me slow time."

He held up his hands. "I confess. I sent TJ out to the park that night. The roaches told me where you were, and I didn't feel good about leaving you alone. I asked him to go there and keep an eye on you. He's the one who gave you the power, the cosmic outlet, probably when he realized he wasn't going to get to you in time to help you."

"You sent Anthony Jones to the park? Why didn't you tell me?

Your lack of interest was one of the reasons I doubted you." *In fact I thought you were the one who killed him.* I kept that thought to myself, now embarrassed for doubting him.

"Tons of reasons." He counted on his fingers. "*Traitor in the house. Get you ready for tournament. Kid brother in hell. Didn't really matter.* The list goes on. Fact is, that poor man died because he did me a favor."

"No," I said, "he did *me* a favor." I looked up at Will, who smiled down at me. "He has to stay there, doesn't he. We can't get him out."

"The mirrors are meant to capture and contain. Nothing can get in. Nothing can get out. But even if Smith and Wesson came up with something extremely clever, the Dark Lords would come for him. Will would be forced to pay his due." He put his hand on the thick, gold frame. "No. Will's safe there. But he has to stay there. Forever."

Chapter Thirty-Two

EVENTUALLY, AS THE day grew older and faded with the birth of night, an air of quiet unease filled the manor. The truth stewed among us all. Mama betrayed the house. She betrayed Will and me. I avoided touching the house, unsure if it, too, felt such sadness, such betrayal, afraid it would be overwhelming. It had known Mrs. White for many years.

It seemed the world felt our grief. Outside, a distant storm began to rumble. Dim flashes lit the dining room, splashing their light across Will's face.

Nathan sat at the head of the dining room table, reading Mama's contract with one hand while gnawing on a drumstick in the other. We'd ordered some Popeye's chicken for dinner. We were missing a cook, after all. He looked up at the grandfather clock in the corner of the room. It read twenty to midnight.

Jeeves came in to fill our wine glasses. We drank a lovely gewurtztraminer with the meal. Seemed uniquely Southern; fried chicken, mashed potatoes, peanut slaw, and a hearty white wine.

"He's cutting it close, don't you think?" Nathan said to Jeeves.

Jeeves didn't answer while he filled our glasses and put the wine back in the iced bucket at our table's side. "Shall I call him, sir?"

Nathan sighed. "No. It's his last free decision. He can run if he wants." I had no idea what they were talking about. This time I didn't care. My own sadness kept me quiet.

"He would be an idiot," Hercule added. He spoke with his mouthful, eating crumbs from our chicken's breading. "This is his home now. Only here is he safe."

Whatever. I munched away. Even though I wasn't hungry I knew I should eat. It had been an exhausting day.

Nathan tossed the contract on the table. "She promised them a pristine soul," he said to Hercule.

"In return for?" asked the *cafard*.

Nathan rolled his eyes. "Nothing of real value. The contract says 'unfettered and unbounded power of poison', but as far as I know she already had that. Mama was nothing short of amazing with potions. I always assumed that included poisons."

Hercule humphed. "I believe she longed to be a darkling again."

With a shrug Nathan reluctantly agreed.

After a beat or two I asked. "What pristine soul? Will's?"

"They already had his soul," Nathan explained. "Or rights to it, anyway."

"So, whose soul did she promise?"

He tossed his glasses on the table and rubbed the bridge of his nose.

"Is not obvious, *madame?*" Hercule said. "She promised them *yours.*"

I dropped my chicken bones on my plate. Then it struck me. "Wait… are you telling me she betrayed Will, betrayed me, betrayed the entire house, all to be, what, the grand poobah of poison? That's insane."

"*Unfettered and unbounded,*" Hercule retorted. "Were you not paying attention?"

A bright flash lit up the room. Thunder rumbled just a few seconds later.

Nathan ignored the bug, "Will's deal was, 'Give me time and I'll feed you for eons.' But she went to them and said, 'If you take him now, not only will you get me to serve you, but I'll bring you someone young and new and strong and so pure you can mold them into whatever you want.' The Dark Lords would have a hard time saying no to that."

"How was she going to do that? Kill me?"

"She didn't want to kill you. She wanted to turn you." Her, Malador, Esmeralda ... I began to see a pattern. "All she had to do was seduce you to the dark side." He sipped some wine. "She set all this up. She set *me* up. She pointed tiny fingers at me for you to find, like the terms of the executorship which lead you to think I wanted this house, or blaming me for putting Will in the painting ... even bringing us home early from tournament would look like something bad on my part. Finally, she put a piece of proof in my briefcase," he waved the contract, "for Mrs. Black and the spiders to discover, knowing that you'd stewed long enough and were ready to cross the line. If you had killed me, if you'd taken my life ..." He shifted in his chair. "You'd be theirs."

I dropped my eyes in shame, recalling the hatred I felt. *I came so very close.* A long, low rumble rattled the windows.

He looked thoughtful, suddenly, raising his fingers to his lips. He thought out loud, "I'm still unclear how she did it. I mean, I get that she poisoned both Todd Collins, er, I mean *Tom Cruise* and Tony Jones, granted. I can even fathom her giving TJ the poison, like in a fruit, or cookie, say, in the guise of a gift."

"But?" I asked, since I got the impression he wanted someone to.

"But how did she even know Tom Cruise? I don't think they ran in any of the same circles. And I certainly don't know how she'd convince him to shoot you in the park."

"Ah," Hercule said. "We do. Bring it in, *mes enfants!*"

Across the floor it came, a book, shivering its way towards the table. Mr. Marble reached down and plucked it from ...

I dropped my chicken bones again as a dozen cockroaches scattered in every direction. I clenched my eyes in disgust. Nothin' but wine for the rest of the night for me.

"We tossed her room," Hercule said. "We found her notebook."

"She kept a diary?" I asked.

"*Oui*. And I took the liberty of reading it." As Nathan sat deeper in his chair and started to read, Hercule continued, "She did it through the use of the dolls. What is it you call it, the controlling of the doll?"

I sat back. "Voodoo? Mrs. White used voodoo to get Tom Cruise to kill me?"

"*Oui*." The *cafard* turned to Nathan. "Do you see that? We did not know she was so strong with that talent." Nathan didn't move. "Nathan?"

Nathan looked in a trance, reading a page. Then snapped the diary shut. "I'm sorry, what?"

"Did you read about—"

"No," he cut Hercule off. "I'll read it later."

It appeared he'd found something of interest, something that disturbed him but before I could ask Jeeves cleared his throat. "Madam," he said, "Detective Sergeant Frost is here to see you." Jack, he called him earlier today. *Jack ... Frost*. I rolled my eyes. I noticed Jeeves glance at the clock. Just a few minutes until midnight.

I looked at Nathan. "Did you know Jeeves and Frost were father and son?"

Nathan sat back, mouth agape. "No." He chuckled, "been a big news day, hasn't it?"

"Have him join us," I told Jeeves, who bowed and fetched the detective.

D.S. Frost entered with as stern a demeanor as he'd left with. "Care to join us?" I asked. He didn't move.

Nathan wiped his hands then gestured to a chair. "Please, have a seat."

The sergeant thanked him and sat, folding his hands on the table. "I came with some news," he said to Nathan. "She's disappeared."

"Who?" I asked. He didn't answer. Didn't even look at me.

"Who?" Nathan repeated.

"Mrs. White. She vanished while in custody. Officially, she's escaped and we are searching for her. I was sent here to warn Mrs. Witherspoon. But unofficially, I doubt she'll ever come back."

"Why?" I asked. The detective didn't acknowledge me again.

"Why?" Nathan repeated. "Oh, wait, I know this," he shook his head as if clearing it. "She broke the terms of her contract. She failed to bring Winki to them, so her life was forfeit. They took her. One of the many penalties for doing business with the DL."

"The DL, sir?" D.S. Frost asked.

"The Dark Lords," he said.

Uncomfortable moments passed. The detective refused to look at me, his face ruddy and hot.

"I take it," Nathan said to him, "you gave notice?"

"I intend to. First thing in the morning."

"You can't wait. The deadline is midnight."

D.S. Frost swallowed. "Very well. I shall call them now."

"Call who now? Give notice to what?" I asked. *Why won't he talk to me?* "What's going on?"

Nathan explained. "He can't work in the public sector anymore. It would be irresponsible. He'll get someone killed."

"What?" I asked, a bit heated. "How?"

"For the love of Zeus," Hercule flamed, "*Get on with it!*"

"Winki, you found him out," Nathan said. "The energy is out there now, his name, his ability, his face. He's a target, and will be for the rest of his life. Innocent people could die if they got in the way." I didn't understand, and my ignorance must have shown. He leaned in closer to me, trying not to be heard by the spikey-haired angry man.

"He's exposed. You exposed him. He can't talk to you until you've claimed him."

Of all the ridiculous ... "Of course he can talk to me, he just *won't*. What's with these stupid rules?"

"No, he really can't. The law is made to prevent him from negotiating terms of his ... service." *Service?* "Once exposed he has to wait until you claim him. And if you don't before the end of day," He nodded to the grandfather clock that read nearly midnight, "you're effectively passing. Then *anyone* can claim him."

"I don't understand. I discovered who he was at the tournament. I've known all along. Why, now, won't he talk to me?"

"Knowing and exposing are two different things. You exposed him. Now he waits."

"You call that waiting?" Hercule yelled. "Dogs wait better than that. Get on your knees, you lowly excuse for a primate, and bow before your new master!"

"Hey," I said to the bug, "That's enough." A bright flash lit up the room. "I don't get this," I said loudly to be heard over the roar of thunder.

"You've exposed him as a healer. If you don't claim him, anyone can. Good or evil, light or dark, he will work for anyone." Then Nathan muttered, "One of the reason no one likes healers."

"Fine," I huffed. Frost told me he didn't want to serve someone dark. He warned me, in fact. "What do I need to do?"

"You need to claim him," Nathan said. "You need to declare him as your property."

"*What?!*" I looked at the clock. Light flashed again, and its subsequent roar was immediate. It was two minutes until midnight. "I'm not taking a man as property. It's illegal. You know that, *lawyer-of-mine.*"

"Not in this world. Not in this community."

"Kneel before her!" Hercule yelled again. "Now, or she will hand you over to Malador, himself."

"I will do no such thing!" I turned to Nathan. "Can't you give him a new identity? Change his name, get him relocated." Frost hung his head, keeping his eyes on the floor. "Isn't that what you want?" I asked him. He didn't move.

"His face is known."

"*You* hid. You changed your face. People didn't recognize you!"

One minute until midnight. "If you don't want him then leave the room. Just walk away," Nathan said sternly. "Malador will happily—"

"Of course I don't want him working for Malador." I hollered. "Both of you knock it off. I don't … I mean, I *can't* own a …" I couldn't say the word. "It goes against everything I believe in."

"Fine," Nathan hissed, "justify it anyway you can. Call it whatever you want. A cheap employee, or an internship, whatever makes you feel good, but don't leave him in the wind. For my sake if nothing else. Winki, he saved my life. Don't make him pay for that, indentured to whoever or whatever comes for him."

"All right," I held up my hands. I looked at the man across the table. "I claim you ... or whatever."

"No, Winki. You have to capture him." I let out a long sigh. "Stand up." I started to.

"No no no!" Hercule argued. "He must go to her. He must show his willingness to serve. He must demonstrate his subservience."

"*Hercule*," I yelled, smacking the table, close to him to make my point, at the same time that light and sound blinded and deafened everyone. Nathan ducked a little to nature's retort. "I said enough," I told the bug.

But the healer did as he'd been told. He came to my side of the table and knelt next to me, eyes cast to the floor.

"Take him by his wrists." Nathan urged. "Quickly." He looked up at the clock.

Without being told or ridiculed by the roach, Frost put his wrists together, in a pious gesture. His usually white cheeks hot with blush.

I put my hands on his wrists. The clock began to chime. "Repeat after me," Nathan said. "Healer, your life is mine."

I hesitated.

"Do it!" Nathan commanded.

"Healer, your life is mine." *I really hate this.*

"To do with as I please."

I swallowed. "To do with as I please."

"From now until the end of your life."

I grimaced.

"Say it!"

"From now until the end ... of your life."

I felt a small but painful pulse course through me, and for a moment, just with the faintest of images, I could have sworn I saw shackles bind his wrists. The healer groaned, head bowed into his forearms.

"It's done," Nathan said solemnly. "You can let go."

The last chime of midnight struck. The healer buried his head in his hands. Jeeves, with tears on his cheek, came to his son and placed a soft, fatherly hand on his back. *Bloody hell, I hate this.*

"Magnificent!" Hercule said, dancing. "A slave! A healer! Now, you mangy dog, show you place. Grovel before me, the Great Hercule!"

"I said, enough!" I smacked the table again just as the outside exploded in rage, this time shaking the building and rattling the chandelier above us. I noticed Nathan push himself away from the table, away from the fixture.

"He is a filthy creature, *madame*," Hercule hissed. "He is *loathsome* and an *abomination* to all the talent of—"

"Enough!" The storm beat me to it this time. Lightning hit a tree outside the dining room, sending an enormous chunk of wood through the window. The rest of the room jumped, moving away from the bits of flinging glass, wood bits, and the wet wind. But I didn't move, didn't care. I pointed to the bug and over the torrent I screamed the words: "*Everyone in this house will treat everyone else with the utmost respect. No one deserves to be called names, no one deserves to put down, and absolutely no one is better than anyone else. Is that clear?*"

The bug sat motionless. I could feel the cold rain dripping down my back. All eyes, big as saucers, were on me.

"Have no fear, Jack, you'll see," Jeeves consoled him as they moved to the dry side of the room. "She'll be a good master."

I cringed at the word, and spun to the butler. "And no one will use *that* word in *this* house. Is that clear?"

I didn't wait for an answer. I'd had enough. I stomped my way out of the room and gave my last command for the evening. "Someone, *clean this mess up!*"

Chapter Thirty-Three

THE SUN'S RAYS burst into my bedroom as joyous and radiant as the first time the stars lit up the sky, some fourteen billion years ago. We were incidental. The rise and fall of empires, the building of cities and roads, the ebbing and flowing of life on this rock meant nothing to the sun.

Clearly, I felt bleak about the world. This world, this new stupid world with its stupid rules and rituals and tournaments and … slavery. *Slavery*. Here, in the now. In my house.

With a groan I rolled over. On the pillow next to me was the cockroach. I don't jump when I see him anymore, although I wasn't wild about him sleeping in my bed.

"Go away," I ordered. He did not. Stupid bug. "Why were you so cruel to D.S. Frost, I mean, Jack last night?" I asked, accusingly.

"So you would do exactly what you did." I rolled over, my back to him. "That man lost everything," he continued. "More than you can possibly fathom. He lost his employment. He lost his freedom. He lost his dignity. I know what that is like, *ma chère*. I, too, had to give up everything. I thought it might be a small blessing if he knew he lost it to someone who would, at very least, stand up for him."

A soft knock at my door made me moan. "Go away."

"As you wish, madam." Jeeves.

"Wait a moment." I scrambled out of bed and found a sweatshirt and some shorts to put on. "Come in."

Jeeves, tray in hand, ambled into the room. From the scent that emerged my eyes widened. "Beignets!" My stomach roared with approval.

As he set the tray on my little table beneath the window he said, "Jack and I went to the Cafe Du Monde early this morning and purchased enough for the household. Coffee?"

"Please." I sat, opened the cover, exposing the puffy pillows of powdered-sugar pleasure. Man, I love these things! Nothing like a whole bunch of powdered-sugar to help brighten a sour morning.

After he poured me some coffee he produced a notepad. "I take it we have quite a morning report?" I asked.

"It can wait, if you prefer."

"No, no," I said through a yawn. "Go ahead."

Jeeves cleared his throat. "Firstly, I took the liberty of helping Jack move in last night. He is ... getting settled."

I shook my head. "I hate this, you know. I mean I'm sure he does, too, but I don't understand any of these stupid rules." I looked up at him. "Did you know who he was from the beginning?"

"Yes. From the first moment he walked through that front door I recognized my son. And I suspect he recognized me." He lowered his pad, and while standing perfectly erect, tilted his head a bit. "It was the first time I laid eyes on him since he was taken away. He was only eight year old."

"Taken away? What, like, stolen from you?"

"That is the way of things, madam. Once a child is found out to be a healer they are taken to a special school, and trained how and when they can use their talent."

"Because surely you would have been an irresponsible parent," I huffed, attempting to make a point on the complete nonsense my ears heard.

"I am not a healer. I would be incapable of preparing him for his life."

"Life. His slavery, you mean."

"It is what it is."

"It's wrong. It's insane. All of you are insane," I accused.

"Quite."

Hercule managed to find the table top, crawling towards my coffee. He pointed to the sugar cube on the saucer. "*Chére?* Are you going to eat that?"

I put it on the table for him. "Enjoy," I said, still bitter about the topic.

"Which brings us to item two," Jeeves said, "your education, madam. Now with the tournament behind us we can properly teach you how things are, and how they've come to be. Mrs. Black will teach you etiquette."

"Probably should have had that before the tournament," I said, with a mouthful of doughnut making a puff of fine sugar spray across the table.

"Not just manners, but protocols and decorum. It will attune you to the community. You will be able to pass someone on the street and know they are one of us. Although," he said quietly, "manners are clearly needed."

Nope, not insulted at all. "Will you teach me anything?"

"History. Why things are as they are."

"Things are screwed up."

"I only offer explanations, not justifications. I have a number of books for you to read. I will drop them off later today."

That's when it hit me. Schooling. I grimaced. "Okay. What else is on the list?" I waved my hand, hoping he would move along.

"We need a cook."

I rubbed my face with my powdered sugar hands. "Yes, we do. Suggestions?"

"Until we find a replacement I can have meals catered for the house."

"Can Nathan help with that, finding a replacement? I assume he has his fingers in all sorts of talented pies." Jeeves hesitated, which made me pause. "What's wrong?"

"He's in a bit of a state himself, at the moment. After you retired last night, after he and I fixed the window, he made a phone call. To a partner, I believe, in his firm. He spoke only one word. 'Limelight.'" I sat back, waiting. "I think his wife became a widow at that moment. He, like Jack, was exposed. His family now faced great risk. He's always known that leading the double life of a normal would have a penalty if discovered. Once found out that he was really Edward Witherspoon he had to make his family disappear." My eyes widened at the words. "*Relocated*, madam. New names, new home.'"

A thousand questions slammed into my brain. Why didn't he run with them? Why didn't he move them in here? But I stopped myself from asking. They always had reasons. More to the point, "How is Nathan?"

"Depressed, as you might imagine. I recommend avoiding him for a few days. Give him some time."

I gave an understanding nod. "Anything else?"

He cleared his throat. "Jack."

"What about Jack?"

"He was hoping you'd be open to the idea of him having a vocation."

"He wants to continue working for NOPD?"

"No. That, he knows, he cannot do. Late night calls, long investigations. He acknowledges that would conflict with his duties here. But I informed him that the house ultimately protects you, so a healer wasn't necessary twenty-four hours a day. He's thinking of becoming a private investigator, madam."

I smiled. *Jack Frost, PI.* "I like the idea. He'd do well." I sipped some coffee.

"Thank you, madam." He closed his little book, gave a small bow, then turned to leave.

"Jeeves?" I stopped him. "I want to watch a DVD this morning, in private. Please prepare the media room. No bugs, no people, no eavesdroppers."

"Indeed, madam." He almost sounded insulted.

~ ~ * ~ ~

I popped the DVD into the player, flopped into one of the plush leather chairs facing the screen, took a deep and steadying breath, and hit *play*.

Half of Will's face popped up on the screen as he hit the record button. He sat back. And smiled.

"So, wife. Clever girl I knew you would be. If you're watching this you figured it out. You've done your first tournament, and survived. And I know that because, again, you're watching this." He licked his lips. Those perfect lips. "No doubt you heard about what happened last year. Well, for me," he looked up into the sky, "just a few weeks ago. It really wasn't as bad as they say. Oh, trust me, it was bad," he chuckled. "But its all about what's in here," he pointed to his head. "Do you know how I made it through that?" He paused with a small smile, the same one that's in the dining room. "You. I thought of *you*." I flushed, recalling how his memory didn't save me from Malador. "I knew it would end, sooner or later, and that I'd leave the damned Citadel and I'd come home. To your sweet face." He shifted nervously. "Lucky for me I when I'm done here I get to come home to you. And I'll hold you close. And kiss your neck." The thought sent chills down my back. I love the way he kissed me. "And tell you how much I adore you. Don't feel sorry for me. I feel sorry for you. All you have is the painting."

I hit the pause button. This felt harder than the last time. He said there were several recordings ... would they each get harder as time went on? As my separation from him grew?

I wiped my eyes and hit *play*. "Okay," he said, "that's not all you have. You have a family. You have a warm and caring group of people in this house that will do anything for you. Cherish them. Cherish your time with them." He opened his mouth as if he were going to say something more, but changed his mind.

"You may have noticed that I know a bit more than I should. I've always been clever. But, I did get a bit of a, well, cheat. I had much of my future foretold to me. In my conversion. For two years I spent time with this old crone of a woman. A mage." Thoughts flashed over his face. "God, at first I hated her. I'd cover my ears, I'd scream obscenities at her. But she wore me down. Gentle. Patient. By the end I'd love sitting with her, talking, listening. Sometimes just being in her presence was like being near a blast furnace, it was so strong, so purifying. Cleansing. I hope you get to meet her someday. Not the way *I* did, of course," he laughed. "Anyway, she told me who I was. What I was. Showed me how ... peaceful and wonderful and *just* my life could be."

He leaned forward, putting his elbows on his knees. "Winks, she told me that I would have three trials, three miserable experiences in my life that I had to endure and I had to triumph over. And if I could, if I succeeded, I'd find peace. Real peace. The kind only the noble and just get to know. The first, she said, would be almost immediately, at my hearing with the DL. She told me they would threaten me, but I had to endure it. I had to save Edward. That that act would unbind a good deal of what I'd done. And win me a beautiful and smart and cunning bride." His smile melted my heart.

"The second, she said, would be a sign, and one I needed to take seriously. That I should consider the ordeal to be the beginning of the end, and get my affairs in order. She told me I would make a mistake and only I could keep it from taking my sanity." He hung his head and rubbed his palms together. "I think that's what happened at the tournament. I made a mistake. I almost lost my mind. And now ...," he gave a small laugh, "and now I'm making DVDs for you."

I uncomfortably shifted around in my seat as I chewed on a fingernail.

"The third trial, she said, would be the longest. It would be dark and cold and she apologized for that. She couldn't change it. And it would last years. I got the impression she meant decades. Maybe even centuries. But I needed to have faith that all the wheels were in motion, all the players have their roles, and the acts would unfold— her words exactly. And that someday ..." He sat back, folded his arms. "Well ... I can't tell you that part, not yet. You have more DVDs to find."

I couldn't let the comment go. "What mistake did you make?"

"Good question. Trust. Blind trust. And by blind I mean I just didn't see. Winki, it wasn't my healer. Just because someone is wearing one of those cloaks doesn't make him ..." His eyes went distant. I could tell he was lost in the memory, the misery. *Bloodly hell*, it was just a few weeks ago for him.

"It's over, Will."

He looked at me. "Yes. It is." He took a deep breath. "I think I'll finish these recordings tomorrow. I just got to get home to see you." He wiped his face harshly with his hands, as if trying to wake himself up. "I'm sorry to say that because you can't see me."

"I have the portrait."

"I don't think a portrait would work for me. But you're a lot stronger than I ever was.

"Listen to me, this is what's important on this DVD. It wasn't the healer, *my* healer, who led me to Esmeralda. They killed him on my behalf, before I had my faculties back to defend him. I don't think I'll have the time to right that wrong. So I'm asking you, please. Don't let that poor man, whoever he was, go unspoken for. Talk to Nathan. I don't mean vengeance. I mean recognition. I mean clear his name. Make sure they know. *They killed an innocent man in the Citadel.*"

I folded my arms. "I promise. I'll find out who he was. I'll make them remember."

"Then," he said, rubbing his lap, "all that's left is the riddle for the next disk."

"Just spare me and tell me where it is!" I insisted.

"Where's your sense of sport, woman?"

"Would you at least put it on this plane?"

"I make no promises, dead man's prerogative. Now pay attention." He cleared his throat. "*The sentence, the burden, and the falter make three. The fourth is where your next clue will be.*"

I dropped my head back with a moan.

"Take your time, Winks. Don't rush these. In fact, the more you learn before collecting the disks the more you'll gain from them." He leaned forward to turn off the machine. "I love you."

The screen went black.

** End Book One **

ABOUT THE AUTHOR

Jax Daniels was born in Chicago, raised in Denver, educated in Berkeley (go Bears!), worked in the Bay Area and Seattle, and currently resides in New Orleans. She and her husband live in an Uptown townhouse they call "The Tower" with their pug, Savannah. Other passions include yoga and making stained glass creations.

Tweet me: @JaxDNola
Like me: facebook.com/jaxDNola
Read me: www.winkiwitherspoon.com
Find me: www.jaxdaniels.com
… bug me: www.bugsmind.com